5-
9-06

DEEP BLUE

D1023142

Also by Tom Morrisey

Turn Four

Yucatan Deep

TOM MORRISEY

A BECK EASTON ADVENTURE

DEEP BLUE

BOOK 1

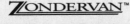

GRAND RAPIDS, MICHIGAN 49530 USA

ZONDERVAN™

Deep Blue
Copyright © 2004 by Thomas Morrisey

Requests for information should be addressed to:

Zondervan, *Grand Rapids, Michigan 49530*

Library of Congress Cataloging-in-Publication Data

Morrisey, Tom, 1952–
    Deep blue / Tom Morrisey.
        p. cm. — (A Beck Easton adventure)
    ISBN 0-310-24407-2 (softcover)
    1. Women graduate students—Fiction. 2. Women genealogists—Fiction.
    3. Treasure-trove—Fiction. 4. Florida—Fiction. 5. Divers—Fiction. I. Title.
    PS3613.O776D44 2005
    813'.54—dc22

                                                                    2004019910

Excerpt from "There Is a Reason" by Ron Block © 1999 by Moonlight Canyon Publishing/Bug Music, BMI. Performed on Rounder Records by Alison Krauss + Union Station.

Excerpt from "Jesus Paid It All" adapted from lyrics by Elvina M. Hall. Originally published in *Sabbath Hymns* (1879).

All rights reserved. No part of this publication may be reproduced, stored in a retrieval system, or transmitted in any form or by any means—electronic, mechanical, photocopy, recording, or any other—except for brief quotations in printed reviews, without the prior permission of the publisher.

Interior design by Beth Shagene

Printed in the United States of America

05 06 07 08 09 10 /❖ DCI/ 10 9 8 7 6 5 4 3

For Al Lee:
a talented writer,
a courageous Marine,
and a friend who stuck
closer than a brother

For where your treasure is,
there will your heart be also.

MATTHEW 6:21 KJV

PROLOGUE

Pale and leaden in the predawn light, the spring looked like nothing special, like a pond of rainwater standing in the tan limestone basin. It was only when a body got close that you saw what made it different: the surface of the water all dancing and rippling from the flow surging up from the depths, a small run draining the overflow into the tea-brown waters of the Itchetucknee.

Jonah Winslow paused, gazing at the rippling headpool, and dragged his threadbare sleeve across his forehead. The spring looked as it had when he'd first seen it, a full four decades earlier.

He shifted his burden, a Confederate Army foraging bag, thick canvas sagging with the weight of what it carried. Then he turned and looked back at the slender young woman who was picking her way among the tree roots, planting her slippered feet with care. She came to a halt beside him and her face was white in the halflight, a striking contrast to the blackness of Jonah's own, white and finely featured, like the china dolls the old slave had watched her play with as a child.

"Oh, Uncle." She shook her head and looked up at him, blue eyes wide. "Let us go home. This is far too dangerous."

"Now, child." He kept his voice low, the voice he'd used to calm her through all the hard years. "If I've done this once, I've done it a hundred times. Wasn't I just in there yesterday, getting things ready?"

Cecilia Donohue blinked and said nothing.

"Besides," Jonah said, "after tomorrow morning, we won't have a home. Carpetbagger's coming. Time to do this chore."

He set the bag at his feet and stripped off his faded chambray shirt, his chest still damp from the walk. Next, he untied the rope that he wore as a belt and stepped out of his patched cotton trousers.

Jonah Winslow made no pretense at modesty. Nor did the young woman avert her eyes. Jonah knew that Cecilia Donohue loved him like family, yet it no more upset her to see him naked than it would have to see any of her father's cattle or horses just as nature had created them. Jonah didn't blame her for this. It was how she'd been raised, who she was.

Cecilia glanced down at the forage bag.

"It will be safe here?" It wasn't the first time she'd asked.

"Yes, ma'am." Jonah Winslow turned and met her gaze, careful not to glance away as he spoke. "I wrapped it in cheesecloth. Crimped a sheet of lead foil 'round it—last sheet we had. Then I coated the whole thing with beeswax. It can lay there for years if it has to. But it won't have to."

He turned and walked down into the spring, wading deeper and gasping just a bit as he stepped off a ledge and the cool water rose to his waist. He kept going until he was shoulder deep, and then he turned and looked back at Miss Cecilia, standing there with the sky growing gray behind her.

"Hurry back, Uncle Jonah," she whispered.

"Two minutes." Jonah's throat felt thick, his words gravelly. "Won't take no longer than that, Miss Cecilia."

He turned back to face the boil of the spring and the two dark openings that gaped at the bottom of the pool. Slowly, deeply, he began to pull in great, long draughts of air.

One breath ... two ... three ...

Jonah's shoulder ached from the forage-bag strap, and he thought about the first time he'd done this, the summer of his fifteenth year, when even the work of loading an entire wagon with water barrels could do little to tire him. He and young Master Cameron, the boy who would one day be Cecilia's father, had come here in the midst of a drought to fetch water. Afterward, they'd gone swimming to escape the heat, and the young master had dared Jonah to dive down into the dark opening that yawned beneath their bare feet.

Jonah had known what the other boy must have been thinking. Most of the plantation's slaves were deathly afraid of the springs, of the "haints" said to live there, waiting to draw swimmers to their doom.

But while Jonah had listened carefully to every circuit preacher who had ever come through and knew there was a devil and evil within the world, he also knew talk of haints was foolishness. Even so, when he'd first dived down, he no sooner touched the rim of the cave than his lungs were burning for a breath. He'd gone gasping to the surface, and the other boy's laughter had so angered him that, on the next try, he had not only gone into the cave—he had swum far back in it, found the junction that led to the other spring opening, and come rocketing out the other side.

It had been a clever trick, one that had sparked an idea with young Master Cameron. The very next Sunday, the plantation owner's son had enticed twenty neighbors to pay a nickel apiece to watch "Donohue's buck"—that was what they'd called him—perform his daredevil feat. And once they'd figured out how to prolong the excitement, Jonah and the young master had been able to coax as much as two nickels apiece from the pockets of their audience.

Four breaths . . .

The eastern sky was getting some color now, the fairest shade of pink, the sailor's color of warning. Jonah squeezed his eyes shut and resisted the urge to shake his head. *Fifty-three summers—too old for this foolishness.* He glanced back at Miss Cecilia, standing there at the spring's edge. *Known her all her life, raised her after her momma passed. I'm her only hope.*

It was a simple proposition. If the men from up North found what was in the forage bag, they'd take it. Take it and its secret and doom Miss Cecilia to a life of poverty. *Got to do it; got to hide this thing.*

Five breaths . . .

It wasn't that Jonah Winslow was afraid to die. He knew by heart the Scriptures that promised him heaven, and if heaven was better than this world for white folk, it was even more so for a man raised a slave. Master Cameron and his family had been as good to Jonah as the times would allow, but they had still treated him as property. Jonah had seen his brothers grow stooped and bent from long hours in the fields, seen his only sister sold away up to Georgia.

Six breaths . . .

Jonah loved the young woman at the spring's edge like his own blood, more than that, if such a thing was possible.

Seven . . .

He took this one as deeply as he could, held it, and dove for the bottom of the spring.

Springflow pushed and tugged at the fringe of Jonah's hair, the water feeling heavy around him, the weight of the forage bag pulling him down like an anchor. Shifting the bag around to the small of his back, Jonah crawled along the boulders on the bottom of the spring basin, snaking across the flats and into the dark, gaping mouth of the cave.

Pig bladders. That was the trick that had allowed Jonah to stay down so long on those two-nickel Sundays: pig bladders, like what they'd blown up to use as kick-balls when he was a boy. He and Master Cameron had pumped the bladders full with a bellows, pumped them close to bursting because the water would shrink them at depth. Then they'd tied them to window sash weights and hidden them in the caves on the morning before a dive. That gave Jonah air to breath. It let him bide his time underwater, exploring the darkness while he breathed down first one bladder and then the next.

Now, groping in the flooded blackness some forty years after he had learned that trick, Jonah found the four bladders he'd brought into the cave the evening before. He wasted no time as he untied the first one and sucked down a deep draught of air, welcome even with the biting taste of the bladder on it. He gathered the rawhide thongs that held the other three bladders and struggled back into the darkness, the haversack trying to slide off his back, the sash weights bumping on the bottom, and the bladders tugging in the current like invisible, runaway kites.

It was on one of those long-ago dives, biding his time down in the underwater darkness while all the white folk waited up above in their Sunday-best, that Jonah had first found the side passage. Its entrance was low and overhung, easy to miss for a body finding his way by feel, but wide enough that he'd felt comfortable about going in. And there, ten feet back in that passage, his hands had fallen upon a flake of rock that pulled away easily, revealing a shallow, natural limestone shelf—the perfect hiding place for something small and valuable.

It was the first place he'd thought of when Miss Cecilia had come to him with her secret.

Jonah's lungs burned again for air. He let his breath go in a single whoosh, untied another bladder, and breathed it down in two deep breaths. This time, he was still hurting afterward. He thought through what he had to do, how the current would help push him back to the surface. *One breath's all I'll need ... all it'll take to get me back to the light.* He gulped down the air from the third bladder, as well.

The last bladder in tow, Jonah found the side passage, dipped under the overhang, found the slab, and moved it away from the wall. His hand landed on the ledge, and he pulled the forage bag over his head and placed it in the hiding place. Checking to make sure it stayed, he pivoted the slab back and rested his hand there for a moment. *Please, Lord, keep this safe.*

Done. That was done. Now it was time for Jonah to get himself out; he was the only man in North Florida—maybe the only man in the world—who could come back and retrieve this thing for Miss Cecilia.

Jonah kicked his way back, one hand up to find the overhang and guide himself beneath it in the dark. He felt the tug of a stronger flow—the main passage. Time to breathe the last of his air.

Jonah exhaled through his mouth and nose, feeling the bubbles whisking across his stubbled face in the darkness. He reached up to the bladder, found a rawhide thong, and pulled it down.

The bit of leather went slack in his hand.

No. His heart plummeted. *No!* He must have left the tag end long when he'd tied the slip knot to secure the bladder—and now he'd grabbed the wrong end in the blackness, pulling the knot free.

Arms flailing, Jonah groped with both hands in the jet-black water, but he knew it was useless. The current would have the bladder thirty feet down the passage by now.

Fighting panic, empty lungs screaming for a breath, he kicked out into the flow and swam for all he was worth—kicking and clawing for the cave entrance and the sweet summer air just beyond.

Oh, Lord. Oh, please. Please, sweet Jesus. Just get me there . . . the entrance.

With nothing in his lungs, Jonah's lean body sank, bumping the stone and clay bottom of the passage. He scrabbled, floated up, and then sank again.

Keep going. Can make it. He urged himself forward. Heavy as he felt, the current had the power to flush him from the cave mouth and back to the surface. Red dots, flaming blossoms of color, swarmed before his eyes.

His lungs screamed for air.

Little bit more . . . not far . . . not far at all . . .

He saw traces of light now, tinges of purple and rose on the rough, scalloped wall of the passage. *Gettin' there. Close.* He gritted his teeth, stifled the urge to breathe. He could already picture himself crawling out of the headpool like a half-drowned muskrat, Miss Cecilia *tsk*-ing over him, and weeping; telling him he shouldn't have tried, both of them weeping and happy.

Then there was the whisper of a touch, like a tentacle, at his ankle. It went tight, ensnaring him. Gripped fast, he stopped, the outflow rushing all around his naked body in the gloom. *No! Ain't no haint in this cave. Ain't no . . .*

Jonah tugged again and felt something thin cutting into the skin above his ankle. He stifled a scream, and water seeped past his clenched teeth. He probed along his leg for the snare that held him fast.

One of his discarded air bladders must have lodged in a rock or a crack, and a loop of floating rawhide thong had snagged him. He gripped it with both hands, yanked with the full strength of fear, and pulled free. His foot was still caught in the cord, but the bladder and its attached weight were moving with him now, drifting down the center of the passage. He reached down for the cord, then shook his head.

Don't go messing with that now. Tend to it later. Got to get out. Already his vision was darkening; dizziness was creeping in on him. The sash weights bumped along below him, the deflated bladder catching and rolling rocks on the passage floor. His chest muscles rippled as they tried vainly to draw in . . . something. *Anything.*

He turned a corner. Ahead, dimly, he could see the entrance to the cave, a purple sky gleaming through the darkness.

His throat throbbed now as he tried to gulp down air that simply wasn't there. He bit his lips and thick blood spread across his tongue. The entrance loomed before him, close—so close that one good kick would see him through.

Jonah pushed, and the surface of the headpool roiled not twenty feet above his head. Treetops beckoned through an oval window of clear water: treetops and clouds and a dawn-pink eastern sky.

He sprang for the light—and stopped short.

Jonah tried once more, but again his leg was tethered. He reached down and yanked with both hands, but all he did was pull his body down. A waterlogged tree limb and chunks of limestone lay at the foot of the cave entrance, and one of the sash weights he was dragging had lodged there. It was stuck, wedged deep, down between two huge rocks. And it held him fast, like a man clapped in irons.

Jonah pulled again, but it was no good; he was weak as a kitten now. He reached down to free himself, but the outflow of the cave, strongest in the closeness of the entrance, blasted his arms up, high above his head. Then it kept him that way, like a man shouting "hallelujah" in a church.

Jonah's clenched teeth slacked, and water coursed into his nose and mouth. He swallowed, and spring water, so sweet on the hot days of summer, burned like molten metal in his throat. He tried to scream, but nothing came out—only the tiniest of bubbles that wobbled up and around the little sunfish darting in the clear water above him.

The sun, big and bold and blood-red, had risen. A shaft of crimson sunlight speared through the water and reached Jonah Winslow's face.

He was sad now. Sad that he had ever taken Cameron Donohue's teenage dare. Sad that he had ever gotten up the nerve to explore the flooded cave and its darkness. Sad that he had come here, a weakened, old, work-broken man, to try and do something that would have tested a young man in his prime.

But mostly, Jonah was sad about Miss Cecilia, waiting up there, not fifty feet away. He had failed her, left her all alone in a world for which she had not been prepared.

Tears flooded his eyes and melted into the cool, fresh flow of the spring. Then the first ribbons of water trickled into his lungs, and he felt the joy of release, the bright, expectant warmth of homecoming.

His eyes went wide as the sunlight flared yellow and the head-pool dissolved into blackness.

TWIN SPRINGS

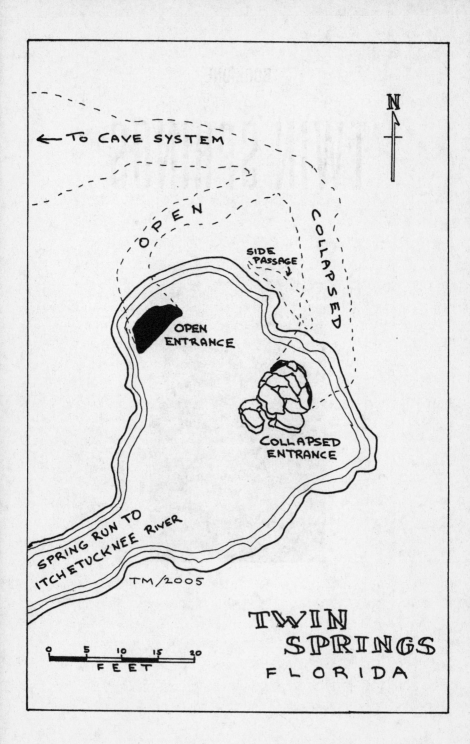

← TO CAVE SYSTEM

N

OPEN

COLLAPSED

SIDE PASSAGE

OPEN ENTRANCE

COLLAPSED ENTRANCE

SPRING RUN TO ITCHETUCKNEE River

TM/2005

TWIN SPRINGS

FLORIDA

0 5 10 15 20
FEET

CHAPTER ONE

JULY 14, 2005
LURAVILLE, FLORIDA

The single-story house was plain and pale yellow, about as architecturally distant from a Miami-Beach art deco as one could imagine. The vegetation across the road was pulp pines, not palm trees, and there was no beach littered with bronzed bodies. In fact, there was no beach, and no body, at all.

Jennifer Cassidy had been to Florida before—she'd come here for spring break at the insistence of a persuasive college roommate. But this nondescript house, sitting alone on a minimally landscaped lot, didn't offer a hint of the glitz and glamour she'd come to associate with the Sunshine State. In fact, were it not for the Bermuda-grass lawn and the palmettos planted along the drive, it wouldn't have appeared Southern at all.

Jennifer slowly drove the fifty yards of concrete driveway and stopped the rental car in front of a detached garage. She moved the shifter to "park," turned the rearview mirror her way, and took a quick glance.

She looked ... efficient.

Her blonde hair was cut short, short and tufting every which way in a responsible sort of punked-out style. She twisted the mirror down, and her eyes, clear and vibrant blue—the kind of blue that made people ask if she wore colored contacts—peered back at her. The rest of her face had that no-makeup look, like the face of somebody who'd gotten up while it was still dark out, made the thirty-five-minute drive to Detroit Metro Airport in something more like twenty, and had still only barely caught her flight.

All of which was absolutely true.

This was no time for the full treatment. She dug the essentials out of her purse and made two quick passes with her blush and just the barest hint of mascara. But that still looked too unfinished, so she got out her lipstick, squinted at the mirror, and applied two smooth, stay-between-the-lines strokes. Then she finished the job with a soft-chomp on a napkin fished from her Burger King bag.

The face in the mirror still looked efficient, younger than her twenty-four years, and vaguely boyish, mostly because of the hair—what there was of it. She turned the mirror back to where it was supposed to be and put her makeup away. On the journey to "beautiful," "cute" was about as far as she'd ever gotten, and she'd learned to comfort herself with the sentiment that things could be worse. She turned the key, silencing the engine, and then rummaged in her bookbag for the webpage she'd printed out back in Ann Arbor; the address was the same as the number on the eave of the garage. This had to be the place.

Jennifer opened the car door and grimaced at the heat. *Okay, maybe I am in Florida, after all.* But it sure wasn't the Florida they put in the tourist brochures. The largest body of water she'd seen on the drive down from the airport was the Suwannee River. And the landscape had consisted mostly of stands of scrawny pine trees and open fields dotted with cattle—not the polled Herefords she'd grown up with on the farm in Ohio, but scrawny, humped and wattled creatures that looked as if they belonged in India.

The yard was quiet; no breeze. Just a few birds, probably asking one another for sunscreen. Slipping on her sunglasses, Jennifer took note of a sign that said "SHOP," and followed the paved walk around the side of the house.

Then she stopped in midstep and wished she'd spent more time with her makeup.

Because there was a man seated at a table on the brick patio, and he wasn't just any man.

This guy was a hunk: nice, strong profile, good jaw, and a head of brown hair that was just coming due for a cut and going light at the ends from the sun. He was wearing khaki shorts, aviator sunglasses, and a faded blue T-shirt that fit snugly enough to show that he was in shape and then some. His arms, tanned and garnished with blonding hair, looked almost too muscular for the tiny, bent-nose pliers in his hand. He looked older than Jennifer, but not much. She guessed that he was in his thirties, early to mid.

Probably early.

He was working on something with black rubber hoses and shiny metal fittings. It looked like a piece of scuba gear, one of those things divers used to get air from a tank. Jennifer searched for the word ... *regulator*. He was working on a scuba regulator.

"I'll be with you in a second," he said without looking up. "I'm at one of those points in this rebuild where you have to hold your tongue just right ..." He tinkered with the device for the better part of a minute, and then he set it aside and stood, wiping his hands on a shop towel. "Sorry about that. I'm Beck Easton. Call me Beck."

"Jennifer. Uh, Cassidy."

They shook hands and Easton stepped back, giving Jennifer a long, slow look from head to toe—long enough to take her from flattered to mildly irritated.

"Let's see," he said. "Five-two?"

"And a half."

"And what? A hundred and fifteen pounds?"

Jennifer lifted her chin. "A hundred and fourteen, actually."

Easton nodded and walked around to her side. "Good tone. Do you run? Work out?"

"I bike a lot, swim when I can." Jennifer considered a quick sprint back to the car.

"That's great. Strong leg muscles help. We can put a 104 on you for the intro section and go to steel 72s, maybe even 95s for the Full-Cave."

"Huh?"

"Not that you have to do it all in one shot," Easton told her, hand up. "Take your time. Work your skills between courses. Do you have your C-card and logbook with you?"

"My what?"

"Your certification card and logbook."

Jennifer removed her sunglasses and squinted. "My certification card certifying what?"

Easton cocked his head and looked at her. "Well, that you're a trained diver, of course."

"Oh. I'm not. You see ... that's why I'm here."

He removed his own sunglasses. Green eyes—nice. "I'm sorry. You want open-water lessons, then? I can do that, but I've got to tell you, a group class down at Ginnie Springs will be a lot cheaper ..."

"No." Jennifer waved her hands and cut him off. "No—I'm not here to learn to dive. I'm here to hire you to do some diving for me."

"Research diving?"

"Exactly." In fact, that was all she wanted him to put on the credit-card receipt. One word: "Research."

"Well, sure." Easton nodded. "I do some of that. Although I've got to tell you, for hydrology, things like that, there's better people. What sort of research do you have in mind?"

"I need you to find something."

Easton rubbed his nose, crossed his arms. "Find what?"

"I ... I don't know."

Easton looked at her in silence. When he spoke again, his voice was low. "Can I ask how you found me?"

"Well, I did a Google search on 'cave diving' and 'Live Oak,' and found an equipment company called Dive-Rite. When I called there, I talked to a man named Lamar, and told him I needed a good diver who won't blab what I'm doing. He said I should come see you."

"O-kay ..." Easton smiled, just a bit, and glanced at the patio table. "Here, let me get this stuff out of our way. Can I get you something to drink?"

"Sure." Jennifer grinned. *Man—is this guy good-looking.* "That'd be great. Would you have a beer?"

Easton shook his head. "Soaking suds and blowing bubbles doesn't mix," he told her, tapping on the regulator. "I've got Coke, Diet Pepsi, root beer, and I think maybe even some Dr Pepper—had some locals diving with me last week. Or I've got some iced tea that I just made up. But I've got to warn you—it's sweet."

She grinned even more. "Sweet tea's fine."

"Great. Grab a seat. Facilities are in the shop if you need 'em."

The tea was still a little warm, so Easton heaped two heavy glass tumblers full of ice, added a stout wedge of lemon to each one—he never had figured out what good it did to slide a wafer of lemon onto the rim of a glass—and poured the tea in, the ice crackling as he did it. A car door slammed out in the driveway as he did this, and when he slid open the door to return to the patio, he saw why: his visitor now had a large black-nylon catalog case next to her and was removing thick file folders from it.

"Looks like this is going to get involved." He set a glass on a paper napkin in front of her and took a seat on the opposite side of the table.

"Well, it's ... complicated." The young woman took a sip of tea and smiled her approval. "Where do you want me to start?"

Easton glanced at the sky. "Plenty of daylight left. Start at the beginning."

"Okay." Jennifer wiped a bead of condensation off her glass and then looked up at Easton. "I'm a graduate student at the University of Michigan, the School of Information Science."

"Like IT—information technology?"

"That's part of it." She grimaced just a little as she said it. "But information science deals more with application than infrastructure. It's about sleuthing out facts, finding where the information is hiding."

"Like being a detective."

"More like a librarian." Jennifer laughed. "Sometimes both. Anyhow, I'm a second-year MS candidate, but this is my first year at U of M; I transferred in from Case Western. That put me low on the totem pole for any kind of assistantship work over the summer, but I was trying anyway—so I could keep my apartment and, you know—avoid going home and waiting tables in Wapakoneta."

Easton nodded and wondered if she was going to ramble. True, female customers at a cave-diving operation were few and far between, and this one was cute as the proverbial button, but he preferred to deal with people who could get to the point.

"Anyhow, it was starting to look as if that was just what I was going to be doing. But then my department head called me in, and there was this attorney in his office, looking for research help." She handed Easton a business card:

LOUIS F. SCARVANO

Attorney at Law

SCARVANO, MARTOIA AND WOODWARD, LLC.

1 Peachtree Centre—Ste. 3459, Atlanta, GA 30309

"I know the address." Easton handed the card back. "High-rent. I'd expect that anyone who hangs a shingle there could afford to keep his own paralegals on staff."

"He can and he does. But he didn't need legal research. He needed a family history."

"He traveled to Michigan to have you do his family tree?"

Jennifer shook her head. "Not *his* family history ..." She pulled a glossy photograph out of an envelope and handed it across to Easton. "... Hers."

Easton took a look and straightened up just a bit. The picture was obviously a copy of a much older image. Yet even rendered in shades of gray, and partly obscured by creases, the woman in the image was a stunning, raven-haired beauty with eyes that seemed to reach out and lock with his.

"Who am I looking at?"

"Cecilia Sinclair, although she was still Cecilia Donohue when that picture was taken. Daughter of Cameron Donohue, who owned a plantation near Branford. That's near here, right?"

"About half an hour away."

Jennifer returned the photo to its envelope. "That was shot the day they announced her engagement to Augustus Baxter—"

Easton shook his head. "You said her married name was 'Sinclair.'"

"Henry John Sinclair was her second husband, originally from Baltimore, although he and Cecilia moved to Ann Arbor after the war. That's why Mr. Scarvano came to U of M for his research; Cecilia Sinclair's personal documents are kept in the archive library there, and you need a stack pass to access them."

Easton nodded. This was making sense. "And you, being a grad student, have a pass."

"Exactimundo. Cecilia's first husband was originally from Georgia."

"So that's the Scarvano connection—his client is from Georgia, one of Baxter's descendants?"

Jennifer's face went to something that was halfway between a grimace and a scowl. "I asked him, and he wouldn't say—attorney-client privilege."

Easton nodded for her to go on.

"Anyhow, Augustus Baxter's father was a plantation owner, like Cecilia's, and apparently that's how they met; their fathers knew one another; Baxter was invited to Cecilia's cotillion—her coming-out ball—chemistry happened and they got engaged. Baxter even took a job at a bank in Jacksonville, to be nearer to Cecilia. They were only engaged three months, which would have been scandalous back then, except for the fact that this was 1861. Florida had already seceded from the Union, and Baxter had accepted a commission as a captain with the First Florida Cavalry. There were a lot of hurry-up weddings down here that year."

"You seem to know a lot about the period."

Jennifer smiled. "I was a dual-major undergrad—English and history. And I've always been interested in the Civil War. Not so much the battles, but the culture. How it affected people."

She took a sip of her tea. "Cecilia was a diarist, and she wrote every day, even when paper got scarce during the war. I read her journal—pretty sad story. Her father was in the war as well, and he got injured, came home, lingered, and eventually died of his wounds. Then Augustus Baxter was killed outright in a skirmish in Virginia, and that left Cecilia alone to run a plantation that was drowning in debt and hadn't cleared a dime in more than four years."

"So she lost it to banks up North?"

Jennifer nodded. "You've got it. Northern banks bought up the loans from failing banks down here. Then the banks up north hired traveling agents who went around selling off estates, liquidating the assets. And that's what happened with Cecilia. They swooped down and sold her home right out from under her."

Easton took a sip of his own tea, lemony and sweet and satisfying. He couldn't believe he'd grown up drinking it plain. "So where does Sinclair come in?"

"I don't know." Jennifer frowned. "In the journals that I have, August of 1865 shows her destitute and scraping for a living. That's how that volume ends. Yet when the next one starts, it's later in the same year—1865—and she's up in Michigan, happily married, comfortable and living on an apple farm. That's one of the mysteries."

"One?" Easton shifted in his chair. "There's more?"

Jennifer nodded, eyebrows up.

"There's a big one." She opened a thick three-ring binder and leafed through photocopies of pages covered with a refined and feminine handwriting. She stopped, read a little, and tapped the page. "On the night before their wedding, Baxter is staying down here, at the Donohue plantation. He comes to Cecilia after dinner and tells her something. In fact, she says that by the time they get done, it's midnight. She doesn't record exactly what it is that Baxter tells her, only that it is a secret important both to them and to their country—which was the Confederacy at the time—and that he is entrusting it to her in case something happens to him after the war."

Easton looked at the binder. It had to be a good three inches thick. "And she doesn't say any more about it in all of that?"

"I think she was so concerned that she was afraid to even mention it in her own journals," Jennifer told him. "In fact, she doesn't bring it up again until it's pretty clear that the South's goose is cooked." She leafed to a section near the back of the binder. "When she gets the news of Lee's surrender at Appomattox, she wonders if 'our Secret may yet save us.' And a few months later, when the war officially ends, she wonders 'what may become of our great Secret, for which so many lives were given, and if it has not yet saved our nation, may it perhaps save us?' Meaning herself and a freed slave she calls 'Uncle Jonah,' who was the only other person left on the plantation at that point. And then she mentions it one more time."

"Which is?"

Jennifer leafed to the last few photocopied pages. "August 6, 1865—Cecilia's just about at the end of her rope. The house has been all but emptied: furniture, paintings, even any clothes of value. And now she's two days away from having to leave the house itself. She's kept this secret, whatever it was, hidden throughout four years of war. Now she's about to be cast—well, she doesn't know where. And she doesn't see how she can keep the secret safe anymore, so she confides in the only friend she has left: the former slave, Jonah. And she adds in a postscript that Jonah has come up with a plan that gives her hope."

Easton tapped the table. "But she doesn't say what it is. Am I right?"

Jennifer glanced up from her binder. "You are. Cecilia's sick with worry. Too afraid to even confide in her diary, for fear that somebody might find it in the days to come. But the next day, she has no such worries. Jonah is dead, drowned in an underwater cave where he was hiding whatever it was. He was trying to breathe off these ... like sacks of air that he took down with him. And something went wrong. He drowned. So now Cecilia's last friend is dead, the secret is gone, and she has no way of getting to it. She closes with, 'All is lost and I am alone.'"

Easton leaned forward and looked at the binder. "And that's where it ends?"

"That's where this volume ends." Jennifer closed the binder. "As I said, when the next one starts, it's Christmas of that same year, and she's married and living on the farm in Michigan."

"Poor farmers or rich?"

Jennifer frowned at the material on the table. "I'd have to say very rich. When Cecilia died in 1931, she left a lot of money to charity—half a million each to the drama departments at U of M and Eastern Michigan University, more than a million, all total, to various missions organizations. She even left eight hundred thousand dollars in trust to help restore Ford's Theater. Pretty odd for a daughter of the Confederacy, but I guess she decided it was time to bury the hatchet. She didn't have any heirs—she and Sinclair had a son, but he died in a streetcar accident in Chicago in 1893. And Sinclair himself had died years earlier, in a shipwreck on the Great Lakes in ..." Jennifer checked her notes. " ... 1868."

"So Sinclair—did he come from money?"

"I don't know. His Bible—not a family Bible, but the one he carried—is with the papers that were left with the university, and it has lots of marginal notes in it. Looks like he memorized verses, kept notes on what he was working on. But the only personal information I can find in that is their wedding date: October 14, 1865. And the first public record I've found of him is in the social pages of the *Ann Arbor Beacon* in November, announcing that they've set up housekeeping and are receiving visitors."

She paused, her shoulders sagging a bit as she looked at Easton. "You think they came back and got it, don't you? Got the money, or jewels, or the deed or whatever it was, cashed it in and went up to start a farm in Michigan ... a hundred and forty years ago."

"It's sounding like it." Easton reached over and tapped the binder. "Does it say in here what spring they used as their hiding place?"

Jennifer searched the binder and read for a moment. "Here it is. Cecilia only mentions the name one time: Twin Springs."

Easton sat back in his chair.

"What?"

"Well ..." Easton put his hands atop his head, fingers knit. "It's sounding even more like it. There are springs down here that aren't often dived, but Twin's not one of them." He wondered why a researcher wouldn't have caught this, and then shook it away. The world of cave-diving was so closed that you'd almost have to be part of it to be privy to the information. "It's on private property, but even so, over the years there've probably been two, three hundred divers through that spring and the system behind it. If anything is down there to be found, I've got to think they would have found it by now."

Jennifer Cassidy looked as if someone had pulled the plug on her. She rubbed her forehead, reached for her tea, and looked absently at the empty glass.

"Here. Let me freshen that."

Easton picked up both glasses and headed back into the house. He glanced out the window at Jennifer, chin on her palm, the picture of defeat. All of his life, he'd thought of himself as a "ready, aim ... fire" sort of person. But Jennifer Cassidy seemed like more of a "ready, fire ... aim"—the sort he'd long since learned to avoid.

So why was it that he felt so badly for her and wanted to find some way to give her hope?

He wasn't sure. But as he was filling the second glass, he remembered something that might let him do just that.

◥

When Easton reappeared from the house, a fresh glass of tea in each hand, he was smiling. Not just smiling—grinning.

Jennifer scowled just a bit. *The cave-diving business must do pretty well. Here this guy has just talked himself out of a job, and he looks happy as a clam.* Finally, her ire got the better of her. "So what's got you so cheerful?"

"Twin Springs," he said, still smiling as he handed Jennifer her glass. "It isn't 'twin springs.' Not really. There's only one aperture—one way into the cave system. There used to be another spring head; you can see where it was and still feel some flow coming out of it. But it's collapsed—the entrance and a fair amount of passage behind it."

"And that's good because—?"

"Because the passage didn't collapse until sometime in the 1890s."

"Are you sure?" Jennifer straightened up a bit.

"Positive." Beck sat down, ignoring the drink in front of him. "As I said, Twin Springs is on private property. And most times, you take what a landowner tells you with a grain of salt. I mean, people tell you they have a 'spring' on their land, and, half the time, you go out to see it and it's not a spring at all. It's usually a sinkhole, no water coming out. But the guy that owns Twin Springs? The land's been in his family for more than a century; they probably picked it up from whatever bank it was that seized it from your Southern belle, there. And because Twin Springs was once obviously two springs, I once asked the owner if he knew what happened to the second one."

"Did he?"

"He did." Easton looked straight at her. "It was dynamited."

Jennifer lifted her head a bit. "Why would somebody want to blow up a spring?"

"To relieve boredom, I guess. Back in the 1890s, there was even less to do around here than there is now. The locals' idea of a good time on a Sunday afternoon was to head out to a spring with a picnic lunch and a barrel of beer. And then, for after-dinner entertainment, they'd chuck sticks of dynamite into the water, watch it geyser up. Only a matter of time before somebody made a lucky shot, landed their stick in the aperture, and the explosion collapsed the cave."

"So there's a fifty-percent chance that what I'm looking for is behind all that rock?"

"I wouldn't go counting your chickens just yet." Despite what he'd just said, Easton leaned forward, one arm on the table, obviously warming up to the idea. "But you can tell, even today, that the second aperture—the one that they blew—was once much larger than the first."

Jennifer waited for a moment, then asked, "And that's important because ...?"

"Because of something called Bernoulli's Principle." Easton held up both hands, the fingers of his left in a tight circle, the fingers of his right touching loosely. "If you figure that the same cave system is feeding both apertures, and one is smaller than the other, the water coming out of the smaller one will have to accelerate to balance the flow. It's the same thing that happens when you turn a shower head from a coarse to a fine setting—it sprays harder, because the flow is coming through a smaller opening."

"Okay." Jennifer nodded slowly. "I follow that. But why would that mean that the larger opening is the one we want?"

"Because ..." Easton's grin grew larger "... if I were diving in that cave on a breath-hold, I'd want to go against the lowest resistance possible on the way in."

Jennifer could actually feel her eyebrows rise. "The one that was collapsed."

"In the 1890s." Easton nodded twice. "They had diving suits back then, but I've never heard of anyone using one in a spring. Scuba wasn't invented until the Second World War. And the exploration of these cave systems around here didn't really get going until the sixties. Yeah, if your information is right—and if this secret, whatever it is, is waterproof—I'd say there's a chance that whatever your man put in the cave is still in there."

They sat back, looking at one another. In the distance, some bird asked another about sunscreen.

"Where are you staying?" Easton asked.

"I haven't gotten around to finding a place yet."

He laughed. "You really planned this out, didn't you?" He stood up and reached for her catalog case. "I've got a bunkhouse built onto the other end of the shop for people taking lessons. Nobody's in there right now. Let's get you settled. We can dive in the morning."

CHAPTER TWO

The two men lay prone in tall weeds, their bodies still as death itself. One man was lanky and ropy muscled with close-cut, jet-black hair under an olive-drab boonie cap, and skin the color of roasted coffee. He held a green parabolic microphone that was about the size of a pot lid. The smaller man, compact sport binoculars to his eyes, wore a smeared mask of charcoal to cover the paleness of his face. A wisp of blonde ponytail hung from beneath a black stocking cap; and a bushy, tobacco-stained mustache completely covered his upper lip. Other than their headgear, the men were dressed identically in olive-drab field jackets and cargo pants, brown jersey gloves, and worn, scuffed combat boots. Both men were sweating heavily, but neither moved to wipe a brow or whisk away the mosquito that settled first on one and then on the other.

The smaller man kept the binoculars to his face long after the man and the woman had moved away from the glass-topped table on the brick patio and moved out of sight, around the end of the plain yellow house. Finally the smaller man lowered the binoculars, rubbed his blonde mustache, and glanced at the westerly sun. He looked at his darker companion, who pointed at the parabolic mike and then rocked his hand from side to side: *Not good—only so-so.*

The smaller man tucked the binoculars into the bellows pocket of his field jacket and then pointed with his thumb, back over his shoulder. As if on cue, both men checked their watches. Then, without turning away from the house, they began to inch back slowly through the tall weeds, crawling with exaggerated care.

CHAPTER THREE

It seemed as if half of Branford started its day at Polly's. Pickups, vans, and sport-utility vehicles of various vintages crowded the gravel parking lot outside the restaurant. Inside, the crowd was mostly men, and Jennifer felt their gazes as she and Beck checked out the buffet; strangers were apparently a rarity at Polly's.

The long steam table was a cardiologist's nightmare: pork sausage, huge trays of bacon, scrambled eggs with onions and bell peppers, biscuits, gravy, waffles dusted with powdered sugar, a heaping tray of pastries, and a large basin of white stuff pooled with butter, which Easton identified as hominy grits. They found a table, and a word to the waitress brought Jennifer a plate of melon slices, cottage cheese, and fresh strawberries.

As she spread a paper napkin on her lap, Jennifer stole a look at a neighbor's stack of waffles. "Haven't these people ever heard of cholesterol?"

"Heard of it?" Easton sat down across from her. "Sure. But you don't see many dying from it. These folks make a living cutting pulp pine and doing the kind of factory work you can stop thinking about the minute you hit the parking lot—and some don't work at all unless they have a bill to pay. Otherwise, they go fishing. The world may think of them as rednecks and crackers, but they're very laid-back rednecks and crackers. It's like forest fires—you can have a whole forest full of dry trees, but you won't have a fire unless lightning strikes or someone tosses a match. People here may have all the fuel for a heart attack, but hardly anybody's got the stress to trigger one."

Jennifer sipped her chicory-laced coffee and nodded at Easton's philosophy lesson. If the truth were to be told, Easton's 5:00 a.m.

start to his day was about four hours earlier than what she'd become accustomed to at the university. And the lackadaisical lifestyle he'd described was anything but evident in his own surroundings. The equipment in his dive shop had been stowed with military precision; his compressor and breathing-gas-blending area gleamed like a hospital operating room. The bookshelves in his office were neat, the volumes arranged alphabetically by author.

Even his bunkhouse had been neat as the proverbial pin, the knotty-pine paneling gleaming and smelling of lemon oil, the four military-style cots tightly sheeted and scented faintly with laundry detergent. When she'd dropped her pen, she'd found it under the bunk on a floor so freshly polished that she doubted it had ever felt the foot of a dust bunny.

Jennifer compared that to her apartment back in Ann Arbor and her study carrel at the library—both piled with binders, paper, and old books feathered with buck-slips. Neat was nice, but come on—who had the time to polish paneling?

Then again, Easton's office also had pictures of him in uniform with other earnest, extremely fit young men, and a framed diploma from the United States Naval Academy. Maybe neat-freak got programmed into you at places like that. Still, it weirded Jennifer out just a bit. It reminded her of her mother, who had been known to iron underwear.

Jennifer reached for her fork and Easton cleared his throat. "Mind if I pray before we dig in?"

"Pray? Uh—sure. Go ahead."

Easton bowed his head. "Heavenly Father, we ask that you bless this meal and the day we now begin ..."

Jennifer sneaked a peek at the man: eyes closed, head nodding slightly as he spoke. Biceps like firm bread loaves strained the sleeves of his Navy Experimental Dive Team T-shirt. He couldn't have shaved more than two hours earlier, but he already had the faintest shadow of a beard.

Mr. Testosterone. Praying. Jennifer was still working on that when Easton concluded, "... and we ask that all we do this day will honor you."

Jennifer, unsure of how to react, forced a smile and picked up her fork.

"I called Alton Edwards last night," Easton said as he stirred his coffee. "He's the farmer who owns Twin Springs. I told him I wanted to try opening the second aperture, see what was back in there. He said he didn't care as long as we didn't stop up the spring. Also said he'd clear it with the DNR—the Department of Natural Resources. Which I doubt will actually happen. In Jake's mind, it's his spring, and the state's got no business telling him what he can do with it. Folks around here tend to be a tad independent."

He sipped his coffee and looked at her over the rim of the sturdy ceramic mug.

"Are you sure you can't give me a better description of just what it is we're looking for in this cave?" He set the mug down.

"I'm sure," Jennifer met his gaze without blinking. "I know that, whatever it was, it was small enough that Jonah Winslow was able to take it in there by himself, back in 1865. Other than that, all I know is that it was something very important to Cecilia Baxter."

"I see." Easton finished his breakfast in silence.

Jennifer began wondering just how sound an idea this all was. Here she was, in back-of-beyond Florida, sort of surreptitiously— okay, *more* than sort of surreptitiously—spending her client's money in a search for something that she couldn't even identify. It had made perfect sense back in Ann Arbor in the wee, small hours of the night when she'd made the decision to come down here. Now she wasn't nearly as sure.

Besides, when she'd gotten up this morning, she'd put on a two-piece swimsuit under her cutoffs and polo shirt, figuring she might end up in the water at some point during the day. Now the

Lycra was chafing, the small of her back was getting moist despite the air-conditioner laboring in the far wall, and she was feeling out of her element—doubtful.

She pushed away the half-eaten bowl of fruit, Easton put some money on the table and Jennifer wordlessly nodded her assent. They got up and left, and Jennifer again felt the eyes following her out of the room. Easton may have had the inside line of the locals, but he didn't have the whole line—fishing wasn't the only thing these guys were interested in.

Easton's truck was a brand-new Ford F-250, fire-engine red with a matching shell that covered a pickup bed full of tanks, suits, regulators, and swim fins. The truck stood tall on off-road suspension, so getting in meant scaling the side of it, and Jennifer did that, grateful for the stainless-steel step and the grab-handle. Otherwise, she would have been reduced to asking the cave-diver to lift her up to her seat.

"Music's in the console," Easton said as he started the engine. "We've got a little drive. Pick out what you'd like."

The console held two rows of CDs. One was music by groups like Nickel Creek and the Oakridge Boys, plus a few Vince Gill albums and other music that Jennifer vaguely recognized as bluegrass and country. She checked the second row and looked over at Easton.

"Who're Rick Braun and Fred Bishop?"

Easton glanced at her over the tops of his sunglasses. "Jazz . . . trumpet."

"Oh." Jennifer picked out a Garth Brooks and put it in the CD player. Sound-effects thunder rumbled softly out of the speakers, and a guitar began to play.

The CD was starting its third song when Jennifer noticed Easton glancing into the rearview mirror. He did it a second time, and then a third.

"Something wrong?"

"Maybe. Anybody know that you're down here?"

"No, not really." Jennifer glanced back over her shoulder. "Just my client's secretary. Why?"

"I think we're being followed."

Jennifer leaned forward and checked the mirror on her side. A dark blue sedan was trailing behind them, about a half mile back on the asphalt road. "Maybe they're just going the same way we are."

Easton shook his head. "I don't think so. They pulled out of the agricultural inspection station just before we crossed the bridge over the Suwannee. And they've followed us through two turns since."

"Is that unusual?"

He checked the mirror again. "The ag station inspects commercial trucks, not cars. And if these folks are headed to town, they wouldn't have made the last turn. Let's try this ..." He took the next right, drove along for another half mile, and then made a left turn onto a winding gravel road.

Jennifer peered at her mirror, trying to see through the dust. "Are they still with us?"

"Yep." Easton kept glancing at the mirror as he drove. "And this road doesn't go anywhere except back to the highway we were just on." He turned to Jennifer. "You sure you haven't left something out that I ought to know?"

"Scout's honor." Jennifer turned on her seat and looked through the back window, but the truck cap's dusty Plexiglas showed her little more than what she'd seen in the mirror. "All I told my client was that I was coming down here to do some onsite research. I didn't tell them anything further—but then, they didn't ask either. So I left it at that."

Easton nodded. They got back to the main highway, made another right, and went about a half mile down the road before turning left onto another thinly graveled road. This made a series of bumpy jogs, and soon they were driving through scrub pine and hedges. Easton slowed and turned onto a faint dirt road. There was a sign beside it:

PROPERTY OF
NAT'L SPELEOLOGICAL SOCIETY — CAVE DIVING SECTION
NO ENTRY WITHOUT PERMISSION

Easton followed the two-track into a small opening and parked next to a tiny pond with a log in it. He killed the engine. "Let's get out for a minute."

Jennifer climbed down and looked at the pond. It didn't look like much—just clear water with some rocks in the bottom of an oblong basin. "This is the spring?"

"It's Cow Spring," Easton said walking around the front of the truck. "One of those 'springs' that's not really a spring. It's an in-line sink; the water comes in from one side and goes out the other, doesn't drain off into a run. The Section—the Cave-Diving Section—bought it a few years back, to keep it open for cave-diving, but no. This is not the cave you're interested in. We're just waiting."

They heard the sound of tires on gravel and saw a flash of dark, metallic blue paint as the sedan drove by on the road outside.

"I didn't think they'd follow us in." Easton turned and looked Jennifer straight in the eyes. "You really have no idea who these people are?"

"Not a clue."

"Because if you do, now's the time to say. Especially if they might mean us harm."

Jennifer's pulse quickened. "Harm?"

"Rob us." Easton glanced back toward the road. "Cap us."

"Cap?"

Looking back at the road, Easton pointed his finger and dropped his thumb, like the hammer of a gun.

"You mean . . . *kill* us?" Jennifer felt as if everything inside her had dropped an inch or two.

Easton nodded.

"But I'm just a grad student . . ." Jennifer touched the truck and held herself steady for a moment. "Man . . . I mean, I—I never thought about anything like that. And I really don't know who they are. Should we call the cops?"

"We could." Easton glanced at the road again. "But personally, if whatever's in that spring is interesting enough to draw this kind of attention, I'd like to go see what it is. And getting authorities involved is just going to complicate things. So I'd like to go have a look before we do anything else. Wouldn't you?"

Jennifer thought of the Marine Corps memorabilia back at Easton's dive shop. And he was a pretty good-sized guy. Her own personal Marine: that gave her a confidence that might otherwise have eluded her.

"Yes, I would." She straightened up and nodded firmly. "I would, very much."

"Okay," Easton reached into his shirt pocket, pulled out his sunglasses, and put them on. "Let's go."

They got into the truck and backed out, turning away from the gravel road.

"Aren't we going out?"

"We are," Easton reached down and pulled a lever on the floor. "But we're taking the back way. They'll probably be watching the entrance."

"So what's to keep them from getting curious, driving in, and following us again?"

Easton grinned, his eyes still on the rutted two-track path ahead of them. "They don't know the country. Otherwise, they wouldn't have followed us on that turn. And then there's this." He turned off the two-track and came to a steep ravine with basketball-sized rocks across its bottom. Easton drove slowly down the dirt bank, pitched and wobbled across the shifting rocks, and then, all four wheels spinning for grip, clambered back up the other side.

"You can't get across that without a four-by-four," he said as he shifted the truck back into two-wheel drive. On the stereo, Garth Brooks was singing a rollicking ballad about a long-haul trucker and his good-looking, unfaithful wife.

"Well, Jennifer." Easton grinned. "Let's go have a look at your spring."

CHAPTER FOUR

TWIN SPRINGS, FLORIDA

The water had long since seeped into Easton's wetsuit and warmed, so he felt comfortable as he floated in the Twin Springs headpool. Holding his breath and moving his fins slightly to keep his position, he peered at the bottom through the twin lenses of his dive mask. He sculled to his side to inspect the largest boulder in the spring's collapsed aperture from a new angle. The lifting straps around it appeared to be in position, and the steel cable seemed secure, so he lifted his head. "Okay, take up the slack. The red button. Good—you've got it. Keep her coming."

On the bluff above, Jennifer Cassidy stood next to the pickup, drawing a hand across her brow in the heat. As Easton signaled, she worked the remote control to the truck's bumper-mounted winch. The steel cable straightened, water dripping from it to the headpool's surface.

Easton swam over and put his hand on the cable. All the slack had been taken out of it, and it was stiff as an iron bar.

"Okay. Slowly, now." He dipped his face beneath the water again.

Wisps of mud and silt began to waft up from the rubble. As Easton watched, the boulder shuddered, and then slid a full inch before the rocks around it began to tumble, silt rising up in dusty tan clouds around them. He raised a clenched fist, signaling Jennifer to stop, and the boulder ceased its motion.

Easton jack-knifed and made a smooth surface-dive, kicking down to where the straining straps embraced the three-thousand-pound block of gray limestone. Up top, the F-250's rear axle was chained to a pair of live oaks, although it didn't look as if that precaution would prove necessary. The boulder was wedged between two other blocks, but once it cleared them, nothing would prevent it from sliding cleanly across the white sand of the spring basin. Since sliding took less energy than lifting, the task appeared well within the capacities of the truck's two-ton winch. Easton popped back to the surface and took a breath.

"We're looking good. Go ahead and pull 'er out."

Jennifer nodded and the winch resumed its mechanical whine.

Easton lowered his dive mask to the water again. Around the boulder, silt began to billow up in earnest, like the smoke of an underwater fire. Easton backed off to the side of the headpool and watched. He'd tied a bandanna to the cable at the water's surface before they'd begun; when the red cloth was five feet above the water, he raised a fist again and Jennifer stopped winching.

The water was completely silted now, as if someone had dumped a double-handful of dirt and sand into an aquarium. But Easton knew it wouldn't last long. The sand would settle quickly, and the rest would wash away. Already, the turbid water was being carried down the spring run to the river, as the cave pumped thousands of gallons of clear water up from its depths each minute. Within ten minutes, the water was clear enough for him to drop down and take a look.

An aperture now yawned where the pile of rubble had been. Just a few feet inside, more boulders blocked the way, but Easton had expected this. He knew from his inspections at the old junction that breakdown—the cave-diving term for collapsed rock—blocked what once had been the main entry passage to Twin Springs Cave. But he reasoned that, if a free-diver—a person diving without scuba equipment—had placed something in the old main passage, it wouldn't be far from the entrance. So he didn't have to clear the whole channel; the first few yards would probably suffice.

They repeated the winching operation a dozen times, Easton using a scuba regulator and a small "pony bottle" of air to breathe on as he hooked up the last boulders, some twenty feet back into the passage. Then, when those too were free and a new pile of rocks decorated the sands of the Twin Springs basin, he signaled Jennifer to secure the winch. It was time to go exploring.

Easton swam to the side of the headpool and donned a dive harness and a belt containing a toaster-sized battery pack. Then he picked up a scuba tank and, rather than mounting it on his back, he simply clipped it to his harness with a nylon tether. He put his regulator in his mouth, set the black bezel on his Mickey Mouse dive watch to zero, and slipped beneath the surface of Twin Springs.

The water was nearly clear again. Only a few particles of silt still hovered in the water of the spring basin, like dust motes turning in a summer-warm room. Easton switched on all three of his lights, then shut the back-ups off again, satisfied that they would work should the need arise. He left his primary light burning and, pushing the tank ahead of him like a small hand-propelled torpedo, sank to the basin floor.

He unclipped a dive reel from his harness, pulled two yards of white nylon guideline from it, and tied it off onto one of the boulders. The tank had a yellow snorkeling vest strapped around it, and, taking his regulator from his mouth, Easton blew a little air into its inlet tube, rendering the steel tank weightless. Maneuvering it underwater now was as easy as handling a plastic toy. All set, he pointed the tank at the yawning darkness and finned his way back into the cave.

Immediately, his light picked up something gray and metallic on the passageway floor, sticking up from the breakdown. Easton hooked the tank valve on a rock to keep his place in the current and reached down between two boulders to wriggle the object free.

It was a lead weight, a window sash weight, by the look of it. He hefted it and guessed it to be about four pounds—far too large to be a jerry-rigged fishing sinker. There was no cordage attached, meaning either there never had been a line, or the weight had been tied with something organic that had rotted and disintegrated in the room-temperature water.

Easton set the weight atop a stone block and went on. The rubble angled almost to the ceiling at this point, as he had not cleared the passage entirely; he'd just made enough space to get through. He pushed his tank through a gap in the rocks and wriggled through after it, breathing hard as he threaded his way against a constant flow of water.

In the blue-white, haloed circle cast by his halogen divelight, rock lay jumbled along the stone passageway, and a thick layer of silt carpeted the floor between the boulders. His light traced open channel for about fifty feet; after that, the rubble reached to the ceiling again. Easton wondered just how much dynamite those folks had chucked in here, back in the thirties. There was enough collapsed limestone to construct a good-sized house.

He slowly played the light around the passage. Up ahead, a dark, shadowed sliver, an opening almost like a low, rough-hewn doorway, appeared behind some of the rubble. Using his fingertips, Easton pulled himself closer in the steady flow, careful not to let his fins disturb the silt slumbering beneath him.

The sliver materialized into a side-passage, nearly closed off by the breakdown on the floor, but still large enough to admit a diver. Easton pulled his guideline taunt, wrapped it off around a finger of rock, and pushed the tank beneath a shallow overhang and into the small, close passage.

Silt still blanketed the floor, although not as much. The flow was lower, and once he'd cleared the entrance, the side-passage was relatively free of rubble.

Easton dipped under a low portion of the passage, and passed a slab of limestone leaning precariously against the wall. As his fins brushed it, he heard a loud "clunk." He stopped, looked back. The slab had fallen across the passage, blocking his exit. He wasn't concerned; it had moved easily enough, so it wouldn't be hard to push out of the way when he left.

The passage rose, tall and narrow. Easton turned on his side, right shoulder up, and wriggled through, his body touching rock at his chest and shoulders. Finally, even that was difficult, and he was satisfied that no one could have come this way before him. So far on this dive, nothing had turned up but rock, rubble, silt, and the single sash weight; whatever had been hidden away in this cave either remained hidden or had been removed long before. Crabbing his way around in the passage, exhaling completely to get past one tight spot, he turned back the way he had come and began reeling in his guideline.

Despite the noon heat, Jennifer shivered as she looked down at the waters of Twin Springs. She'd read in Cecilia Sinclair's diary that one man had already drowned here. Easton seemed to know what he was doing, but still ...

Beck Easton had set up his equipment with methodical care, double-checked everything, even though it was obvious that he had done dives like this a thousand times before. When he'd donned his wetsuit, he'd looked like a factory worker putting on his coveralls, the motion automatic, like something he no longer had to think about.

Jennifer's thoughts lingered on an image of Easton pulling on his wetsuit, the morning sun painting shadows on the muscles of his tanned back. Then she stopped herself. *Where had that come from?* Beck Easton was hired help, nothing more.

Then again, she had liked how decisive he'd been when he'd thought they were being followed. Maybe his actions had just been theatrics, a bit of melodrama to impress his client. For all she knew, the people in that blue car could have been bird-watchers, or lost tourists. She'd met men before who liked to embellish. Men she didn't like.

But Jennifer didn't get that sense with Beck Easton. Her intuition told her he was the real deal. And while she had the objectivity of a trained researcher, she trusted her intuition.

She glanced at her wristwatch and then took it off and put it inside the truck. Choosing her steps carefully with her bare feet, she climbed down the steep gully to the spring basin, pulled off her T-shirt, and laid it on a sun-warmed rock. Then she unzipped her cutoffs and slipped them down, kicking them off on the spring's limestone verge.

The two-piece swimsuit underneath, purchased for that long-ago spring break, hadn't raised a single eyebrow on the beaches of Fort Lauderdale and Miami. Yet, sensible as it was, it was still considerably less than the one-piece Jennifer had worn for family trips to the lake back home. To tell the truth, it made her just a little self-conscious. But the day was hot, the water looked inviting, and there was no way, after chaffing in the suit all the way through breakfast, that she was not going to use it when she had the chance.

Walking around to where the basin dropped steeply into the headpool, she dove in, sliced through the water, arced back up to the surface and gasped. Seventy-two degrees or not, the water felt freezing after the ninety-three-degree air. But she stayed in, despite the chill. It was a relief to be out of the noonday heat, and it gave her a strange comfort to share the same water as the quiet and confident Beck Easton.

Jennifer peered through the shimmering surface at the cave entrance. Every few seconds, bubbles slipped from the lip and wobbled to the surface of the pool. Those would be the exhaust bubbles from Beck Easton's scuba equipment, and Jennifer figured that, as long as they kept rising, he was still breathing. She floated on the surface of the pool, watching the bubbles as they shimmered up to her. She found herself silently moving her lips, asking, hoping that they would keep coming. Then she caught herself and stopped.

After all, she hadn't prayed in years.

Easton reeled in line and retraced his path. The water on the way out was not as clear. That was standard fare in virgin cave passage; no matter how careful a diver was about not disturbing the silt on the floor, the exhaust bubbles from the regulator would hit the ceiling and scour minuscule particles of algae and loose grit from the rough surface of the limestone. Once freed, the tiny bits of matter sank slowly to the passage floor, creating an underwater snowstorm.

Visibility plummeted to just under five feet. With particles raining down in the small side-passage, Easton nearly rammed the fallen limestone slab with his tank, making it out with his light only at the last moment.

Even leaning across the passage, the big slab couldn't prevent him from making his exit. There was room both at the top and at the bottom of the passage to wriggle through. But his guideline had drifted high, where the toppled block had trapped it. Unwilling to cut a perfectly good line, Easton vented the buoyancy compensator and set his tank down on the floor, raising a small cloud of silt. Bracing against the walls with his fins, breathing on the long-hosed regulator, he gripped the limestone block to lean it back against the wall.

Then he saw it.

His divelight, mounted on the back of his right hand, lit the right-side wall as he pushed the big slab out of the way. When it did, it illuminated a ledge, and on the ledge was something—something that was roughly rectangular, and lighter in color than the surrounding rock. Puzzled, Easton moved closer to get a better view.

It wasn't a rock. It was manmade—an old canvas bag of some sort. He could just make out faint letters, "CSA," printed on its surface.

Easton leaned the slab of limestone back, against the opposite wall of the passage and reached for the bag. When he tried to lift it, the ancient canvas disintegrated, vanishing like sodden tissue-paper into a waterborne cloud of dust.

But whatever had been inside the bag was still there. Unwilling to risk ruining that as well, Easton studied it for a minute before touching it.

At first glance it looked almost like a rock, darker than the limestone behind it, the object's surface a deep gray in color, mottled here and there with lighter blotches.

Changing the angle of his light, he saw a crimped seam. Metal? It looked almost like tinfoil, but it was darker in color, with only the barest hint of luster. And it was coated with something translucent—what, he didn't know.

Easton touched it gingerly. The surface felt malleable, soapy in texture. Wax? He poked the object tentatively and, satisfied that it wouldn't fall to pieces, lifted it off its ledge.

It was heavy. Surprisingly heavy, even in the water. About the size of a thick book, it had to weigh better than ten pounds. He turned it over, looking for markings or writing of any kind. There were none, just three carefully crimped seams.

Easton hefted the object and thought for a moment, gauging his distance from the cave entrance. Even if all the intervening rubble were to be removed, he still believed it would take him nearly a minute to dive from the surface and swim back here to this spot.

A minute in; a minute out. Fifteen seconds more to move the limestone slab back and hide that heavy canvas bag. All told, at very minimum, two-and-a-quarter minutes underwater, fighting the outflow of a second-magnitude spring. Easton checked his depth on his wrist-mounted Ni-Tek computer: the digital numerals showed 42 feet. It was quite a dive for any day and age, and if Jennifer Cassidy was right, and this object had been down here since the end of the Civil War, it was an absolutely amazing, very nearly incredible, feat.

Easton thought about the cave-diver—because that was most certainly what that person had been—who had made this trip ahead of him. Three-quarters of a century before scuba, breathing, according to what Jennifer had read, from "bags of air." Easton's hat was definitely off to him.

Easton loosened his harness, put the mysterious object under his chest-strap, and then cinched the webbing tight. Satisfied that the parcel was secure, he pushed the limestone slab back upright, retrieved his air supply from the passage floor, pushed the purge to vent some air from the tank's buoyancy compensator, and continued his exit.

Back in the main passage, the water was much clearer, the stronger flow having long since flushed any bubble-scoured matter down the system and out of the entrance. In his element and relaxed, Easton let himself drift with the outflow, reeling in his guideline and snaking his tank through the piles of broken limestone that rose from the passage floor.

He reached the restriction atop the largest pile, retrieved the object from under his chest-strap, passed it and his tank through first, and then wriggled after them, the cave's flow pushing against his fins as he went. On the other side, he resecured the object and made his way back to the entrance.

When he came back out into the light, his dive watch showed that he had been down for barely ten minutes, his computer recording a maximum depth of 46 feet. It was safe for him to go directly to the surface, but, true to his training, Easton settled to the white-sand floor of the basin. A three-minute safety stop, even when the computer showed you were clear and safe to ascend, was the diver's equivalent of an-apple-a-day.

He looked up and saw Jennifer floating at the surface. She gave him a fingers-only wave, and he lifted a hand in return. It was the first time he'd seen her in a swimsuit, and she was worth a second look.

How was it that his colonel on Okinawa had put it about young women her age? She was at that time of life "when their flower is open its fullest." It was an apt description.

Easton's thoughts turned to his wife. She had been gone for nearly four years now, and he still carried a Statue-of-Liberty-sized torch for her. A few close friends had urged him to move on, but he'd found that advice impossible to follow. Other women—even the thought of them—just naturally got measured against the woman he'd married, and they universally had come up wanting. Nor had the passage of time lessened this—if anything, it had strengthened it.

Still, there was something about this Jennifer Cassidy. Maybe it was her looks, or maybe it was her headfirst, out-the-window, way of dealing with issues. Maybe it was both. Whatever it was, Easton had to admit that he was finding this woman attractive. Very much so. And coming on as it had, in the space of less than twenty-four hours, the feeling startled him.

He shook the thought away. Jennifer Cassidy was his client. Nothing more. You had to keep the business side of your life separate from the personal side. Anybody knew that. He looked up again as his exhaust bubbles wobbled toward the surface and broke around the slender, youthful form of Jennifer Cassidy.

A sunfish swam across his field of vision, interrupting the reverie. Easton checked his watch; five minutes had passed since he'd emerged from the cave. He smiled behind his regulator. He'd long had a tradition that anything less than fifteen minutes did not constitute a dive; it either lasted that long, or he refused to log it. And now his new client, floating fifteen feet above him, had distracted him long enough for his bottom-time to pass the magic number.

Easton picked up his tank and swam to the shallow end of the basin. Jennifer was waiting there, her wet, blonde hair slicked back from her forehead, expectation alive in her bright, blue eyes.

"Did you find something?"

Grinning, Easton quickly unhooked his tether to the tank, shed his battery pack, loosened his web harness, and took out the mysterious object. Instantly, he was enveloped in a blonde, tanned, bikinied hug, a wonderfully warm kiss on his cheek.

He laughed. "I take it this is what you were looking for?"

"I don't know ..." She accepted it from him, and her eyebrows rose. "Wow ... It's heavy, isn't it?"

"It is. So what do we do, take it back to the shop?"

She looked at it and nodded. "That'd be best. Get it into a more controlled environment, subdued lighting, out of all this heat. But, then again ..." She squinted and tapped the object. "Do you have a pocket knife with you?"

"Up in the truck."

"Let's go."

Ten minutes later, Easton had toweled himself off and pulled on blue canvas shorts and a faded gray T-shirt emblazoned with the seal of the Navy Experimental Dive Team. Jennifer spread her cut-offs on the tailgate between the two of them and carefully set the object Beck had retrieved on top.

She accepted Easton's stainless-steel Leatherman multipurpose tool, a scratched and battered specimen that had obviously seen some use. Opening it to its smallest blade, she scraped away a bit of the outer substance on the object and sniffed the blade, holding it out so Easton could do the same.

"Smells like honey."

"That's right." Jennifer nodded her head. "Beeswax."

"So they wanted to waterproof whatever's inside."

"So it would appear." She worked the knife's blade under the crimped metal, which lifted easily. "It looks like tinfoil," she muttered.

"Lead," Easton corrected. "See? It's dark gray all over, except for where the knife has scratched it, and there it's bright."

She shot him a sidelong glance.

"Cutting Xs in bullet heads," he said. "It's a Marine thing. But believe me, I know lead. That's lead."

Jennifer turned back to the parcel and carefully pulled the metal apart at the seam. It was thicker than tinfoil, but it tore as she began to lift it. Tsking, she carefully slid the knife under the foil and lifted it that way.

Under the heavy foil was a layer of cloth, or several layers by the look of it, with a heavy, stiff finish.

"Oilcloth," Easton said. "Some places, they still make waterproof packaging out of it."

Jennifer pulled the foil completely back, then used the knife blade to lift back the edge of the oilcloth. "Look at that. It's not even brittle." She looked Easton's way, her eyes wide with surprise.

"No air," Easton told her. "Things get brittle, oxidize, because of prolonged exposure to air, and especially air and heat. Cave environments reflect the average topside temperature of their locations, and around here, although you might not believe it today, the average annual temperature is room temperature. If your Southern belle's journal is correct, this thing has been sitting undisturbed for more than a hundred and thirty years in a constant, airless, seventy-two-degree environment."

Jennifer pursed her lips as she nodded. "Perfect archival conditions ..."

"Freshwater'll do that," Easton agreed. "I have an uncle who's a marine archaeologist—he and I used to dive the Great Lakes together. And the Lakes are more like cold storage—average bottom temperature is around thirty-six degrees. One time we brought up a jar of preserves from a shipwreck—when we opened it back at his lab, it still smelled like fresh apples."

But Jennifer didn't seem to be listening. She'd set the object on her lap and was unwrapping the layers of oilcloth. Beneath them was another fabric, this one a plain cotton calico. When she lifted the last layer, she gasped and set it back down.

"What is it?" Easton leaned nearer.

"Take a look."

Easton lifted the printed cloth. A half-dollar-sized gold coin and an eight-inch gold bar gleamed in the afternoon sunlight.

"Holy smokes ... are they real?" Jennifer put on her reading glasses to examine the gold bar as Easton reached for the coin.

"This isn't lead." He turned it over in his hand. The front was simple: a cameo of a woman with a classical Grecian hairdo, wearing a crown inscribed with the word "LIBERTY." Thirteen stars were arranged around the woman's head and under her image was a date: 1856.

The other side was more complicated. An ornate eagle—a shield in front and rays of light bursting from behind—was framed with filigree. It held an olive branch and two arrows in its talons. Over its head was a halo of thirteen stars, and under the fan of its tail was a small "S." Running above the design were the words "UNITED STATES OF AMERICA" and beneath it, "TWENTY D."

"It's a gold double eagle," Easton said. "San Francisco mint."

"Double eagle?" She frowned. "I only see one."

"True. But the ten-dollar gold piece also had an eagle on the back. This is worth two of those, so ... it's a double eagle."

Jennifer peered at him over the top of her glasses.

"Every shipwreck in the Great Lakes was rumored to have gone down with a safe full of double eagles in the captain's stateroom." Easton shrugged. "As far as I know, none of them ever did, but somewhere along the way, I made it my business to learn what one looks like."

Jennifer showed him the bar. It was about the same size as a Hershey's bar, only half an inch thick. She tapped the end where a tiny corner of it had been cut away, and something scratched into its surface: ".9975 F."

"So," she asked, "any idea what this is?"

"Yeah. I've seen this before." He leaned closer, squinting at the writing, their heads almost touching. "Gold markets in Jakarta, on leave. They'd buy up old wedding bands, watch cases, you name it, and melt them down into bars. Then the brokers would cut off a corner for analysis. That stands for 'point nine-nine-seven-five fine.' That's the same as ninety-nine point seven-five percent pure gold. The broker melts and weighs the sample to make the analysis, and then gets to keep the sample as his fee."

"Think they were doing it that same way back before the Civil War?" Jennifer asked.

Easton shrugged. "It'd make sense. And now we know why we attracted some attention on the way here. That bar is about as close to pure gold as you're going to get. I'd say that you have several thousand dollars sitting there, easily."

Jennifer whistled softly and set the gold aside on the oilcloth. She lifted up the last layer of the calico, exposing a worn, black leather book. The cover was engraved with initials: a Gothic "B," flanked by an "A" and an "S."

"Augustus Samuel Baxter," Jennifer said.

"Who's that?"

"Cecilia Donohue's—Cecilia Sinclair's—first husband, the one who died in the Civil War."

Jennifer used both hands to carefully open the book. It looked old, with water stains on the edges of its pages and creases on its leather cover, but it opened without cracking.

Folded and set between the front endpapers was a typewriter-sized sheet of paper, a fine-lined, black-on-white map, apparently cut out of a larger chart. Open-faced script running nearly off the page identified a long, narrow hook of land as "Cat Island."

"That's in the Bahamas," Easton said. "I've been there. It's a typical Bahamian out-island, about fifty miles long and a decent Frisbee-toss wide. No cruise-ships, no night clubs, no casinos, and so virtually no tourists. Good diving, though. Someday, they'll put in a decent airport, something that can handle commercial jets, and it'll get busy. But right now, the whole island has less than four thousand people. Half fish for a living and half don't. Before the Civil War, I'd be surprised if there was anybody there at all. Ships might've stopped to catch turtles for meat or to take on fresh water, but that'd be about it."

The book was a slim volume, somewhere in the neighborhood of a hundred pages, most of which were filled with a strong, precise, copperplate hand.

"Diary?"

Jennifer shook her head "I don't think so. None of the entries are dated. It appears to be a narrative of some kind."

"Must be some narrative. A man died trying to hide it." Easton wrapped the gold in the calico cloth and placed the bundle next to Jennifer, and then he stood, scanning the terrain around them and the county road, barely visible through the trees.

"Tell you what," he said. "It feels like it's time we got moving. I'm going to get the gear up, out of the spring. Why don't you take a run through that book and see if you can figure out what it had in it that could make it worth dying for."

He climbed easily down the gully to retrieve his tank and his harness, carried them back to the truck, and put them away, securing the tank to a rack so it wouldn't roll. Then he went back to retrieve the salvage straps and his mask and fins. He had just cleared the gully's brink on the return trip, when he saw Jennifer's face, wide-eyed and incredulous.

"You found something," he said. It was a statement, not a question.

Jennifer held up her hand, read a page, and flipped a few pages more. For what seemed to be an eternity she read in silence. Then she lifted her gaze to Easton, her eyes even wider.

"There was this ship," she said, "a few years before the Civil War, a steamship called the *Halcyon*. They stole it, Beck. Hijacked it—Baxter and his friends. And it was full ..." Her voice drifted off, and she glanced around as if afraid to say what came next.

"Beck," she whispered. "The *Halcyon* was full ... of *gold*."

CHAPTER FIVE

Beck Easton's kitchen was equipped with a north-facing skylight that flooded the room and the adjacent dining area with daylight without letting in the glare of the sun. It was perfect reading light, so good that Jennifer almost did not need her glasses to read the handwritten script. But she wore them anyhow. She did not want to miss a single word, and besides, Beck Easton had already seen her in them, so she had no need to masquerade in the name of vanity—a fact that she found rather comforting. Drawing in a breath, she settled the glasses on her nose and began to read aloud.

> My darling Cecilia,
>
> There is neither world enough nor time to express the joy that you gave me this Easter last, when you did me the honor of agreeing to become my bride. No muse is strong enough, no expression sufficiently profound to convey to you the sentiments that my heart has enjoyed in the two weeks since first you promised to bind your future to mine.

"Whoa," Easton chuckled. He glanced over his shoulder as he worked at the kitchen counter, turning two chicken breasts in a marinade. "What color ink is this guy using—purple?"

"This is a nineteenth-century gentleman writing here," Jennifer reminded him. She tapped the book on the table in front of her. "He refers to his engagement to Cecilia, so that would put the writing sometime between"—she reached into her knapsack, took out a printout of her notes, and checked it "—between March 31 and June 15 of 1861—that's when they were married. Besides, Augustus

Baxter's writing to his fiancée, so this is a love letter. The first line he writes is a paraphrase of a poet ..."

"Andrew Marvell."

"Um—that's right." Jennifer looked over the tops of her glasses in surprise.

"Hardly the poet to be quoting to a bride-to-be," Easton muttered as he walked to the refrigerator. "Marvell could be pretty lewd."

Jennifer just looked at him, her head cocked.

"What?" He shrugged. "I read him in my plebe lit class at the Academy."

"And you remember it?"

"Remember it? Sure. Like it? That's another story. Tell you what, why don't you run through that while I cook? Then you can give me the high points."

Easton left to light his gas grill, and Jennifer continued reading. The narrative drew her in; after a page or two, she had to remind herself to breathe. From time to time, she stuck a strip of paper in before turning a page, to mark a spot that she wanted to come back to, or paused to make a note on a pad at her elbow. She dropped into full research mode, that old familiar place in which she lost track of time and even where she was, only lifting her head when she heard the sound of water running in the sink. Easton was washing several bunches of broccoli, trimming the leaf shoots off with a paring knife as he did it. He met her gaze and quirked an eyebrow.

"Uhm ..." Jennifer squelched a gulp as she realized she was staring. She'd never met a man before who fixed fresh broccoli. Or even liked it.

"Okay," she said, hoping he'd mistake the blush in her cheeks for a healthy glow. "Here's our story this far: Augustus Baxter is giving this record to Cecilia on the evening before their marriage. He doesn't want any secrets standing between them."

"A man who communicates. Imagine that."

"No joke. Anyhow, it gets weird right away. There's a guy in here that Baxter only identifies by a single initial—'W.'"

Easton didn't look up as he cut the woody bottoms from the stalks of broccoli. "Want to read me the part where he first shows up?"

"Sure." She leafed back in the record and found her place.

I have spoken before to you in confidence of my dear friend W, whom I came to know when we were classmates in Maryland, and who I dare not name even here, in this most private of missives. Although he had lived all of his life in the North at that time, W nonetheless expressed a profound sympathy for the causes of the Southern states, a predilection that gained the admiration of those of us who hailed from such environs, and raised the ire of the faculty, who were abolitionists and ardent Unionists to a man. While still a beardless boy, he proved his mettle when the headmaster, irate over some chickens missing from the school henhouse, cancelled a much-anticipated holiday. W raided the academy arsenal, outfitted himself and a group of compatriots with muskets, and retired to the woods, refusing to return until the headmaster had relented and returned to us our holiday.

"There you go," Easton said as he set the broccoli into a steamer basin. "Just check the prisons for records around that time of a juvenile delinquent whose name begins with 'W.'"

"Or not. It looks as if schoolmasters were a little more lenient about armed insurrections back then. W apparently got off with a reprimand. It says here that Baxter went to Europe after school— that was a common thing back then, if you had money: the Grand Tour. Girls went with an older female relative as an escort, but a young man was on his own. Anyhow, Baxter runs into this W in London, and apparently W is some sort of celebrity because he's staying in a townhouse that belongs to, according to Baxter, 'an admirer of W's celebrated father.' This is apparently the late 1850s, and W has a bunch of Southern friends who are pro-secessionist. They get together in the evenings at this townhouse and gripe about the North."

"Bickering." Easton set a pot on the stove and adjusted a burner. "That's their social life?"

"Nineteenth century," Jennifer reminded Easton as she watched him open a package of fresh spinach pasta. He was also the first guy she'd ever met who fixed spinach pasta. "Political passion is in vogue. And this is where it gets good. This W has a brother who traveled to California and, while there, apparently met Ulysses S. Grant."

"Apparently?"

"That's my guess." Jennifer leafed ahead in the record. "Here ... let me read it."

> While in San Francisco, W's brother mentioned in a letter that he had met a recently cashiered captain of the infantry, a man named Grant, who had been chased out of his post at Fort Humboldt for drunkenness, and was staying, as was W's brother, at the What Cheer House, a tavern and boarding establishment.

"Grant's a pretty common name." Easton picked up the chicken breasts and headed to the deck, leaving the door open. "It doesn't necessarily mean he's *that* Grant."

"But circumstances suggest it," Jennifer called after him. "Baxter here says that this W's brother was in San Francisco five years after the Gold Rush. Gold was discovered in California in 1848, and the rush began in earnest in 1849. So, five years after 1849 is 1854. Ulysses S. Grant was stationed at Fort Humboldt, in Eureka, until April of 1854."

Easton came back in and slid the screen door closed. "How do you know these things?"

"Everybody knows these things. Every serious student of Civil War history, at least. Grant was a major player later on. But he wasn't in these days. He was promoted to captain one day, then resigned his commission the next over concerns about his alcoholism. He wasn't the only drunk Army officer in the California Territory in those days. Soldiers were deserting right and left to go out to the gold fields. Prospectors were making upwards of fifty dollars a day, panning gold out of streams, in a time when a soldier would stand posts and drill all month for a measly six bucks. It was a losing battle for the Army, and especially for its officers, just trying to keep people in the ranks."

"So why doesn't Baxter say anything about Grant becoming a big wig?" He lowered the heat on the burner as the steamer pot's glass lid began to chatter. "I mean, the Civil War had broken out by the time he wrote this, right? So Grant was the head of the Union Army—"

"Not until 1864," Jennifer corrected. "At the time Baxter is writing this, Grant is still a civilian in Illinois, awaiting call-up for the war. That won't happen for quite some time. And even when it does, Grant goes in as a mere colonel, and he'll only get that because he's a West Point alumnus. No—Augustus Baxter is writing, here, in the spring of 1861, about an incident that took place in 1854. Hardly anybody knows about Ulysses S. Grant at that time, and among those who do, he's only thought of as a washed-up, shiftless drunk."

"This is getting interesting." Easton dropped the spinach pasta into a pot of boiling water, gave it a quick stir, and rinsed the spoon at the kitchen sink. "Where's it going?"

"Grant was apparently drowning his sorrows at the What Cheer House, and W's brother sat down to join him. One of the main jobs of the Army back then was guarding gold shipments, and, a few cups into the evening, Grant spills the beans that some of his brother officers have been skimming the shipments."

"Lining their own pockets?" The pasta pot foamed at the brim and Easton reduced the heat. He leaned against the counter, arms folded, giving Jennifer his full attention.

"They're worried that the North might cave to Southern interests. They're stockpiling gold as a war chest in case they need to take action."

"Take action as in overthrow the government?"

"You've got it."

"So where are they keeping all this gold?"

"That's the key." Jennifer reached for the journal, then changed her mind and decided to stick with her notes. "They were stockpiling the gold in California, but they needed to get it to the East Coast. The transcontinental railroad hadn't been built yet, so the only alternative is to send it by steamship. But this is the part that doesn't make sense. They talk about steaming the gold down to Panama and taking it across there—but the Panama Canal doesn't exist yet—and won't for more than half a century."

"That's true," Easton agreed as he poured the pasta into a strainer. "But now we're getting into one of my areas of expertise. You're right. There wasn't a canal in those days. The only alternative was Cape Horn. That could take half a year, or more, and the waters at the far end of South America were monstrous. Lots of ships sunk trying to round the Horn."

He put the pasta into a large serving bowl and tossed it with a garlic olive oil.

"When *HMS Bounty* tried it—as in *Mutiny on the Bounty*"— Easton set the bowl aside and went out to the grill, talking as he went—"they spent a month trying to make just one hundred miles. But if you steamed from San Francisco to Panama, that only took about a week. Then you'd offload, take your cargo across the isthmus by mule train—that took five days, weather permitting—and reload onto another ship on the Atlantic side. Even with delays for loading, reloading, and waiting for weather to break, you'd still save five months by crossing Panama. And it was a lot less risky."

"Okay," Jennifer said, nodding. She looked up as Easton brought the chicken in from the grill. "How do you know all this?"

"Like I told you at the spring . . ." He grabbed two plates and headed to the table, a dish towel draped across one shoulder. He set one plate in front of Jennifer, the other, opposite her. ". . . I'm a shipwreck junky. I dive them, I read about them, I study them." He continued talking as he retrieved two bowls of salad and a bottle of ranch dressing from the refrigerator, then carried them to the table. "And one of the most famous shipwreck finds of the last century was the *Central America*, found in deep water off the East Coast. The *Central America* was one of the ships that ran the New York–to–Panama leg of the journey. And when it was found, it was carrying gold from the California Territory." He set a bowl in front of Jennifer and shot her a smile. "So let me guess. Baxter and W and their secessionist buddies decide to take this gold shipment?"

"You've got it." She began to shake the bottle of salad dressing as she nodded at the journal. "It says here that W had some money his father had left him. So they—there were five of them—booked passage from London to Nassau, where they hired an engineer who didn't care what they were up to as long as he got paid."

"That takes care of propulsion. But who're they planning to use as a navigator?" Easton took the broccoli out of the steamer, drained it, and set it into a serving bowl as well. "Who's first officer?"

Jennifer checked her notes. "One of the conspirators—a man named Stewart—his father ran a shipping business, Charleston to New York."

Easton tsked as he set the chicken, broccoli, and pasta on the table and then returned to the refrigerator to take out a pitcher of iced tea. "That's coastal shipping. Not the same as open sea."

"Yes . . ." She scanned her notes again and stopped as another consideration came to her.

"What?"

"I was just thinking. These guys are all just kids. Some of them are still teenagers."

He nodded as he poured. "True. But so were the people who won World War II. Sometimes the best person to do something outrageous is a kid who hasn't figured out yet that he's mortal."

His face seemed to darken just a bit as he said that. Jennifer's instinct was to ask about it, but she pushed the urge aside and got back to her narrative.

"They went to Havana," she said, "and found a crew of a dozen Portuguese sailors who were waiting in port for a ship. Baxter says that they waited some time—nearly three weeks. Then they learned from the harbormaster that the *Halcyon*, the ship that they were waiting for, was in Aspinwall, in Panama, having emergency repairs made on her boiler. Finally, after nearly a month, the *Halcyon* came into port in Havana, and the conspirators took the ship that same night. And it says . . ."

She opened the record and reread a passage she'd found earlier. She looked up at Easton. "Baxter says there were only three crewmen on the ship when they took it. How can that be?"

"The same way South African diamond wholesalers ship their goods to Amsterdam and London by sending them in the regular mail," he said, taking a seat. "When you've got something valuable, often the safest course is to avoid drawing attention to it. Especially for the first night in a major port like Havana, three men would have been a typical watch on a freighter back in those days."

Then, having said that, Easton did something that Jennifer hadn't expected. He reached across the table and took her hands.

Her heartbeat immediately doubled. It was pleasant, his fingers enveloping hers, but she wondered what signal she had sent that had invited this. She was still startled, still wondering, when Easton bowed his head.

"Gracious heavenly Father," he said, "we thank you for your protection, and we ask your blessing on this meal and on what is said as we enjoy it. Amen."

He released her hands, but Jennifer kept them on the table for a moment, remembering his touch. Then as warmth flooded her face, she blinked twice and picked up her fork.

"You don't usually pray before your meals, do you?" He moved his salad bowl nearer.

"Uhm ... not for a while." It sounded better than "*not ever.*"

"I didn't mean to make you uncomfortable."

"You didn't. Not at all." *If only you knew.*

"So—what's next?"

"Next?" Jennifer thought about the touch of his hands.

"With our boys." Easton nodded toward the journal. "If they only had three crewmen on that ship, it's a cinch that her boilers were cold. Lighting them and making steam would take hours. How'd they get the *Halcyon* out of the harbor?"

"Oh." The flush returned to her face and she picked up her notebook to cover. "First they tied the crew up at gunpoint and put them in a dinghy that they left anchored in the harbor. Then two of the conspirators stole the harbormaster's tug, which was kept fired up at all times, swung by the city docks to pick up the crew, and then went out to the *Halcyon*, where they raised anchor and towed her out of the harbor."

"And lit the boiler once they were clear of the harbor?"

Jennifer nodded.

"And ... ," Easton stabbed a piece of lettuce, "the crew they picked up went along with this? Why?"

"Baxter says W told them the previous crew had gone back to Panama on another ship—because of the delay—and they needed a replacement crew to get the ship to Nassau."

"Nassau?"

"They knew the crew wouldn't buy New York as a destination— they didn't have enough coal on board. And Nassau was where they were really going. The kid whose dad had the shipping business? He'd arranged to have another ship standing by in Nassau, so they could offload there. Kind of like ditching the car you robbed the bank in, and then picking up another."

"I wouldn't know," Easton deadpanned. "I haven't robbed that many banks."

He handed Jennifer the platter of chicken and then tapped the table.

"So," he asked, "why Cat Island?"

"Hmm?" She tried a bite of grilled chicken and was surprised. *Orange marinade. The man can cook!*

"The chart we found with the record," Easton said. "It was of Cat Island. Nassau is on New Providence. Why leave a chart of Cat with Cecilia?"

"Because," Jennifer allowed herself a smile, "I haven't told you yet about the hurricane."

CHAPTER SIX

"Hurricane?" Easton's eyebrows rose. "All right ... You have my full attention. Feel free to speak with your mouth full."

Jennifer didn't. The grilled chicken was fabulous. She finished chewing, swallowed, and then tapped her notes.

"Let me read you something else first." She wiped her hands on a napkin—a cloth napkin, no less. Beck Easton seemed to have new depths at every turn. Surprised at how much that thought pleased her, she reopened the record and began to read.

Within two hours, the great paddle-wheels at either side of the ship began to turn gradual revolutions; and soon the single-cylinder steam engine was chuffing along steadily, the wheels churning more rapidly, and the line to our tug slackened. Stewart anchored the steam-launch where she was and we took him aboard, taking care to keep our crew belowdecks, as they were under the impression that the work-boat would be returning to the harbor. That done, we steamed along the Cuban coastline until the first light of dawn, and then Stewart pointed us due east, toward the rising sun and freedom.

My cherished Cecilia, how can I describe to you the thrill I felt at that moment? W, armed with a tally-book, a pencil, and a lantern, had gone below to assay what we were carrying. Two hours after sunrise, he emerged, tired but all smiles, and reported to Stewart and me that we were in possession of at least two million dollars in bullion and another million and a half in coin.

"Three and a half million dollars?" Easton whistled lightly. "What would that be in today's money?"

Easton set his salad plate aside and fell silent for a moment. "When the *Central America* sank, she was carrying a million and a half in gold, by her captain's account. And when she was found in the early 1990s, her gold's value was estimated at a billion dollars. Of course some of that was the collector's value of the coins, but what you just read there says that almost half of what the *Halcyon* carried was also in coin. So, theoretically, if this cargo were to pop up today, I'd say it would be worth somewhere in the neighborhood of two and a quarter to two and a half, give or take."

Jennifer's mouth dropped. "Billion?"

Easton nodded.

She tried to imagine two and a half billion dollars' worth of pizza, or textbooks, or blue jeans, or apartment rent, or anything else she'd ever spent money on. It was impossible.

"Okay ... the hurricane." She turned two pages of the record. "They'd only been underway a few hours when the boiler begins leaking. They'd started men on a pump to keep the water at a manageable level. And then Baxter reports this ..."

We turned northward, and had just crossed the tropic when our engineer came back on deck and informed us in a harsh whisper that the boiler was but one of our troubles. Our hull was leaking as well, and the water in the bilge was now rising faster than two pumps could overtake it. He asked Stewart to lay to, so we could effect repairs. But Stewart had his own concerns by this point.

"Do you see that?" He asked the three of us, nodding at a low bank of black cloud that now rimmed our entire southeastern horizon. "I've seen cloud like that before, but only once, and the storm that followed sent my father's largest ship to the bottom of the Outer Banks. No, sir. We cannot afford to stop running, not even for an instant. As it is, I can only hope that we can get in the lee of New Providence before that great, black beast overtakes us."

"Cloud all along the horizon, and they're in a midnineteenth-century side-wheel steamer?" Easton shook his head. "A ship like that might make about ten knots, but even your run-of-the-mill tropical storm will travel three times as fast. Okay. I can see where this is heading already. These guys are toast."

"It gets worse." Jennifer tapped the old black book. "Baxter writes that he goes belowdecks to help the engineer, and they try to repair the boiler while they're underway. But they're only partly successful, and when Baxter goes topside to report this, the storm has already caught them. By this time they're trying to make their way east to"—she checked her notes "—the Exumas. Where's that?"

"Out-islands of the Bahamas," Easton said as he lifted his tea. "They run in a line roughly north and south, and they have shoal water—shallows—to their west. That's good thinking—try to make for the nearest beach and run aground. I take it they didn't make it?"

"Not hardly." She gave up squinting and put on her glasses. "When Baxter reports topside, the guy who's acting as captain tells him they need full steam and ..." She met his gaze above the top of her glasses. "... Well, here—let me read it."

Understanding our peril, I nodded my reply and pulled along the pitching railing, making my way toward the hatch through harsh and slanting rain. But before I was even halfway there, the very deck beneath my feet leapt up, a report sounded from belowdecks as if a cannon had been touched off, and a billow of black smoke issued from the hatchway and roiled in the rain-filled air. Not half a moment afterward, the deck beyond it erupted in a cloud of soot and steam.

I stood dumbstruck. One of our crewmen ran screaming from the black maw of the hatch, his flesh hanging in reddened strips. I moved to leap to his aid, but he rushed straight past me and plunged headlong into the angry sea.

"Man overboard!" I screamed to Stewart. "Come about, man! For the love of all that is holy, come about!"

But a glance told me the futility of what I'd asked. The paddlewheels had fallen still and, without propulsion, our vessel would not answer to her helm.

Then a figure brushed past me. It was our courageous W, plunging into the smoke of the hatch. Startled from my lethargy, I shook off my fears and followed him.

The sound of china clinking across the table broke her concentration. Easton had finished his dinner and was clearing his plates. "This is fascinating," he said, heading to the sink. "But you might want to eat something. Give you strength to finish your sea epic."

Jennifer blinked in surprise and tried another bite of chicken. She hurriedly finished it. The pasta was *al dente* and the broccoli still tender. *If this guy likes to shop, he just might be perfect.* Jennifer blushed at the thought and finished the meal.

Easton took her plate. "That was quick. Do you want seconds, or are you in a hurry to get back to the *Pirates of Penzance*?"

"Yes," Jennifer said. "No, I mean ... it was wonderful, but one was plenty."

Easton smiled down at her and Jennifer felt warm. What was it about this man that flustered her? He refilled her glass with tea, and she wondered when she had drunk the first one. Murmuring thanks, she turned back to her notes. "Okay, so the boiler had blown up ... "

"And she didn't sink immediately?"

"No." She squinted at her notes. "They lost the crewmen that were working in the engine room, they started taking water, and they had a fire. But they got the fire out and shored up the holes, and kept working the pumps."

"They were very lucky." Easton began loading the dishwasher and shooed Jennifer away when she rose to help. "Most steam engines of that era were like bombs. When they blew, the ship went with them. But obviously the storm caught them."

"It did. Baxter says they could barely hold on to man the pumps. The ship almost rolled a couple of times, and one of the crewmen broke a leg when a bulkhead fell on it. The wind scours the masts away, and W takes one of the crewmen with him to re-lash the ship's two dinghies to the deck. The crewman almost gets washed overboard, but W saves him. And then, just when it seemed at its worst, everything goes still, and ..." She glanced up and reached for the journal. "I'd better read this part. It's pretty cool."

When I was a boy, my father took me on a summer's trip to see the great Falls of the Niagara. One evening, hours after dinner, a guide rowed me in a skiff under a moonlit sky to the churning cauldron at the base of the giant cataract.

That sight, magnified a thousandfold, is what I beheld when I stepped out onto the *Halcyon's* deck. A monstrous wall of cloud, as plumb as the side of a house, was rising to the very heavens, angry seas churning at its base. There was motion within the vapor, like water falling, and the scale of the thing struck our company speechless.

Above us, stars twinkled in the clearest sky I had ever beheld. The moon was out, and its blue light on the cloud-wall only added to the illusion of a cataract.

As we watched, the great wall of cloud slowly receded, and the seas around us calmed. In a matter of minutes, we were riding on water as placid as a mill-pond.

At length, finding my tongue, I breathed, "It is a miracle."

"It is not."

We turned toward Stewart, who had spoken. Even in the pale moonlight, I could read the concern etched deep upon his face.

"This storm is far from over, gentlemen," he told us. "We are in the eye: a circle of calm at the center of the hurricane. In less than an hour, and I would hazard much less, the weather will return, and its fury will be the equal of anything we've seen. It may even be greater if the storm is gaining strength. But the wind will be out of the west when the storm returns, driving us toward shoalwater. We need draft. We must get below and pump this vessel dry."

The creak of a floorboard broke her concentration. Easton had left the kitchen and walked quietly into the darkened living room. She scowled. "Yo, buddy! What's up? Am I boring you, here?"

"Not at all." He was standing a few feet back from the window, studying the road in front of the house. "I love a good sea story. Just thought I heard a car, that's all. Go ahead—finish."

She found her place in the narrative and then glanced up again. Easton was still in the living room. "You coming back?"

"In a sec," Easton said. "But I can hear you just fine from here. Tell me why we've got a map of Cat Island."

She opened her notebook and cleared her throat. "Baxter goes on for several pages about the storm," she said. "The ship gets driven all night by the storm, it's taking on water, and it runs aground at first light. The rest of the crew and two of the con-spirators jump into the water and try to swim to shore—it's just a hundred yards away. But the storm is still raging, so W keeps Stewart and Baxter from trying.

"He talks them into using the ship's one remaining dinghy and making an all-out dash for the shore. They do, they all get knocked out of the dinghy, but they hang on and kick it to shore. And then, just as they get there, the dinghy rolls in a wave and Baxter gets hit in the head. He passes out, and when he comes to, it's morn-ing and there are only the three of them left."

"Three left out of seventeen, and the ship's aground," Easton said from the living room. "Yeah. I'd say that qualifies as a disaster."

"Well, you don't know the half of it," Jennifer told him.

"How's that?" He was moving in the living room, walking toward the other end of the house.

"Remember the Exumas?" Jennifer called after him. "The islands they were trying to make a run to?"

She scowled. *What's he doing?*

"Uh-huh." At least now he was walking back toward her.

"Well, they missed them."

CHAPTER SEVEN

"So." Easton set something on an end table in the darkened living room and came to the kitchen doorway. "You're telling me they passed the Exumas in the storm and drifted all the way to Cat Island?"

Jennifer nodded.

"Hang on a sec." Easton disappeared down the hallway again, and when he returned he carried a broad sheet of paper, which he set on the table. It was a chart of the Bahamas.

"The Exumas are here." He pointed to a chain of islands extending roughly southeast to northwest. "And Cat Island is over here." She followed the line he drew with his finger to a smaller duplicate of the island on the chart he'd found in the cave: a long, skinny bit of land with a clublike hook at its base. It was at the other side of the map.

"Wow." She glanced from the Exumas to Cat Island, and back again. "These guys were way off course."

"No joke." He nodded thoughtfully. "Then again, they were in the teeth of a hurricane—no way to get a star sighting, unless someone had the presence of mind to do it while they were in the eye. And by that time, it would have been pointless. No engine, no mast to raise a sail. They were adrift—no way to navigate."

Easton straightened from the table and walked back into the living room, picking up the object he'd left on the table.

Jennifer peered after him into the darkened room. The thing in his hand was black, with a lens on the front of it, like a small camera or monocular. He turned toward the window and lifted the device to his eyes.

"Shall I come with you?" she called after him. "Continue this in there?"

"No. You're fine where you are. Go on."

Jennifer thought about what Easton had said: . . . *thought I heard a car.* Her stomach gave a little lurch. But the man seemed calm, and that soothed her, so she continued.

"Okay. Baxter wakes up, and it's just him, W, and Stewart. The sky's blue, the air's warm . . . Baxter's lying on the beach well back from the sea; there are trees down and palm fronds all over the place. But other than that, it's just a beautiful day. Then he gets up, walks over a dune, and sees their ship . . ."

The *Halcyon* had rolled as the hurricane spent its fury upon her. Our once proud ship now lay upon her side, the wreckage of one paddle wheel uppermost, like a great bashed and battered tambourine. She lay stern-to toward the shore, her rudder completely clear of the water, her bow submerged beneath the brilliant blue sea. With the storm waters receded one could, I saw, easily wade out to the wreck. Stewart had clearly already done so; he was standing on the beach with a map case and a chronometer at his feet, and a sextant in his hands. Just beyond him, W was returning through waist-deep water, balancing a wooden cask upon his shoulder. I walked down the sloping sand and W and I reached Stewart at the same time.

"Well, hello, old fellow," W greeted me cordially. Then, turning to Stewart, W set the cask down and said, "Here's freshwater. There's more where this came from. And what of you? Have you determined our position?"

"I have," Stewart told us. Stooping, he unrolled a chart and held the corners down with conch shells. "We are here— Cat Island, at the top of this bay at the lower end of the island. And gentlemen, I have news beyond all hope!"

"How is that?" I asked.

"Not a soul lives on the southern half of this island," Stewart said. "But the northern half is inhabited! There are plantations, a town ... If we raise a mast on our dinghy, we are only a morning's sail from humanity!"

"That is good news," I said.

"It is," W agreed. "Of course, we shall not be making that journey."

"We shan't?" I asked.

"Why not?" Stewart added.

"Gentlemen," W smiled. "Have you so quickly forgotten the purpose of this journey? Men have died to get that gold this far. The gold on that vessel has been purchased with blood, and I for one am not about to abandon it."

"Wait a minute," Easton called from the living room. "All that gold? No way do they fit it in a dinghy. No way do they fit it in *ten* dinghies. How are they planning on getting it off the island?"

"They aren't." Jennifer grinned. "That's why we've got the map. They stashed the gold on the island."

"Stashed the ..." Standing in shadow, he took a step closer to the doorway. "With three guys? That would take weeks."

"It did. It helped that the ship was on its side in shallow water. They were able to take the dinghy right into the hold, load it up, and then wade it back to the beach. And from there it didn't have to go far. They dug a trench, shored the sides with timbers from the ship, and buried the gold just above the high-tide line. Baxter says they lived on fish and coconut milk while they got the job done."

"Buried treasure." Easton laughed. "Unbelievable. What'd they do about this ship? The island's inhabited—Stewart just said so. Somebody's bound to sail by eventually, and that wreck's going to stick out like a sore thumb."

He stepped back into the shadows of the living room and held the cameralike object to his eye again.

"They thought of that," Jennifer craned her neck, watching, as he seemed to scan the terrain. "They burned it. Waited for a cloudless night to do it."

"It's obvious they didn't want the townspeople to know that they were there," he said. "Somebody figured out that the light of the fire would reflect from the clouds. Smart."

She marked her place with her fingertips and looked up at him again. "Okay. And what's a 'neap tide'?"

"An extremely low tide. Happens when the moon's at right angles to the sun." He kept the device to his eyes as he spoke. "If they torched the wreck at any other time, there'd eventually be sections of it sticking out of the water when the tide went out. This way, you'd have to be practically on top of the wreck to spot it."

"Okay ... that makes sense."

"So where did they do all of this?"

Jennifer checked her notes. "'At the deepest bend in the beach on Fernandez Bay,'" she read. "Baxter wrote down the bearing to the highest point on the island. It says '170 true.'"

Easton kept looking into the night. "So what did they do next? Sail to the town?"

Jennifer peered into the living room, back to her notes, and drummed her fingers on the kitchen table, wondering what the deal was with the camera-thing. "W is afraid it'll raise too many questions. He talks the other two into rigging a mast on the dinghy and sailing to Nassau."

"That's gutsy. Or crazy."

"I'd have to agree." Jennifer opened the record again.

After all that we had been through, the first two days of that journey were the most effortless possible, with a modest but following breeze, gently undulating seas, and bright skies for Stewart to steer by each evening.

Our one concern was the sun, which had already burned us black on Cat Island, and was relentless in the tiny open boat.

By and by, we took to slipping over the side, one after the other, in the heat of midday, the better to escape the glare of old Sol.

And so it was that, our third day out, when I had just returned to my place in the dinghy, and Stewart was taking his turn over the side, that W and I were alarmed to hear our old friend cry out in pain, and then to turn and see him dash beneath the surface as if pulled down by a hundredweight of lead.

Instantly we looked over the side to see a gray form sounding for the blue.

"Shark!" W exclaimed, and over the side he went in a brave attempt to reach our friend and wrench him from the jaws of the monster.

Alas, that was not to be. After several minutes of diving and resurfacing, W pulled himself, heartbroken, back into the dinghy, and we went no longer into the sea for our relief.

"And then there were two," Easton muttered. "I take it thay made it to Nassau?"

"They did. They'd brought some of the coins with them, and they used the money to buy clothes and get passage back to England. When they got back to America, no one was the wiser as to what they'd been up to—not until Baxter shared the secret with Cecilia."

Jennifer took a deep breath and set the narrative down. She drummed the table again. "Yo!" she called. "Buddy! What's going on in there?"

Easton took the device away from his eye. Jennifer saw a slight green glow on his cheek as he did so. He didn't turn his face from the front window.

"You'd better come in here," he said. "See for yourself."

She looked down at the record and then back into the living room. *What? I'm telling him where a few billion dollars in gold is hidden and he wants me to do some sightseeing?* Reluctantly, she pushed her chair back, and walked into the living room, reaching for the light switch.

"Leave the lights," he told her softly, still peering out into the darkness. He handed her the device. "Here. Take a look. About sixty feet past my mailbox, far side of the road."

"Mailbox? It's pitch black out there. I don't even *see* a mailbox."

"Use the goggles." Easton's voice was barely audible.

She put the device to her eyes and gasped. Trees, shrubs, gravel, and Easton's driveway culvert all showed up as if displayed on a monochromatically green high-definition TV. The mailbox showed up bullet-sharp; she could read the route number and the name "Easton," applied in adhesive lettering, and she could almost make out part of a headline on a newspaper rolled up and hanging part way out of the pigeonhole underneath. A reflector on the side of the mailbox glowed like a malevolent eye.

"Wow," Jennifer breathed. "It's like CNN."

"Sort of," Easton said. "TV crews use the civilian versions, made for watching wildlife."

"And this is what? The military version?"

"This is a little better than the military version."

She took the night-vision device away from her eyes and looked at him, eyebrows arched.

"Did you see them?" He nodded toward the darkness.

"See who?" She was whispering, even though she wasn't sure why.

"Far side of the road, about sixty feet beyond the mailbox."

Jennifer put the goggles to her eyes again. A small deer wandered out of the brush on the far side of the road, lowered its head, cropped off a bit of grass, and then raised its head as it chewed, its eyes glowing like something out of a horror movie as it turned her way. Beyond the deer, down in the ditch at the side of the road,

Jennifer picked up the slightest bit of movement. She made out two people on their bellies in the ditch. Both had binoculars. Both were pointed her direction.

She blinked and stared again through the night-goggles.

The two people stared back.

CHAPTER EIGHT

"Who are those guys?" Jennifer took a step backward as she kept the night-vision goggles to her face.

"You're okay." Easton put a hand on her back. "They can't see you—it's too dark in here. As to who they are ... I was hoping you could tell me."

Jennifer lowered the goggles, frowned at Easton, and then put the device to her eyes again. The two men were wearing vaguely military-looking jackets and billed caps. They dipped their binoculars and appeared to speak to one another but, in the shadows under the bills, not even the night-vision goggles could resolve more than a vague suggestion of eyes, mouths, noses, and, on the man nearest the road, a decidedly bushy mustache. But those details, vague as they were, were enough for her.

She met Easton's quizzical gaze. "I've never seen these guys before." She stopped and drew in a sharp breath. "The people in that car this morning ... It's them, isn't it?"

"That'd be my guess."

She bit her lip, squinting. "They've got to know what we're after ... nothing else makes sense. But how?" She took another look through the goggles, then, letting them down again, she shook her head. "How would they know about the record? Or the gold? *We* didn't even know about that until after we'd opened the parcel."

Easton was still peering into the darkness. It was almost as if he didn't need the goggles to see what was out there. "Maybe they're farther down the road on this than you are," he whispered, reaching for the goggles. "Or maybe, at least, they think they are.

At any rate, all they're doing is watching. They haven't moved in forty-five minutes, and they aren't very good at this sort of thing."

"What makes you say that?"

He nodded toward the men. "They had enough smarts to ditch their vehicle down the road out of sight, but not enough to get well back and hide themselves in the brush. And they aren't using night-vision gear, like these. The goggles emit in the same spectrum they receive in. If they were using night gear, I'd see a glow when I glassed them with these. I don't."

Jennifer stifled a shiver. "So now we do what?" She stared into the blackness, up at Easton, and into the blackness again. "Call the cops?"

He shook his head. "We can if you want, but if you've got people trailing you, I don't see any reason to make them smarter at it. If they're low on the learning curve at this stuff, I'd say it's best to leave 'em there."

Jennifer didn't say anything. She sat in the darkened living room and looked out at the night. She was close enough to Easton that she could detect just a hint of aftershave, which was comforting, but not comforting enough. She wrapped her arms around herself and rocked back and forth a little bit.

Finally she found her voice. "Let's talk about this."

Easton checked their watchers one more time with the night-vision goggles and then nodded. They went back into the kitchen and sat at the table. The gold bar, the coin, the record and the map were on the tabletop, off to the side where she had moved them to make room for the dinner.

"I guess the first question," she said, "is who does all of this belong to?"

"I'm no expert on the subject," Easton replied, "but Twin Springs is on private property. So I'd have to say it belongs to the landowner."

"Yeah." Jennifer's heart sank a bit as she said it. "I'd have to agree."

"Alton's a good guy, though," Easton added. "If I give him the gold bar, I'm sure he'll let us hang onto the rest—and keep his mouth shut—until you've finished your research."

Jennifer rummaged in her bookbag and came up with her passport, its blue cover still stiff and new. "I got this a couple of years ago. There was this overseas study program that I never quite saved enough money to take. I've been carrying it ever since, just—well, just in case, you know? I've never actually used it."

Easton glanced at the passport, "And now you think this might be a good time to go to where? The Bahamas?"

Jennifer shot him a smile. "Want to come?"

"I could," he said. "Not right away, but in a week or two."

"But we're in Florida. The Bahamas is like . . . right over there." She waved her hand the direction she assumed to be east.

"That's true, but I've got a business—clients scheduled. And I'm always in Florida. And the Bahamas are that way." He pointed at right angles to the direction Jennifer had indicated.

"Knowing that there might be a gazillion dollars in gold on a beach on Cat Island—that doesn't make you want to change your schedule and go now?"

Easton studied the gold on the tabletop. "You can go now if you want. But if you want me with you, I'll need to make some arrangements first. I don't think there's any hurry."

Jennifer took a breath. The compressor on the refrigerator began to hum softly. "You . . . ," she drew in a breath, "you don't think that this gold is still there, do you?"

Easton shook his head. "I'm sorry."

"But we've only got four people who knew about it." Jennifer tapped the record book. "Baxter—who died in the war. W—who Cecilia says is also dead by August of 1865. Jonah—who died hiding it. And Cecilia . . ."

"Who lived well into the twentieth century."

The refrigerator clicked off.

Easton put his elbows on the table and rested his chin on his palms. "This woman was an apple farmer? And yet she left a small fortune to colleges and charities at the dawn of the Great Depression? I'd say that there is an excellent chance that she searched for it. Found it. And there's one other thing ..."

His tone said it wasn't good news. She braced herself. "What's that?"

"The place where you said that they buried the gold? On the deepest bend of the beach on Fernandez Bay?"

She nodded, reluctantly.

"Well, I've been to that exact spot," he said. "And the last time I was there, it had a resort sitting on top of it."

CHAPTER NINE

TALLAHASSEE REGIONAL AIRPORT

With her dark hair pulled back under a scarf and sunglasses covering her brown eyes, the woman slunk low in the seat of her plain, tan, rental Cavalier and watched Jennifer Cassidy curb-check her single plain blue suitcase.

"Marisol"—that was the name the dark-haired woman was using for this operation, a name so like her real one that she had no problem thinking of herself that way. Marisol knew it would pay to keep as low a profile as possible. Her bronze skin and slight *cubana* accent, attributes that would have blended her right in down in Miami, made her stick out like a sore thumb in the predominantly Anglo population of northern Florida.

Marisol surveyed her surroundings, stopping every ten degrees as she turned her head, just as she had been trained, to take in every detail.

There was no sign of the two men she had come to think of as *estupido et mas estupido,* "dumb and dumber," which amazed her, but she imagined that, given the laws of probability, even such clumsy oafs as those would occasionally do something right.

She had picked them up instantly in the darkness outside the *anglo*'s house, even before she had switched on her night-vision goggles. The ruckus the two men made settling into their observation position in the ditch, snapping twigs and rustling leaves, had been enough to draw her attention to them.

She, on the other hand, had been so inconspicuous that the small deer wandering out of the thicket had nearly brushed against her as it foraged for tender shoots among the grasses.

That was no accident. Marisol worked hard on her craft, and that included her surveillance. She ate a bland vegetarian diet, not because of any health regimen or moral commitment, but because doing so naturally reduced her body odor to almost nothing. She wore no scents, no perfumes, did not smoke and avoided both alcohol and candies with equal discipline. For the detail the night before, she had worn crepe-soled boots that were virtually noiseless under any circumstance, and her face-mask and three-D camouflage would have rendered her undetectable even in broad daylight. By starlight, she'd been no more than another shadow.

Secreted in the Florida night, she could have walked up on *estupido et mas estupido* and eliminated either one without the other being the wiser, but she had left them alone. Her orders were specific: observe but do not intervene ... for the time being.

The *anglo* had been another matter. His use of a night-vision device the evening before had come as a total surprise. Had the man not switched the unit on before raising it to his eyes, she most certainly would have been spotted. As it was, she had barely had time to switch her own goggles off to keep him from seeing her. And that trick with the four-wheel-drive the morning before had thrown even her off his trail. It was something that wouldn't have happened if she'd had air assets available, but she had not. This mission had not been so critical as to require them.

That, too, was subject to change. Still, Marisol was glad that the girl had left the *anglo*'s place. If the Cassidy girl had stayed on, even one day longer, Marisol would have had to break cover and request information on Beck Easton; otherwise, it would be too dangerous to proceed.

But with him out of the picture, it was another scenario entirely. The girl was unskilled at this game, and Marisol knew that she could tail her closely without arousing her suspicion. The only reason she did not was the opposition. They were ignorant and they were clumsy, but they were not entirely without skills.

Her rental car checked in, Jennifer Cassidy schlepped her backpack and laptop case through the lobby of Tallahassee Regional Airport, looking for a sign that could direct her to her gate. It took her just a moment to then realize that the gates were all in one place. She estimated that she could easily kick a soccer ball the length of the terminal—and she'd spent both of her high school seasons on the bench.

Her passport still rested in her backpack pocket. There was time to go to the ticket counter and cancel her flight and use the credit card her client had given her—use it to buy a ticket to the Bahamas.

She resisted the temptation. Easton would be available in a week or so, giving her time to think things over a little more. And she had to admit that heading down to the islands with her own personal Marine sounded a lot better than trying to be the Lone Ranger. Especially with the creeps that had been lying in the grass the night before. She'd slept in Easton's guest room while he had sat up all night, watching. He'd told her that they had finally withdrawn sometime before dawn. *Creepy.*

Jennifer marched straight ahead, past a coffee shop, a shoeshine stand, a game room, restrooms, a nuts-and-yogurt place, and a restaurant. The security checkpoint was small, just two metal detectors and two X-ray machines, and only one of each was operating. A line of people, mostly men in suits, was waiting to go through, and Jennifer joined them, obeying the sign that told her to take her laptop out of its carry-case. The security people, all in identical blue blazers, looked like retirees moonlighting on their pensions, but they apparently took their jobs seriously; they were asking the businessmen to remove their shoes and send them through the X-ray machine in gray plastic bins. It took five minutes for Jennifer to get up to the checkpoint.

"Put your computer in the bin please," the woman at the machine said.

"Want me to take my shoes off too?"

The woman glanced at Jennifer's canvas sandals. "No. That won't be necessary."

Jennifer sent her computer and her bookbag through the X-ray machine and then walked through the metal detector.

"Sir!"

Jennifer turned. The woman was talking to someone on the opposite side of the X-ray machine.

"Sir! That gate is not being used! You'll have to step back in line."

Jennifer stood on tiptoe to peer over the top of the machine. A man with a bushy mustache and a blonde ponytail stood in the gate of the second metal detector, staring over the operator's shoulder toward the monitor in front of Jennifer.

"Say what?" The man shrugged as if confused.

"*In ... line!*" The security guard jerked her head toward the queue.

"Oh. Sure thing, lady."

The bushy mustache meant something to Jennifer, but she wasn't sure what. She walked on and collected her computer and bookbag from the steel rollers. She opened her carry-case and tucked her laptop inside.

Then she froze.

The man hadn't been some confused tourist in the wrong line. He'd been staring into the X-ray machine monitor, looking at what was in her bags.

Bushy mustache. The man she'd seen through Easton's night-vision goggles had a bushy mustache. Jennifer gulped silently. *Chill pill, Jen. Lots of men have mustaches.* She tried to calm herself.

Clammy and breathless, she glanced at her ticket envelope and headed for B–5, the gate indicated on her boarding pass. It was at the end of a broad corridor, past a cocktail lounge and a set of restrooms, and while a gate attendant was on duty at the podium, the door to the jetway was not yet open. So she sat, choosing a chair that faced the hallway leading back to the security check-point.

A few minutes passed; the man appeared again. He walked briskly to Jennifer's gate, accompanied by a tall and muscular black man. *Bushy mustache, two men. Not a coincidence.* Jennifer's mouth went dry. Her heart rapped against her ribs.

Clammy and tense, she fished a paperback out of her bookbag and pretended to read. The men took their seats in the row opposite her.

Jennifer's mind raced. Airline security was so tight that even nail files were forbidden in the passenger compartment of a jet-liner, but what if the men had found a way to smuggle a weapon on board? And, if the men were flying to Detroit, any small assurance of safety would vanish once she stepped out of Northwest's McNamara Terminal, on the other end of the flight.

She bit her lip and squeezed her book to keep her hands from shaking. What to do? She could alert the authorities, but what could she say? That she had found the key to a long-lost pirate treasure? That she thought these men were after it? How plausible would that sound?

Not very.

As Jennifer watched, a woman with shoulder-length ash-blonde hair sat just behind the men. Jennifer looked at the woman and thought that, for the next few hours, she'd give anything to trade places with her—to be someone these two men were not interested in at all.

With her black hair tucked under the ash-blonde wig, Marisol was reasonably certain that *estupido et mas estupido* wouldn't take any special note of her, but she wore a pair of blue-lensed glasses as added insurance.

Hacking into the airlines' reservation computer sounded just a little too sophisticated for a pair like the men sitting ahead of her.

So she figured they had simply done as she had, and booked seats on every Northwest flight to Detroit over the next seventy-two hours.

The gate attendant announced pre-boarding for their flight. *Estupido et mas estupido* stood and walked to the jetway.

They were using a "leading tail"—smart. Maybe whoever had trained these two had actually taught them something. Preceding a surveillance subject—going where he or she would logically be going—tended to reassure people who might suspect that they were being followed.

Marisol was tempted to step up behind the two men and read the names on the men's boarding passes. She resisted the temptation. Besides, she had no reason to suspect that the subject had "made her"—identified her—so it was safe for her to keep the girl under observation.

Marisol waited until the subject stood and moved into line for boarding, then she stepped in directly behind her.

Everything went smoothly until they got right up to the podium. The gate attendant studied Jennifer's boarding pass, gave her a pasted-on smile, and said, "Thank you, Miss Cassidy. Would you step over to the side, please?"

Marisol resisted the temptation to curse. The girl had done something to get selected for a spot check.

It was part of every commercial airport's terminal security routine. A certain percentage of all checked luggage was set aside for physical inspection, and every so often, a passenger would be pulled from the boarding queue for a detailed check. While it was no longer random, as it had been in the past, security guards or gate attendants could identify suspicious individuals in the boarding area—those who made last-minute flight changes, or those who appeared nervous or overly secretive—for a recheck.

Marisol had no idea why they didn't pick *estupido or mas estupido*, or even her, with her dark glasses. But they hadn't. As luck would have it, they'd fingered the girl.

Marisol made a show of glancing into her purse, shaking her ash-blonde-wigged head, and heading back to where she'd been seated while waiting for the flight. Once there, she bent over and began looking on the floor, as if searching for a lost object, all the while keeping track of the girl out of the corner of her eye.

The security agents were really giving the girl's things the full monty—rifling through the pages of her paperback novels and asking her to turn on and operate her laptop computer.

Finally, when the last of the passengers in line had boarded the aircraft, the disguised woman realized that she could not linger any longer without drawing attention to herself. Suppressing a grumble, she stooped, pretended to retrieve a lost object from the departure-lounge carpeting, and walked back to the jetway. The girl was a fairly meek person; according to the brief, she was studying to become a librarian or something of the sort. She wouldn't be so daring—or stupid—as to try to smuggle contraband past a security checkpoint.

Cursing her luck, and with a last glance back at her subject, Marisol boarded the aircraft.

"Would you have a photo ID, miss?"

Jennifer glanced toward the jetway, and then back at the security guard. The woman looked matronly, but stern. "But they already checked my photo ID—at the metal detector."

"Yes, miss. I know. This is just a routine recheck. Your ID—may we see it, please?"

Flustered, Jennifer unsnapped her wallet, took out her Ohio driver's license and then, for good measure, added her University of Michigan student ID.

The security person checked the two forms of identification against Jennifer's boarding pass.

"Wapakoneta is your permanent mailing address?"

"Yes," Jennifer cast another worried glance toward the jetway. "My university address is on my student ID."

"Don't worry, miss. They won't roll back the jetway until we tell them to. Would you mind opening the outside pockets on your backpack?"

They asked her to unzip the nylon pouch that she used to carry her tampons, and even had her open her little jar of moisturizing lip balm. Finally, after passing a metal-detector wand over Jennifer and her belongings one last time, the guard thanked her and told her she was free to go.

Biting her lip, Jennifer powered down her laptop, started to put everything away, and then, conscious that a whole planeload of people was waiting on her, just dumped all her loose belongings back into her bookbag and zipped it shut. She shrugged it onto her back, gave her boarding pass to the gate agent, and hurried into the semidarkness of the jetway.

The sloping corridor of the jetway was empty except for a coveralled ramp worker with a clipboard in his hands, standing at the bottom of the tunnel-like passage with his back to Jennifer. Moving at a quick trot, Jennifer made the left turn at the end of the corridor and was just about to step into the jet when she felt a hand land on her shoulder.

She turned. It was the ramp worker. She looked up, at his face. It was Beck Easton.

Jennifer gaped. "What are you do ..."

"Shhh. Do you still want to go to the Bahamas?" He kept his voice low, a whisper next to her ear.

Jennifer glanced toward the plane, where the flight attendant had her back turned, talking to the crew on the flight deck.

"Now?"

"Now," Easton told her. "Let's go."

BOOK TWO

FERNANDEZ BAY

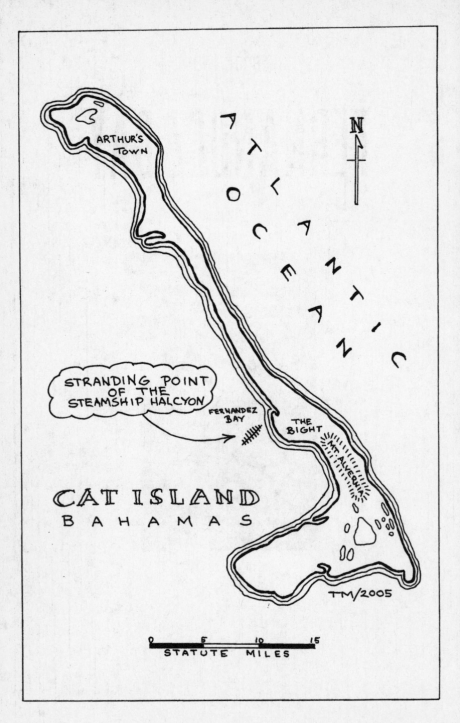

N

ATLANTIC OCEAN

ARTHUR'S TOWN

STRANDING POINT
OF THE
STEAMSHIP HALCYON

FERNANDEZ BAY

THE BIGHT

MT. ALVERNIA

CAT ISLAND
BAHAMAS

TM/2005

0   5   10   15
STATUTE MILES

CHAPTER TEN

Hot, humid Florida air wrapped itself around Jennifer as, fighting her swaying bookbag and clutching her laptop case, she followed Beck Easton down the steep stairway on the outside of the jetway. Blinking in confusion, she kept up as he made his way around the nose of the big airliner to its far side, where a luggage tram was parked. Easton pulled back the rubberized canvas side-curtain on the nearest car and motioned with his hand.

"Get in."

She peered into the metal-floored baggage car. It looked pretty hot and dusty. "In there?"

"Sorry—the limos were all booked. Yes, in there. Quick as you can. We can't be hanging around out here."

She climbed in and found a seat on top of a suitcase. Easton climbed in after her and pulled the side-curtain closed.

"Hey, Beck," called a male voice from outside of the tram. "Where're you parked, dude?"

"South ramp," Beck called back. "This end."

"You got 'er, man. Hang tight."

The tram lurched forward and started rolling.

"Wait!" Jennifer grabbed Easton's arm. "My luggage! It's on the plane!"

"Calm down. You're sitting on it."

Jennifer looked down. Sure enough, she was sitting atop the blue Samsonite pullman that her parents had given her when she first headed off to college. She grinned at Easton, who was stripping off the Northwest flight-line coveralls. Underneath, he wore a pair of canvas shorts, a faded polo shirt and boat shoes, without socks—the same sort of thing that he'd been wearing when Jennifer had first encountered him, two days earlier.

"They were in there," she said. "The two from last night."

"That figures," he said. "Did they get on the plane already?" He rolled the coveralls up and wedged them between a pair of duffel bags.

She nodded.

"Good. Then they're on their way to Detroit. It'd call too much attention to them if they tried to get off now."

Jennifer thought about that for a moment and drummed her fingertips on her suitcase. "You know," she finally said, "if you'd wanted to go to Cat Island today, all you had to do was tell me so last night."

"Couldn't do it." Easton shook his head. "We knew you had people watching you. I had to assume they'd follow you. We needed to lose them, and if I'd let you in on the plan ... Well, there's an art to deception. The easiest way to convince these guys that you were going back to Michigan was to let you think you were going back."

"What if they were listening in last night?" she asked. "If they, you know, bugged the house, then they know everything."

He shook his head. "I've got ways of detecting listening devices, and the house was clean. I think we're in the clear, now."

Jennifer nodded, then she did a double-take. "What do you mean, you've 'got ways of detecting listening devices'? Why would you have that?"

Easton grinned. "Your tax dollars at work," he said. "I did some spec-ops work ... back in the Corps. You'd be surprised, the things they train you to do."

A breath of air was drifting around the edges of the baggage car's side curtain, but even that was on the warm side of muggy. Jennifer reached for the curtain.

"Leave it," Easton told her. "Nothing's supposed to be peeking out the side of a baggage cart. We're hiding, here."

"So," she said, fanning herself with her hand. "My security check was your doing?"

He nodded. "The chief of security here at the airport is a retired warrant officer I was stationed with back on Okinawa. He ran the shore patrol. We saw each other. Often."

Jennifer tapped her knee and admired Easton's shadowed profile as they bumped along. "And," she said, nodding toward the front of the tram, "what about Jeeves, up there? Was he in the Army with you too?"

His eyes narrowed. "The Corps," he said. "And no, Jason's not anybody I met in the service. I taught him to cave dive a couple of years ago."

The whine of the tram dropped by an octave or two, and Jennifer rocked to the side as they turned in a semicircle. The motor noise stopped and there was a clunk as the hitch of their car bumped against the next one in line.

"South ramp," The young man called from outside. "Thank you for flying Air Jason."

Easton pulled the side-curtain back, and Jennifer blinked as the sunlight flooded in. She got out, dusting off her legs, and Easton reached in and grabbed her suitcase. He led her to a high-winged, single-prop, tail-dragger airplane, painted dark blue above and light below, in the manner of World War II naval aircraft. But apart from that eccentricity, the airplane looked brand, spanking new.

"This is how we're flying to the Bahamas?" She stared at the small plane.

"Yep." Easton swung her suitcase into the back of the airplane.

"Where's the pilot?"

"You're looking at him." He pulled sets of nylon chocks away from the front wheels.

"My tax dollars at work again?"

"Not this time." Easton walked quickly around the airplane, checking the edges of the wings, the tires, and the control surfaces. "I've been flying since I was sixteen."

She watched him. "We're just going to jump in and fly there?"

Easton nodded as he raised a cowl on one side of the engine, pulled a dipstick, glanced at it and replaced it.

"Is this even legal?"

"As long as they don't catch you," the tram driver said cheerfully. "You all set, Beck?"

"That I am, Jason. Much obliged."

The kid got back onto the tram and drove away, toward the main terminal building.

"Don't let Jason egg you on." Easton helped Jennifer up into the right seat of the airplane. Stowed seat belts showed where the rear seats had been removed; the back of the airplane was full of dark nylon duffel bags, scuba tanks, and Jennifer's suitcase and hand luggage, all lashed securely into place with wide nylon cargo straps.

"I've got a flight plan filed," Easton continued. "Part of the way, at least. All perfectly legal. Here, put these on. It's going to get noisy."

Jennifer accepted a pair of pale green headphones. She settled them over her ears and watched as he did the same with an identical set. Mimicking him, she positioned a flexible, foam-covered boom microphone just in front of her lips, feeling vaguely like she was about to cover the drive-through window at McDonald's.

"Can you hear me?" Easton's voice sounded like it was coming from inside her head.

"Yeah," she said. "But don't I need a visa, shots, something like that?"

"Clear!" Easton called out his open door. Then he shut it, pressed a button, and the prop on the front of the airplane made two jerky turns and then caught with a whirring roar, a puff of blue smoke wafting back past the bubble-shaped window in Jennifer's door.

"No." Easton's voice came over the headphones, making it sound as if he was inside her head. "Americans don't need a visa or anything special to visit the Bahamas. Your passport by itself will be fine."

Jennifer nodded as Easton fiddled with the radio, and a flat voice issued from it for about twenty seconds; the only words that Jennifer caught were "westerly" and "knots."

"Tallahassee ground," Easton called. "Cessna One-Niner-Five-Two-Echo, Have ATIS. Taxi Alpha South Ramp to runway One-Eight."

"Roger, Five-Two-Echo; taxi Alpha to One-Eight," a disembodied voice replied. "Hold at the line."

Easton clicked a button on his steering yoke twice. Then he pushed in a long-stemmed knob on the instrument panel and the engine note rose. The plane began moving. In moments they were dipping and swaying along an asphalt roadway. Jennifer craned her head as high as she could, but she still couldn't see anything over the engine cowl but the fogged disc of the spinning propeller and blue sky. Her ears felt clammy under the rubber headphone covers, and she looked for a way to open her window but found none.

"Hey, buddy," she said into the microphone. "Do we have AC in here?"

Easton grinned. "Mother nature's own." He was studying a chart strapped to a kneeboard. For a moment, Jennifer was alarmed that he wasn't touching the wheel. Then she saw his legs moving and realized that he was steering the airplane with a pair of pedals on the floor. She glanced down at the floor on her side— she had a wheel as well, but no pedals. She looked again and saw that her set was folded up, out of the way.

"Once we get up to altitude, the temperature will be twenty, thirty degrees cooler," Easton told her. "Just bear with me for a bit."

They came to a stop. Easton pressed the tops of his foot pedals as he pushed in the knob on the dashboard. The engine roared and kept roaring as he flipped switches on and off, pressed one foot pedal and then the other, and pushed, pulled, and turned his steering yoke. Then he reduced the engine speed, flipped to a new setting on the radio, and pressed a button on his yoke.

"Tallahassee Tower, Cessna One-Niner-Five-Two-Echo, departing runway One-Eight, left turn after takeoff."

"Five-Two-Echo takeoff One-Eight, left turn after climb," came the disembodied reply.

"Five-Two Echo." They slowly made the turn and lined up with the runway. He turned a small knob on the instrument panel and grinned at Jennifer. "Ready?"

She nodded.

Pushing the throttle control all the way in on the dash and then keeping his hand on it, Easton held the yoke in a deceptively casual manner as the airplane moved down the runway, rapidly gaining momentum. In a moment, Jennifer felt the tail rise off the ground, and then she could see everything in front of them—the runway scrolling toward them, small cone-hatted light fixtures rushing by, off in the scrub grass to either side. Then the rumbling beneath them stopped abruptly, and the ground just seemed to drop away.

"Whoa," Jennifer breathed.

"Yeah," Easton agreed. "We're about eight hundred pounds under our maximum useful load, right now, plus I've got a STOL kit installed, so we've got lift to spare."

"'Stall kit?'"

"S-T-O-L. Stands for 'Short Take-Off/Landing.' We can land in five hundred feet, fully loaded. Take off in eight."

He tapped her arm and pointed to the window as they banked and climbed. "There goes your flight."

Jennifer leaned toward the window as a red-tailed airliner rolled, toylike, down the runway below them and then angled up into the air. She let out a long, deep breath.

Easton pressed a keypad under a four-color display in the center of the instrument panel, and a small moving representation of an aeronautical chart appeared. In the center of the chart was the outline of an airplane.

"So," Jennifer said, glancing around, "you have your own airplane ..."

"Commercial flights allow fifty pounds of checked baggage per passenger. After that, it's your firstborn for every ounce." Easton was moving a wheel-like control between their seats as the ground continued to recede beneath them. "When I'm flying with cave gear, my tanks, alone, can weigh in at a hundred and thirty pounds. A plane like this can fly right in to Akamal or Abaco."

"Where?"

"My point exactly. Fly commercial, and you're going into Cancún or Nassau, and then you've got a whole other set of logistics to deal with, just to get to where you wanted to be in the first place. When I fly this, I'm never more than fifteen minutes from my water. In fact, I've got a set of floats back in the hangar that will put me down right *on* my water. But I don't use those in the Caribbean. Sea-plane landings will get you shot at in the tropics; people think you're a drug-runner."

Jennifer took in the moving-chart screen on the panel, the headsets, the vintage military paint scheme. "So this isn't just a big-boy-toy thing?"

Easton met her gaze and grinned. "No. It's absolutely that, as well." After a moment, he added, "CD player's on the bottom of the panel. Flip the switch where your headset cord goes into the intercom, if you want to listen."

Taking the hint, Jennifer turned the switch and reached for the zippered nylon case as he handed it to her. She opened it and suppressed a groan. Easton's airborne CD collection seemed to be the twin of what he kept in his truck.

She selected a CD by somebody called "Alison Krauss + Union Station," and was pleasantly surprised by a hauntingly pure female voice with a violin and acoustic guitars in the background.

Jennifer found a volume adjustment on the side of her headphones and turned the music up a notch.

Not bad, she thought. *Not bad at all.*

Lulled by the drone of the engine, and feeling safe with Easton at her side, Jennifer closed her eyes and drifted off to sleep.

> *"In all the things that cause me pain,*
> *You give me eyes that see.*
> *I do believe, but help my unbelief . . ."*

Jennifer blinked awake and took a moment to figure out where the singing was coming from. She turned her headset from the CD player back to the intercom, reached under her earphones and rubbed her ears.

"Pressure bugging you?" Easton asked her.

She nodded.

"Wet your lips, hold your nose, and swallow."

She shot him a look from the corner of her eye.

"Really," he urged her. "Try it."

Glancing toward him again, she tried it. Then she smiled in relief. "Hey! That really works."

"It's called a 'modified Valsalva maneuver.'" Easton pulled up on a handle that looked like a parking brake, and then adjusted the wheel on the console between them. "We're getting ready to land; we've already lost about four thousand feet in altitude. The lower we go, the higher the ambient air pressure is, but your inner ear had equalized to what we were experiencing at altitude. When you swallowed, your tongue acted like a piston. Forced the air up your Eustachian tube to your inner ear. Added air pressure, relieving the discomfort."

Jennifer stared at him. The man was a flying encyclopedia. "Okay, let me guess—you're an ENT too?"

"Nope." He grinned. "An OWSI."

"Ow-see?"

"Open Water Scuba Instructor," Easton said. "The Valsalva is one of the first things you show people when you're teaching them how to dive. Helps with the pressure underwater." He reduced the engine speed, pulled the lever between the seats one notch higher, and pressed the button atop his control yoke to talk to someone he called "Fort Lauderdale Executive Tower."

Jennifer listened as they communicated. It sounded like a lot of bravo-foxtrot-tango talk. *Is all that really necessary? Or do these guys just like to sound like they were in Top Gun?* She strongly suspected the latter.

They banked and a moment later lined up with a runway flanked with white strobe lights. Easton set the airplane down with such skill that Jennifer could barely tell when the wheels met the ground.

"Hang on," he said, his voice almost casual. "Tight left coming up."

He slowed the airplane with the toe-brakes, then goosed the throttle and kicked the left pedal down hard, swinging the tail to the right behind them, and heading them back at a forty-five-degree angle to the way they'd landed. A minute later, he shut off the engine in front of a building with a sign that read "Execuport International."

They hung their headsets on the yokes, and he flipped switches on the panel. "There's a restaurant inside. Why don't you go on in? I'll wait here for the fuel truck, get them started, then I'll be in to join you."

Even in the heat reflected off the sun-faded tarmac, Jennifer was glad for the chance to stretch her legs. She walked slowly, savoring the warmth on the backs of her thighs.

She turned her head, taking the place in. It looked like Florida, or at least the way Florida should look, which was more than she could say for Live Oak. Even here, in a landscape that was mostly asphalt and airplanes, she could see the shag-haircut shapes of distant palm trees, and the perimeter of the airport was planted with thriving, green palmetto and sawgrass. As Jennifer approached the terminal, a small lizard scurried across the sidewalk and vanished into the vegetation.

Jennifer opened the door and stepped into a delicious coolness: American air-conditioning at its finest. The cool air refreshed Jennifer, but it also awakened another need. She spotted the universal paper-doll-in-a-dress symbol and hurried down the broad entry corridor to the ladies' room.

Standing at the sink, eyes closed, Jennifer splashed cool water on her face and neck. Refreshed, she dried off with a paper towel, and then blinked into the mirror.

Yikes. Her hair had been schmushed every which-way by the broad band of the radio headset. *Nice 'do, Jen.* She pulled a short-bristled brush out of her bookbag and affected the necessary repairs.

She brushed several short strokes, and then stopped, squinting at her reflection once more. She was a little sunburned, a little disheveled, a little drawn from a night of half-sleep and the excitement of her unorthodox departure from the Tallahassee airport.

Drawing a breath, she did a quick mental inventory. Just a little over one month earlier, she'd been on the verge of a long, hot, summer of slim tips and sore feet at the Wapakoneta Trucker's Heaven. Since that time, she'd not only landed an assistantship that did not involve teaching undergrads. She had uncovered a mystery; lied to her client about why she was going to Florida; hired Jacques-Cousteau-meets-Rambo out there on the tarmac; found clues to long-lost treasure; been followed by—she gulped— hit men? Spies? She'd turned in her airline ticket for a boarding pass and then skipped the flight with no way to get back to Ann

Arbor; and then she'd crossed an airport in a manner that she was certain must have violated at least one FAA regulation. Probably more than one.

Now she was farther from home than she'd ever been in her life, on her way out of the country with a man she'd met only two days earlier, and heading to an island where she didn't know a single soul.

All that, plus she was still rendered semi-speechless by the mere sight of Beck Easton, which she was pretty certain wasn't how you were supposed to feel about someone with whom you shared a client-contractor relationship.

She wondered if she was still paying for his services. And if she was, how steep was his price tag? Was she doing something that could cost her the assistantship, get her booted out of grad school, or otherwise ruin her life?

She thought it over.

Probably, she decided.

"You're an idiot," she told her reflection.

"I beg your pardon?"

Jennifer swallowed and turned. The lady who'd just entered the restroom looked to be in her late sixties, wearing a straw cowboy hat, a red flannel vest with little embroidered patches all over it, and a blue, engraved, plastic name tag that read "Mary Lou" and "Cherokee 180 Nation: Fresno Tribe."

"Oh ... hi," Jennifer said, forcing a smile. "Is the ... um ... restaurant far from here?"

"Why, no, dear," Mary Lou said. "It's just right down the hall."

Mary Lou was traveling in company.

The restaurant teemed with red flannel vests, straw stockman's hats, and name tags. The crowd seemed to be married couples. Almost all were of retirement age, and several seemed well along into it. All seemed highly amused, and they were divided nearly evenly into two groups: those who were speaking and those who were laughing. No one in particular seemed to be listening.

"Who are they?" Jennifer whispered as Easton joined her at the hostess stand.

"These folks?" Easton squinted at a name tag as two men walked by, chatting, hands on one another's shoulders. "They're a Cherokee owners' club."

"Cherokee? As in 'Jeep'?"

"Cherokee as in 'Piper,'" Easton smiled. "It's an airplane."

"They're all pilots?"

"Are, or were. As they get on in years, lose their medicals, folks like this tend to fly Winnebagos rather than airplanes, but they keep their friends."

Jennifer glanced around, taking in the sea of graying and blue-white hair.

"Does it bother you?" Easton asked her.

"It?" She turned her gaze back to him.

"The thought of getting older." He looked thoughtful. Serious. "Does it?"

Jennifer felt her face reddening. She looked around worried that some of the people in the club might overhear.

"This old?" She kept her voice to a whisper. "Well . . . sure. Doesn't it bother you?"

Easton pointed to an open table near the window, and they headed that way.

"No," he said as they walked. "No. It doesn't. It looks like they're having a pretty good time."

They skirted around a man in a walker who was greeting someone named "Andy." Jennifer looked back at him after they'd passed and then turned again to Easton. "Aren't you afraid of the day when you'll no longer be young?"

Easton chuckled. "Is that what I am? Young?"

They got to the table.

"Well, yeah," Jennifer whispered. "I mean, compared to these folks, *anybody's* young."

"Jen," he pulled a chair out for her and held it as she sat. "I enjoy being who I am, as I am."

He sat across from her, and the Cherokees filled the room with the buzz of thirty different conversations.

"You know," Easton said after the waitress had come and taken their order. "I did five hundred sit-ups this morning."

"Five hundred?"

"Uh-huh."

Jennifer's mouth dropped. "Why?"

"Because I do five hundred sit-ups every morning."

Jennifer felt her eyebrows elevate a notch.

"But," Easton added, "back when I was on active duty, I used to do a thousand."

Jennifer looked at him in admiration. "Every day?"

"You bet. And you know what? Now that I've cut back, I don't regret the other five hundred. And I won't regret it when I cut it down to two-fifty. Or a hundred. Or ten. I like who I am right now. I really do. And five years, ten years ago, I did some things that, in all probability, I'll never do again. But I've learned since then. I've grown since then. And I wouldn't trade now for then. And thirty, forty years from now, I really don't think I'll regret not being the age I am now. Why should I?"

She didn't often reveal what was in her heart, especially when it came to her fears. But something in Beck Easton's eyes said he would understand.

"Because these people . . . ," she finally whispered, ". . . they're so close."

"To what. To dying?"

Now her face was really red. She could feel it. "*Yes.*" It came out like a hiss. "To dying."

"And that's a problem?"

She wrung her hands, not believing that they were actually having this conversation. "Yes," she finally said. "Dying would constitute a problem."

"Why?"

Jennifer turned to the restaurant window and the palm trees beyond. She suddenly had this urge to be out there, under them, and not having this uncomfortable talk.

One of the Cherokee couples walked by, arm in arm. Easton followed them with his eyes, and the friendly smile dropped from his face for just a moment. It was quick, but it was there. For just a fraction of a second, he looked somber. Hurt.

Jennifer was pretty sure she knew why.

"Have you ever been married?" There it was. The question slipped out before she could stop it.

Easton tented his fingers and rested his chin on them. "Yes," he said after a long pause.

Maybe too long a pause. Jennifer's heart headed for Australia.

"And are you still . . . ?" Her voice was two sizes too small. ". . . Married, I mean?"

Again, he didn't answer right away. His attention was on the older couple as they exchanged a word and a laugh with another man and woman.

"No," he finally said. His voice didn't sound all that large either.

Four of the Cherokees started singing.

Easton smiled. "Good," he said, his voice back to normal. "The burgers are here. Let's pray, okay?"

CHAPTER ELEVEN

The long, sand beaches of Fort Lauderdale receded beneath the bubble window on Jennifer's side of the plane. Below her, small dancing boats ran parallel to the shore, white wakes trailing like diminishing brushstrokes. The ocean dropped off into deep water, the turquoise of the near-shore waves giving way to ever darkening shades of blue. And ahead, as far as she could see, was blue, the sea meeting the sky in a horizon so obscure that it was impossible to say where one took up and the other left off.

She didn't switch her headphones to the CD player this time, because doing so would also cut her off from communication with Beck, and if he had anything to say—like, "Get ready to swim"—she wanted to hear it.

He'd invited her to pick up whatever she wanted to in the flight service's snack shop, and she'd done that, selecting a twelve-pack of Mountain Dew Code Red, a tin of butter cookies, and a couple of bags of chips—sour-cream-and-onion flavored for her, mesquite barbecue for Beck, because he looked the type.

While she was in the pilot's shop, she'd watched him through the window as he began his preflight inspection on the airplane. He started at the pilot's side door and walked slowly around the airplane, feeling the fuselage surface, carefully checking the leading edges of the tail, moving the control surfaces up and down and side-to-side, and peering closely at every hinge. Twice—once under the wing and once under the engine cowling—he drained liquid into a clear test-tube-like container, held it up to the light, and then disposed of it on the tarmac. He'd checked several things in the engine compartment and had felt the entire length of the propeller with both hands. Then he'd taken a folding step stool out of the back of the airplane and climbed up and inspected the top of each wing.

He'd started checking the airplane when Jennifer had gone in to shop, and he'd still been checking it when she'd come back out. That was when it hit her: They were going to be flying over water, with no place to land but islands.

The very thought had been enough to send her back inside for one more trip to the ladies' room.

Now they were—she checked the altimeter—five thousand feet above the ocean, and there were no islands to be seen. On the screen in the center of the instrument panel, the little airplane was flying over a similarly blank expanse of blue.

Jennifer cleared her throat.

"What's up?" Easton raised a brow her direction.

She stared out at the ocean below. "How do we know where we're going?"

Easton pointed at the little screen in the panel. "GPS," he said. "Global Positioning System. Several years back, the Defense Department put up a system of satellites in geosynchronous orbit, all around the globe. It's designed for military use, but civilians can access it as well. We have a receiver in the top of our wing that tracks as many satellites as it can find, triangulates a position off of them, and converts it into visible data on this screen. I punch in the airport code of our destination, and it automatically navigates toward it. So we are now ..." He hit a button on the GPS and a page of numbers came up. "... two hundred eighty-five statute miles from New Bight Airport on Cat Island, which is on a heading of one hundred forty-seven degrees from true north from here. GPS says we'll arrive in two hours and six minutes, which means that we've got a bit of a tailwind, since this beast cruises best at one-thirty."

Jennifer cast a worried look at the screen. "What happens if this little GPS thing breaks?"

Easton smiled. "We can also navigate by radio signals with a system called VOR," he said. "If we lose all electrical power to the panel, I have a battery-powered handheld radio that can also home in on a signal. And if all else fails, I have a compass ..."

He pointed to an instrument atop the panel that looked a lot like what Jennifer's dad had on the dash of his GMC Suburban.

"... And the compass doesn't need electricity to run. From Fort Lauderdale, if you fly due southeast, you inevitably start hitting islands in the Bahamas. And a lot of them have airstrips."

Jennifer frowned. "You said, 'If we lose electrical power to the panel ...'" She paused, wondering if she sounded as worried as she felt. "Uh, if we do that ... doesn't the engine stop?"

Easton shook his head. "Airplane engines run off magnetos, not alternators and generators. And we have two magnetos. I'm running off both right now, but we can run fine on either one by itself."

"Well," she murmured, looking out the window at the small specks of whitecaps, far below. "At least it's a nice, brand-new airplane."

"Brand new?" Easton laughed, more a hoot than a laugh. "The flight manual is in the glovebox, there, just above where the CD player is mounted. Take it out and have a look."

She turned the knob, opened the little piano-hinged door, and took out a blue leatherette volume about the size of a small-town phone book. On the cover, in gold letters, it read: "1968 Cessna A185F Skywagon."

"Nineteen sixty-eight?" She gasped. "That's like, the Nixon administration, isn't it?"

"No." Easton frowned in thought. "I don't think Nixon took office until sixty-nine."

Her jaw dropped. "So," she said slowly, staring at the flight manual as if waiting for it to change. "I'm flying over the ocean in an airplane that was built before I was born?"

"Don't feel too badly," Easton told her. "It was built before *I* was born too."

She clutched the flight manual tighter and tried to ignore her white knuckles. Her voice came out in a croak when she asked,

"Do you know anything about the person who owned it before you?"

"Oh sure," Easton said. "Know all about him."

Jennifer relaxed a notch.

"It belonged to a South American drug dealer."

Jennifer dropped the flight manual. The plane hit a pocket of turbulence and the blue book slid under her seat. She reached forward to retrieve it and was caught by her seat belt.

"Leave it," Easton said. "We'll get it when we land."

Jennifer straightened. "You're ... you're kidding about the drug dealer, right?"

He shook his head. "I've got a friend who flies for a missionary service over in Kenya," he said, "and while he was home in West Palm on leave, he got word that the DEA had seized three 185s that got shot up—"

"Shot *up*?"

" ... just a little bit, in a drug raid down in South Dade. Anyhow, they wanted to auction them off, and he wanted one for his missions work—these 185s are just what the doctor ordered for airlifting light loads of medical supplies—but the Feds only wanted to sell 'em together, as a lot. So we went together and picked up all three for just eighteen thousand bucks—people are often leery about bidding on seized aircraft, because you never know if the maintenance books on them are on the level, you know?"

She felt a little faint.

"Anyhow, I had a couple of guys who were ATs—aircraft technicians—and they wanted to learn to cave dive, so we worked a trade. My buddy and I pitched in to help do the grunt work, take things apart, do the lifting and whatnot. These guys took all three planes down to the last nut and bolt, did a ground-up overhaul and restoration. All it cost us was parts ... which, admittedly, was still a little over four times what we paid for the airplanes."

He leaned forward and moved a lever on the panel from "Left Tank" to "Right Tank."

"We got some deals," he said. "Like the paint? One of my guys' customers was restoring a Navy Corsair, and he bought way more than he needed. And when he found out what we were doing and that one of the planes was going into missions work? He just gave us his excess. It took us nearly a year to do all the work—nearly the entire length of my buddy's home leave—but when we got done, we had three totally refurbished airplanes. They had new interiors, new avionics, completely overhauled mechanicals throughout. Our total investment was around ninety-eight thousand dollars. We sold the third plane to a dentist over in Daytona ..." He fiddled for a moment with the knurled wheel between the seats. "... for a hundred and seven, rolled the profits back into my buddy's missions deputation, and walked away from the deal with two free airplanes in absolutely perfect condition."

He grinned. "All it cost me was a little sweat and some cave diving."

She smiled weakly.

"And," Easton added, "I have good news."

"What's that?"

"There's a life jacket strapped to the bottom of your seat, and it's new too."

It was okay, but I never did put my full weight down on the seat. That was one of Jennifer's father's favorite one-liners about flying. And it had begun to make perfect sense by the time Andros— one of the most westerly islands of the Bahamas—rose low and green on the horizon.

She turned to Easton. "Is there an airstrip?"

"Sure." He pushed a button and zoomed the GPS out. "Here's one on the north end of the island, about ten minutes' flight. Why? Need to make a pit stop?"

"No." She shook her head. "It's ... just nice to know, that's all."

Easton laughed. "I'm with you," he said. "It's always nice to know where your nearest field is."

Andros was wide. By the time they got over it, it seemed to stretch nearly from horizon to horizon. But big as it was, it wasn't nearly as reassuring up close as it had seemed from a distance. The afternoon sun glinted off of fingers and pockets of water all over the place. The island seemed to be more water than land.

"Lots of sinkholes all over Andros," Easton said, as if reading her mind. "Lot's of 'em offshore, as well. The island's famous among cave divers for its blue holes. There's been quite a bit of heavy-duty exploration done here, over the years."

The beaches of Andros disappeared behind the Cessna's tail. Jennifer looked at the GPS, which was still zoomed out. A thin chain of islands was creeping in from the lower right-hand corner.

"Is that the Exumas?"

He nodded. "Yep. That's where Baxter and his buddies were trying to beach the *Halcyon*. And they must have been about this far north. Down south? Great Exuma and Little Exuma? They're practically a solid wall across the water, stretching for miles and miles. But up here, next land we'll see is a group of little islands with lots of water in between where you can slip through. See the color of the water?"

She looked out. "It's really blue," she said. "It's like ... what do they call it? Indigo blue, dark. Why? Different color bottom?"

"More like no bottom," he said. "Not in any practical sense. That's the Tongue of the Ocean, the deep water Stewart spoke of in Baxter's narrative. More than a mile deep. So deep that the Navy uses that water to test nuclear submarines."

They flew in silence for about twenty minutes. Then Easton spoke up. "Check the water now."

Jennifer leaned toward the window again. The water was lighter. Not nearly as light as the sky, but nowhere near the midnight blue of the sea they'd flown over earlier. "So," she said. "How deep is this?"

Easton glanced out. "I'd say two hundred fifty, three hundred feet. Water's deceptively clear in these latitudes. Sunlight can still hit a white-sand bottom that far down and reflect back up. But the bottom's coming up, that's for sure. Another ten minutes, and we'll start flying over tongue-and-groove coral formations, like an underwater tank trap for a deep-draught old-time steamship. Down there, in a blow—a tropical storm—in one of those? Uh-uh—it doesn't get any badder than that."

The upper Exumas were just what he had said—scattered little biscuits of stone, sand, and palm trees, washed by waters that were a thousand shades of aquamarine, green, and blue. Dark shadows of coral danced under the shifting waves, and at one point Jennifer spotted a shape, like an exclamation point without the dot, swimming from one coral head to another.

"Is that a shark?"

Easton didn't even bother to look. "If you think it is, then the answer's probably 'yes.' Lemon sharks, white-tipped, black-tipped, sandbar, bulls. These waters are like Sea World without the controlled feedings."

She shivered.

"Thinking of Stewart?"

She gave him a small nod.

"Long time ago, Jen. You ever been to the Bahamas before?" She shook her head, and he went on. "Well, you're going to be ..." He pushed the button on the GPS. "... in twenty-seven minutes. See the clouds directly ahead of us?"

She nodded.

"Look below them. See the land?"

"No." Jennifer squinted and looked again. "Wait ... yes. Okay. Got it. Looks like a bumpy pencil line."

"That's where we're headed. Cat Island, coming up."

CHAPTER TWELVE

SANTIAGO DE CUBA, CUBA

"Idiota!"

Umberto Alcázar beat the expensive Iridium satellite phone against the intricate mosaic-tiled surface of his terrace's patio table; one swat, two swats, three. He listened to make sure the phone was still working, and then beat it against the tabletop one more time for good measure.

"Por favor, me . . . " the voice in the receiver began protesting.

"Oh, speak English, you fool," Alcázar said to his caller. "I'm sick of your lisping Spanish. It makes you sound as if you bat from the wrong side of the plate."

Alcázar enjoyed the moment of silence that followed. It meant that his euphemism—understandable in both baseball-crazy Cuba and her estranged neighbor to the north—had hit the mark.

"Fine."

It was amazing. Scarvano's voice was being encoded, relayed to a secure transfer node in Canada, uplinked to a satellite, bounced back down to an Iridium router base in suburban Chicago, uplinked to a second satellite, bounced to Alcázar's phone, and decoded. Yet, after all that, Alcázar could still detect the dual inflections in that single syllable—the meekness of the servant who knew he was being overpaid, and the haughtiness of the high-powered attorney who was accustomed to running the show.

"Fine," Scarvano repeated. "I just want to assure you that our people lost the girl due to a security check in Tallahassee. We had every reason to believe she was boarding the airplane, but she didn't get on, and we couldn't break cover by leaving the airplane ourselves—"

"The *anglo*," Alcázar interrupted. "This Easton. What do you know about him?"

"Well ..." Scarvano's voice sounded evasive. "We know he's former military, and—"

"*Idiota!*"

Scarvano stopped talking.

"Former military?" Alcázar took a deep breath. "I made a phone call to the Minister of Intelligence's office this morning. They ran a check. They tell me that this Easton *hombre* graduated—not just attended, but *graduated*—from the United States Navy's BUDS in Coronado, California. Do you know what that means?"

Scarvano's silence said that he did not.

"He has had Navy SEAL training, you imbecile!"

"B-but our information indicated he was in the Marines ... "

"Silence," Alcázar hissed. "Where do you buy your intelligence from? Kmart? Marines sometimes undergo the SEAL training ... to ready them for covert operations."

Scarvano fell silent again.

Alcázar calmed himself by taking in the view from his rooftop terrace. On his left, the ancient parapets of *Castillo el Morro* guarded the sun-sparkled blue waters of Santiago Bay. Far to his right, green mountains slept, rugged and hazy in the warm afternoon. And between them, enfolded upon its many hills, was the second largest city in all of Cuba, a warm-blooded city on his nation's southeastern coast, a city with twice the tradition of coarse Havana, and three times the other town's beauty.

Alcázar looked at the city, quiet in the heat of the afternoon, and consoled himself with the fact that no one in all of Cuba, not even *El Barba*—"The Beard," the way everyday Cubans referred to their longtime leader—had such a view. Alcázar had been many times to the presidential palace in Havana and to *El Barba's* fabled retreat on the Isle of Pines, and they had had nothing to compare with this, no vista that allowed one to see in one sweep the beauty of the Cuban land and the souls of the Cuban people.

"All right," he said into the telephone, calm now. "Out with it, old friend. What else are you not telling me?"

Through all the cutouts and encryption software, he heard the other man take a deep breath. "Well," Scarvano began slowly, "we have learned through our sources that Easton owns an airplane."

"An airplane?" Alcázar asked it as nicely as if he were asking for a second cup of coffee. "And what are you telling me, my friend? That, in addition to being trained for covert operations, this Easton is also a pilot?"

"Yes."

Alcázar's calm vanished in a bright red mist. He slammed the phone against the tabletop one more time.

"*Where?*" He growled it. "Where have they gone?"

"We have ways of finding out," Scarvano assured him earnestly. "We know his N-number—the identification number for his airplane. If he filed a flight plan, if he flew through airspace that required him to use his transponder, if he paid a landing fee or purchased fuel, there will be a record of it, and we will find them."

Alcázar could feel his eyes narrowing. "You listen to me," he said, his voice low. "You are on very thin ice here, my friend. I want to know where this *americana* and her Marine have gone, and I want to know what they know, and I ... do ... not ... care ... not one iota ... how you learn this. Do you understand me?"

"I do," Scarvano said.

"Then make it so."

Alcázar punched "End" on the satellite phone, dissatisfied that he had no receiver to slam it into.

He tossed the phone onto the padded seat of one of the handmade, wrought metal patio chairs, stood up, and walked to the low wall surrounding his terrace. It was a good view. The best in all Cuba. Worthy of the most powerful man in all Cuba. And he was not that. He was not even in the top five.

All that would change when he got his hands on what the little blonde college girl and her enigmatic ex-Marine were following.

They had never expected that the girl would go chasing after the *oro*—the gold—by herself. But a professional had to be prepared for such contingencies. This Scarvano had the reputation of being a professional. Well, he'd better be.

Alcázar calmed himself with his view.

At his feet, *Santiago de Cuba* slept in the afternoon sun. *The Basilica de Nuestra Señora del Cobre*, the holiest place in all Cuba, was here. This city was a historic place, a place steeped in tradition, a place steeped in ... honor. José Marti was buried in this city. Marti, the greatest national hero that Cuba had ever known.

And if things went as they should, a new hero would soon rise up from this city, a hero that would forever save this nation from returning to the vulgarity of the nation that lay less than a hundred miles to the north.

And if that hero became wealthy beyond measure in the process?

Well, what of that? It was only as it should be.

Alcázar patted his shirt pocket. He was out of cigarettes again. Two dozen of the finest cigars in the world rested in a table humidor, not three steps away, but he kept those purely for his VIP guests; among the government officials of Cuba, Alcázar was that rarest of rarities—a man who hated cigars. They stank up the restaurants of his country and fouled the air at meetings. As far as he was concerned, the nation's entire production could go to export, and if—when—he became *presidente*, most of it would. At three hundred dollars a box, cigars could buy his country a lot of needed medical supplies. That, or a lot of bullets.

He started back into the house for a fresh pack of Marlboros— an embargoed product that he had flown in weekly from Canada— and then he stopped.

Two strikes. That was another baseball metaphor equally understandable in both Cuba and the giant to her north. And Louis

Scarvano and his fancy, genteel Atlantan, silk-stockinged law firm had two strikes against them: first they had lost track of the girl and her *americano* helper on the Florida back roads; now they had lost her again at the airport. And she was his best—his only—chance of getting his hands on what he needed to help and to purify his country. It would not be good for Alcázar to be in Cuba if Scarvano's hired help increased the count to three. It was time to get—how was it the Americans put it?—hands-on.

He picked up a phone, not the satellite phone with its bulky, club-like antenna, but the small cordless model that was linked to his house line. He pressed the speed-dial number for his office.

"I need to consult with our professor at McMaster," he told his assistant. "Put me on the first flight tomorrow for Toronto ... open return. No—I don't know how long my business there will take."

CHAPTER THIRTEEN

CAT ISLAND, COMMONWEALTH OF THE BAHAMAS

"That's Fernandez Bay."

Easton banked the Cessna so Jennifer could take in the view from the passenger's side. She didn't see anything that looked like the seaside resorts that had dotted the beaches back in Fort Lauderdale, just a handful of cottages spread out above the high-water mark on the sand.

"Is that where we're staying?"

"Fernandez Bay Village," Easton said, nodding. "Guy named Armbrister built the bungalows on spec back in the sixties, planning to sell them as vacation property. When they didn't sell as quickly as he'd hoped, he opened a resort, instead. Good choice; they book up a year or more in advance. Quite the clientele. You come here after you get tired of the rest of the Bahamas. Rock stars, actors ... and people like us. It's laid back, out of the way, and private. Plus it's got the best kitchen in the out-islands."

"How'd we get in, if they book up so early?"

Easton grinned. "Just blessed, I guess." He leveled off and pointed at a low peak. "Mount Alvernia."

There seemed to be buildings of some type on top, but it went by too quickly to be sure. "Doesn't look high enough to be a 'mount.'"

He laughed. "It is if it's the highest point in the Bahamas. It's, I don't know, maybe a little over two hundred feet above sea level. Seems higher from the ground."

He keyed the radio and announced, "New Bight traffic, Cessna November-One-Niner-Five-Two-Echo, downwind for runway Three-Four."

The radio rustled with static, and Jennifer shot Easton a look. "Nobody's answering."

"Tower's closed in the afternoon," Easton said. "They only show up for the commercial flights and those come through in the morning. The radio call's just a courtesy, in case any other traffic is in the area. It's not Miami, you know?"

He slowed the airplane, extended the flaps, and made two turns to line up with a sun-cracked concrete runway. A minute later, he made yet another feather-smooth landing.

It soon became clear someone had been listening on the radio. Minutes after Easton cut the engine, an older Toyota Land Cruiser pulled in next to the plane, its fenders powdered with dust.

"Beck! Great to see ya! Bring your gear?"

To say the man who met them the moment they'd stepped out of the plane was enthusiastic was the ultimate in understatements. He greeted Easton with a handshake that seemed to devour his entire forearm. Then he answered his own question by peering into the windows of the airplane.

"Great! You did!" He turned, still grinning, toward Jennifer. "Crikey! She's a looker! Who's this?"

"Jennifer Cassidy," Easton smiled. "Allow me to introduce Kerry Whittaker, divemaster extraordinaire and, apparently, our greeter from Fernandez Bay Village."

"Great!" Whittaker offered Jennifer a more genteel version of the handshake he'd given to Easton.

"Ow, she's a keeper, Beck," he said, turning to Easton. "Good on ya!"

"Subtle, Kerry," Easton grinned. "Very subtle." But he did not, Jennifer noticed, make any effort to set the divemaster straight.

A pleasant warmth filled her face. "So," she said, covering her fluster, "you're English?"

Whittaker winked at Easton. "Awesome! She's got a sense of humor, as well!"

"That she does," Easton agreed. Edging past Jennifer to start taking the bags out of the plane, he whispered under his breath, "He's Australian."

She turned to Whittaker. "So ... Sydney?" It was the only Australian city she could think of.

"Adelaide." Beaming, Whittaker turned to help Easton unload the airplane.

"Umm," Jennifer bit her lip. "Shouldn't we be seeing to, you know, customs and immigrations?"

"Oh, Lionel's up in Arthur's Town today," Whittaker said. "Leave your passport at the lodge with Donna, and he'll stop by tonight and stamp it."

Jennifer blinked. "The customs agent makes house calls?"

"He lives in New Bight." Whittaker shrugged. "He'll get it on the way home."

"But how will he know we're here?"

Whittaker chuckled, but it was Easton who answered. "Coconut telegraph. By dinnertime, everyone on the island will know that we're here."

Whittaker kept talking while they loaded up the Land Cruiser, while he helped Easton chock the wheels and tie down the airplane, and while he drove the two of them ten minutes down the road to the resort.

Whittaker and Easton sat up front in the right-hand-drive Land Cruiser, while Jennifer sat in back. The SUV's climate control system consisted of four windows, rolled all the way down. All she could catch of what was being said in the front seat was the general buzz of conversation, punctuated at regular intervals by Whittaker's uninhibited, braying laughter.

She gazed through the open window. Low scrub trees and bushes crowded up to the crumbling asphalt road on either side. Tiny, double-rutted driveways provided irregular interruptions to the wall of vegetation and the briefest glimpses of blue sky and sea. Every couple of minutes they'd pass a picket-fenced yard that enclosed a strutting population of chickens. A few minutes later they came upon an open area framed by a stone arch, and after that the trees closed in again.

All that changed when they turned into Fernandez Bay Village. The tropical foliage was still lush, but cultivated, and manicured pathways led away from the gravel turnout. It was almost as if they had left the Third World and re-entered the First.

"Tell you what," Whittaker was saying to Easton, "I'll have the guys take your bags to your cabin, and I'll put your dive gear in the shop. Want me to air up your tanks?"

"No need," Easton said. "I topped them off with Nitrox before I left this morning."

"Brilliant!" Whittaker pumped Easton's hand. "Well, you know the drill, mate. See you at dinner, right?"

After a mock salute Jennifer's direction, the divemaster headed off to find some luggage help, and Jennifer turned to Easton. "Just how many times have you been here, anyhow?"

Easton laughed. "Not as many as you think, but a few. I came here on some leaves back when I was in the Corps, and one time, when I showed up, both of the resort's dive staff had just quit to take a job in Nassau, and Kerry, there, literally came in on the same flight as me. So, as I'd been here before, I helped him service the air station in the shop, over there, and do the visuals on all the resort's tanks. Then I spent my whole leave showing him dive sites."

Jennifer tilted her head toward him. "That was pretty nice of you."

"Not at all." Easton shook his head. "Diving was what I was here to do anyhow, and it turned my vacation into an adventure. And the resort showed their appreciation."

They started walking toward the resort's main lodge building. "How?" she asked.

Easton shrugged. "That was about ten years ago," he said. "And I haven't paid for a stay here since." He held open the entrance door to the lodge. After she stepped in, he led her through a sitting area and a library and out onto a verandah.

She blinked as her eyes readjusted to the sunlight. Then she gasped. They were standing next to a small cabana bar. Swept pathways and palm trees occupied the immediate area. Beyond them was an empty white-sand beach that arced off to a picture-perfect horizon in either direction.

But it was the sea that took her breath away. It was transparent turquoise and filled with light. The swells lifted and dropped, as if living and breathing, before dissolving into white-capped wavelets on the sand.

"Beck!"

Jennifer turned as a blonde woman in her early forties headed toward Easton. An instant later, she kissed him on the cheek. She smiled at Jennifer, then kissed her on the cheek as well.

"Welcome," she said. "I'm Donna."

"Jennifer."

Donna turned back to Easton. "Oh, Beck. She's absolutely adorable."

The color on Easton's cheeks deepened. Was GI Joe, here, blushing?

He cleared his throat. "You sure we're not putting you out?"

"Not at all," Donna said. "One of our regulars had both sides of Sunset booked for his family next week. He got called to an emergency board meeting. He'd already paid in advance, so he told us to keep it—said he'd get reimbursed. So the cabin's available, and it's paid for. Enjoy."

Before Easton could thank her, Donna had turned back to Jennifer. "Sweetheart, we have a tradition, here. The cabana bar is self-serve, on the honor system, and your welcome cocktail is complimentary, so help yourself."

"Thank you." Jennifer stepped into the little bar, poured a small bottle of Schwepp's tonic water into a glass—it only seemed appropriate, given the setting—added ice and a lemon wedge, and eyed the bottle of gin. She glanced toward Easton. "Beck? What can I get you?"

"Nothing for me, thanks. Want to go look at the cabin?"

Still has his work hat on, Jennifer thought, her heart sinking. *This is all just a job to him.* She decided tonic water by itself would be fine, pasted on a bright smile and walked with Easton down the conch-shell-lined path. The path soon gave way to sand, and the sand to the beach itself. She took off her sandals and, holding them in one hand, sipped the cool tonic water, the soft, warm sand feeling delicious between her toes. Trusting that Easton knew where they were going, she took in her surroundings as they walked.

The beach curved gently, south to southwest. In the distance, it was interrupted by some marshy plants—the mouth of a creek, she imagined—and then continued its curve to a distant point. To their left, up past the mounded high-water mark of the beach, stood a row of wooden cottages, each standing out with its own unique design, some simple, others larger and more elaborate. Near one of the smaller cabins a hammock was slung between two palms. A few feet away, a paperback book rested on a side-table next to a rattan chair. Jennifer sighed. A little piece of paradise.

She was still taking it all in when Easton stopped. She halted as well and cast him a curious glance. He was staring at the cabin in front of them. A small signpost in front read "Sunset." Their cottage.

Easton's face was blank, unreadable. For a moment, he didn't speak, then he inclined his head toward the door. As soon as they stepped under the porch overhang Jennifer saw that the low, plastered building had two entry doors: The cottage was divided into two separate accommodations. She didn't know whether to feel relieved or disappointed.

The front doors were open, and Beck glanced inside the room to the left. "Looks like your bags in here," he said. "Other one must be mine. Do you have anything you could hike in?"

Jennifer nodded. "I have my running shoes."

"Those'll do. Why don't you change? I want to get a look at something while we still have light."

"Let me powder my nose, and I'll be right with you."

A few minutes later they were walking along the beach, and she was enjoying the sun on her shoulders. It felt ... romantic. She ventured a look toward Easton. He had a small green daypack on his shoulders, and his eyes were hidden behind his sunglasses.

All business.

They left the sand, cut through the lodge, and headed to the Land Cruiser, which had its keys in the ignition.

It felt strange to climb into the left front seat as a passenger. But if Easton found it odd to be driving a manual-shift SUV from the right-hand side, he didn't show it. He started up the sturdy little vehicle and drove back down the same worn asphalt road they'd been on earlier. In just a few minutes, they turned in at the stone arch she'd noticed when they arrived.

Leaning forward, she peered up at the top of the arch, where worn wooden letters spelled the name MT ALVERNIA.

"Mount Alvernia," she mused. "You know, when you mentioned it in the plane, I had this feeling I've heard that name before."

"Probably have," he said. The Land Cruiser bumped down a rutted two-track path. "Lots of Franciscan monasteries are called that. It's where Saint Francis had his hermitage, near Assisi."

Jennifer laughed.

"What?"

"They teach you that in the Marine Corps?"

"Sure." Now he was laughing with her. "Right between physical hygiene and marksmanship—'History of the Ascetic Orders of Western Religion.'"

They stopped in front of the ruins of a stone mansion. Easton grabbed the rucksack and led Jennifer through the gaping front entrance.

"What is this place?"

"Old sea-island cotton plantation," he said. "It went up in the late nineteenth century and burned down back in the nineteen-twenties. Never got rebuilt. The rain patterns here on Cat aren't the best for cotton. We're just cutting through the house ... the bush is overgrown on either side, so this is the easiest way back to the path."

"Path?"

Easton nodded. "Up Mount Alvernia."

They walked through a grove of trees. "Looks as if these were planted here," she said. "Are they fruit trees?"

Easton shook his head. "They're cascarilla, found all over the island—some wild and some planted, like these. The local people strip the bark off and sell it. It's used in medicines, perfumes. You know the Italian liqueur, Campari?"

"Uh-huh." Jennifer kept to the path, trying to match her stride with his.

"It's made with cascarilla," Easton said as he walked. "And most of it comes from these islands."

They walked silently for a moment. Around them rose the sounds of birdsong and the creaking of unseen insects. Then what Easton had just said hit her. "The people here strip bark off of trees to sell it? That's how they make a living?"

Easton stopped and turned to her. "They have to. Plantations like this one folded a long time ago. Today, if you live here, there are only two basic ways of making decent money—tourism and drug trafficking. If you aren't into one of those, you live by subsistence and basic agriculture, or you sell gas and groceries to people who have less money than you. Those are your choices. There's more separating these people from North America than water, Jen. They've got wonderful hearts, most of them, but here on the out-islands, the world has sort of stranded them and left them all behind."

He turned and nodded at a rock outcropping ahead of them. "Here's where we head up the mountain."

Steps were carved into the rock, some as much as two feet high. More than once, Jennifer had to use her hands to get from one level to the next. "Whew," she panted after just a few minutes into the climb. "Who put these in? Goliath?"

"They were carved by hand." Easton wasn't even winded. "Each step probably took two, three days—maybe more. When you're doing that, you don't limit yourself to a six-inch riser."

As they climbed, they encountered carvings in the rock next to them—a haloed man praying, the same man standing before what looked like a judge. In the next one, he was being whipped. It was only when she got to a carving of the man carrying a cross that she understood that the carvings were scenes from the Passion—the day Christ was crucified.

She paused to catch her breath, then looked up. A sense of awe came over her. What she'd seen fleetingly from the airplane was now visible: flying buttresses, gothic windows, a steeple. "Is that a cathedral up there?"

"It looks like it," Easton said, "doesn't it?"

Jennifer furrowed her brow at the odd answer. But two minutes later, as they stepped out onto the small summit plateau atop Mount Alvernia, Easton's words made sense. The "cathedral" was a tiny stone structure, no more than twenty feet from its base to the steeple-top. From a distance, it had looked huge, like some gigantic medieval house of worship. But up close, it bore the rough marks of hand-shaped stone. Still, there was a certain elegance, almost a delicacy, to the structure.

"Wow." Jennifer found herself speaking a hush. "What is this place?"

"It's called the 'Hermitage,'" he said. "It was built more than seventy-five years ago by a Franciscan priest named Father Jerome. He was a Scot, educated as an architect, who came to America and joined the Franciscans back in the early part of the twentieth century. They sent him as a missionary to Cat, and he spent his time helping the people here build churches. He traveled all around the eastern out-islands—here, Eleuthera, Long Island, San Salvador, Great Exuma, Rum Cay. It didn't matter whether the people were Catholic, Anglican, Baptist ... whatever. If they were Christians and they needed a church, he'd build them one. People here say that he built more than two hundred church buildings during his ministry. If you see a stone church on the island today, he built it."

The wind picked up a little and sounded through the small stone chapel, a low, howling moan.

"Then," Easton continued, "when he got older, Father Jerome petitioned the Vatican to allow him to retire as a hermit here on Cat. He built this chapel to live in and carved those steps and the Stations of the Cross that we passed as we came up, all the while living on fish and fruit—whatever he could forage from the island. When he started getting feeble, back in the early nineteen-fifties, he built this sepulcher ..." He nodded toward a small domed structure in front of them. "Local women used to climb up here to bring him bread. They were the ones that eventually found him, dead of old age. He was lying on a bench, carved into the wall in the chapel, that he used for a bed. I guess the whole island showed up here to bury him."

The wind moaned again through the chapel. Jennifer wrapped her arms around herself and shivered.

"Take a look inside, if you want," Easton urged. "It's pretty amazing when you realize that one man built it by hand."

Jennifer walked inside. There was a stone kneeler erected in front of a hand-carved cross, next to a window that looked out to the open, blue sky. The bench Easton had talked about appeared to be only about four feet long—even someone her size would have to curl up to sleep on it. She passed through a low doorway, came to a hand-lashed wooden ladder, and followed it up to the steeple, where she moved, almost reverently, to the windows. To the north and to the south, the island stretched to the horizon. But to the west and to the east, the sea stretched out before her.

Tranquil waves washed the western shore, while on the east, the Atlantic side, she could see the angry dash of whitecaps.

She took a moment to absorb the view and its primitive beauty. Then, reluctantly, she climbed back down the ladder and left the chapel, trailing her fingertips on the sun-warmed stone walls.

"It's so clean," she said in a half-whisper. "Place like this, back home? There'd be spray paint and beer cans all over the place."

"Not here," Easton said. "Everyone around the island pitches in to keep it patched and swept. Other than that, the only reason anyone comes up here anymore is to pray."

"Is ... that what we're here for?" Jennifer asked tentatively. "To pray?"

He shook his head. "I don't need to be anywhere special to pray." He turned toward the beach. "But we need the vantage point. Remember, how the record said that Stewart took that compass bearing on the highest point of the island? Well, that was after a storm—the trees were down. It's hard to see this hilltop from the beach now that everything's grown back. But if we shoot a reciprocal heading—the opposite of what Stewart recorded—we should get a good general idea of where they buried the *Halcyon* gold."

Easton handed her an odd pair of binoculars with a circular housing jutting up between the two lens barrels. "These are bearing-reading binoculars," he said. "Look through them, straight at the horizon."

Jennifer squinted into the eye-cups. "Hey! That's cool! There're numbers just above what I'm seeing."

"That's your bearing."

"They're jumping every which way."

Easton touched her bare arm, and Jennifer's heart did a little flip-flop.

"Put your elbows against your ribs and then take a breath and hold it, to keep the glasses steady."

Jennifer followed his instructions. The numbers and her heart both settled down.

"Okay," Easton said. "The reciprocal heading to 170 degrees is 350. I've already adjusted for declination. Pan left and right until you get three-five-zero in the readout, and when you do, push the button under your right index finger."

"Okay ... the numbers went away, and I got a green light."

"That's good. That means you have the bearing. Now slowly lower the binoculars until you come to something besides ocean. If the green light goes out, you'll get a red arrow, and if it does, just inch it in the direction the arrow's pointing until the green LED comes back."

"Okay." It was easier said then done, like trying to work one of those puzzles where you're guiding a little ball through a maze. But eventually she got the hang of it. The light stayed green and something beside ocean crept into the bottom of the image.

"Oh, no ..." She lowered the glasses, studied the beach, and then turned to Easton. "The first thing I get," she said, "is the roof of the main lodge at Fernandez Bay Village."

"That's what I thought," he said.

Jennifer pursed her lips. "Maybe the gold is buried there and the lodge got built on top of it."

"Not a chance."

Jennifer stifled a scowl. "Why not?"

"Remember I said that Armbrister put the main lodge building up in order to start the resort, after he wasn't able to find buyers for the cottages?"

"Sure."

"Well," Easton shrugged, "if he was building the lodge for financial reasons—in order to recoup his investment—and he struck gold when he dug the foundation, then he wouldn't have needed to start the resort. The gold would have resolved any financial concerns on its own. So the mere fact that the building is there tells us that the gold had been moved by the time construction began on it."

Jennifer raised the binoculars and rechecked the compass reading. "What if he didn't dig deep enough?"

"We're in the hurricane belt here, as Baxter and company found out. When you build on the beach in these islands, you dig all the way down to bedrock ... all the way down. If the gold is there, no way could it have been missed." He shook his head. "It was long gone before they started building down there—if it ever was down there at all."

Jennifer opened her water bottle and took a sip, her eyes on Easton. "What do you mean by that?"

"If that gold was as big a secret as they said it was, maybe Baxter left some deliberate misdirection with his bride. Throw the federals off track. That way, if he got captured and they came snooping around when Cecilia was by herself, they'd be led on a wild-goose chase." He shrugged the rucksack onto his shoulders. "The same wild-goose chase we're on. Only, back in the eighteen-sixties, it would take them weeks, even months, to learn that they'd been duped."

Jennifer sipped her water, considering his hypothesis. "No," she said after a moment, "I don't agree. I've read Cecilia's journals. They loved one another. He wouldn't lie to her. Not even for his country."

"Maybe you're right," he said, settling a faded khaki ball cap on his head. "It appears we'll never know."

He nodded toward the western horizon. "Sun's low," he said. "We'd better get going. It gets dark quickly in these latitudes."

Jennifer finished her water and tucked the empty bottle in Easton's backpack. He started walking, and she followed, turning one last time to look at the lonely little stone chapel on its windswept hilltop.

CHAPTER FOURTEEN

Fernandez Bay Village's dining room was the open beach in front of the main lodge. A half dozen tiki torches shed their flickering orange defense against the encroaching twilight, and five round tables, each seating six guests, had been arranged along the high-water mark. Jennifer sighed; it seemed a setting custom made for romance and relaxation. Two dinghies were pulled up on the beach, evidence that the resort had company from the sailboats moored in the bay. Most of the guests mingled around the tables, chatting and making the introductions so necessary in a place where people arrived and departed on almost a daily basis. Two guests were in the cabana bar, pouring themselves drinks and marking chits on a tablet clipped to one of the posts.

Jennifer turned to Easton as they passed the cabana bar. "I'm going to have a drink. Can I get you something?"

"No, thanks."

She'd been surprised a few minutes earlier when he'd come to the door of her cabin, not in his habitual canvas shorts, but in long trousers—freshly ironed, white cotton slacks over brown-leather closed-toe *huaraches*, a tan canvas belt, and a pale, blue, lightweight, long-sleeved shirt that he called a "bonefishing shirt." Whatever that meant.

"My dress whites," Easton had said with a grin. And then he'd explained. "The out-islands are peculiar that way. In Nassau or Freeport, you'll see people at lunch in T-shirts and cutoffs. But out here, it's like the clock's been turned back twenty or thirty years. I don't think anyone would care if you're wearing shoes or not, but the tradition is that men wear long pants to dinner."

Though Easton had assured her she looked fine, she'd gone back inside and found a pair of tan culottes that could pass for a skirt in low light, a peach sleeveless top that survived unpacking and repacking with a minimum of wrinkles, and a pale green gauze jacket because Easton had said the evenings were sometimes cool.

Easton's broad smile after she returned had caused another heart-flutter. "Fabulous," he'd said, his eyes reflecting his approval. "Mrs. A. will be very pleased."

"Mrs. A.?"

"Oh, you'll see."

Jennifer started for the cabana bar, stopped, and turned back to where Easton stood, the beach and the ocean behind him. "Tell me something," she asked him in a low voice. "Do you ever drink?"

Easton arched his eyebrows. "Ever?"

"Ever."

He acted as if he were thinking it over. "No," he finally said.

Now Jennifer raised her eyebrows. "A teetotaler Marine?" She surprised herself by asking.

Easton laughed: a deep, attractive laugh. "Present tense only," he admitted. "If you mean have I ever been a drinker in the past, then yes; there are a few bars in Bangkok that probably built additions with the proceeds from my tabs. I had a few legendary benders. More than a few. One time, I woke up and I was in a tattoo parlor and this guy was getting ready to put a bald eagle on me."

Jennifer shrugged. "That's not so odd. Lots of people get tattoos."

"Yeah," Easton nodded. "But this guy was about to put a bald eagle on my forehead. Some of my so-called friends had a pretty bizarre sense of humor."

"Your *forehead*?" Jennifer put her fingertips to her mouth. "Is that what put you on the wagon?"

Easton shook his head, and Jennifer found herself admiring that dimple in his chin all over again. "Oddly enough, it's not," he said. "At first it was because I got in a job in the Navy where I was continually on call."

"On call for what?"

"I can't tell you."

"Okay ..." She drew in a deep breath, studying his expression. It gave nothing away.

"And then," he continued, "it just never worked out that I was in a position where I might not have to have my wits about me. I got into teaching cave, and you don't drink one day and blow bubbles the next ..."

"So basically," she said, "you haven't been able to relax for two decades?"

Easton gave her a thin smile. "It hasn't been quite that long. More like a decade and a half. And it's not completely vocational. Some of it—much of it—is spiritual."

Jennifer blinked.

A broad smile lit Easton's face. "Mrs. A.!"

Jennifer turned to follow Easton's gaze. A white-haired woman walking slowly down the beach path appeared to be in her late sixties, although Jennifer got the sense that she might be much older. She was wearing an airy batik muumuu that might have looked shapeless on others but was absolutely elegant on her. A strand of pearls with matching earrings set off sparkling eyes and an easy smile.

"Wow ...," Jennifer whispered. "She's beautiful."

"Isn't she?" Easton agreed.

"Is she some kind of royalty?"

"Of a sort," Easton said. "Her name is Francis Armbrister, which is her married name. She was a fairly successful film actress in her day."

"How'd she end up here?"

"I'll let her tell you," Easton said. "Shall we?"

He offered her his arm, and she took it, her heart doing its acrobatics all over again when she touched him. Easton escorted her to a table on the far end of the beachside dining area, where Mrs. A. stood regally, waiting for them, gesturing at a table set for eight. Jennifer relinquished her escort so he could pull the older woman's chair back for her.

"Why, thank you, Beck," Mrs. A. said. She didn't effuse, and she didn't act surprised. She was obviously a woman long accustomed to such things. "Please—join me."

Easton walked around the table and offered the same courtesy to Jennifer, who tried to act as if she was also accustomed to such things. Two other couples joined them as, around the other tables, the rest of the guests were taking their seats.

Mrs. A. smiled at Easton. "Beck, would you honor us by asking grace?"

"I'd be happy to." Easton stood, and Jennifer scooted back her chair to stand beside him. Then she noticed that only the men were rising; the women had remained in their seats. After a quick peek toward Easton, she bowed her head.

"Heavenly Father," he began, his eyes closed, "we thank you for this food. We ask you to bless it, this gathering, and the memories that we share here and build here this evening. In Christ's precious name we ask this."

"Amen," the guests answered together.

"Thank you, Beck," Mrs. A. said. "That was very nice."

Jennifer tried to contain her surprise. It had been an amazingly polished bit of oration for a guy who made his living by swimming in holes in the ground.

She didn't say so. She didn't say much for the next forty-five minutes. And it wasn't just the excellence of the food—" . . . black grouper caught this afternoon by our cook's two sons," according to Mrs. A.—or the magic of dining under the stars, bathed by blossom-scented breezes, next to a man who was interesting her more and more by the minute.

It was the company—all of the company—as well. On her other side was an older gentleman who said he "used to fly," and whom

Mrs. A. corrected by saying, "Don't let Ian's humility snow you, dear; before he retired, he was commandant of the entire Royal Air Force ..."

Ian's wife was an associate publisher with a Canadian news weekly. The man next to her—"Reggie ... I'm in real estate ..."—turned out to own most of Cable Beach, the section of Nassau that contained some of the Bahama's most prestigious casino hotels. And then there was Mrs. A. herself—the first genuine movie star that Jennifer had ever met.

It was like tuning into some fascinating talk show. Between the RAF commandant's exploits in the Falklands, his wife's stories of her days as a foreign correspondent, and the casino developer's tales of sport-fishing in Bimini with people Jennifer had only seen on *Entertainment Tonight,* her only contribution to the dinner-table talk was an occasional, "Really?" Yet when she said it, the company around the table reacted as if she had just made the most witty observation imaginable.

And when Mrs. A. talked about meeting her husband during a film shoot, it turned positively magical.

"He told me that he had property left to him by his family in the Bahamas," the older lady reminisced. "He said that he was thinking of selling it. And I told him, 'You will do no such thing. You are going to marry me and take me there. Tomorrow.' And he did."

By the time she'd enjoyed the last bite of key lime pie, Jennifer was as relaxed as she had been in months. And it had happened, she realized, despite the fact that she never managed to get over to the cabana bar for that drink.

So she was beaming and relaxed when, after the rest of the guests had taken their coffees for a walk down the beach, Mrs. A. leaned toward Easton and said, "Beck, Donna wasn't here that first time you had Sunset Cottage. She didn't realize where she was putting you two. Would you like to be moved?"

"No." Easton lowered his head as he shook it. "We're fine."

"Are you sure? Hummingbird House came open this evening. It's nearly as spacious, and I can have the boys move you. You won't have to lift a thing."

"Really," Easton assured her. "We're fine."

A second later, Kerry Whittaker was drawing Easton away from the table, wanting to introduce him to someone, and Jennifer and Mrs. A. were left alone.

"The cottage is wonderful," Jennifer told the older woman. "Why would we want to be moved?"

Mrs. A. looked at her silently, and then she shook her head. "So you don't know," she finally said.

She frowned. "Know what?"

Mrs. A. touched her fingers to her lips. "Dear me," she said. "I fear that I have said far too much already."

"Mrs. A., ... please. You can't leave me hanging like that."

The older woman shook her head again, and then she finally said, "I suppose you're right. My late husband always said that, when you open a can of worms, the only honorable thing to do is to empty it."

She leaned toward Jennifer. "I was afraid that the cottage might hold bitter memories for your young man, Jennifer."

Distracted by the "your young man" comment, it took Jennifer a moment to ask, "What bitter memories?"

"Sunset Cottage, dear," Mrs. A. said, her hand on Jennifer's. "I'm afraid it was where Beck stayed with Angela."

"Angela?"

"His wife, dear. On their honeymoon."

CHAPTER FIFTEEN

Mrs. A. excused herself, and that left Jennifer at the table alone as the other guests got up to stroll the beach. Finally, she got up to go . . . she wasn't sure where.

The cabana bar was sounding like a viable destination.

"Oh . . . Jennifer?"

Night had completely fallen, and Jennifer couldn't see who had called her until the woman was very near. "Oh . . . hi, Donna."

The resort manager flashed her a smile. "Lionel stopped by," she said. Jennifer must have looked as puzzled as she felt because Donna quickly added, "For your passports—he stamped them." She held out the two blue, leatherette-bound documents.

"Oh, of course." Jennifer smiled weakly. "Thank you."

"Not a problem." Donna hurried off to catch up with a couple of other guests.

It was easy to tell which passport was which. Easton's was visibly dog-eared and looked thicker than hers. Curiosity was enough to nudge her out of her self-pity. She moved closer to a flickering torch and opened his passport.

There was her answer; Easton's had extra pages sewn into it. He had entry stamps for Japan, Switzerland, Australia, Yap, Palau, South Africa, Belize, Saba, Dominica, lots of stamps for the Bahamas, and even more for Mexico—so many that they had overrun the seventeen pages originally allotted for them, and additional pages had been sewn in.

It looked like the record of a very full lifetime of travel. Jennifer leafed to the front, checked the date of issue, and saw that Easton's current passport was a renewal, only four months newer than hers.

For some reason, that just made her feel like more of a rookie. She opened her own passport and scrutinized the single Bahamian entry stamp: gray ink, carefully affixed and perfectly legible, squarely applied within the lines.

"Got our passports?"

Jennifer turned. She hadn't heard Easton come up behind her. "Yeah. Donna brought them out to me."

"Great." Easton took his and tucked it into a shirt pocket without a second glance. "Well, want to call it a night?"

"Sure."

A stroll down the beach in the starlight, a soft breeze rustling invisible palm leaves, silky sand beneath their feet, the sweet scent of frangipani blossoms on the air, the chorus of tree frogs calling in the darkness ... It should have been the most romantic setting possible, but all of that was dampened by the knowledge that they were returning to a place that could only be a downer for Beck Easton.

No words passed between them as they walked up toward the cabin from the beach. They got to their doors and Easton put a hand on her shoulder and gave it a light squeeze. "See you in the morning, then."

"Sure." Jennifer retrieved her key from her culottes pocket and walked to her door. She put her hand on the knob, and it swung open. She halted midstep and frowned.

That's odd. I could have sworn I locked it.

She reached for the light switch. And then she screamed.

CHAPTER SIXTEEN

Easton was on the move in an instant. He covered the distance between his room and Jennifer's door in three swift strides. She was still standing at her door, key in hand, facing away from him.

He gently turned her around, and she clung to him.

"What is it?" He took a step backward and stooped a little so he could meet her terrified gaze. "What's wrong?"

"A m-man," Jennifer stammered. "In ... in my room." She pointed. "He pushed me out of his way and then ran ... off into the bushes."

Easton held her firmly by the chin and looked her in the eyes again. "Run to the lodge," he said. "Tell Donna. Then stay there until I'm back."

"Back? Back from where?"

But he was already on the move again, dashing into the deep shadows of the shrubbery. He sprinted flat-out, wishing he was wearing something more substantial than the thin-soled, woven-leather *huaraches*. He came to a halt, peering into the darkened bush in front of him and listening.

A diminishing rustling led off to his right, away from the beach.

That was good enough for Easton. He squared himself off in the direction of the sound and sprinted blindly inland, into the leaf-thick darkness.

Easton ran with his arms high, in front of his face, waiting for the slap of branches or the razor-sharp slash of sawgrass. It didn't come, and he realized that he was on a path.

His eyes were still not adjusted to the darkness; his night vision had left him when he'd turned on the lights in the cabin. But who-ever he was chasing would be in the same boat—Jennifer had turned on her room lights when she'd frightened the intruder away. So Easton slowed, letting his eyes adjust, and gradually, the ghostly white ribbon of a sand pathway materialized in the almost nonexistent starlight.

He took off running, flat-out, again. Twigs snapped again—closer this time—and he homed in on the sound. Now he could just make out who he was chasing: white T-shirt, dark trousers, white basketball shoes.

Lungs burning, Easton fought to keep up the pace, closing on his quarry. The man—Easton could see now that it was a dark-skinned man—burst clear of the brush and Easton raced behind him onto uneven, broken asphalt, the main road of the island.

Still running, the man glanced back at Easton. At the same instant, a flash of light flickered through the leaves ahead of them. They closed on a curve in the road. A heartbeat later, twin blinding lights caught them both.

"Look out!" Easton shouted as loudly as his air-starved lungs would allow. But he was too late.

The screech of brakes filled the air, and the man disappeared into the blackness between the headlights, reappearing a moment later like a limp rag doll, tossed to the side of the road.

Arms pumping, head up, Jennifer ran down the white-sand beach like death itself was pursuing her—which, for all she knew, it was. After a hundred yards, her right sandal fell off. She wobbled a few steps more, kicked off the left sandal, and kept right on running.

The tiki torches had been extinguished, and the strings of party lights on the cabana bar were dark. But lamps still burned in the main lodge building, and Jennifer headed toward it, still racing barefooted up the hard sand path and slowing only long enough to yank open the wood-framed screen door.

"Help!" Jennifer shouted as she dashed into the sitting area. "Hey! Is anybody here?"

Donna hurried in from the kitchen, a menu planner in her hands. "What is it?"

"Break-in . . . ," Jennifer panted, trying to catch her breath. "A man . . . in our cabin. He took off."

Donna took a step forward. "Where's Beck?"

"Chasing him."

"Oh, no . . ." Donna dropped the planner and scooped a cordless phone off the sideboard. She hit a speed-dial button, listened for a moment, then said, "Kermit? It's Donna at Fernandez Bay. One of our guests surprised a burglar. He's chasing him right now."

There was the buzz of a response on the handset, and Donna said, "Thank you. We'll be here."

"Now what?" Jennifer asked.

Donna nodded toward the phone. "We wait."

Outside, beyond the graveled parking turnout, there was the ghost of a shout, the screech of brakes, and the distant suggestion of rending metal.

Heart plummeting, Jennifer headed through the door. It slammed behind her as she ran toward the sound.

"We have to wait," Donna called after her. "For the constable . . ."

"Go ahead," Jennifer shouted back, and with that, she was out into the night again, running toward the road.

When she spotted Easton, he was in front of a stopped car, on his knees at the edge of the road, alive. Jennifer felt a warm flood of relief. Then she saw that Easton was pushing down with both arms on another person.

Her first thought was that he was strangling the burglar. Then he leaned forward, and Jennifer understood. He was giving CPR.

A middle-aged couple stood outside the car, doing little to help the situation.

"*Er lief direkt von mein Auto,*" the man was saying. "*Ich konnte nicht anhalten!*"

"*Machen Sie sich keine Gedanken,*" Jennifer told him. "*Er ist ein Dieb. Setzen Sie sich in Ihren Wagen und warten Sie dort . . . schnell!*"

The man looked at his wife, who shrugged. They got back into their car.

"*So*," Easton grunted as he went back to compressing the man's chest, "*du sprichst deutsch.*"

Jennifer inched closer. The man was young: barely into his twenties, from the looks of him. He was a black Bahamian and he wore no watch, no ring, no jewelry of any kind. His face was bristled with a day or two of beard, and the tight, black curls of his hair were beaded with sweat from his flight.

"I don't speak a lot of German," she said. "I read and write enough to pass my graduate fluency exam." She swallowed hard. "Is he ... going to be okay?"

"You speak—" Easton continued his chest compressions. "— enough to tell those folks ... not to worry. Because ... this poor guy ... 'is just ... a thief'?"

Jennifer suddenly realized how heartless that sounded. She felt the color rising in her cheeks. "Oh, man ... That came out wrong. I thought it would get them out of your way."

Easton gave her a glance and went on with his CPR.

"Can I help?" Jennifer asked.

"Do you ... know CPR?"

She bit her lip. "No."

"Better let me ... go solo."

A flashing blue light swept across the trees at the curve. Moments later, a white Subaru rounded the turn and came to a halt next to the German tourists' car. A portly man emerged from the van and knelt on one knee next to the body. The blue lights from the van washed across the constable's ebony face.

"Beck ...," the constable said.

"Kermit ..."

"It was your cabin he was breaking into?"

"That's ... right ... " Beck grunted as he pressed rhythmically on the young man's chest.

The constable touched Beck's shoulder. "Stop. Let me check him."

Beck sat back on his heels and wiped his brow with his forearm as the constable felt for a pulse, listened at the young man's nose, and then touched the base of his skull and gently rocked it, first one way and then the other.

Soft and low, the constable whistled between his teeth. "His neck is broken, Beck."

Easton tsked and set his lips, silent for a moment. "I thought it was. I just didn't want to give up until someone else double-checked ... made sure."

The constable nodded, looked up at Jennifer and then back at Easton. "I'm going to have a word with the driver over there."

"He's German," Jennifer said.

"Yes," the constable said. "I speak German. Why don't you two go wait at the lodge, and I'll be up directly?" Then he glanced down at the body and shook his head.

"You know him," Easton said.

"He's a Blakely boy, from up Arthur's Town way. I don't recall his Christian name just now, but I've seen him around, trips up there." He shook his head and said, "We'll speak up at the lodge. Go ahead. I shan't be long here."

The sound of the ambulance had come and gone. Sitting in the lodge, Jennifer rubbed her feet absentmindedly. Easton sat to one side, and Kermit sat across from them both, his notebook open.

When Jennifer and Easton had walked back to the lodge, she had taken one step onto the gravel turnout—the same parking area that she had sprinted across in her bare feet just minutes before—and cringed. The gravel was sharp-edged, crushed limestone, not pebbles. Easton had wordlessly picked her up and carried her, bride-across-the-threshold style, to the small porch behind the lodge.

It should have been romantic or sexy or sweet or even funny, but it had been none of those things. It had simply been comfortable. Safe.

And now Kermit, the constable, was writing in his notebook, taking her name—he already knew Beck's—and their permanent addresses. "Is anything missing from your cabin?"

"I doubt it," Easton said. "I think we surprised him just as he'd broken in. He didn't drop anything."

"I thought as much." The constable reached into a paper bag. "All he had in his pockets was this." He pulled out a Zip-Loc bag that contained a white feather and what appeared to be ashes.

"What is it?" Jennifer leaned forward to get a better look.

"A curse," Easton said. "That's the general term here for any token or enchantment. Cat Island has a long history of *obeah*."

"Oh-what-ah?"

"A form of witchcraft," Kermit explained. "Unique to these out-islands. The fellow probably thought this curse would render him invisible." The man looked serious. Kermit, obviously missing her incredulous expression, turned to Beck. "Resort break-ins are very rare here, as you know. Too many Cat Islanders depend on the tourist trade for their livelihoods. Have you any idea what this fellow may have been after?"

Jennifer's eyes went wide, and she held her breath as Easton answered.

"Jennifer uncovered some information during her university research that led her to me in Florida. With the landowner's permission, we searched some property near my home that led us to information about a shipwreck that may have occurred here on Cat about a century and a half ago. We left that information with my bank, in Florida, but my guess would be that someone hoped we had it with us."

Jennifer swallowed. This was more information than she wanted to share with the police; too many people knew her business already. But after all, a man was dead, and she supposed they owed the constable as much information as would help.

"So ... you think he was sent to do this," Kermit said, writing in his notebook again. "Any idea who sent him?"

Easton glanced toward Jennifer as she shook her head. "We know someone is interested in this, but we don't know who."

Kermit put the ashes and feather back into his evidence bag, frowned, and closed his notebook. "Will you be on the island long?"

Easton smiled. "Is that a genteel way of asking if we are going to be attracting any more trouble for you?" When Kermit shrugged, Easton continued, "No. I don't think we are going to find much here."

The constable stood to leave, took a few steps, then stopped, inclining his head. "What is the name?"

Easton and Jennifer exchanged a glance. His expression said he was as puzzled as she was.

"The shipwreck," Kermit said. "What was her name?"

"The *Halcyon*," Easton said.

Kermit's eyebrows shot up, but he didn't elaborate. He took a few more steps toward the lodge's door, and then turned again. "Tomorrow is Sunday. Have you made your plans for church?"

"No," Easton said. "Is the Frenchman still running the mission up in Arthur's Town?"

"On home leave," Kermit said. "And Arthur's Town is twenty-six miles away. Come and be my guest at my church—New Bight Christian. I can pick you up in the morning. Ten o'clock. May I do that?"

"Certainly," Easton said, shaking his hand. "We'd appreciate that."

"Good," Kermit smiled. "I believe that you will find it most interesting."

CHAPTER SEVENTEEN

For the third time in one evening, Jennifer walked with Beck Easton down the same stretch of sand. The first time, she had been enchanted; the second, disappointed.

This time? She wasn't really sure. The man beside her—someone whom she'd thought of as first attractive, and then intriguing—had shown her two new facets. First, he had been her knight in shining armor, leaping blindly into the thick island foliage in pursuit of the intruder.

And then, the next time she had seen him, he had been on his knees, literally trying to breathe life back into the same man that he had been chasing.

Something caught her eye in the starlight, and she stooped.

"What'd you find?" Easton asked.

"My sandal." She held it up. "I lost it, sprinting down the beach. The other one should be around here, somewhere."

She stooped and peered. And then caught her breath. Creatures—a whole colony of scurrying little shapes—were moving on the sand. She grabbed Easton's firm arm in both of her hands and squeezed it. Tightly.

"Hey!" He met her eyes, his own filled with concern. "What's wrong?"

"Something's moving ...," she said, "a whole bunch of somethings. On the sand."

He laughed. "Ghost crabs."

"Ghost what?" She gripped his arm a little tighter.

"Crabs. They come out at night, scavenge on the beach."

She kept hold of his arm. "Are they dangerous?"

Easton moved his arm out of her grip and slipped it gently around her shoulder. "If you're a newly hatched sea turtle, yes," he said. "They're very dangerous. But I think we're a little too large to be on their menu."

Jennifer moved nearer to him and put her hand on his, touching his fingers, keeping him close.

They walked that way for a minute or more, and then Easton took his arm back and stooped. When he stood, her sandal was in his hand. "Here's the other one."

"Great ..." Jennifer knocked her sandals together to get the sand off of them and then slipped them on. "Thanks," she smiled, and they walked the rest of the way in silence.

She stopped at her cottage door, the key in her hand. "Would you mind ... ?"

His smile said he understood. "Checking?"

"Checking. Yes."

Easton put his key back into his pocket and edged past her into the room. As Jennifer watched, he peered into the closet, the bath, and even the shower. Then he came back to the door. "All clear."

"Thank you." Jennifer rose on tiptoe and gave him a peck on the cheek. Then, heart racing, she turned his head and kissed him full on the lips. She felt his arms begin to slip around her, but then he stopped and backed gently away.

Jennifer's heart sank.

"I'm sorry," she said. "If I was too ..."

"No, no ..." Easton stopped her. "That was fine. That was ... more than fine."

Jennifer took a deep breath. "I'd feel more comfortable," she said, struggling to keep her voice above a whisper, "if you slept here tonight."

Easton didn't say anything for a moment.

"Sure," he finally said. "Let me get my chair and a blanket out of my place. I'll bunk out here, in front of your door."

Gallant.

"You don't need to do that," she told him, slipping her arms back around him. "I've got plenty of room ... inside."

Easton took a deep breath. His eyes were full, sad. He gently grasped Jennifer's arms, but he didn't move away. For several silent moments, he searched her eyes. Then he swallowed hard.

"I can't," he said finally.

She squeezed her eyes shut and stepped away from him. Her chest was so tight it physically hurt. "Sorry," she said, her voice flat. She opened her eyes and shook her head. "You're still carrying a torch, aren't you?"

He touched the empty third finger on his left hand and let out a long, slow breath. "Well," he said. "I suppose I am."

"So why don't you try to get back together with her?" She was surprised at the bitterness in her voice.

His brow furrowed, and he put his hand to his mouth, his fingers curled in a loose fist. His eyes glistened in the entryway light, and he blinked and took a deep breath.

"Oh," Jennifer said, her voice softer. "She's remarried?"

He shook his head slowly. "No," he said, his voice gruff, but surprisingly strong. "She's dead."

The silence that followed was nearly deafening. Jennifer could hear the whisk of the ceiling fan turning in her room, the chirping of the crickets and the peeping of the frogs, the lapping of the waves on the packed sand of the beach.

"Oh. Oh, no ..." She could barely manage a whisper. "Beck, I'm so sorry."

Easton seemed not to hear her. "She ...," he said, "Angela ... did interior design. Offices, workspace, that sort of thing. That's how I met her. I was running a dot-com after I got out of the service. I was on the verge of chucking it all when Angela came in to help lay out a new programming wing. We met, it clicked, and I stuck on, just so I could be in the same building with her."

He crossed his arms, looking out into the darkness.

"We made a plan together. I proposed, she said yes, and I exercised all my stock options at once, sold for cash at a peak, and quit. We moved to Florida, built the house, and the idea was that I was going to teach cave diving, and she was going to freelance for some designer friends. That worked well, and then she got pregnant.

"It was ... it was great. We both agreed that we wanted her to stop working early. We didn't need the second income; I was doing okay, and besides, my stocks had set us up pretty well. But one of her friends called and begged, and she agreed to take one last assignment, to do the floor-planning for a brokerage firm in New York City. It was only going to take one trip up there to look at the space, in the night before and out that afternoon. She scheduled the meeting for first thing in the morning, so she wouldn't have to worry about missing the flight back ..."

He fell silent again. The ceiling fan seemed to grow louder.

"What happened?" Jennifer whispered it, but even that seemed like too much.

"That was 2001," Easton said. "I took her to the airport up in Jacksonville on a Monday. September tenth."

"Oh, no—"

"Oh, yeah. The meeting was the first thing the next morning. She'd marked it on our kitchen calendar: One World Trade Center ..."

He turned and looked at Jennifer, pain etched on his face.

"I know details," he said. "Lots of details. Trust me. You don't want to hear them."

"Oh, Beck ..."

Jennifer wrapped her arms around him and pressed close, resting her cheek against the broad Vs of muscle in his back. She held him tightly, her tears wetting the cotton of his shirt. "I didn't know," she said.

"How could you? I didn't tell you."

For a long moment they stayed that way, her arms wrapped around him. Then he turned and pulled her closer. She felt the slow, strong beat of his heart through the cotton of his shirt. Then he stepped back slightly and, with his fingertips, turned her face up toward his.

"It's not just Angela's memory that's stopping me, Jen," he told her. "Trust me—I find you very attractive, and there was a time when I . . . well, there was a time. Let's just leave it at that. But I'm different now. I have this—this faith. I'm responsible—to you, to me, and most of all, to Christ. I just don't do what does not honor him. As great as it would be to sleep on the inside of your door tonight, it would be wrong. And while I'm not perfect, the best way for me to live is to turn away when I know a thing is wrong. So I've got to turn away."

Through a blur of building tears Jennifer saw the solid strength of his expression. What he had just revealed seemed beautiful and foreign and endearing and frustrating to her, all at the same time.

Easton opened the door for her, then moved back to let her enter. "Goodnight, Jen."

She reached up, touched his cheek, and then kissed the spot. "Goodnight. You . . . uh . . . you don't have to sleep in front of my door. I'll see you in the morning, okay?"

Easton smiled and Jennifer stepped inside, closed the door, and just stood there. A moment later, she heard the scrape of a chair on the paving stones outside. Beck Easton, being true to his word, was guarding her. *Prince Charming.* Only the thickness of the door separated the two of them.

She turned off the light.

"Goodnight, Beck," she whispered into the darkness.

CHAPTER EIGHTEEN

When Jennifer awoke, blue sky was peeking through her window. She stretched, yawned, and got up, opening the front door. The chair was gone, and so was Easton.

Wrapping her arms around herself, Jennifer stepped outside and looked down the beach.

It was morning in name only. Although the sky was a brilliant, cobalt blue and absolutely cloudless, the sun had yet to clear the shallow central ridge of the island, so the entire beach was still in shadow. Standing on the cottage's wooden stoop, it appeared to her that the broad sweep of sand was also deserted, but after a moment Jennifer noticed movement. When she looked more closely it was Easton, an ankle locked to either side of a smaller beachside palm tree, doing his morning sit-ups.

Just watching him made her tired, so she returned to the room's tiny kitchenette to brew a carafe of coffee.

When she came back out to the stoop, having short-stopped the first cup, she saw that Easton was on his feet, just above the waterline, punching, blocking, and kicking, as if fighting an entire army of invisible opponents.

Sitting down on the stoop, pulling her nightshirt taut so it reached all the way down to her ankles, she sipped her coffee and then rested her hands and her head on her knees, Easton still in her line of vision.

He moved with an uncanny smoothness, his head, shoulders, and hips always staying at precisely the same level above the wave-flattened sand. It was as if he were moving on rollers. His fists corkscrewed as he punched, in and out, and his kicks, most of which were at head-level, were not mere swings of his legs, like kicking a football. When he brought his leg up, his foot was tucked and his leg remained doubled back until his knee was on a line with his target. Then and only then would his foot shoot forward, a quick, snapping movement that was a mere blur in the early morning light.

The movements were powerful, explosive, and again Jennifer found herself getting winded, just watching him. Finally, after about fifteen minutes—a guess, as she had left her wristwatch inside on the nightstand—she got up and returned to the kitchenette for a second cup of coffee.

As she came out with her brimming cup, Jennifer wondered whether she ought to fish another mug out of the cupboard and run a coffee down the beach to Easton. It seemed like a deliciously domestic thing to do.

But Easton had progressed to more elaborate movements. He leapt high, his feet a good four feet off of the sand, and did an outward-sweeping kick of his right foot against his open left hand. A second after he'd landed it, the sharp pop of the impact echoed down the beach. He landed in a deep crouch, swept one leg above the sand in a complete circle, and then leapt again, describing a three-hundred-sixty-degree block with his stiffened forearms as he spun in the air.

No, she decided. *This does not look like a man who needs coffee.*

Easton finished in a deep, elongated pose, and then returned to a neutral stance, bowed—out of habit, Jennifer assumed, as there was nothing whatsoever in front of him—and straightened up. He stripped off his shirt, dropped it to the sand, ran straight ahead until he was in waist-deep water, and began swimming, reaching with long, clear strokes for the empty blue horizon.

Jennifer watched with half-breaths as Easton shrank to a mere dot on the broad, blue sea. Finally she saw him turn and begin to swim north, still very far out, but parallel to the shore. Figuring that the man was in his element, Jennifer brushed off her feet with her open hand, and went back into the cottage to collect her bath things.

She showered and then wrapped a towel around herself and risked a peek through the front door. The coast was clear; Easton was nowhere in sight, and there, hanging from the thatch of the porch roof, was a beautiful, simple, natural cotton dress with intricate embroidery—birds, flowers, vines, and filigree—running down its entire length. She ducked quickly out the door and brought it back into her room. It looked Mexican, and when she checked for a label, there was none. It was handmade.

She held the dress up to herself and quickly checked the size; it looked perfect. Smiling, she put it on, slipped on her sandals, brushed out her hair, spent just a little longer than usual with her makeup, and then went next door and knocked on Easton's room.

He opened the door, and Jennifer whistled. Easton was wearing dark slacks, a dress shirt open at the throat, and a dark pair of loafers. With socks, no less. It was the first time she'd seen him in socks.

"Well look at you," she said in a fake Cockney accent. Then she twirled in the dress. "And what're you trying to do here, gov? Make a lady outta me?"

"When in Rome," Easton told her. "I've got a feeling we're going to stand out as it is at New Bight Christian. These slacks and shoes are Kerry's—lucky we're the same size. And Donna says you can keep the dress; some rock star's girlfriend left it here last month. She didn't want to pay to have it shipped to England. And nobody on the resort staff has a size five in their family."

"How'd Donna know I was a size five?"

"If you were at a party, and a woman showed up who wore a size four, would you notice?"

She grinned. "Yeah. I guess."

"Well, there you go. We'd better get down to the lodge. Kermit's picking us up in twenty minutes."

Church in New Bight was unlike any Jennifer had ever seen.

Not that she'd seen that many. Her family had mostly been Christmas and Easter churchgoers. But even from that limited experience, she had clear expectations: church was supposed to be two songs by the choir, followed by forty minutes of sermon, and then one more song by the choir, followed by the trip to a restaurant for brunch.

But at New Bight Christian, the whole congregation stood in for the choir, and it wasn't just two songs. It was ... she wasn't sure. A lot. Accompanied at times by dancing.

And when the pastor—a shrunken, elderly black man with a fringe of gray hair and a broad, cheerful smile—took the pulpit, what transpired was not so much a structured sermon as a free-form conversation. The stooped and elderly man opened a Bible that looked to be as old as he was, peered at it as if reading it for the first time, and then, when the church was completely hushed, asked one question, "What ... must I do ... to be saved?"

That was all it took. Twenty people answered him at once. Most said, "Jesus." Some said, "Believe." A couple said, "You know." And one lady, sitting at a little portable electric piano—if it had been playing during the singing, Jennifer hadn't heard it—simply shouted back, "You *tell* it."

The preacher asked the same question, only with a different inflection: "What must ... *I* do ... to be saved?"

"Preach it!"

Jennifer looked up, startled. It was Easton who had answered. He was smiling, relaxed, at ease. Then someone echoed Easton's cry from the far side of the little church.

That was the way it went, for the next two hours. The preacher said one thing and the whole congregation answered. More than once, a person in the back asked a question, and the wry minister smiled as if he welcomed, even expected, the interruption, and then answered. Several times, so many people called out at once that it was impossible for Jennifer to tell what any were saying.

It grew warm in the quaint little limestone church—one of Father Jerome's moonlight-architecture projects, Jennifer assumed. A woman two seats down handed her a stick-and-cardboard fan with an advertisement for a local gas station on it, and she put it to use. Trying to get in the spirit, Jennifer tried one "Amen!" herself, but the reaction—forty or fifty ebony faces, turning and grinning broadly at her—so startled her that she stayed silent for the rest of the service.

There was only one truly coherent part of the message, and that was when a woman asked from the back, "What about sporting with a man not your husband? Come on! You *know* Jesus teaches *that's* a sin."

And the preacher answered her, "No, Molly. Jesus teaches that even *thinking* about such a thing is a sin."

Then somebody sang out, "Oh-oh," and the whole congregation laughed except Jennifer, who shrank a little in her seat, color rising in her face. *Just thinking about it is a sin?*

She wasn't surprised when the pastor came back to meet her and Easton after the service. They were, after all, obviously visitors— the only white faces in the congregation. But she was surprised when he greeted her as, "Miss Jennifer Cassidy, all the way from Wopakoneta, in faraway Ohio."

Jennifer blinked in surprise. "Kermit told you who I was?"

"He did," the pastor answered. "But I already knew. I validated your passport last evening." He took her hand. "Lionel Watters, pastor of New Bight Christian Church, and also Her Majesty's immigration agent for the Bight. But please … you will call me Lionel. None of my people here will do that, and, respect aside, it is a great pleasure to hear one's own Christian name."

Then turning to Easton, he asked, "Tell me, did you know that of all the churches constructed on this island, this is one of just three that has not only a steeple, but an actual belfry?"

"I did not," Easton admitted.

"It is true," Lionel said with a slow nod. "Quite. Limestone is very easy to come by in the Bahamas; our islands are formed from it. But bells are extremely costly, and yet our humble little church has one. Tell me, would you care to see it? I think that you would find it most interesting."

With those last two words, the pastor had Jennifer's full attention. It was the exact phrase the constable had used the evening before: "... most interesting."

"Sure," Easton smiled down at the cheerful old pastor.

The three of them made their way through the thinning crowd to the back of the church, where a rough-hewn wooden ladder led up to a square opening in the ceiling.

Lionel inclined his head toward the ladder, and Easton climbed up, disappearing into the hole. Thirty silent seconds passed, and then Easton's face reappeared. "Jen? I think you'd better come up here and take a look at this."

"Go ahead, miss," the old pastor said, nodding at her dress. "Don't you worry. I shall avert my eyes while you climb."

The ladder felt sturdier than it looked. Still, Jennifer stopped once her head and shoulders were clear of the belfry's floor. Just as the pastor said, a well-polished bell hung from a heavy beam in the belfry. But other than that, there was nothing, not even bird droppings because of the wire screens fitted into the stone windows. Easton stood on the far side of the bell, but as soon as she reached the top, he walked around and held out his hand.

He was smiling, his eyebrows arched. "You need to see the other side of this."

Mystified, Jennifer stepped up onto the belfry's creaking floor. She edged around the narrow platform, and looked at the heavy, brass bell. On it was raised lettering:

HALCYON
1854

Lionel would not hear of the Americans dining anywhere but with him. He had insisted, though, that the story of the bell wait until after dinner, an amazing repast—prepared by his granddaughter—of baked chicken, fried jacks, fried plantains, mixed greens, and a sweet, white bread, all served on a plank table under a latticework sunshade. The meal was accompanied by hot tea and a sweet drink that Lionel described as "jelly coconut, milk, and water—and sinners add gin, but today we did not."

"So . . . let me tell you the story of that bell," the old pastor said when they'd finished eating. He led them to a set of pastel Adirondack chairs arranged in a semicircle in the midst of an herb garden. A few feet away in a fenced yard, a number of speckled chickens, no doubt the compatriots of those the pastor's granddaughter had fixed for dinner, scratched at the ground, oblivious to the fact that their numbers had dwindled.

The two men stood, smiling at Jennifer. She slowly got the message: they were waiting for her to sit first. So she settled into the nearest chair, smoothed her skirt, and smiled back.

"You know about Father Jerome," Lionel said, as he took a seat. It wasn't a question; he was obviously aware that Easton had visited the island many times. "And as you have no doubt surmised, our little church was one of the products of his ministry."

He smiled, and the laugh lines deepened at the corners of his eyes.

"That always troubles the theologians who come to visit us," he said. "That a Catholic priest would offer to build churches for the likes of us—and that the likes of us would accept. And I know that there are worlds in which neither of those things would happen, but the out-islands of the Bahamas are not one of them. And do you know why that is?"

"Because you're not pretentious," Jennifer said.

Lionel laughed again.

"Oh, you compliment us, Miss Jennifer! You do! But there is another element here that those outside our islands rarely consider."

"*Obeah*," Easton said.

The pastor nodded slowly. "Precisely. And while I never heard Father Jerome say as much, I believe that was his thinking. I am certain that it was my grandfather's thinking when he accepted the good father's help.

"You see, Miss Jennifer, it is as my grandmother used to teach me—'When Christians squabble, it is the devil himself who dances.' And every church that was built on these islands was another brick in a wall against demon worship and witchcraft. So it is that I am the third generation of my family to preach from New Bight Christian's pulpit, in a church built for us by Father Jerome, our brother in Christ."

A hummingbird whirred in and hovered at a flower not six inches from the old man's elbow. His wizened face relaxed into another smile as he watched it drink.

"The priest had the gift of poverty," Lionel continued in his low, musical voice. "And although he would accept charity in his hermitage, it was not so during his active priesthood. He would not hear of the islanders feeding him, not even when he was building our church. It was not because he did not wish to impose; it was because he desired the simplicity. He wanted his life to be composed of nothing whatsoever but ministry and prayer."

"So what did he do?" Jennifer asked. "Live off the land?"

"In a manner of speaking," the pastor said. "Although, when one lives on an island, it is more a matter of living off the sea. That, at the very least, is what Father Jerome did. He was, by all accounts, one of the best hand-line fishermen on Cat Island. And that is how he came by the bell. He was fishing off the beach at Fernandez Bay, after a storm, when his line snagged on something on the bottom. The bottom there is usually sand, which does not snag a hook, so that engaged his curiosity. Because of that, and because he was a very poor man who could not afford to lose a hook and line, the good father leapt into the sea and swam down to investigate. And what the hook was snagged upon is the very bell that you saw today."

Lionel's granddaughter, a quiet, slight, and pretty young woman, wordlessly approached and left a wooden tray with a plastic pitcher of iced tea and three glasses.

The old man's eyes sparkled as he thanked her, and she departed as quietly as she had come.

"Nor was the bell the only thing the priest found." Lionel poured a glass of tea and handed it to Jennifer. "He said that a large quantity of rusted iron—beams and strips of metal—lay scattered upon the sand. They lay in a gully uncovered by the waves of the storm, and once again covered over, I imagine, long since. I have sailed over those shallows many times, and I have never once seen anything other than white sand."

"Did he find anything else?" Jennifer asked.

Lionel sipped his tea. "You mean," he said after a moment, "did he find any gold?"

Jennifer glanced toward Easton who was doing a remarkable job of appearing unflappable. She, on the other hand, was sure that she was not—she could almost feel the color rising into her face.

"In point of fact, he did," Lionel said. He reached into his pocket and brought out a gold coin. He passed it, open-handed to Easton, who studied it for a moment before handing it on to Jennifer.

"Double eagle," she murmured, turning it over. "And the date's the same—1856." It was identical to the coin they'd discovered in the cache in Twin Springs, except the coin they'd found had looked new, while this one was well-worn, the "LIBERTY" on the woman's crown rubbed nearly smooth, and the bottom of the date running into and joining the fluting around the rim. She handed the coin back to the pastor, who let it lay on his open hand.

"Do you know your Bible?" the pastor asked. Easton nodded, and the older man continued. "Then you are familiar with the first phrase of James 5:16?"

"'Confess your sins, one to another ...,'" Easton quoted.

"Precisely," the pastor said, delighted. "And Father Jerome was a man who took that injunction quite literally. He confessed to me that, when he discovered that coin—it was literally lying under the bell—he forgot, for the moment, all about the church he was building and his use for the bell, and he made dive after dive after dive, looking for more coins, but there were none to be found. When he realized that he had violated the spirit of his vow of poverty, he forced himself to carry that coin in the folds of his tunic for years: to carry, but never to spend, as a reminder of his fallibility and, I suppose, as a form of penance."

"How did you come to possess it?" Easton asked.

"The day I left for seminary," Lionel told him, "Father Jerome came to see me after breakfast, just before my father drove me up to Arthur's Town to catch the mail boat. He told me the story of that coin. He said he had carried it long enough, so he gave it to me to help with my education."

"But you never spent it," Jennifer said.

"No," the old man shook his head. "I kept it as a reminder of home ... and pure, Christian love. And all through my studies, even during those winter nights in England when I studied in my sweater and my overcoat, because I had no coal for the fire, I consoled myself with the fact that I was not poor, because I was a young man with gold in his pocket."

He fell silent and, somewhere in the foliage of his garden, a cricket began to sing.

"You have seen another coin such as this?" Lionel turned the bright coin over in his aged and callused hand.

"We have," Easton said.

"Then here is the greater wonder," the old man's eyes crinkled at the edges again. "So have I."

More gold? Somewhere else? Jennifer leaned forward so far that she almost fell off her chair. *Is it nearby?*

"It was after I had concluded my studies," the pastor said, laughing. He turned to Easton. "Do you know New Smyrna Mission, in Nassau?"

"The orphanage?"

"Precisely. It was started nearly a century and a half ago by a Dutch missionary. When I came back from England, my ship arrived in Nassau on a Tuesday, but the mail boat to Eleuthera and Cat Island would not depart until Thursday. And of course, being a Bible student, a hotel was beyond my means, so I stayed at the mission while I waited for the boat." He shook his head and laughed at the memory. "You know how it is here during the rainy season? How it can be pouring one hour and sunny the next?"

Easton nodded.

"Well," Lionel laughed again. "As I was walking to the mission in my one suit, carrying my one suitcase, that is the very weather that I got. The rains came, and I tell you, in the space of ten steps, I was soaked clear through to the skin. So of course, as soon as I got there, the first thing Brother Browne did was to fetch me some dry clothes and give me a place to change before I caught my death.

"As I changed, I placed the contents of my pockets—my New Testament, my wallet, my pen, and, of course, the coin—on the dresser top. And when Brother Browne came in and saw the coin, he just froze. Seeing the look on his face, I thought perhaps the mission was in great need, so I offered him the coin, but he said no, it wasn't that. He took me into his office and there, in his desk drawer, was the twin of the coin I have here—same type, and same year, only mine was weathered and worn, while his looked as crisp and sharp as if it had just come out of the mint."

Like the one we found in the spring. Waiting until the pastor had taken a sip of his tea, Jennifer asked, "This Brother Browne ... did he say how he came by his coin?"

"Indeed he did," Lionel smiled. "It had been passed down to Brother Browne from Dr. Jan Vandernoord, his maternal great-grandfather, the Dutch physician who started the mission. The doctor had arrived in Nassau that spring, only to discover that the support with which he'd been provided would not be sufficient to build on New Providence, where construction, then as now, was very costly.

"And as he was contemplating this dilemma, soldiers from the fort brought to him a man, an American who had collapsed while completing a transaction at the bank. The American was suffering from yellow fever, and the doctor spent a month nursing him back to health. In gratitude, the American left him with a gift of fifty gold coins such as this, all the same, all fine and new. The doctor kept one as a reminder of God's faithfulness and provision. The rest he used to build and start his orphanage, that very same year."

"In 1856," Easton said.

The pastor looked up, puzzled.

"Oh, no," he said. "The year that the orphanage was founded is chiseled into the keystone over the main entry. I remember seeing it as I came and went. It was 1865."

The year of Cecilia's change.

Jennifer gaped at Easton. "This American ..." The words came tumbling out as she turned again to the pastor. "Did Brother Browne tell you his name?"

"Oh, yes." Lionel smiled. "It was Sinclair. A Mr. Henry John Sinclair."

CHAPTER NINETEEN

Washington in the summer displeased Umberto Alcázar.

It was not the heat of the place. He had a lifelong familiarity with heat. Rather, it was the humidity, and the sweaty, T-shirted tourists everywhere. He found it quite distasteful.

He was traveling with a Chilean diplomatic passport and had no choice but to enter the country through Washington. Since September eleventh, even diplomatic passports got a second glance in New York, and immigration officials in Miami could instantly discern the difference between a Chilean-English accent and that of a speaker born and raised in Cuba.

So that left Dulles, the port of entry just outside of Washington, DC. Diplomatic passports were as common there as fleas on a dog—there were separate counters for those holding such documents, open even for the predawn flight from Toronto. And the ears of those who had grown up in the tidewater region were far less attuned to the nuances of Spanish inflection than those who had spent their youth in the bilingual intensity of Miami and South Dade.

The third-country passport allowed Umberto Alcázar unhindered entry into the United States of America, something that his Cuban travel documents had been unable to do for all of his adult life. Better still, his *corps consulaire* status gave him the equivalent of an unrestricted visa and granted him immunity from several inconveniences to which even America's own citizens were subject: things such as detention, search, arrest, prosecution, and most forms of income tax.

Alcázar enjoyed a further advantage in that his Chilean diplomatic passport had not been arranged through any of Cuba's several secret services. This was good for two reasons: first, because he was reasonably convinced that someone in the Chilean government was selling Western intelligence the numbers of all travel documents so obtained, and secondly—most importantly—because this meant that no one in the Cuban government was aware that he was presently in the United States either.

Probably the most amazing part about the entire arrangement was that it was perfectly legal. Perhaps "perfectly" stretched the point, but it was legal, nonetheless. For 7,900 American dollars a head, Alcázar had purchased Chilean second citizenship for himself, his wife, and two extremely young women whose company he occasionally enjoyed, and whose birth certificates had been officially altered to give the impression that they were his children. And then, for a mere 26,000 more, he had purchased a vice-counsel's credentials, granting diplomatic immunity to himself and every member of his strangely cobbled-together family. It had all been arranged through a suburban Seattle law firm that specialized in obtaining such things from Chile and more than a hundred other cash-flow-starved Third World nations.

The document gave Alcázar a great sense of freedom. He could rob a bank here at gunpoint, and American law enforcement officials would be powerless to detain him or search his vehicle for the—what was the word the Americans used in their gangster films?—*Loot.* Yes, the loot.

Then again, America was the last true superpower remaining on earth. The American government could always ask Chile to revoke his documents and, with them, his status. If Western intelligence learned who he truly was and how he had come to be here, Alcázar imagined that they would do so rather swiftly. So he opted for discretion and kept a very low profile.

Carry-on bag hanging from his shoulder, he walked to the Delta counter and purchased a ticket to Atlanta, paying with an American Express Gold Card—cash raised suspicions. Then he stopped at a twenty-four-hour travel boutique in the terminal, bought a prepaid cellular phone, and used it to call Hertz and arrange a car in Atlanta.

That was one thing he truly loved about America—the freedom of movement.

It made what he had to do so much easier.

Marisol walked across the quadrangle of the University of Michigan, past the bell tower. Few students were out. It was summer session, and despite the early hour it was hot and muggy, the kind of weather in which breathing seemed to take an extra effort. But the weather didn't bother her; it felt like home.

Nor did she worry about being seen here on the campus of a Big Ten university. Foreign students were common at Michigan. Already, in the space of five minutes, she had heard conversations being conducted in Farsi, in Hindi, and in a lightly inflected Spanish that her highly attuned ear identified as Guatemalan. Her long hair and slender figure got her a glance or two from the few men she passed, but other than that, she had no worries about standing out. In the multicultural environment of a major university, she was just another ingredient in the melting pot.

At least she looked young enough to be a student. The same could not be said of *estupida et mas estupida*, who were holed up in an Embassy Suites near I-94. And that was fine with her; the more they stayed put, the easier her job became.

It had given her a moment of concern when her contacts had text-messaged her on her T-Mobile PDA phone two days earlier, informing her that her subject had been spotted boarding Easton's plane in Fort Lauderdale, and that flight-tracking radar had later shown them to be flying into the Bahamas.

The Bahamas was problematic for her; it was a British commonwealth, and that posed operating issues. But then she'd noticed that *estupida et mas estupida* had stayed put, so she'd gone with her instinct and done the same. The latest intelligence showed her subject departing Cat Island shortly. Had the Americans found what they were looking for, they would not be gone so soon. And if they had not found it, it stood to reason that the girl would soon be coming back here.

Some late-night bar-hopping the evening before had led Marisol to a club where a group of law students were discussing a seminar they were taking on civil rights. A bump and a flustered apology were all it had required for her to relieve one of the women of a wallet, which had contained both a university ID and the law student's class schedule. Then, after doctoring the ID with her own picture and relaminating it, Marisol had what she needed to do her job.

She glanced at her watch. She was better than an hour early. And she had completely inspected her operation area, memorizing the various lines of sight, cataloguing every possible avenue of escape, and silently reciting her "legend"—her cover. She had completed her preparations. Plenty of time to get a bottle of mineral water, sit, and wait.

When the doors opened, she would head over to the graduate research library and make her request to look at some of the diaries of Rosa Parks. Marisol had already checked, and she knew exactly where the university kept them.

They were upstairs, on the secure floor—the archives collection.

CHAPTER TWENTY

ABOVE THE EXUMA SOUND

Jennifer jerked awake as Easton's airplane bumped through a pocket of turbulence. She lifted the headset, and the whirring roar of the engine flooded in. Wincing, she popped the headset back over her ears. Beyond the bubble window, miles and miles of empty blue ocean stretched to a razor-sharp and cloudless horizon.

"Have a good nap?"

Easton sounded way too awake for—Jennifer checked the blinking Fossil watch on her wrist—five minutes shy of eight in the morning. Then again, he was the one flying the airplane, so wide-awake was probably a good thing.

"Yeah," Jennifer murmured. "Where are we?"

"Still about thirty-five minutes out from Nassau," he said, pushing a button on the GPS.

He looked relaxed, confident, in his element. Jennifer had risen at five-thirty to finish packing, but he had not only awakened earlier; he had already finished his five-hundred sit-ups and was well into the shadow-boxing thing that he did, kicking and punching in the predawn gloom when she peered down the beach, searching for him.

"So," Jennifer said, "you think this missionary will know anything?"

"One way to find out." Easton pulled back lightly on the yoke and, turning his head, caught her staring at him. "What?"

"I was just wondering about all that Kung-Fu back on the beach."

He laughed. "Not Kung-Fu," he said. "Karate. I studied it the whole three years that I was on Okinawa, and then kept it up afterward. What you saw me doing was *kata*—part practice, part visualization. Good way to wake up both body and mind."

Jennifer rubbed the back of her neck and yawned, trying to wake up her body and mind.

"Let me guess," she said. "You're a black belt, right?"

"I'm a *go-dan*," Easton told her with a nod.

"Go ...?"

"Fifth-degree black belt."

"Oh." She was waking up a little. "How many degrees are there?"

"Five."

That figures. She straightened, the seatbelt rubbing her neck, and asked, "So, tell me, Beck—how does this all look to you? Think we're on a wild-goose chase?"

Easton shrugged. "I think we're on a cold trail," he said. "That's for sure. Then again, it was cold when we found it. And we know more now than we did when we came here. We know that the gold's gone from Cat Island. If it had still been there, the Armbristers would have found it when they built the lodge. We know that your southern belle's second husband seems to be as tied to the missing gold as the first. We know that at least some of the gold got to Nassau."

Jennifer listened in silence—he was paralleling her thoughts. The airplane's engine droned on.

"Cecilia and Sinclair got married in October of 1865," she finally thought out loud. "And yet Sinclair was picking up the loot that same year. Sounds as if they didn't waste any time in hustling him down here."

"Yeah, but ..." Easton left the thought unfinished as he adjusted his throttle setting.

"But what?"

Easton shrugged. "The directions to the cache and the map were in the spring," he said. "And it seems safe to assume that Cecilia didn't jot down a duplicate set of directions. She'd be running the same risk—that someone would discover the secret."

"Yeah?"

"So," Easton glanced toward her. "How did Sinclair locate the gold? Cat Island is a pretty big place."

Jennifer thought about that for a moment. "All she'd have to know is 'Fernandez Bay, just past the high-water mark,' and one compass heading off the highest point around," she said. "Maybe she just memorized it."

"And Sinclair came traipsing down here on the strength of a recollection?"

"For a fortune in gold?" Jennifer asked. "Wouldn't you?"

Easton didn't answer.

Jennifer stretched and looked down at the ocean.

"Well," she said. "One thing's for sure. The gold is dug up and gone. There doesn't seem to be much point in chasing it any farther."

"Maybe not," Easton agreed. "But we have to put down in Nassau to refuel, anyhow. May as well invest in a taxi ride while we're at it—go take a look at the New Smyrna Mission."

"Please, please, have a seat. I'll be with you just as soon as I've finished with this very brave gentleman here."

Jennifer watched quietly. The missionary didn't look like a missionary. Not that she was sure what a missionary was supposed to look like, but this guy wouldn't have been the least bit out of place back on the University of Michigan campus. He looked lean and fit, and his blue jeans and short-sleeved khaki work shirt were a little faded but hung well on him. Both his hair and his beard were cropped short and sun-bleached brown, with hints of gray creeping in on the edges. His face and arms were deeply tanned, and she could see the yellow hint of a wedding band under the thin latex surgical gloves that he wore.

His patient was a six-year-old boy, sniffing back tears and biting his lower lip stoically as the missionary swabbed the youngster's scraped knee with a Mercurochrome-dampened pad of gauze. The missionary finished cleaning the wound and consulted a folder at his elbow as he unwrapped an adhesive bandage.

"Well, Robert," the missionary said to the boy as he bandaged the knee, "I see on your chart that we just gave you a tetanus booster last October, so, unfortunately, I won't be able to give you another injection today. Is that acceptable?"

The boy nodded solemnly.

"All done," the missionary said, stripping off his gloves. "Still friends?"

The boy nodded again.

"Then give me a hug."

The child wrapped his arms around the missionary's neck, grinning.

"Off you go," the missionary said. "Tell Miss Cheryl that you can still play—just stay out of the tree this time."

Dropping the gloves in a lidded trash can, the missionary extended a hand. "Sorry for the interruption," he said, smiling. "I'm Harold Prinze. Call me Harry."

Easton followed the doctor's example and made the introductions.

"You're American," Jennifer observed as she shook his hand.

"Guilty as charged." Prinze shook hands with Easton. "Brother Geoffrey Browne, who ran New Smyrna for more than sixty years, took ill about a year ago—his heart. I'd served an internship here between college and med school, stayed in touch ever since, and my surgery practice in New York has done very nicely for me. So I volunteered to come down and run things for a year while the board looked for a permanent replacement. It helps to have a physician on staff here. Kids can be pretty doctor-intensive, particularly kids who were neglected in infancy."

"So you've only been here a few months?" Easton asked.

"Seven, to be exact."

Jennifer sighed, and both men turned. She swallowed and straightened up. "Sorry," she said. "It's just that there've been so many dead ends. I'd hoped ... well, I don't suppose you know anything about Henry John Sinclair, do you?"

"The 'angel'?" Prinze asked with a chuckle. "That's what Dr. Vandernoord called him in his journals, you know—'the angel God sent us so this mission would not go unbuilt.' Sure. I know about him. As much as there is to know, which is not a great deal. What can I tell you?"

"Well, to start with—," she began.

"Wait," the doctor held up his hand. "We have a sister mission in Jamaica that supplies us with, among other things, some wonderful coffee in this bastion of tea. What say I start a pot of Blue Mountain, and we can continue this at our leisure?"

Ten minutes later, they were sitting in the mission's study with fresh mugs of coffee. Jennifer took a sip. "Wow," she murmured.

"Great cuppa joe, isn't it?" Dr. Prinze grinned. "Now ... back to Henry John Sinclair. I heard about him my first time here. Brother Browne was studying Dr. Vandernoord's journals, and he was making it his business to write a history of New Smyrna Mission. Prior to satellite dishes, the television on New Providence was pretty deadly, so our only source of evening entertainment was that history. Brother Browne would read us what he'd written and add his own observations."

He turned and slipped a slim, clothbound book off the shelf behind him.

"If you're asking about Sinclair, then I take it you know the gist of his story," Dr. Prinze said, opening the book. "He was brought to Dr. Vandernoord's residence suffering from yellow fever. The doctor sweated him—all they could do in those days—broke the fever, and nursed him back to health. In gratitude, Sinclair endowed the mission with a thousand dollars in gold double eagles; Dr. Vandernoord used the bulk of it to make up the shortfall in constructing this mission. They broke ground that very month. The mission wound up twenty dollars to the good, so Dr. Vandernoord kept back one double eagle as a remembrance."

The missionary got up and spun the latch on an old-fashioned safe in the corner. "Here's the coin," he said, handing a small clear acrylic case to Jennifer. She turned it over; the coin looked identical in every respect to what they'd found in Florida.

"Brother Browne used to keep it on the wall," Dr. Prinze said. "But the board had it appraised as part of an inventory last year. The 1856-S is one of the most common double eagles ever minted, but even so, Stack's said that one in that condition would fetch better than three thousand dollars."

"Three thousand?" Jennifer's voice broke. According to Baxter's narrative, the *Halcyon* had carried case after case of such coins. Hand trembling slightly, she passed the coin back to the missionary.

"Yellow fever," Easton said. "Isn't that pretty unusual for the Caribbean?"

Dr. Prinze raised an eyebrow—just one. Jennifer had always wondered how it was that some people were able to do that.

"It's highly unusual," the doctor replied. "Yellow fever is endemic to Africa and South America; it's pretty much unknown in the northern hemisphere. My guess is that Sinclair either visited one of those two places, or he was in direct contact with people from those regions. On a ship, for instance. If Sinclair was on a ship full of South Americans, and a mosquito bit him after biting an infected sailor or passenger? That's a possible transmission scenario."

"What else can you tell us about Sinclair?" Jennifer asked.

"Just three things," Dr. Prinze said, tapping the book. "Brother Browne searched the records at Government House, here in Nassau, and they show that Sinclair leased property here in the islands, on—"

"Cat Island," Jennifer said.

"That's right." The doctor's surprise was visible. "The records show he kept the lease for three years. He relinquished the lease through a Nassau solicitor in 1868."

"The year he died," Jennifer murmured.

"And that is something I didn't know," the doctor said. "It sounds as if you've researched the man pretty extensively."

"She has," Easton said, and the doctor, to his credit, pried no further.

"I take it, then," the doctor said, "that you also know about the wedding."

Jennifer looked up. "Sinclair and Cecilia were married here in Nassau?"

The doctor checked the book.

"Yes," he nodded. "Her name was Cecilia—Cecilia Donohue Baxter—and yes, the wedding was here, later that same year, at Government House. That always troubled Brother Browne; here, Sinclair had a friend who was a minister, right on this very island, and yet, when he returned to Nassau, Sinclair chose to get married in a civil ceremony. In fact, there's no record that he so much as stopped in at the mission or made Dr. Vandernoord aware of his presence in Nassau that second time. It suggests that Sinclair and the doctor may have had some sort of falling out."

"More likely," Jennifer told him, "Sinclair and Cecilia wanted to get married right away, but they were trying to keep their presence on the island as low-profile as possible. I think Sinclair was trying to avoid the hoopla."

"Okay," the doctor said slowly. It was obvious that he wanted to know more, but he did not pry.

"You said that you know three things," Jennifer said to him. "What's the third?"

The doctor smiled.

"That he was saved."

Jennifer blinked. "From yellow fever, you mean," she said.

"No," Easton shook his head slightly. "What Dr. Prinze means is that Sinclair was saved from the consequences of his sins."

The consequences of his sins? Jennifer blinked at the odd phrase. Then it dawned on her.

"You mean Hell," she said.

"It's part of it," Easton said. "So is separation from God, living without his presence. Christians know that you can't redeem yourself from those circumstances, but that Jesus can and did. Accepting that, deciding that you're going to make Christ number-one in your life—that's what Christians call 'being saved.'"

"Exactly," the doctor agreed, nodding firmly. "In fact, Dr. Vandernoord recorded the exact circumstances surrounding Sinclair's salvation in his journal."

The missionary leafed forward in the little volume and found what he was looking for. Lifting the book, he began reading aloud in a clear, strong voice:

For three days and nights, my patient's delirium was very nearly constant. He slipped in and out of consciousness, and I strove to make him take liquids when he was lucid enough to do so. But I feared it was not sufficient; the man grew more wan by the hour, and his skin burned to my touch.

When at length he began to writhe and struggle against the fever that held him, I became gravely concerned. Lacking some sudden turn, the man was dying; of that I was most certain. His hot skin had become dry as leather, and he rasped when he breathed like an ancient bellows. And while I know that there are medical colleagues of mine who will smile at the sentiment, I have seen enough people pass out of this world to know that, as they near the end, they experience a premonition of the fate to which they hurry. Those bound for reunion with their heavenly Father are peaceful, tranquil, even joyous, while those bound for eternal separation kick and fight against that dreadful inevitability. And this man was kicking and fighting.

My vocation was to combat sickness, but my commission was to spread the Word of God. So, knowing even as I did it that I ran the risk of choking him, I lifted the American's hot, dry shell to a half-sitting position and raised to his lips a tankard of water, lemon and honey, tipping it his way and taking no notice when the excess dribbled down amongst his bedclothes.

"Friend," I asked him anon, as he coughed from the effects of the drink. "Tell me, friend, is there sin within your life?"

This started him upon a fit of coughing, followed by much groaning, and then a whisper. Placing my ear close to his lips, I heard him whisper, "How fain, like Pilate, would I wash my hands of this most grievous murder ..."

At that, he motioned with his fingers toward the tankard, which I held once again to his lips. He drank deeply, and began to speak with greater strength, telling me that he had shot a man in the back during the American war.

"I have blood-stained hands," he told me. As news had reached even our little island of Lee's surrender and the subsequent fall of the South, I took this to mean that my patient was a Confederate and, from what he had told me, a sniper—one of those marksmen much detested by their comrades, who attack from hiding and seek to create confusion among the ranks of the enemy.

Sniper or no, I told my patient that causing a death in wartime is no murder, but he became even more agitated, saying over and over again, "Who can absolve me? Who?"

And to that I leaned and whispered, as clearly as I could, into his ear, "We all have sinned my friend. But you are absolved at this very moment, if only you repent and believe."

That brought a great stillness over him. He turned his head toward me, and I could see the question clearly, even in his fever-brightened eyes.

"Jesus," I told him. "The son of God, and God incarnate. He went to the cross willingly, to pay for what we could not with his blood. If we accept his largesse, then he nullifies all of our sins; even the one that maddens you here, upon this sickbed. Do you believe that what I am telling you is the truth?"

He nodded.

"Then say so," I told him. "Scripture adjures us to confess him with our lips."

He motioned once more for the tankard, and after he had drunk, he whispered, "Sweet Lord Jesus, thank you for tasting death to pay for my iniquity. I beg the forgiveness that only you can bestow, and I turn now from all other roads ... I take the way that leads me closer to you."

It was as eloquent a prayer as ever I have heard in my life, and surprised me all the more, coming from a man so near to death. Still, it depleted what little energy my new brother had. He fell back in my arms—dead, I thought at first, but when I held the glass of my watch to his nostrils, they fogged it. So I wrapped him close with all the blankets to be found in the house, even though I was certain in my heart that I would be burying both him and them in the morning.

Imagine, then, my surprise when I looked in upon him before breakfast, and found my new Christian brother sitting on the edge of the bed in the nightshirt with which I had dressed him, looking haggard, wan and wasted, but full of life, and as thirsty as a fish out of water.

Dr. Prinze set the book down. He looked like a guy who'd just sunk one, nothing but net, from midcourt. Easton was nodding slowly. Jennifer felt like a tourist who'd just wandered into a shop where everyone was speaking a language she only partly understood.

"Does anyone know what he looked like?" She asked the question as much to fill the silence as anything else.

"We have a picture," Dr. Prinze said.

Jennifer and Easton exchanged a surprised glance.

"It's in here," the missionary said, leafing forward through the slim book. "Right ... here." He turned the book around and handed it to Jennifer. There was a half-page picture of two white men in dark, nineteenth-century suits, together with two black couples.

All of the men had their hats in their hands, and one of the white men had a large black book in his hands as well.

"That's Dr. Vandernoord?" Jennifer gestured toward the image of the man with the Bible.

"That's right," Dr. Prinze said. "He noted in his journal that he asked a local photographer to take the picture on the morning that Sinclair left the mission, as he wouldn't be around when they started construction on the mission the following month."

"Can you make me a copy of this?" Jennifer asked.

"I can do better than that," he said. "Brother Browne just published this history the year before last. Some of the kids from World Help came over and did the formatting and the graphics files on the mission's computers. I've got a high-res scan of that shot, right here on the hard drive."

He opened a drawer, pulled out a sheet of photo paper, and slipped it into the top of his printer. Then he hit a key with a decided tap. "There," he said. "Printing out right now."

The printer buzzed and hummed, and after a minute, the printed photo slid onto the top of the credenza. Dr. Prinze handed it to Jennifer, who turned it slightly toward Easton.

The photo printed out in sepiatone and, enlarged, it showed considerably more detail than the same picture in the book: details of the calico patterns in the women's dresses, and the letters, "HOLY BI ... " on the cover of the book in Dr. Vandernoord's hands. There was even the faintest suggestion of stubble on the doctor's face.

But it was even less useful than the smaller image when it came to Sinclair. He was a slim and fine-featured man with a full mustache and curly dark hair. But other than that, she couldn't really tell much. Of the five faces in the photograph, Sinclair's was the only one not in focus.

"Hmm ..." Easton squinted as he studied the image.

"It could be anyone, couldn't it?" Dr. Prinze said.

"He moved." Jennifer pointed to the other subjects in the picture. "See how the eyes look a little glassy here ... and here ...? That's because they blinked during the exposure. Flash powder wasn't really all that common until late in the nineteenth century, so this was shot with available light. And even under tropical sun, the emulsions of that era were so slow that they would've had to hold the pose for several seconds; maybe as long as half a minute. Sinclair moved, which is odd, because any photographer in those days—any photographer at all—would have stressed the importance of holding perfectly still."

"Could you burn us a copy of that file?" Easton asked the doctor.

"Sure thing." He slipped a compact disk into a drive on the computer, typed in a command, and then put the disk in a sleeve and handed it to Easton.

"Well," Jennifer murmured. "At least now we know exactly where Sinclair was in ... what? When was he first here? October of 1865? November?"

"June," Dr. Prinze said.

"Pardon?" Jennifer shot Easton a look.

"June," the doctor repeated. "Sinclair recovered and left the island the month before Dr. Vandernoord began construction on the mission and, according to Brother Browne's history, construction on the mission began on July twelfth of that year. So the latest that picture could have been taken was June."

Jennifer's jaw dropped.

Easton returned her curious look. "What's wrong?"

She faced him. "The narrative you found? The map?"

He nodded.

"Cecilia's man hid those in August of 1865," Jennifer said. "That's better than two months *after* her future husband was down here, picking up the gold."

CHAPTER TWENTY-ONE

WESTBOUND, OVER BIMINI

"So what are you thinking?"

Easton asked the question without looking toward Jennifer. He was "trimming out the airplane," fine-tuning the thumb-wheel between the seats to level out their flight.

"That Sinclair is W," Jennifer muttered. She fell quiet for a moment. "Either that, or Sinclair is somebody that W told about the money."

Easton shook his head. "Trust your first instinct. The exact location of enough gold to overthrow a government? That's not the kind of information you hand out to just anybody. You'd need to have a pretty special relationship with them."

Jennifer tapped her knee. "Like the woman you're on the eve of marrying." She was thinking aloud.

"Exactly."

She looked down at the sea. A boat was plowing steadily along through the light chop. Easton was flying low enough that Jennifer could just make out a pair of fishing rods bending slightly at the stern. *Trolling*, she thought. It was exactly the way her uncle fished for lake trout, back on Lake Erie.

"So," she asked Easton. "Why '*W*'? How do you get that out of 'Henry John Sinclair'?"

Easton glanced at the chart on his knee and tuned his second radio to a new setting.

"Calling him *W* made sense to Baxter," he said. "And it made sense to his wife."

"And when I know what they knew, it'll make sense to me? Thanks a lot, Confucius."

Jennifer frowned and shook her head.

"What?" Easton asked.

She shrugged. "Have you ever been right on the edge of knowing something? Like you know that you know it, but you don't know what it is?"

Easton laughed. "I actually followed that. And yes, I've been there quite a few times."

"What do you do?"

Easton glanced her way. "I usually just pray—let God take care of it. I can't do anything about it, but he can—it makes sense to me."

"O-kay . . ." Jennifer went back to looking at the ocean.

Two hours later, purse out of her bookbag, Jennifer took stock of her resources while Easton got her suitcase out of his plane. They were on the private-aviation side of Orlando International Airport, where it was, oddly enough, about ten degrees hotter than it had been when they'd left Nassau.

She opened her wallet. She still had the American Express card, but was not looking forward to explaining to her clients why she had to purchase three boarding passes in order to complete two legs of travel. She did have five hundred dollars' worth of traveler's checks that she'd purchased before she left Michigan, but that was her own money, from her savings. If she spent it, she'd use up everything she'd been able to set aside from her summer fellowship thus far.

An airplane down the ramp fired up its engine and Jennifer jumped, just a little, at the sound. It occurred to her that she had left Michigan less than a week earlier. It seemed longer. But when she thought about leaving Easton, one week didn't seem nearly long enough.

She urged herself back to the matter at hand. She wondered if five hundred would be enough to get her home. She would be buying a one-way ticket, day of the flight, and most likely would pay top dollar.

Easton had suggested as they approached the Florida coast that she fly out of Orlando rather than Miami, as it was doubtful anyone would be watching for her in Orlando. And that had made sense, but Orlando-to-Detroit was a popular route; it wouldn't be cheap, either.

She heard Easton closing up the airplane. A moment later, his hand was on her shoulder.

"When you get to the terminal," he said, "you'll need this."

She turned around. Easton held an envelope in his hand: a ticket holder with a Northwest Airlines logo—a lowercase "nwa" in a compass circle—on the front of it. "Your return voucher."

"But how ..."

He grinned at her reaction. "My old warrant-officer buddy," Easton said. "The security guy in Tallahassee? We set it up ahead of time; he had you listed as missing your flight due to a security delay. And it's peak vacation season; there'll be lots of flights back north out of here, this time of year."

Jennifer smiled and relaxed. "You never cease to amaze, Mr. Easton."

She turned toward him and lifted his arms by the elbow, putting them around her. To her great relief, he held her. She rested her cheek against the front of his shirt. "I hate good-byes. Not always. But I hate this one."

"I know what you mean."

She hugged him all the more tightly. "It seems like I'm flying a million miles away," she said, her voice breaking.

"And I," he said, "am a guy with an airplane."

She lifted her face toward his, tearing up as she looked into his eyes. A hundred thoughts came into her head at once, but she gave voice to none of them. She gave him a soft smile as he lowered his face to hers.

"Beck . . . ," she said, turning her head, only allowing his lips to graze her cheek. "Do you really think I'll see you again?"

He slowly released her and just stood there. It was the first time since she'd met Beck Easton that he had looked like anything approaching awkward. "I get that feeling," he said. "Don't you?"

Jennifer began to feel awkward. She thought about the distance between Florida and Michigan and wondered about the likelihood of anything more than an occasional visit over all those miles. *Slim to none.*

"I guess I should settle up with you . . . ," she finally said. "Pay you what I owe you . . ."

"Don't worry about that just now," Easton was looking far down the flight line, where a small twin-engine airplane was beginning to taxi. "I'll bill you later. When I get home."

"All right," Jennifer said. She watched the same plane taxi out. "You have my address, my email?"

"I do," he said, slipping his ball cap onto his head. "And you have mine?"

"Yeah." Jennifer looked into her wallet. "I picked up one of your cards, the first day."

"Okay." He took the cap off and put it back on. Then he picked up her suitcase. "Well, I guess all that's left is to get you over to the shuttle."

"I guess."

Easton nodded, and the two of them began walking, Jennifer stealing one final glance back at the sturdy little blue airplane.

CHAPTER TWENTY-TWO

An electronic bell chimed, the seat belt light went dark, and clouds began to drift between the Boeing 757 and the pine woods and grazing lands of north-central Florida.

Jennifer turned from the airliner window and rubbed her eyes. She'd been gazing out ever since she'd boarded the flight—at first, to see if she could catch a glimpse of Beck Easton's little blue airplane taking off from the far side of the field. And then, when she had not seen it, she had kept turned to the window to avoid conversation or eye contact with another human being. She felt miserable, as if someone close to her had just died, and she simply didn't want to engage in idle chitchat with the flight attendant or the middle-aged lady across the aisle, all smiles in her Minnie Mouse T-shirt.

Easton had offered to accompany her on the shuttle to the main terminal, but she had refused. They wouldn't let him near the gate, anyhow. Plus, she felt near tears, which she hated; she wanted to be stronger than that. So she'd avoided the long goodbye. She simply gave him a peck on his cheek at the shuttle door, and then she was swept off on a carpet of diesel exhaust and air-conditioning.

Easton had been right about being able to find a flight back. Even with the security check, she'd made the flight with twenty minutes to spare, the sole glum face in a boarding area full of smiling, sunburned people. And she'd been given an aisle seat with no one in the window-seat next to her, perfectly conducive to giving in to her sorrow.

Beck Easton. Jennifer stared at the seat-back ahead of her and pictured his face, thought about his confidence, his decisiveness, his willingness to protect her without a second thought. She crossed her arms tightly, closed her eyes, and imagined him holding her. Her throat got very tight, and she took a deep breath, wiped the corner of her eye, and then left her hand there, covering her face.

"Miss, would you like to buy a meal?"

"Pardon?" Jennifer looked up. It was the flight attendant: young, male, close-cropped red hair.

"Soft drinks and pretzels are complimentary," he told her. "But we do have a limited number of meals on board—chicken a la king or beef tips New Orleans. If you want one, it would be ten dollars."

"You mean ... you'd charge me ... for airplane food?"

The flight attendant nodded.

And that was it: the final straw, the crucial crack, the card that brought down the house. In an instant Jennifer felt hot tears coursing down either side of her face. She tried to wipe them away, and her body was racked by one sob, and then another, and another after that. Through eyes fogged by weeping, she saw the flight attendant gaping.

Chill pill, Jennifer told herself. *For Pete's sake, you're blubbering.* But by now her nose was running, and she pulled her bookbag out of the footwell next to her own and rummaged for a Kleenex. When she looked up, the flight attendant had beaten a retreat.

Okay, time to get a grip. She took a deep breath, then another, then one more. It worked. She sighed; she felt like she'd just run a mile.

"Um ... miss?"

Jennifer looked up, thankful that she was again relatively dry-eyed. It was the flight attendant again, a tray in his hand. "Um ... excuse me," he said. He stooped, lowered her tray table, and set a meal—chicken on noodles and vegetables—in front of her.

"Oh ..." Jennifer reached back into her bookbag and took out her wallet.

"No, miss, that's okay," he said. "Compliments of Northwest."

"No, I . . ."

"Really," the flight attendant insisted. "Our pleasure. Want a drink? Beer? Mixed drink? Whatever." When she shook her head, he quickly added, "It's on the house."

"A Coke will be fine," Jennifer told him. "When the cart comes by."

"You're sure?"

"I'm sure," she nodded. "Thank you."

The flight attendant looked relieved as he turned to leave.

The beginnings of a giggle welled up. Jennifer tried to stifle it, but it escaped anyway. Then she tried the chicken. *Not bad. Not bad at all.*

Eating something helped, but Jennifer needed distraction. She opened her bookbag, got out her PowerBook, and—moving the remains of her meal onto the tray table next to her own—opened up the laptop and turned it on.

She was no Agatha Christie. She probably wasn't even a Nancy Drew. But she had a few hours to kill before they landed in Detroit, and she didn't want to spend them crying in her Coke over Beck Easton. And being with Beck Easton, she'd been a little too starry-eyed to do what she'd trained herself to do—to study what she knew so far, organize it, and see if it made sense.

Her first contact with someone who knew of the missing gold had been the diaries of Cecilia Baxter-Sinclair. But that wasn't the earliest contact she knew of. Who was it? Baxter? W? W's brother? No.

Opening a new document in Microsoft Word, she typed:

Ulysses S. Grant

Okay. Who next? She slipped on her reading glasses and continued typing her list:

Ulysses S. Grant—(pre-Civil War)
W's brother—in California
W—same as Sinclair?
Augustus Baxter—Cecilia's first husband
Stewart—dead by shark attack
Cecilia Baxter-Sinclair (nee Donohue)
Jonah Winslow—former slave
Henry John Sinclair—Cecilia's 2nd husband
Dr. Vandernoord—New Smyrna founder
Father Jerome—monk
Brother Browne—New Smyrna historian
Lionel Watters—pastor
Kermit—constable
Harry Prinze—New Smyrna missionary

There. Was that it? No. Jennifer added two more names:

Beck Easton
me

She blinked at the computer screen. It was quite the list. And the more she studied it, the more she suspected that there were other names—names she'd yet to discover—who also knew about the gold. Who, for instance, had Baxter, W, and Stewart spoken with as they waited in Havana for the *Halcyon* to arrive? The Union officers who were transporting the gold in the first place—who had they told about their loss? And Sinclair—he couldn't have gotten to and from Cat Island by himself, could he? There must have been a boat, a captain, a crew. What had they seen?

Lots of holes. Lots and lots of holes.

And what about W? Were he and Henry John Sinclair really one and the same? And was "Henry John Sinclair" the man's real name or an alias? It wouldn't have been hard to cook up a new identity, back before Social Security numbers and computerized records. Plus, it made Jennifer suspicious, the way he'd just shown up, out of the blue *before* Cecilia had hidden the narrative. And the only one Cecilia had shared her secret with—Jonah—had died hiding it.

"Okay, W, who are you?" Jennifer rhymed to herself in a whisper. She thought about what she knew about this enigma: that he had a brother who'd traveled to California, that he'd gone to school in Maryland, that Baxter had written of him as if he'd achieved some celebrity, that he had confessed to Dr. Vandernoord that he'd committed murder, even though the doctor had assumed it to be a killing in the line of duty.

Jennifer tapped the bottom of her laptop. She scrolled up and looked at the list again, stopping on the first name:

Ulysses S. Grant

What was it about that name?

Two seconds later, it hit her.

"Ho-ly smokes," she whispered. She could feel her hair standing on end.

Marisol shifted on the tiny rear seat of the Jeep Wrangler, scrutinizing the plain, two-story, cedar-shingled house: the house matching the address she'd found when she'd hacked the university computer. It was typical college-town housing: a single-family dwelling divided into apartments, its backyard long since graveled into a parking area.

Surveillance from the street was enough to tell her that this particular house had been divided into three apartments. Conversation with a neighbor lady—Marisol had pretended to be looking for a place to rent—revealed that the occupants of a two-bedroom unit on the ground floor, accessed through either a front or a rear door, were a married couple staying on through the summer to finish their master's degrees in psychology; there was a vacant studio apartment in the basement, accessed through a side door, off the driveway; and her target, a single-bedroom apartment on the upper floor, accessed via a rear stairway—an apartment in which no one was currently at home, although a living-room light on a timer had begun burning promptly at eight in the evening.

Now it was a few minutes after nine and well into Michigan's summer twilight. Marisol touched the seat next to her and made sure the night-vision goggles were there, accessible. Having them in the luggage from Florida to Michigan had gotten her the predictable preprinted note from the FAA, letting her know that her bag had been opened and checked, but nothing more. The electronic device couldn't blow up or spray gas, and once airport security had verified that, they were no longer interested.

Marisol shifted on the small bench seat again. The roll bar made it hard to get comfortable, but for this type of duty, that was actually a merit of sorts. If she couldn't get comfortable, she wouldn't fall asleep.

Part of the reason she'd rented the Wrangler was that she was still smarting over how Easton had lost her with his off-road legerdemain. The plain, off-the-rental-lot Jeep might not be the equal of more specialized four-by-fours, but it was better than nothing. If anyone tried the same gambit again, she would be ready.

And airport rental agencies only had new vehicles. In a college town full of beer-and-bologna budgets, most new vehicles would stick out like a sore thumb. But not a Jeep. Because it was one of the few that a college student might scrimp and save for, it would attract no more attention than the mountain bikes chained to fence posts, trees, and light stands up and down the street.

It was logic that had apparently escaped *estupido et mas estupido*, who had shown up half an hour after she had, driving a Crown Victoria that may as well have had a neon sign on top of it, proclaiming, "STAKEOUT."

They had stayed hidden in the shadows of the car well enough through the light of the late afternoon, but both men smoked like chimneys, and that, too, had been a mistake, once the sun had gone down. They both lit their cigarettes with old-fashioned Zippo lighters, and the flames had illuminated their faces well enough for her to positively identify the duo who'd mounted the equally clumsy surveillance in Florida.

Surveillance: that was all they had done with the girl in Florida, and she was relatively certain that was all they were here for ... tonight. It was all she was here for, as well, but if things transpired in a manner out of the ordinary, then she had ways of dealing with that, beginning with the nine-millimeter Beretta handgun that had been delivered by private courier to her hotel room that morning.

Headlights played down the street. Marisol leaned forward, knowing that the mummy-like shape of the front seat would shield her from all but the most careful scrutiny.

The car coming down the street was a four-year-old Saturn, matching the Ohio motor-vehicle registration information that had been faxed to Marisol that morning.

She followed the car with her eyes, trying to catch a glimpse of the license-plate number. That turned out to be unnecessary. The car turned into the driveway of the cedar-shingled house and pulled into the parking area in the back. For a moment, the Saturn's headlights continued to illuminate a brick wall and a set of green plastic trash cans. Then they went dark and the red glow of the tail lamps died as well.

The woman checked the other car. *Estupido et mas estupido* were staying put. Good. She turned her attention to the house. More lights flicked on. The shades were drawn, and while there were things—listening devices and fiber-optic microcameras—that could let a careful watcher know what was going on within the walls of the apartment, Marisol had none of them available to her at the moment. So all Marisol knew for certain was that the

American, the girl, had come home. What she was doing up there, what she knew, remained an open question.

The red light was blinking on Jennifer's message machine like Rudolph's nose gone manic. She didn't care. Dropping her bags at the door, she dug out her laptop, set it on the kitchen table, and unplugged the phone, running the phone cord into her computer instead.

She clicked an icon and autodialed into the University of Michigan's student ISP—the official on-campus portal to the Internet. Pop-ups erupted to alert her of new email, but she ignored these, as well. She clicked her "Favorites" icon and brought up a Civil War history site run by the National Park Service. Keying a name into the search box, she hit "Enter" and waited.

In seconds, a list of entries came up, and she clicked on the one she was looking for. She read an entry, checked her notes on Augustus Baxter, and nodded to herself. Then she entered another search string and waited while a black-and-white photo edged onto the page, a few lines at a time.

Finally the entire graphics file downloaded and resolved into an image at the upper left-hand corner of the computer screen. Hands shaking, Jennifer opened her bookbag and found the photograph that Harry Prinze had printed out for her at the New Smyrna Mission in Nassau. She looked at the screen, then at the photograph, and then back at the screen again.

"Gotcha," she whispered.

She moved her finger on the touch-pad, running the cursor over to the email box. Then she stopped herself. She knew as well as anybody that email was anything but private. It was like sending a postcard that could be read every time the message crossed a server.

Jennifer unplugged the computer and plugged in the phone instead. Finding Beck Easton's card was no problem. It was right on top in the security pocket of her wallet. He'd written his house number on the bottom, and she keyed it in rapidly, wetting her lips. The phone rang once, twice, three times.

"Hi, this is Beck Easton ..."

"Beck!" Jennifer couldn't contain her joy. "Beck, I—"

"I'm sorry I can't come to the phone right now, but if you'd ... "

Jennifer scowled and held the phone away from her ear. She looked at the clock on the wall. It wasn't even half past nine on a Monday evening. Where was he? Maybe he'd turned in early.

Easton's voicemail service beeped at her.

"Beck?" Jennifer said. "Beck, it's ... uh, me. Pick up if you're home, okay?"

She gave it a couple of seconds. Nobody picked up.

"Listen," she continued. "Call me. Call me right away, okay? Better still, get up here just as quickly as you can." She paused, collecting her breath. "Beck," she whispered. "Listen, Beck. I know something new ... "

She took another breath.

"Beck ... I know who W is!"

BOOK THREE

POINTE AUX BARQUES

LAKE HURON

N

WRECK OF
THE SCHOONER
FLORIDA

POINTE AUX
BARQUES
LIGHT

GRIND-
STONE
CITY

SAGINAW
BAY

MICHIGAN
THUMB AREA

0   10   20   30
STATUTE MILES

FORT
GRATIOT
LIGHT

PORT
HURON

SARNIA

ONTARIO
CANADA

DETROIT

LAKE
ST. CLAIR

ANN ARBOR

TM/2005

CHAPTER TWENTY-THREE

Seventh heaven. There was no other way to describe it. That's where Jennifer was, and that is where she'd been since she'd awakened and found the email from Beck Easton:

> Okay, super-sleuth. That worked; you've piqued my curiosity (not that I needed all that much motivation to come up and see you).
>
> Forgive me for not returning the call, but I just got in and it's two in the morning. A couple of my former students drove in just as I got home, wanting to make a dive, and as time doesn't matter much in cave-diving (there's never any daylight in a cave, anyhow), we headed out of here at about eight-thirty and hit a spring down near Branford around nine last night.
>
> Let me repack, make a couple of calls in the morning to make sure all my bases are covered down here, and I'll be on my way. Plan on picking me up at the Ann Arbor Municipal Airport at five tomorrow afternoon, main building. See you then.
>
> Easton

That was it, and that had been enough. True, a "Love, Beck" would have been better. A "can't wait to see you" would have been good, as well. But no matter. Beck Easton was on his way north; he was in the air right now. And he would be setting down at the airport, just a few miles away, on the other side of I-94, in just— she checked her watch—seven hours.

She felt like skipping now as she walked past the bell tower, but she resisted the temptation. A small group of soon-to-be-freshmen were walking along behind a campus docent, taking a summer orientation tour. No need to make them think the campus was populated by madwomen and crazies; they'd be learning that truth for themselves, soon enough.

She raced up the steps to the library and walked through the stacks to the elevator up to the archive section. Humming to herself, she pressed the button for the secure floor and leaned against the wall, eyes closed, as the elevator made its high, rumbling hum.

She'd made a breakthrough the evening before; she'd be sharing it with Beck in just a few hours. It was a good day, a great day: the kind of day that was well-nigh unspoilable.

The elevator doors opened, and Jennifer blinked. The regular archives-section security guard was not at his post. Instead, there was a uniformed Washtenaw County Sheriff's deputy, a shiny aluminum clipboard in his hand. Beyond him, other deputies were taking photographs and pulling measuring tapes. Two men in suits were walking around, speaking into tape recorders in hushed voices.

Jennifer walked slowly into the archive-library's lobby. She didn't see Mrs. Hunter, the archive librarian, and, at first, her heart sank. Then the portly, elderly woman rounded the end of the central counter in a barely controlled waddle, making a beeline, it would seem, for Jennifer.

"Miss Cassidy," Mrs. Hunter said acidly. "Where have you been? We've been calling you at home for better than two hours!"

Couth had never been Mrs. Hunter's strong point.

"I ..." Jennifer faltered. Every face in the room had turned to look at her. "I went to the coin-op and did my laundry. And then I stopped at the Pancake House for a late breakfast. Blueberry, uh, waffles ... Why? What happened?"

"We had a break-in," Mrs. Hunter told her, in a tone that implied that it was Jennifer who had done the breaking. "Sometime overnight."

"Oh, no ..." Jennifer put her knuckles to her mouth.

"Oh, yes," Mrs. Hunter said bitterly. "Only one collection is missing. The Sinclair. The one that you were working with."

The library seemed to shift a little bit.

"The journals," Mrs. Hunter continued, "the letters. The farm records. All that's left are the printed materials. Every single hand-written manuscript is gone!"

Beck Easton slowly brought the nose of the Cessna up as the tire-blackened runway rose to meet him. There was the briefest moment where the airplane felt weightless as he glided in the ground effect, and then he placed the wheels on the asphalt—main gear and tail, all at once—in a transition as seamless as soft butter being smoothed onto warm bread.

Easton switched to his second radio and got clearance to taxi to the two-story, brick terminal building.

Ann Arbor's was a typical small suburban airport. The terminal was surrounded by a waist-high chain-link fence, and there, just on the other side of the fence, even though Easton was twenty minutes early, waited Jennifer Cassidy. She wore a sleeveless white shirt and tan culottes as she watched his plane draw nearer. Her hair shone like gold in the sun, and as she lifted her hand to shade her eyes, he could see that her face and arms were lightly sunburned.

But something was wrong. Her posture said it all: shoulders down just a touch, head just a fraction of an inch too far forward, her free arm hugging herself as if she were chilled, even though Easton knew from the met' report that the temperature was in the mideighties. Taking advantage of the light weekday traffic, Easton taxied to a tie-down within fifty feet of the fence, cut the engine, and had the door cracked almost before the prop had stopped turning. Not bothering to chock the wheels, he started walking and then, seeing the tears in Jennifer's eyes, broke into a trot. In seconds, he was through the gate and Jennifer was in his arms.

"Beck."

Her voice was muffled by his shirt. He slid two fingers under her chin and gently lifted her face until she was looking him straight in the eyes.

"Tell me," Easton said.

So she did. She told him about the library: how the security guard and Mrs. Hunter had arrived that morning to find the lock broken on the door to her study carrel, and an eighteen-inch hole scribed through the double-paned solar glass of an exterior window. She told him how the top had been pried off of the bin containing the Sinclair materials and how the thieves had taken Cecilia's diaries, her letters, the farm ledgers, and all of the CD-Rs she'd had in the office.

"So they did what?" Easton asked. "Roped down from the roof and got in that way?"

"Looks like it. The police said the window-washing platform was still locked up."

"And they got your notes?"

Jennifer shook her head.

"They got the copies," she told him. "I've been burning backup CDs as I go. All of my originals are still on my laptop. And all the printed books—the Bible and some old books on farming—are still at the library."

Easton realized he was still holding her. He relaxed his arms, but she did not relax hers; she continued to cling to him as if she were afraid she might blow away. He gently pried her hands away from his back and held her at arms' length.

"The police questioned you?" Easton asked.

Jennifer drew in a deep breath. "Uh-huh."

"And what did you tell them?"

She let her gaze drift from his. "That I was, well ... researching a family history."

"And?"

She was still looking away from him.

"You know," he said, "any cop in the world—even a first-year rookie—should have asked you, 'Do you have any idea why anybody would want to take this stuff?'"

Jennifer remained silent.

"Well?" he persisted. "Did they ask you that?"

Jennifer took a breath and then nodded.

"And what did you tell them?"

Finally meeting his eyes again, Jennifer bit her lips and arched her eyebrows.

"Jen ..."

A blue helicopter swept in from the north and hovered in front of a hangar about a hundred yards away. Easton fell silent as the chopper hovered about ten feet off the tarmac, blades churning out a bone-rattling thunder, jet turbine whining at full pitch. Following the signals of a ground crewman, the helicopter settled gently onto its skids and powered down, its rotors continuing to spin. Jennifer watched as the helicopter's rotors slowed.

"Jen ..." He squeezed her hands gently. "A couple of billion dollars in lost treasure—sure, that's interesting. But these people are breaking and entering ... I assume to try and find it. Assault and battery can't be far behind, you know? You can't keep a lid on this anymore."

Jennifer kept watching the helicopter, her eyes narrowed and set. "I think ... ," she said finally, "with this much gold at stake ... well, I think it's worth keeping a lid on it if we can find it. Don't you?"

A twin-engine airplane banked overhead, turning onto the downwind leg of its approach. Jennifer turned toward him again, and she met his gaze.

"No, I don't," he finally said. "For three reasons." He paused. "First of all," he said. "You made all these discoveries as an agent—"

"You mean I was working for someone else." There was an edge to her voice.

"The work you were doing was for hire. The proceeds of it belong to your client."

A flush deeper than her sunburn colored her cheeks. "So," she said, "you're saying that just because somebody contracted with the university, just because they're paying me the princely sum of what—about three-hundred-fifty bucks a week?—they're entitled to own a billion-dollar treasure that I discovered on my own initiative? I mean, nobody ordered me down to Florida, you know. That was my idea. I did that myself."

"Who paid for your flight?"

She swallowed hard as if to suppress her anger. But her reddened face showed him that she was fuming inside.

"Okay," Easton said, deliberately softening his voice. "There might be a question of equity. *If*—and it's a pretty big 'if'—if you were to wind up finding the *Halcyon* gold ... if it wasn't split up, sold off, and spent a hundred years ago or more, which is what common sense would say probably happened to it ... then I could see that an impartial judge might suggest that you are entitled to at least part of it. But there's also the fact that this is getting pretty dangerous here, Jen. You've got people following you, people breaking into your office. I hate to see you taking these kinds of risks."

Jennifer suddenly laughed. "O-kay." She poked a finger at Easton's ribs. "Here's a guy who spends his workdays underground, in caves that have zero light and zero air, and on top of all that, he probably does this for probably not all that much money, and he's telling me to be careful? Doesn't that strike you as just the slightest bit rich?"

Easton allowed himself a grin. He closed his eyes and sighed.

"Listen," he said. "For the sake of due diligence ... have you contacted this attorney who hired you, to let him know what's going on?"

Jennifer frowned. "Scarvano? He tried to make me think I was doing a family tree for somebody's rec room. I can't believe he didn't know about the *Halcyon* all along."

"He probably did," he agreed. "But he's still your client. Two wrongs don't make a right." He gave her a gentle smile. "Proverbs 1:31—very loosely translated." Then he paused, shaking his head slowly. "Jen ... if you don't tell him, you could be accused of being derelict in your duty."

Jennifer rolled her eyes. "This isn't the military, Beck."

"Same principle applies. You could be sued."

Two men in sunglasses came walking out of the terminal, aviation headsets in their hands. Easton took a breath and looked at his watch. "It's ten minutes till five," he said. "Atlanta's on the same time as us: your guy's office should be open. Why not give him a call?" Without waiting for a response, he popped a small silver cell phone off the holder on his hip, flipped it open to check the signal, and handed it to Jennifer.

"Just hit four-one-one if you don't have the number," he said.

Jennifer let out an impatient sigh. "I've got it," she said. She opened her bookbag, dug out a business card, and then, with a glance at Easton and a second sigh, she keyed in ten digits and hit "Send."

"Yes," she said after a moment. "Mr. Scarvano, please." She tilted her head, listening, and then replied, "It's Jennifer Cassidy, in Michigan—the researcher he hired."

Jennifer's jaw dropped. "What?" Her eyes widened, bright with fear. "When ... how?" She listened for several seconds and then said, "Yes ... I'm so sorry. Yes ... of course. Certainly. Good-bye."

Jennifer's hand trembled as she closed the phone and handed it back to Easton. He moved closer, meeting her frightened gaze. "What happened?"

"Scarvano ..." Jennifer's voice shook. "The lawyer ... he's dead."

"Dead?" Easton cupped her shoulders in his hands. "How?"

"Someone stabbed him." Beneath the sunburn, her face had turned ashen. "He was murdered."

Easton stayed silent for several seconds. "Okay," he finally said, "do you have anything in your car that you need?"

His expression was dead serious. Jennifer knew immediately what he meant. Without a word, she sprinted to the Saturn, took all of her clean laundry out of the basket and pressed the clothes into her suitcase. She handed him the big, blue Samsonite bag and her bookbag, and he swung them into the back of the Cessna.

Then he leafed through a small three-ring binder. "Wait here," he said and left for the terminal. She could see him dimly through the plate-glass windows, pumping coin after coin into a pay phone.

Five minutes after that, they roared down the runway and into the air. Easton banked the plane into a broad, sweeping turn that pointed the right wing straight down at I–94 and away from Ann Arbor.

Seat belt pressing on her collarbone, Jennifer looked back, between the seats. In addition to her bookbag, her suitcase, and the green canvas duffel bag that served as Easton's suitcase, there were several other faded heavy nylon bags. Under one, she could just make out polished valves and the hemispherical tops of metal tanks. Scuba tanks. She leaned forward, catching Easton's eye.

"Why the dive gear?"

"Same reason I hauled it to the Bahamas—just in case. There's water up here."

They flew in silence for a while and then Jennifer cleared her throat. "So ... is there water where we're going?"

Easton grinned and shook his head. "I'm sorry. I guess I just sort of shifted into exfiltration mode and hauled you out, didn't I?"

"*Exfiltration*? Is that a word?"

Easton pulled his lips tight as he checked the chart on his knee. "Yep," he said. "In the world I used to live in, that's a word."

He punched a short string of characters into the GPS. "And we're flying to an airport west of here. Napoleon. Napoleon, Michigan."

Jennifer glanced down at cornfields as Easton turned a knob on the instrument panel.

"West," she repeated. "So why does the compass say we're flying south?"

"Well ... " He adjusted the trim tab on the airplane and lowered the engine speed just a bit. "I started thinking about how somebody could have tracked us to Cat Island. And the only thing I could come up with was the transponder." He tapped the instrument panel. "When you fly through controlled airspace, airspace with a major airport, like Detroit—or Fort Lauderdale—this radio sends your altitude and N-number every time the radar hits you. An N-number's the airplane's registration number; says who you are. And I ran the transponder all the way to Cat—the DEA takes an interest in every private aircraft that flies into the out-islands, and having your transponder on is one way of showing them you're one of the good guys."

"So—you think somebody else tracked us the same way?"
Easton nodded.

"Is that easy to do?"

Easton drew in a deep breath. "The technology is out there for commercial flights. There are websites you can go to and see the current location of just about every airliner aloft. But private aviation?" He leaned back and shook his head. "That would take some heavy connections."

"So," Jennifer stared at her feet. "These are some serious people that are after us."

"Absolutely." He gave her a quick glance. "This is not just a matter of slipping some cash to some Third-World air traffic controller. Whoever followed us? They followed us through three or four different airspaces. Either they have government connections, or they have one major, heavyweight hacker on the payroll."

He reduced the throttle a little, and the airplane began to descend.

"So right now, we're in uncontrolled airspace. I have the transponder off, and we're nothing more than one of a couple of dozen blips on the screen. I'm going to set us down in Monroe, right there on the edge of Lake Erie, and we'll sit tight for a minute or two and then take off for Napoleon. Any luck, if the bad guys are monitoring the radar, we'll just look like one more recreational pilot setting off on a cross-country joy ride."

This time, Jennifer didn't look out the window as they made their approach and landed. She spent the time watching Easton, following the careful, practiced way he slowed them in steps, lowering the flaps, the wind noise picking up as he banked and then leveled them off. Finally, keeping his hand on the throttle control, he pulled it all the way back, and the engine noise dropped to nearly nothing. Thirty seconds later, there was just the slightest chirp as the tires kissed the asphalt, and Easton retracted the flaps as he steered the airplane down the runway with his feet. He took the first taxiway turnoff. They made their way slowly to the small tie-down area, where he cut the engine and Jennifer opened the door for ventilation. For half an hour they sat quietly as four small planes taxied out and took off.

After the fourth plane had left, Easton recranked the engine. Two minutes after that, they were back in the air and headed northwest.

"I feel like we just pulled behind a billboard," Jennifer said, "and waited until the cops drove past."

"The aviation equivalent." Easton dialed the trim-tab into its cruising setting, adjusted the fuel mixture, and punched the characters "3NP" into the GPS. "That's exactly what we did."

The Napoleon airport was one step away from reverting to a cow pasture: two grass airstrips, some dilapidated hangars, a collection of small airplanes—some with foil-and-cardboard sunshields visible under their Plexiglas, and a gravel parking area that held half a dozen cars and trucks.

While Jennifer was still stretching and blinking after the flight, Easton walked over to an old red, open-top Ford Bronco in the parking area, felt under the front wheel well, and came up with a key. He drove the sturdy four-by-four over to the plane and offloaded all their bags and equipment into it. Then he tied the airplane down, chocked the wheels, put a mask-like nylon cover over the windshield, popped a couple of bright red plugs into the engine-cowl openings, and snapped a can-like metal collar around the tail wheel.

"Okay," he said. "Hop into the Bronco; we're good to go."

Jennifer hopped in. Almost literally. Then she regretted it. The excitement she felt wasn't right. A person she knew had just died. Not just died; he'd been stabbed. The whole, gory, excruciating, *et tu Brutus* deal. And his was not the first death around her, around what she was doing, in the last—what?

Week. In the last week.

Yet here she was in this funny old proto-SUV convertible, riding down the road to she-didn't-know-where with Beck Easton. On the run. And it was all more than perfectly all right with her.

What was the word they used for situations like this? *Conflicted.* That was it. After all she'd been through, she supposed she ought to be feeling sad or scared or outraged. But she wasn't feeling any of them. She was just glad to be back with Beck Easton again.

Right now, with the sun on her face and the wind in her hair, and pines whisking back on either side of the road, their scent strong in the air, she was very close to what she would call happy. And it was not the first time in her life that she had noticed that happiness often came packaged with its own certain measure of guilt.

Driving after a single reference to a hand-drawn map that had been left in the Bronco's glove compartment, Easton took them down a short section of highway, turned left at a fork in the road, and continued a mile or two farther before turning onto a broken asphalt road that soon gave way to gravel, and then two dirt ruts. He never stopped to shift into four-wheel-drive, but he did slow down as they rocked and swayed down the tree-crowded path.

Then the trees opened up and there was water—lots of water—about a hundred yards away on either side. It looked as if they were on a peninsula in a fairly large lake, a peninsula with giant pine trees and granite boulders poking up through a carpet of brown pine needles. And at the end was a two-story log cabin with a wraparound porch.

"What do you think?" Easton asked. "Lake's called Center Lake."

"Wow." Grabbing the top of the windshield, Jennifer stood in the roofless vehicle and took in the old cabin. "If it was just a little bit bigger, I'd be looking for Hoss and Little Joe. We're staying here?"

He nodded. "Belongs to an old wreck-diving buddy of mine. Same guy that owns this Bronco. He teaches at Spring Arbor, a university not far from here. I called him from Ann Arbor."

She got out of the old SUV and gazed across the lake. The far shore was a good half mile away, and while houses were visible there, the shoreline immediately adjacent to the peninsula was thick with pine trees and undeveloped. "Man ..." She shook her head. "Professorships pay better than I thought."

Easton laughed. "His grandfather left this place to him—this and enough of an annuity to pay the taxes on it. He told me that he finally got Caller ID on his house in Jackson so he could screen out the real-estate developers. Said he wants to hang onto the place so his kids can enjoy weekends at the cabin, same as he did when he was growing up."

Jennifer nodded, thinking that it was exactly the sort of thing that her father would do for her.

"I doubt that whoever may be trying to find us has a deep enough dossier on me to know my associates from years ago," Easton explained. "And if they can track my transponder signature through air-traffic-control records, I've got to figure they can track hotel registrations, credit card records, that sort of thing. This is the closest I can come on short notice to making us invisible. I'm not saying that we're completely untraceable—if it's a government that's trying to locate us, they'll find a way. But as far as your average bad-guy-on-the-street is concerned, we're gone. Here, I'll get your bag."

The inside of the cabin was comfortably cool; an air-conditioner hummed and whirred in a frame set into the living-room wall. But the rest of the place harkened back to an earlier time: old creased leather sofas facing one another across a hooked run and, at the back of the room, a huge fireplace fashioned from rounded river stones. Setting Jennifer's bag down at the base of a wide stair, Easton walked into the kitchen and opened the refrigerator door.

"Thought so," he said with a grin when he returned. "Jim—my buddy—keeps the fridge stocked—in warm weather, he's out here every weekend. We can lay low, then restock it before we leave." He grabbed Jennifer's bag and headed up the stairs. "You can bunk up here—the loft has its own bath. I'll use the couch downstairs."

They carried the rest of their things in from the Bronco, and then Jennifer got them a couple of Cokes out of the fridge. The sun was getting low, and she could hear the occasional whine of motorboats passing on the lake outside the living-room windows. She handed a Coke to Easton and then opened her own. "So," Jennifer asked him. "What's the other reason?"

Easton looked up. "Pardon?"

"Back at Ann Arbor—when I asked you if I should be trying to find the gold, you said, 'No,' and you said that you had three reasons. But you only gave me two. So what's the other reason?"

He stepped closer to the window, glanced at the lake, and then looked back to her. He sat on the couch and patted the seat next to him. "Have a seat."

"Oh-oh." She settled onto the couch. "That bad, huh?"

"That good," he said. "Potentially."

"Potentially," she repeated slowly.

Easton folded his hands and took a deep breath.

"What?" She laughed: a short laugh.

"What's the most important thing in your life?" He looked straight at her, not a hint of a smile on his face.

"Most important?" It was one of those moments when one wanted to buy a little time. "At this very instant?"

"You've got it."

She swallowed. "You." She barely whispered it.

The window air-conditioner cut out abruptly and the room fell silent. Outside sounds—the hum of an outboard on the far side of the lake, birdsong, a distant dog barking—gradually drifted in.

"Didn't expect that, did you?" Jennifer hated it that she grinned sheepishly as she said it. "You thought I'd say 'finding the *Halcyon* gold.' Right?"

Easton nodded.

"Well, you're close." Jennifer leaned toward him and nudged him in the ribs as she said it. "The gold is number two."

He clasped his hands behind his head and looked up at the age-darkened log rafters.

"So what about you, Beck? What's number one in your life?"

He lowered his gaze to meet hers, and his expression was gentle. Maybe too gentle.

"I'm sorry." She looked at the floor and then forced herself to face him. "No answer required. It's not me, is it?"

"It's not. And it's not the gold, not diving, not caves ..."

"It's your ... It's still Angela, isn't it?"

He sat forward, unclasping his hands. His eyes brightened at Angela's name. "She was a very special lady." He took a breath. "But no. It's not her either."

Jennifer couldn't help but register her surprise. "This isn't going toward God, is it?"

"You bet. There are several places in the gospels where people physically left their families—the people they love the most—so they could, quite literally, walk with Jesus." He studied his folded hands as he spoke. "And once, when a rich man asks Jesus how he can attain holiness, Jesus tells him to sell everything he has, give the proceeds to the poor, and come follow him. Number one—my number one—has to be Jesus ... has to be God."

Jennifer looked around. "Well, Beck, not to be a smart aleck or anything, but I don't see any Jesus to walk with anymore."

He smiled. "Maybe not in a physical body—or at least not in his. But I feel called to carry him." He put his hand over his heart. "And to be a picture of him to the world around me. Is this making any sense?"

She thought back to how he'd acted with her over the past week, his kindnesses—and his restraint. "Yeah. I think it does. But if you follow that line of thinking, don't you eventually turn into some sort of monk?"

"Some people do." Easton lifted his gaze and locked eyes with her. "Jen, I'm not saying that a person can't have loved ones or wealth. The Bible makes it clear that God is perfectly okay with that. But God's not okay with things that take precedence over him."

"Like the gold, you mean?"

"I'm not called to judge you, Jen. But I wouldn't be doing a good job of showing you how much I care for you unless I helped to make you think."

The room fell silent again. Out on the lake, there was the sound of a motor and of laughter; through the blinds, Jennifer caught a glimpse of a water skier, blue water, sunshine. She knew that Easton was hoping she'd be thinking about heaven. Stuff like that. But what she was thinking about was what he'd just said: *showing you how much I care for you.*

She felt her face reddening and decided she'd better switch gears.

"You know, I've read the Bible myself." It was true—sort of. She'd had an aunt who'd taken her to Sunday School a few times during farm vacations. "And I seem to remember a story in there about a guy who sells everything he has so he can buy a field that has treasure buried in it."

"It's a parable. Jesus is talking there about knowing for certain that you're going to heaven."

The sound of the ski-boat receded. Jennifer stared at the floor and felt Easton take her hand. When she raised her gaze, his expression was still warm, kind.

"I didn't mean to make you uncomfortable," he said.

"Well, I asked the question, didn't I?"

"You did, but I eventually would have brought it up, anyhow. It's not the sort of thing I'd withhold from someone I care for."

There is was again: *someone I care for*. She felt the color rising anew in her face—she hated it that she blushed so easily—and looked away for a moment, blinking. Between the Jesus talk and the declarations of affection, she was feeling more than a little dizzy.

"Well, I have one other question." She forced the brightness into her voice, trying to cover the abrupt change of subject. "Aren't you going to ask?"

"Ask?"

"Who W is."

Easton sat up. "Oh—man ... I forgot. Yes. Out with it. Who's W?"

Jennifer grinned. She took a breath. It seemed anticlimactic to just blurt it out, but there wasn't any other way. "It's Booth."

"Booth?" Easton frowned.

"John ... *Wilkes* ... Booth."

CHAPTER TWENTY-FOUR

DETROIT

Umberto Alcázar rolled the throttle all the way forward on the Four Winns bowrider and made his way swiftly up the Detroit River, passing the towers of the Renaissance Center on his left and the huge electric sign for Canadian Club far to his right, on the Windsor side of the river.

Alcázar liked boats. As a boy, he'd lived around boats, and he knew them well. This one was not at all to his taste—far too small, too gaudy. Too American. But it had been available to rent by the day, and it would suffice for the work at hand.

He heeled the vessel into a broad, sweeping turn and stayed near the western shore, aiming for the channel separating Belle Isle from the Michigan side of the river. He passed under the Belle Isle Bridge and pulled the throttle back, coasting to the main dock of the Detroit Yacht Club, where two men, one slender with a blonde mustache and one more heavily muscled and black, waited. The *anglo* was carrying a salesman's sample case, and the other was wearing a jacket, despite the morning heat.

Gun, Alcázar thought.

No matter.

The Cuban brought the boat to a full stop the moment that it kissed the dock. He grasped a piling, holding the eighteen-foot boat steady. "Well," he said to the Americans. "What are you waiting for? Come on. Get in!"

The two men clambered heavily into the boat, and Alcázar nodded toward the catalog case. "Put it in the seat," he said.

The men stared at him with blank expressions, and Alcázar reached over and flipped the passenger seat forward, revealing a storage space large enough for the case.

"No way," the blonde man said. "It stays in my hands while we talk."

"We talk out there," the Cuban said, nodding toward the north. "In the middle of the lake. If you don't cover it up, it will get wet. Don't be dramatic. Stow it."

Keeping his eyes on the Cuban, the blonde man set the bag into the space, released the handle, and flipped the seat back into place. "Man," the *anglo* said, clumping heavily into the seat. "You have seen way too many movies."

"Perhaps," Alcázar shrugged as he put the stern-drive into reverse and backed them out into the channel. "But I know ways to listen to a conversation in the *restaurante*, I know ways to listen in the hotel, and I know ways to listen to *hombres* walking in the park. But two miles out? In the middle of a lake? With the wind and the chop and the sound of an engine idling? *That* I do not know how to listen in on. Nor does anyone else."

With that, he shoved the throttle forward, noting with satisfaction that, by doing so, he managed to drop the menacing black man heavily into the left rear seat.

The Cuban kept the throttle wide-open as they ran down the length of the island, up the river, and then past the river's head, past the red and green channel markers, and out into the open, wave-washed expanse of Lake St. Clair.

He ran the boat at full speed, its bow nodding steadily as it crashed from wave to wave on the minimal surface of the stepped hull. On a fine day such as this, there was no part of Lake St. Clair that was truly out of sight of land, but the part that he aimed for was distant from any shore and well removed from the freighter channel and the few fishing boats out on this weekday morning. When he got there, he dropped the throttle to idle and put the stern-drive into neutral, letting the boat drift.

He unlatched the walk-through hatch on the windshield. "What you have in the bag, that is all of it?"

"The whole shot," the *anglo* said. "We left the printed materials, but all the letters, the journals, the stuff that was written out by hand? Yeah. We got it right here."

"Nothing left to go back for?" Alcázar latched the windshield open, leaving a space where one could walk through and go to the bench seats in the bow.

The black man laughed. "No," he said. "I don't think we'll be going back."

"I understand that the police were summoned," the Cuban said as he stepped to the other side of the windshield, to the bow.

"Why wouldn't they be?" The blonde man shrugged. "We had to break in, man."

"Yes," Alcázar said and sat in the bow, positioning himself on the upper edge of the seatback, his feet on the cushion. "But if you had been a little more careful about how you got in, if you had picked locks instead of breaking them, if you had taped the glass back into place, perhaps pulled the drapes to cover it? Well, it might have been several hours—days or weeks, maybe, before anyone noticed anything."

"Listen, Juan Mandez," the skinny blonde said. "We were hired to tail. For surveillance. Not for a B and E. And nobody saw us doing it . . ."

"Say again?" Alcázar cupped his hand to his ear, despite the fact that he could hear this ill-mannered *americano* just fine.

"I don't even know what we're doing here." The little one with the mustache walked to the bow. "Scarvano hired us. Not you."

The black man followed. It would be tough to stand in the bobbing, drifting boat, Alcázar knew. They would want to sit.

They did, exactly as Alcázar was sitting, up on the tops of the seats, their feet resting on the seat cushions. It was just as he had expected, the insolent hoodlums not wanting to sit lower than him, not wanting to appear subordinate to him. And now, with the two men on one side of the boat and him on the other, their side was riding lower. They steadied themselves with their hands.

"I hired Scarvano," he said in a tone he hoped was not unfriendly. "You surely remember that I was in his office when he told you I was coming. Trust me, Señor Scarvano and I are in absolute agreement."

"Like the man said, it's not how we operate," the black man said.

Alcázar turned his head slightly, facing the one who had just spoken. This was good, a natural reason to turn, because he had already decided that it would be the black man—the one with the gun—who would have to go first.

"And we want extra for the B and E," the black man said.

"Do not worry, *amigo*," Alcázar said with a smile. "By the time we are finished here, I guarantee you will have no complaints whatsoever."

He slid his hand behind the seatback next to his own, the one he had unsnapped before picking these two up. He found the checkered rosewood grip of a Colt Woodsman *pistole* that he had purchased at a gun show just the evening before, taking delivery with a driver's license and a permit that had cost him five times as much as the gun.

The Colt was a laughably small-caliber weapon, chambered for a .22 Long Rifle round only a third of a thumb-nail wide.

But from two feet away? In the heart or in the head? Why, it would be every bit as lethal as a .357 Magnum. Only the Magnum would have a report that would carry all the way to Detroit, while the small pop of the .22 would not even be audible to the fishing boats trolling one mile distant. Not in this breeze.

Alcázar smiled. He loved to use tools that were perfectly matched to the job.

CHAPTER TWENTY-FIVE

CENTER LAKE

"Booth? John Wilkes Booth?"

Jennifer nodded. Easton searched her face; if she was pulling his leg, she was doing a darned good job.

"All right ... and you got *W* out of this ... how?"

Jennifer's smile brightened. "Ulysses S. Grant," she said. "What does the *S.* stand for?"

"Oh. I've heard this, before—somewhere. It doesn't stand for anything."

"Right—know why?"

Easton shook his head.

"Because his real first name was Hiram," Jennifer said. "Only he never used his first name. His family, his friends, everybody called him by his middle name, which was 'Ulysses.' In fact, when his congressman appointed him to the United States Military Academy, he'd never heard Grant called anything else, so the congressman assumed 'Ulysses' was his first name. The congressman guessed that Grant used his mother's maiden name—Simpson—as his middle name. So *Ulysses S. Grant* was written on his appointment to West Point. Grant tried to have it corrected once he got there, but there wasn't any protocol for doing such things, so it was left as originally written. In time, 'Ulysses S.' was the name under which he was commissioned, and at that point it became official."

Easton had never heard any of this before. "This is interesting. But what it has to do with John Wilkes Booth is—?"

"—is that it made me remember that, except for his later stage career, Booth never used his first name either. His family and friends called him 'Wilkes.' In fact, when he first began acting, he didn't want to go in on the coattails of his father and brother, who were among America's leading actors at the time, so he briefly used the stage name, 'J. B. Wilkes.' Plus, I've compared a photograph of Booth to the picture from the mission. There are a lot of similarities."

"That picture from the mission could be anyone—"

Jennifer held her hand up, palm out. "We know that Augustus Baxter and Booth attended school together in Maryland. Booth attended St. Timothy's Hall. So I checked the notes sent up from Georgia on Augustus Baxter, and guess where he went to school?"

"St. Timothy's Hall."

"Correctimundo." Jennifer leaned forward, hands together. "Baxter wrote in his narrative that he met W again in England. History doesn't tell us where John Wilkes Booth was from the winter of 1855 to the autumn of 1856, but England is plausible—Booth's mother and father were both from England.

"Later, after the war has begun, Baxter writes in the narrative to Cecilia about W being well-known in his profession; by that point, he was the leading man of the American stage. And later on, news reaches Cecilia of W being killed. But how would she know that? Men were dying by the thousands in the Civil War. For W's death to stand out enough to make news, it would have to be something extraordinary. Like W was somebody famous—or infamous. And when Sinclair is lying in bed, delirious with yellow fever, at the mission in Nassau, he begins whispering Shakespeare—"

"*Richard the Third*," Easton added.

"That's right," Jennifer said. She paused. "I had to look that up. How did you . . . ? Oh, never mind. The point is, who but an actor would quote Shakespeare in his delirium?"

The air-conditioner kicked noisily back to life again.

"Okay." Easton took a deep breath, composing his thoughts. "Abraham Lincoln was shot by Booth on April fourteenth and died of his wounds the next morning. I remember that because my history teacher used to joke that that was why the government made April fifteenth tax day—so the country would always be sad on the anniversary."

Jennifer shook her head slowly.

"Okay, odd teacher," Easton continued. "But later, Booth was found on, um, let's see ... "

"Early on the morning of April twenty-sixth, in a tobacco shed on the Garrett farm, outside of Bowling Green, Virginia."

He smiled. "I'll take your word for it. And that's where he died, right?"

"That's what the history books say." Jennifer was beginning to grin.

"So," Easton cocked his head a bit. "How is it that he then goes on to run around the Bahamas and turn up in Michigan, married to this Southern belle—"

"Cecilia."

"—Yes, her—eight months after he's shot to death in Virginia?"

Jennifer clasped her hands and held them to her mouth. She looked like a kid at Christmas. "Because ... " She patted Easton's knee for emphasis. "There has always been doubt that it was Booth who died in that tobacco shed down in Virginia."

"Oh, man," Easton glanced skyward. "This isn't going to be one of those conspiracy things, is it? Are you going to start telling me about the Freemasons or something?"

"Only if you want. But really, look at the facts that are left. "First," Jennifer began to tick the points off on her fingers, "after shooting Lincoln, Booth doesn't run out the way he came, he jumps off the balcony onto the stage—"

"Breaking his ankle in the process."

"Leg," Jennifer corrected. "Or so it seemed at the time. But why jump onto the stage at all? There's a door right behind him. I think he does it because he's one of the best-known actors in America. He even pauses to shout out a line, '*sic semper tyrannus*'—'Thus always to tyrants'—before he gets out of Dodge. It's like he wants everyone in the theater to register the fact that he's John Wilkes Booth, and that he just shot the president. Several historians have referred to it as Booth's last 'performance.' But why draw that much attention to yourself if you're trying to escape?"

Easton nodded, urging her to go on.

"Shortly afterwards, a rider shows up at the Navy Yard Bridge, leading south out of Washington, a military sentry challenges him, and the rider replies that he is John Wilkes Booth—the full three names. Then the rider hangs around a full ten minutes to wait for David Herold, another one of the conspirators, to join him, even though 'Booth' knows that a massive manhunt must already be underway. It's as if they want to make absolutely certain that the entire Army of the Potomac will follow them off into the countryside."

Jennifer ticked a third point off on her fingers.

"At four the next morning, a man with a broken leg shows up at the home of Dr. Samuel Mudd to be treated. Mudd's a moderately well-off physician; he's been to the theater often. He even knows Booth personally. Yet he later swears, over and over again, that he did not recognize the man that he treated, which is preposterous, if the man was Booth. It would be as if, today, one of the world's most famous actors, like, uh . . ."

"Mel Gibson."

"Okay. There you go. If Mel Gibson were to show up in the emergency room, to get treated by a doctor who had been to dinner parties with him previously, and the doctor were to later swear under oath that he did not know who he was. It was either one of the most stupid, clumsy lies ever concocted or Mudd really didn't have a clue as to who the guy was—which means that the patient couldn't have been Booth."

Easton pursed his lips before asking, "Is there more?"

"There is," Jennifer said. "Union troops eventually track Herold, together with a man assumed to be Booth, to the tobacco shed on the Garrett farm. When they do, the unit's lieutenant sends Sergeant Boston Corbett, the most unstable member of the company—a guy who will later be declared legally insane—around the back of the shed to light a fire to smoke them out. He does, and 'Booth' yells out that Herold wants to surrender. Then, according to the record, Corbett, through the smoke and the flames, thinks he sees Booth aiming a gun at the doorway, so he fires, delivering the fatal gunshot. Bear in mind that the sun hasn't come up yet; nobody's gotten a clear look at the man. By the time anybody else gets to see the guy thought to be Booth under broad daylight, he's bloodied, smeared with soot, and contorted by pain. Anybody would be hard to recognize under those circumstances."

"Wait a minute," Easton said. "I thought that the government positively identified him."

"By his possessions." Jennifer made a sweep of her hand. "He was carrying Booth's wallet, Booth's diary, a letter to Booth from a female fan, a check made out to Booth from a Canadian bank, and a stick-pin given to Booth by another actor."

The air-conditioner shuddered itself off again.

"Interesting," Easton nodded. "But—"

"Hold on." Jennifer held up her hand, palm out. "There are two more things. One—the government paid a bounty for capturing Herold, but not for capturing Booth. It's as if they weren't convinced they'd gotten the right guy. And two—the Army buried Booth's body under the floor of a prison. It wasn't exhumed and released to his family until 1869, by which time it would have been unrecognizable, because it was never embalmed. The story is that Edwin Booth had the family dentist verify that the body was Booth's but think about it ... "

"If you knew that the body wasn't your brother's," Easton murmured, "would you volunteer that information to the authorities so they could hunt him down and kill him?"

"Precisely."

Easton got up and walked to the window. He turned, and before he could speak, Jennifer asked him, "Want to hear what I think really happened?"

"Sure."

"Sit." She pointed to the seat next to hers, on the couch.

Easton sat.

"Okay." Jennifer nodded. "People always wonder, if Booth was so ardent a Confederate, why didn't he enlist? But in fact, records show that he did. He joined the Richmond Grays as an officer, so he could witness the hanging of John Brown. And the story is that he later resigned his commission before the unit fell in with the Confederacy. But Asia Booth—his sister—reported he had told her in secret that he was still working for the South well into the war, buying quinine, which was needed to fight malaria, and personally smuggling it through the blockades."

"Why would he do that?" Easton lifted his open hands. "He's a celebrity. I mean, I can see that he would use his wealth to buy scarce supplies for the South. But why smuggle them himself? He could hire a blockade runner. There'd be no need for him to assume the risk."

"Unless it was a dress rehearsal," Jennifer said. "Like maybe he was trying different routes, finding the weaknesses."

"Makes sense." Easton nodded. "Go on."

Jennifer stood and began to pace as she spoke. "Despite what we might have heard in school, the Lincoln assassination was not merely a case of some wacko shooting the president. Rather, it was the only successful element of a spectacularly unsuccessful Confederate plot to throw the entire federal government into chaos. Lee may have surrendered at Appomattox, but the war was not yet over, not technically. There was still a Confederate government; Jefferson Davis was still president of the CSA, and Confederate troops were still in the field. And the original plot was put together not to assassinate Lincoln, but to kidnap him. I mean, you were in the military. Think about it; if you want to confuse an enemy and buy yourself some time, what's the first thing that you try to do?"

"Disrupt the chain of command," Easton said, almost without thinking.

"Exactly. And that was what the conspirators intended to do—snatch Lincoln and forestall or frustrate a surrender. Except Lincoln's schedule kept changing. One time, when Booth was waiting outside of Washington to kidnap Lincoln on his way to a hospital visit, Lincoln was actually having lunch in the very same hotel where Booth was staying! A real comedy of errors. So finally, when time was running out, the conspirators decided to go with their 'Plan B,' which was to assassinate the president, the vice-president, and the secretary of state, all on the same evening."

"The entire federal leadership," Easton murmured.

"That's right. Numero-uno would go to the Speaker of the House, and without the support of Seward, the Secretary of State, the Speaker's too low on the totem pole to govern with any popular support. It's a brilliant plan, but there has always been one question that has plagued historians, and that is, 'Why?' I mean, the South's broke, and even if her Army could be pulled back together, there're no funds left to buy munitions. Disrupting the government and delaying the surrender makes no sense, unless—"

"—Unless," Easton said, "the Confederacy has a huge stash of gold that they can retrieve in the meantime."

Jennifer nodded emphatically.

"So they were what?" Easton asked. "Trying to re-arm the South?"

"I don't think so." Jennifer shook her head. "That was probably the plan in the beginning, but I think four long years of war changed all that. I did a little research into that gold ship you were telling me about."

"*The Central America.*"

"That's the one. It was carrying twenty-one tons of gold when it sank: gold that was going to back up the paper issued by banks all up and down the East Coast. It was enough gold that its loss was sufficient to trigger a minor recession, because there wasn't enough precious metal to back the paper. Yet the opposite could hold true as well. Remember, the *Halcyon* contained almost three times as much gold as the *Central America*. Just imagine what would have happened if Booth and company were to dump all of that gold onto the New York gold exchange, all at one time."

"It'd lower the value."

"Enormously." In her excitement, Jennifer pounded her fist into her open hand. "And in 1857, when the *Central America* sank, paper money was issued by banks, and the abrupt change in value caused banks to go under. But by 1865, the United States was issuing the paper money—greenbacks, the value of which was ultimately tied to the value of gold. And if the gold market collapsed ..."

"The government would collapse."

Jennifer smiled. "It would be brought to its knees, that's for sure. The Confederacy would become the least of its worries. Congress may even have voted to allow the South to secede, just to save the country the costs of reconstruction. A victory without firing so much as one more cannon."

"So Booth may have thought that, by killing three government officials in what he still viewed as a fully declared war—" Easton looked up, recognition dawning on his face, "—he was winning that war and potentially saving hundreds of thousands of lives." Easton's gaze locked on hers. "If what you're saying is true, we may need to rewrite history."

"Most historians believe that even if the Confederacy had prevailed, the South would have eventually repatriated," Jennifer said. "And if Booth's complete plan had succeeded, history might even have viewed him as a hero. But as it turned out, Seward was only wounded by his assailant, the guy assigned to kill the vice president chickened out, and the Lincoln assassination didn't panic the North—it galvanized it.

"The Union made capturing Jefferson Davis a priority, which they did less than a month after the assassination. The last Confederate units were captured in late June of 1865, while Booth, traveling as 'Henry John Sinclair,' was still sick with yellow fever in Nassau. By the time he was well enough to raise a crew and go after the rest of the gold—which is, I assume, what he came to Nassau for—it was game, set, and match for the Confederacy. Booth was left with no use for the gold." She paused. "Except for himself."

"And for the widow of his very best friend," Easton added.

"That's right. I figure he risked a trip to Florida to rescue Cecilia from the carpetbaggers, and the rest, as they say, is history."

"Or chemistry." Easton got to his feet and looked out at the lake, now golden in the setting sun. He turned back to look at her. "So who died in the tobacco shed?"

"John Phillip McGraw."

"Who?" Easton's head was starting to hurt.

"John Wilkes Booth's understudy," she said, obviously pleased with herself. "He was the same size as Booth, the same build. They were said to sound alike and, with a little bit of work, they even looked somewhat alike. It's said that new playgoers who saw McGraw going onstage for Booth often weren't even aware that a switch had been made."

"And this McGraw was a southerner?"

"A Virginian, and outspoken in his support of the South."

Easton nodded. "Keep going," he urged.

"I figure that the Sinclair identity was laid down for Booth long in advance. He probably had papers, bank funds to draw on, the works. D-day comes, Booth gives his personal effects to McGraw, and McGraw becomes the rabbit for the greyhounds."

"One problem," Easton cocked his head. "Booth broke his leg on the stage. The guy killed in the farmhouse had a broken leg, did he not?"

"And John Wilkes Booth was an actor." Jennifer was grinning broadly now. "The way I figure it, something happened and McGraw broke his leg before the assassination attempt. By that evening, he can't walk. But the plan has to go through; it's the one night that week that Lincoln's going to be in the theater. So, to make sure that everything matches up, Booth, who's an actor, *acts*. He pretends to injure his leg when he lands on the stage."

They stared at each other. Then Jennifer drew in a deep breath. "The only thing I have trouble with," she said, "is that for the plan to work, McGraw had to die. That was the only way to stop the North from looking for Booth until the end of his days. And that's the part I wrestle with. I mean, can you imagine someone holding another person in such regard that he is willing to go to certain death for him?"

"Yes," Easton said without hesitation. "Yes. I can."

Jennifer blinked. "Well," she shrugged. "There it is."

Easton shook his head in amazement. He went to the window. The sun was setting over the lake, turning the blue water to burnished crimson. "That's one whale of a theory, Jen."

"But still just a theory," she said. "If I were to publish, based on just what I have now, the notion that John Wilkes Booth lived on for three years after the assassination and died in a shipwreck, I would be laughed right out of academe."

Easton turned from the window, heart sinking. "You want to keep pursuing this." He didn't even bother to phrase it as a question.

"You bet I do! Why wouldn't I?"

"Because people are following you. Because people are getting killed."

"One person got killed," Jennifer said. "And we don't know for sure that Scarvano's death is even related to us. I mean, he's a lawyer, for Pete's sake! Could have been a coincidence. Could have been a client who wasn't satisfied with the service."

Easton did his best to stare bullets at her.

"Besides ..." She walked across the room and put her hand on his arm. "Besides, aren't you the least bit curious who these people are? I mean, why do they want the gold?"

"Well, probably, because it's gold—"

"Point conceded," she laughed. "But aren't you the least bit curious as to how they found out about it?"

He was quiet for a moment. "No," he said. "Not enough to pursue it any further."

"Really?" She was running her finger up and down his bare arm now. "How about something nice and safe?"

"How safe?" He moved his arm away. He hated that he was even discussing this.

"Well," she said eagerly. "We have Booth and Cecilia, living here in Michigan. We have Booth dying in Michigan waters. I went on the Internet and threw out kind of a really wide net on Google, searching for anything that I could find that had to do with Booth and Michigan. And I found something."

"What?" Yes, he was definitely discussing it. He was being played like an accordion, and he knew it.

"The Lincoln Rocker."

This stopped him. "The what?"

"The rocker that Abraham Lincoln was sitting in when he was assassinated." Jennifer was nodding as she spoke now. "Where do you think it is?"

What is this, a trick question? "Ford's Theater."

"Wrong!" Jennifer was positively beaming. "The one they have there is just a replica. The real one got held as evidence during the conspiracy trial, and then it got bounced to the Smithsonian. Then, in 1921, the widow of the owner of Ford's Theater petitioned to have it returned to her, and it was. Eight years later, in 1929, right about the time of the stock market crash, she sold the chair at auction. It wound up in the Henry Ford Museum, right here in Michigan—Dearborn, Michigan."

"Makes sense," Easton shrugged. "'Ford' and 'Ford.'"

"I'd agree," Jennifer said, in a tone that indicated she wasn't about to. "Except that there is no relationship between the Ford theater family and Henry Ford. They just happened to share an extremely common surname."

"And now you want to go check out this chair—"

"The rocker. Yes. If we do that, I'll be satisfied that we've exhausted every available avenue. May we? Please? Please?" She was virtually simpering, which Easton would have found irritating, except he was buying it.

"And after that," he said, "you'll drop it, and we can lay low until this thing has completely blown over?"

"Yes." Jennifer held up two fingers, pantomiming scout's honor. "I promise. If nothing comes of it, I'll drop it."

Easton said nothing. He knew when he'd been had.

CHAPTER TWENTY-SIX

Three dormer windows faced east in the cabin's loft, guaranteeing that the first light of dawn would find its way into Jennifer's bedroom. Pulling on some sweats, she made her way quietly down the stairs and wasn't surprised at all to find the living-room couch unoccupied. Yawning, she padded barefooted into the kitchen and started a pot of coffee, short-stopped a cup, added milk and sugar, and then walked into the living room, stepping to the windows.

The sun was just rising over the pines on the eastern shore, a steadily brightening yellow that turned the lake water to molten gold. Jennifer glanced down the stone beach to the point and, sure enough, there was Easton, plunging into the still water and then pulling with long, steady sweeps of his arms for the center of the lake. She wondered how cold the water was. This was Michigan, after all, closer to the equator than to the North Pole—but only just barely.

"Brrr," she whispered, then turning from the window, headed across the room to pick up her bookbag at the end of the couch. Easton's blanket was folded at the end, his pillow stacked on top. Unable to resist, she put her face to the pillow, breathing in the faint scent of Ivory soap and what she could have sworn was Aqua Velva—the same aftershave she'd given her father for years. Then, feeling slightly foolish, she put the pillow aside and took out her PowerBook. She found an outlet and phone jack under the table next to a big, overstuffed plaid chair by the window. *Perfect.*

Showered and dressed, Jennifer was greeted by the homey smells of toast and bacon as she descended the stairs a second time. She found Easton in the kitchen, frying eggs in a crackling, sizzling pan.

"Hey." Easton flashed her a smile as he turned the eggs. Like Jennifer, Easton was already dressed; he seemed to be the master of the three-minute shower, which she found absolutely inconceivable; it took her ten just to shampoo and condition. "I'm making a cholesterol-bomb for breakfast; that okay with you?"

Jennifer looked around at the rough log walls, rafters, and roof beams.

"Given the surroundings." She clucked her tongue. "I'd say that it's probably mandatory."

They didn't dine; they dove in. Jennifer was beginning to understand Easton's morning workout routine; if this was the way he ate every day, he probably needed it to keep his heart from stopping. It was the kind of meal that made you want a nap afterward.

But that wasn't about to happen.

"I figure we're about ninety minutes from Dearborn," Easton said. "What time does the museum open? Nine?"

"That's right," Jennifer nodded.

"Okay." Easton glanced at the Mickey Mouse dive watch on his wrist. He picked up their plates and headed for the sink. "I'll clean up here. It's seven right now; what say we leave in half an hour?"

"All right." Jennifer got up to brush her teeth, and then she stopped midstride. It was only seven?

She studied the Fossil watch on her wrist. Sheesh! What time had they gotten up?

"Dr. Cassidy, I'm Chuck Sopata, senior furnishings curator for the museum."

"It's just Jennifer," she hastily corrected him as they shook hands. "I'm afraid 'Doctor' is a ways down the road for me. And this is my associate, Beck Easton."

"Call me 'Beck,'" Easton said, shaking the man's hand.

"Jennifer, Beck—great! I prefer Chuck, myself," the curator said. Then, with a tip of his head, he gestured down the entry corridor. They followed him into a gigantic hall filled with steam locomotives, automobiles, aircraft, and towering factory machines. The curator didn't look much like what Jennifer had expected: no Harris tweed jacket, no elbow patches or woolen necktie. He appeared to be a reasonably fit man in his late thirties, and he had a ponytail. His outfit consisted of tan Dockers slacks, Birkenstock loafers, and a dark blue polo shirt embroidered with the single word "STAFF" in red.

"So," he said, turning and smiling as they walked. "Your email said that you were looking for acquisition background on the Lincoln rocker, and I've pulled all the files on it. But would you like to see it first?"

"Sure." Jennifer nodded.

"Great! It's just past the museum store, down here, between the Rosa Parks bus and the Oscar Meyer Weinermobile."

"You have an Oscar Meyer Weinermobile?"

The curator laughed.

"To say our collection is eclectic," he said, "would be a considerable understatement."

They passed a restored Montgomery city bus and a collection of small exhibits, "Henry Ford's Collectibles," ranging from a small tool chest to a broadsheet copy of the Declaration of Independence. Just past this, and slightly cattycorner from the Weinermobile, was a black exhibit case that had thick polycarbonate sheeting on two sides and heavy green velvet curtains as a backdrop. The case was topped with a sign that said "LINCOLN'S CHAIR" and contained images of the sixteenth president and the case's contents. It was so understated that, had the curator not led them to this spot, Jennifer probably would have passed without noticing it.

The rocker was upholstered in red silk damask that had frayed heavily and faded to pink in several places. On the front of the overstuffed, pillow-like seat cushion, white cotton batting showed through. The frame of the rocker was honey-colored wood, thick and jig-sawed without any attempt at ornamentation, save for the headboard, where a design was either stamped or carved. It looked as if the artist had set out to embellish the top of the rocker with acorns, and then switched to a gourd motif at the very last moment.

The only other object in the case was a mounted copy of the Ford's Theater playbill for "Our American Cousin," dated April 14, 1865. But this accessory, standing upright next to the rocker, only underscored the rocker's cockeyed posture. Its back leaned to the left of its seat. Or perhaps the seat had settled to its right. Jennifer changed her position a couple of times, squinting from different angles.

The curator stepped closer. "If you filter out the theatrical lighting and the backdrop, it looks like the kind of thing you'd haul straight to the curb if you found it in your attic, doesn't it?"

"How'd you know what I was thinking?" She laughed, glad the dim museum lighting hid her blush.

"Because that's the same reaction most people have," he said with a smile. "They also want to know if the stains are blood."

"Are they?" She couldn't help asking.

"There are two small bloodstains on the upholstery," he said. "One, at about shoulder level on the seatback, is almost certainly Lincoln's blood. There's another on the front of the seat cushion, and that one is anybody's guess. There was a brief struggle in the box after the shot was fired, and that could be from someone's skinned knuckles or bloodied nose. For all we know, the second blood spot is Booth's. The rest are just the results of neglect and poor storage. Most are water stains."

He stepped closer to the case. "You might not think it at first glance, but the museum has put considerable energy into stabilizing this piece. We've covered the upholstery with a sheer fabric to take the strain off the silk, and the case itself is temperature- and humidity-controlled, as the rocker itself is made of organics— wood, silk, and cotton—all of which had begun to deteriorate by the time we received it. Of course, we'll never restore it; to do that would destroy the historical significance."

He reached into his pocket and took out a key with a circular paper tag. "Would you care to see the back?"

"Thank you, but this is fine," Jennifer said, still thinking about the bloodstains. "We're really more concerned about the documentation."

"Sure thing. It's right this way." He led them across the hall, past the Weinermobile Cafe, to a door hidden in the paneling, taking them down two flights of stairs and then into a hallway crowded with filing cabinets and banker's boxes.

"Sorry for the clutter," he said as they walked. "We keep talking about computerizing all the documents and moving all the originals to a fireproof warehouse off-site. It'd save room and make things more accessible for researchers, such as yourselves. But I'm afraid it'll be a while before the budget trickles down that far. Ah—here we are."

He took them into an office that, with the exception of a thin-screen computer monitor and an ergonomic keyboard, looked as if it could easily have dated back to the time of Henry Ford himself.

"Wow," Jennifer murmured.

"I know," the curator laughed, settling into a wooden desk chair and motioning his guests to a pair of straight-back, age-worn wooden armchairs. "Our director keeps saying he's going to bring potential donors to my office—give them the impression that money's tight? Actually it is. But not this tight. I just like old things. My house looks this way, too. Thus the job."

He walked his fingers through a stack of folders on his desk.

"Here's what we're looking for." The curator opened a file folder and slipped on a pair of wire-rimmed glasses. "There's manufacturing documentation; the rocker was a fairly costly piece, in its day, but it was factory-built, nonetheless—part of a set. Are you interested in that, or should I jump straight to the chain of ownership, from Ford's Theater to here?"

"Yes ... that ... please," Jennifer said. She gave Easton a quick grin.

"To the point; I like that," the curator smiled. "Okay. Here goes: the rocker was originally purchased by Henry Clay Ford, treasurer of Ford's Theater. It was part of a set that was used variously as part of the stage properties, lobby furnishings, and home furnishings for the Ford residence, which was in the same building as the theater. During the trial of the assassination conspirators, Ford testified that the rocker '... had been in the reception-room, but the ushers sitting in it had greased it with their hair ... '

"We've verified that, by the way—there is still a significant amount of heavily oxidized nineteenth-century pomade in the fabric on top of the chair; that's the stain everyone mistakes for blood at first glance. Anyhow, Ford initially had the chair moved to his bedroom to keep it from being damaged by his ushers. And then, when the other parts of the set were placed in the box to make it ready for the president, Ford testified, 'The only reason for putting that chair in the box was that it belonged to the set, and I sent for it to make the box as neat as possible.' One assumes they put a doily on it, to hide the hair-grease from the president."

Jennifer nodded, wishing the man would cut to the chase. To her side, the toe of Beck's boat shoe began a slow, silent tap.

The curator took a deep breath and continued. "The War Department took possession of the rocker as evidence following the assassination," he said, consulting his notes. "After the trial had concluded, it was kept in the office of Edwin Stanton, the Secretary of War, until 1866, when the War Department conveyed it to the Smithsonian, which immediately stuck it in a basement.

In fact, from the position of the water stains, I'd say it wasn't even sitting upright during this time—it was probably piled in a heap with a bunch of other items."

He scanned his notes again. "And that's where it sat for the next sixty-three years. In 1921, Blanche Chapman Ford, the widow of the Ford's Theater owner, petitioned the government for the rocker's return, claiming it had no further value as evidence, and eight years later, in 1929, the government apparently agreed, because they gave it back.

"That's the year of the Crash, of course, and while this is guess-work on my part, I'd say the financial climate had something to do with the fact that Blanche didn't hold onto the rocker for long. It was sent to auction in New York, where it was purchased for twenty-four hundred dollars—doesn't sound like much, but it was nearly two years' salary for a factory worker in those days. And the purchaser donated it here ... to us."

"So," Jennifer asked, "the purchaser was ...?"

"Let me just check and make sure there was no condition of anonymity connected to the donation," he said. He leafed through the file and smiled. "Nope. No request for anonymity. The rocker, together with a model three-sixteen roll-top desk manufactured by Lambert and Hudson of Grand Rapids, was donated to us by a Mrs. Cecilia Donohue Baxter Sinclair, of Ann Arbor."

"Bingo!" Jennifer slapped her knee.

The curator laughed. "I take it," he said, "that's the answer you were looking for?"

Jennifer nodded, grinning.

"The desk," Easton said, and Jennifer looked up. It was the first time he'd spoken since they'd entered the curator's office. "Do you still have it?"

"Yes!" The curator seemed surprised by the question. "It was one of the terms of transfer—the rocker and the desk, on the con-dition that neither one will ever be sold or disposed of. They must be kept on grounds and cannot be loaned. Which has caused us no end of grief, by the way. The National Park Service has been trying to buy or borrow the rocker ever since Ford's Theater underwent its major restoration, back in 1967."

"Hmm." Easton leaned one arm on the other and cupped his chin. "Is the desk valuable?"

"As an antique?" The curator scratched his ear. "Marginally— it depends on condition; I've never actually seen it. But as a museum piece, I can tell you flat-out that the answer is, 'no.' The furniture shops in Grand Rapids turned out desks like that by the hundreds of thousands back in the eighteen-nineties. We would have shipped it off to auction immediately, I'm sure, had we not been required to keep it."

Jennifer and Easton stared at each other, then at the curator. Jennifer cleared her throat. "Isn't that unusual?"

"Well," the curator shrugged, "anyone who could afford to spend twenty-four-hundred for a chair in 1929 would be, by definition, wealthy, and while I certainly wouldn't say this at a member's banquet, wealth and eccentricity do seem to go hand-in-hand."

"Could we see the desk?" Easton asked.

"See it?" The curator looked even more surprised by that question. "I don't see why not. Just let me make sure we can get to it."

He peered through his glasses at the file, found what he was looking for and marked his place with his finger while he dug his phone out from beneath a pile of mail and keyed in an extension.

"Phil? Chuck Sopata here. Would you have time to pull an item out of storage for me? You would? You're the man! The crate number is one-nine-two-one-dash-six-two-two-eight ... Yes, bigger than a breadbox—bigger than several, in fact. It's a roll-top desk ... Forty-five minutes? Wonderful. Thanks, Phil." He hung up the phone and closed the file.

"Well," he smiled at Jennifer and Easton. "What say we go grab a cup of coffee at the Wienermobile Cafe?"

Crate number 1921–6228 appeared to be the original packaging in which the desk had been shipped to the museum: a stout wooden case double the depth of an upright piano. There were stenciled arrows indicating which end was up, a caution to "LIFT FROM BENEATH," and a hand-scrawled address that read "EDISON INST., DEARBORN." The crate had been left on a loading dock, where daylight could reach it. A steel pry bar was lying next to it, which the curator stooped and picked up. He ran his fingers along the side of the crate, found a seam, and glanced up and smiled.

"I love this part." Putting the pry bar into the seam, he pulled and nails screeched as one side of the crate gaped open. He handed the bar to Easton, who did the other side, and the whole front of the crate came loose. The curator pulled it off and he and Easton set it aside. A strong odor of camphor came wafting out.

"Potent," Jennifer said, stepping away and waving her hand in front of her face.

"Mothballs." The curator pulled double handfuls of excelsior out of the crate. "My predecessors used to throw a box or two in whenever they recreated items for storage. That's how they kept the mice out. The downside was . . . well, you're smelling the downside. But it should air out pretty quickly here, with the dock doors open and all . . ."

He pulled out the last of the excelsior and stepped back. "There we go," he said. "One . . . pretty beat-up and ugly . . . roll-top desk."

Jennifer and Easton walked around to the front of the crate. "Wow," Jennifer said. "You weren't a-kiddin'."

The desk looked like something that had seen hard daily use for half a century or so. The finish had been worn away around the drawers, and the roll-top hung slightly canted in its tracks. Some of the fittings had been replaced with others that did not quite match, the varnish was aged and cracked, and a jagged split ran half the length of the desk's top.

"You kept . . . this?" Jennifer asked.

The curator shrugged. "Terms of transfer. A deal's a deal."

"Okay if we look through it?" Easton asked.

"Help yourself," he said. "Should be empty, though. We never put furniture into storage with contents."

It took the curator a few tries to do it, but he finally succeeded in getting the roll-top all the way up. The various pigeonholes and drawers inside the desk looked in better condition than the exterior, but only marginally so.

As Jennifer watched, Easton began opening drawers, one after the other, feeling under the bottom of each one, and then reaching inside to feel the space above. Jennifer felt as if she should join him, but he seemed to know what he was looking for, so she contented herself with looking on.

Next, Easton pulled each drawer completely out of the desk and peered into the spaces behind each one. Then he began to replace them, one at a time, feeling the sides and bottoms, and putting a finger down the corner on the inside and then doing the same on the outside. He was on his third side-drawer when he stopped and gauged it again.

He carried the drawer over to the open loading-dock door, and squatted down to examine the wood in the sunlight.

"What did you find?" Jennifer walked over to join him.

"Here," he glanced up at her. "The inside. See?"

Jennifer stooped beside him. The drawer had a blank wooden bottom. There was a small nick in it, but other than that, it looked absolutely unremarkable.

"No, I don't."

"I do." It was the curator, now standing beside them. "The bottoms of the other drawers are supported in grooves at all four sides," he said. "Standard construction. But this one is only supported front and back—there are seams on each side."

"That's right," Easton said. "And the inside of this one is shallower than the other three side drawers." He shook the drawer lightly from side to side. A tiny "click-click-click" came from within. Reaching into his pocket, he came out with a small black-handled pocketknife and opened it with a sweep of his thumb.

"May I?" Easton asked the curator.

The museum official chuckled. "You know," he said, "if that were any other piece in the collection, I would be having a coronary right about now. But this? I've found better junk in garage sales. Go ahead."

As Jennifer watched, Easton slipped the tip of the knife into the nick in the drawer and pulled. There was the tick of wood against wood, and the bottom of the drawer moved; now there were seams on three sides. He slipped the knifeblade into the back of the seam and lifted. The bottom of the drawer came up with it.

"It's a false bottom," Jennifer said, and both men nodded. Easton lifted the shelf even with the upper edge of the drawer, grabbed it between his thumb and the blade, and pulled up and out. The false bottom lifted free, revealing brown paper underneath.

An envelope. Jennifer's heart began a tapdance.

"Um, at this point, I think we'd better take this into a lab," the curator said.

"I—" Jennifer paused to swallow and wet her lips—"agree."

With the curator leading the way, they carried the drawer back into the museum offices and stepped into an empty room with old black Bakelite counters and soft, even fluorescent lighting.

"May as well do this right." The curator handed white cotton gloves to Jennifer and Easton and then pulled on his own. He reached into the old drawer with two pairs of plastic forceps and lifted the envelope out. Laying it on the counter, he reached within the envelope and slid out two sheets of handwritten paper, one crisp and clean except for two crease marks, and one wrinkled and blurred; it looked as if it had been left on a windowsill in the rain. Jennifer stared; she could actually hear her heartbeat pounding in her ears now. The handwriting was neither Cecilia's nor Augustus Baxter's.

Then the curator reached into the envelope with the forceps again and pulled out a sepiatone photograph. "Wedding picture," he said. "Think the woman is Cecilia Sinclair?"

Jennifer took a look.

"I know she is," she said, awe softening her voice.

"The man looks very familiar too," the curator murmured. "Is that Mr. Sinclair?"

"Um-hmm," Jennifer said, aware of Easton's pointed look. Sinclair's face was identical to the history book photos of John Wilkes Booth.

The curator opened a cabinet and took out a halogen reading lamp, turning it on and setting the crisper of the two sheets of paper under it. All three of them leaned forward and began to read.

5 November 1868
My Dearest Cecilia—

My captain has told me that a mail boat will come out to meet us in the river as we pass abreast of Detroit. I am tempted to simply disembark there and come see you—you will be so close! The thought that after all these travels, you will be a mere two or three hours' ride away is enough to madden me. But I must see this voyage through, and then I shall never again leave your side.

My darling, before leaving Albany, I dispatched to you a rail shipment of a dozen chests, filled with mementos of my halcyon days. They will be, I trust, sufficient to brighten all the days of your life, should circumstance prevent our reunion.

But I speak too darkly. Two weeks more and I shall surely be home to you. The wind freshens from the south, and our captain feels certain it will see us swiftly up the St. Clair and thence out into the lake. The sky is as bright as any I have ever seen, and it is a fine day to be upon the water, but it would be finer still if spent within your arms.

The mate calls now for the mail. I must put up my pen. Two weeks longer, my love. I shall mark each day and count every minute.

Yours forever,
John

The curator was the first to speak. "I've heard there's a mail boat that still meets freighters in the river today, delivering the crew's prescriptions and perishables, and dropping off and picking up their mail. The freighters drop a bucket on a rope—the letters are inside. I bet they did it the same way in the nineteenth century."

Jennifer barely heard him. She was too focused on that one phrase "... mementos of my halcyon days ..."

The curator set the letter aside and picked up the next, holding it at two corners with the forceps. "This one's about to fall to pieces," he mumbled. He removed a letter-sized sheet of thin, glare-proof glass, laid the letter atop it, and then moved an identical sheet over the paper. Finally, he slid the glass-sandwiched letter under the reading light.

7 November 1868
Beloved wife,

Paul writes in this book that he was shipwrecked thrice and survived all. I am praying to our Lord and Savior that, if it be His desire, I might survive one less than that number. But it does not appear that I will.

Since midnight last, our ship has been battered by storm after wretched storm. We were heavily laden and rode low in the water as it was, but sometime after midnight, blown off-course and barely in control, we struck a submerged shelf of rock and began to take in water faster than our stalwart crew could pump it away.

Through a break in the clouds, we saw, far to the south, a light, which the captain identified as that of Fort Gratiot. This caused him no lack of distress, as he had reckoned our position to be some seventy-five miles north, and he could not understand how we had become so hopelessly lost. But it gave him cheer, as well, because the proximity of the light should have meant that the western shore was quite near, and we could beach our vessel before she sank. Yet we have beaten west, against the wind, for two hours now, and still we are in deep water. Although the waves continue to mount, we get breaks in the clouds now and again, and the captain is on deck with his sextant, trying to fix our position from his glimpses of the stars as the clouds tear past.

My truest treasure, dear Cecilia, is not within this sinking ship at all. It is in heaven, in the certainty that I am going there. And it is in the certainty that you shall one day join me there. I have done much in this life that I regret, but I forever rejoice at the opportunity you gave me to lead you to the throne of our Lord.

If this letter reaches you, then I will have passed from this world. Do not be too sad, my wife, as I am going to the feet of the only One who could possibly love me more than you. And I beg that whoever finds me will convey to you not only my remains for interment, but this letter and the book that goes with it. That which is written in those pages has been the record of your salvation. Search it closely in your hour of need. Should circumstances require it, that which is written there can save you yet again.

Your loving husband,

"The signature's too badly smudged to read," the curator observed. "But isn't that odd? It's obviously the same hand, but he signed the last one 'John,' and, on this one the signature looks as if it begins with a 'W.'"

"Maybe it's a pet name." Jennifer flinched as Easton poked her in the ribs.

"So," the curator said with a frown. "Who's Paul?"

"The apostle Paul," Easton said. "Where he says 'Paul writes in this book that he was shipwrecked thrice . . .' That's a reference to Second Corinthians. This letter was left with a Bible."

"Well," the curator said, straightening. "That's quite a touching snapshot into two lives from long ago." He smiled at Jennifer and

Easton. "You two have given me a memorable day. What can I do to thank you?"

"Can you make us copies of the letters and the photo?" Jennifer asked.

"Absolutely," he said. "Let me run these down the hall to Imaging. If nothing else is on their agenda, they should have them for you in just a few minutes."

Twenty minutes later, as Jennifer and Easton left the Henry Ford Museum, the bell in the tower above them tolled the noon hour. They walked along the edge of the large green, toward the parking lot, neither one speaking.

"You seem lost in thought," Easton finally said.

"I am," Jennifer admitted. "Some—lots—of what we just heard is not adding up."

"Same here." Easton halted and turned to face her. "You first."

"Okay." Jennifer gazed up at the museum's clock tower, a replica of the one atop Independence Hall, and nibbled on her bottom lip, thinking. "For starters," she said, "Booth is obviously coming home with the gold, and he's coming home with the lion's share of the gold . . ."

"Tell me how you figure that."

"Well, the first time Booth goes through the Bahamas as 'Sinclair,' he's alone, he shows up in Nassau just a month after the assassination, and he takes sick just as soon as he gets there. I figure that he was just making sure the gold was still there, picking up enough to bankroll the expenses of coming back to recover the whole stash later on, and on top of all that, he was scoping the territory. Maybe the original plan had been for him to haul everything back, but he's now lost his outside support, no government behind him, and he's probably too weak to go back to Cat again on that trip. So he improvises a back-up plan and heads back to the mainland to rest up and to check on his buddy's widow."

"Okay . . ." Easton stepped to one side while a group of schoolchildren in blue T-shirts trooped down the sidewalk, chattering happily.

Jennifer let them pass before she spoke again. "Booth gets to Cecilia sometime in late August, or early September. I don't know why it takes him so long, but I suspect that, since hostilities only completely ceased at the end of June, he probably came in by a circuitous route, maybe through Canada. Anyhow, he finds Cecilia, and takes her with him, they get married in Nassau in October, and by December, her old hometown newspaper reports that she has set up housekeeping in Ann Arbor. So there's roughly a month before the wedding, and a month after, where they might have been in Cat, collecting more of the gold. But I don't think they collected much more than they needed to buy a farm, build a house, and set aside a nest egg. I mean, there's only the two of them, he was near death in June, and she's been malnourished for months. How much gold could the two of them possibly have picked up by themselves?"

"All right." Easton blinked in the sun, unfolded his sunglasses, and slipped them on.

"So, at that point, most of the gold is still on the island," Jennifer continued. "Sinclair and Cecilia get their farm going and wait for things to settle down. There's a huge market in gold around this time. Within the year, two speculators—Jay Gould and Jim Fisk—will try to corner the market. So the time's right to go back. Booth finds some way to bring a shipload of gold into New York harbor—"

"Spices," Easton said.

"Pardon?"

"Talk to any smuggler, and he'll tell you that the way they do it in the movies, telling customs that you have nothing to declare, is never the way it's done," Easton said. "If Booth's smart—and it seems that he is—he'll have his captain declare some kind of cargo in New York, preferably a relatively valuable cargo, to provide a reason for being in the islands. And Booth told Dr. Vandernoord that he'd been in Dominica. Remember the casparilla trees on Cat Island that the people harvested as a flavoring?"

Jennifer nodded.

"Dominica's like that, and then some," Easton said. "Cinnamon, cloves, you name it. Dominica grows and exports them all. Spices are one of the few things that he could have brought in by the boatload from the skinny latitudes and not raised suspicions. So, I figure that Easton carried enough cloves, or whatever, to give customs something to look at, and then he declared the whole ship as a load of spices, paid a tariff, and offloaded. That's just a theory, but it works. It gets the gold inside the United States."

"Okay." Jennifer took a breath. "He's in New York. He has a boatload of gold. How does he get it home? If he puts it all on a train, he's letting it out of his hands. If he uses wagons, he's prone to highway robbery—literally. The only way he can stay on top of things is to use a boat, and to travel with it. So he risks using wagons to take the gold to Albany, where he puts a small reserve on a rail car—"

"Small? It was a dozen trunks," Easton reminded her.

"True, and that's probably a ton or two, literally. But compared to the total of what was on the *Halcyon*, it's just a tiny fraction. He takes the gold by barge to Buffalo, using the Erie Canal, and there he offloads it onto a ship that he's purchased previously."

"Whoa," Easton said. "Back up. He bought a ship?"

Jennifer nodded. "When I first started going through Cecilia's papers, I found documentation that Lloyd's paid on the loss of a frigate called the *Florida* in 1869. At the time, I dismissed it as an investment; Cecilia put money in a lot of different things over the years. But the timing's right. If the ship was lost in November, it'd easily be the following year before the insurance paid on the claim."

"And Booth would have bought insurance on any ship that was going to sail the Lakes," Easton said. "No reputable Great Lakes captain would consider sailing without insurance. Point Pelee, the Detroit River, the St. Clair—there are just too many places where it's easy to strand a ship. You'd need insurance to get a salvor to tow you off."

They started for the parking lot again, stepped back to let a family with a child in a wheelchair past, and then kept walking, past a wide lawn with tall oak trees. Canada geese waddled on the grass, honking at a man who came too near with his video camera.

"Okay," Jennifer said, squinting up at Easton. "Your turn, buddy."

"All right." He ran his hand back through his hair. "One thing both letters beg is where Booth was going. In the first one, he's sending mail from Detroit and saying he wishes he was home, and he mentioned the run up the St. Clair River, which is north of Detroit. Then, in the letter he writes as the ship is going down, he talks about being north of Fort Gratiot Light. That puts him in Lake Huron."

"Which means he's not taking the gold home," she said.

"Can't be," he agreed. "If he's going to Ann Arbor, he would have tied up in Detroit."

"So where's he going?"

"Beats me." Easton shrugged. "Where do you sell that much gold?"

Jennifer stopped walking. "He's already left there," she said. "New York—the Gold Room. In 1868, it's the only gold market in the country."

Easton turned her way. "What did you do if you didn't live in New York?"

She scratched her head. "Well, there were gold brokers in other major cities. They used telegraphs to act as sort of agents for the Gold Room. There would have been brokers in San Francisco, in Denver, certainly and—"

She pushed Easton in the arm.

"Chicago!" A passing family turned and stared as she shouted out, but she didn't care. "He was headed to Chicago! Don't you see? John Wilkes Booth couldn't hang around New York to sell his gold—there were too many people there who might recognize him! But most of his career was spent on the East Coast. In

Chicago, he'd have a fair degree of anonymity. He might have to pay a commission to unload the gold in Chicago, but it's worth it, if he doesn't get recognized."

"Okay." He inclined his head, frowning.

"What else?" Jennifer stepped around in front of him and looked up, into his face. "There's something else about this that's troubling you, isn't there?"

"There . . . is." Easton was staring past her, at the ground.

"Spill."

"Okay." Easton dug his hands into his pockets. "From what we heard from Lionel and Harry in the Bahamas, it seems to me that, if Dr. Vandernoord had Booth in his care for the better part of a month, he would have led him through some sort of discipleship, grounding him in the truths and principles of what Jesus taught. After all, he's a missionary, right? And I have to believe that, after Booth led Cecilia to Christ, he would have educated and nourished her in the same fashion."

"Makes sense," Jennifer agreed.

"Well, what doesn't make sense is that he would tell her to go to the Bible if she needs salvation again."

"Why not?"

"Because—" Easton kneaded his fingers, put his hands on top of his head—"salvation is not like a Magic-Fingers motel bed, Jen. It's not as if your quarter runs out and you have to plug another one in."

"Well . . ." She let her gaze drift from his and studied the geese walking on the lawn. "When we were in the Bahamas, reading the doctor's journal, you mentioned being saved from the consequences of your sins—from Hell and all—right?"

"That's right."

"So . . ." She wanted to face him but couldn't. "What happens if you sin again? Don't you have to start over?"

"No!" Easton rubbed his head with both of his hands and then kneaded the bridge of his nose. "Actually, some people might agree with you, but most theologians would not. And Dr. Vandernoord was a Baptist missionary—he certainly wouldn't. Do you remember in the Bahamas, when I told you how I was ... tempted?"

Jennifer stopped watching the geese. "Yes?"

"When he taught his disciples, Jesus was most concerned not with what they said or did but with what they kept in their hearts. In fact, the word, 'heart,' shows up in the New Testament nearly a hundred times, about half of those in the gospels."

Easton took off his sunglasses. His eyes seemed to hold Jennifer's.

"One of the things Jesus said was that the things that pass through our hearts carry the same weight as the things we have done. Just as Lionel preached down on Cat. That ... having those sorts of feelings for you ... was the same as acting on those thoughts. And what does that tell you?"

Jennifer grinned. "That we should have gone for it!"

"No." Easton put his palm to his forehead and shook his head. "That's not where I was going. I'm just saying, how often do we consider things like that, or anything else improper, unethical, or unacceptable—and then choose not to act on it?"

"You're asking me?" Jennifer let her gaze drift to the sidewalk. "Gosh. I don't know. Constantly?" She looked up. "Am I—" she felt the smile drop from her face—"am I that bad?"

Easton touched her cheek. "You," he said, "are that human. It's why we need God. And that's why it's so good that God is omniscient—that God knows everything, including the sins we have not yet committed. And since Jesus is God, when he went to the cross to pay for our sins, he paid for them all. That's what I believe, and I'm sure that's what Booth believed. We may have to seek forgiveness—I know that I do every day—but the way that I, and most Christians read the Bible, we never have to seek a second salvation. Which is why Booth's note to his wife makes no sense at all. Read the Bible? Sure. But not in some perpetual request for what you've already been given."

Jennifer studied the geese again. "So, if I were to accept Christ as my ..."

"Savior," Easton offered.

"Okay," she mused as a drake flapped its wings and frightened away a crow. "If I were to accept him as my savior right now, then, no matter what happened ..."

"Then heaven is certain for you," Easton said. "The Bible makes that clear. It doesn't necessarily promise you sweetness and light for the rest of your life, but it does promise you that for the rest of eternity."

"The Bible!" Jennifer didn't say it. She shrieked it. People down the whole length of the green turned and looked. "Don't you see?"

Easton's expression showed that, clearly, he did not.

"Booth obscured his message," Jennifer said in a loud whisper, "because he knew that other people—whoever finds his body—will see it before Cecilia does. The second salvation he's referring to is not spiritual. It's financial."

Easton nodded slowly. "It's financial," he said.

"Yes." Jennifer was hopping up and down, and she didn't care who saw her doing it. "He wrote the location of the wreck in his Bible!"

"So why are you so excited?"

"Because!" Jennifer grinned broadly. "I've got the Bible!"

CHAPTER TWENTY-SEVEN

JACKSON COUNTY, MICHIGAN

Marisol flipped on the cruise control so the Jeep would not slow and attract undue attention. She drove past the Napoleon Municipal Airport a second time, dark glasses covering her eyes, head turned as little as possible, verifying that Beck Easton's airplane was still there, tied down, wheels chocked, and windscreen shielded. The distinctive paint job made it possible to locate the Cessna in a glance.

On the second pass, she could clearly see that the grass around the airplane was undisturbed, with no tracks left in it from the aircraft's wheels. That cinched it; the Cessna had been there all night, or at least the majority of it, and it had not moved since.

Conclusion: the subjects had arrived in this airplane, but they most certainly had not departed in it.

Yet a thermal scan of the cabin at the lake showed no signs of human occupation. And the most sensitive listening devices at her disposal gave Marisol nothing more than the signature of a relatively noisy air-conditioner. A physical inspection of the cabin would be absolutely conclusive, but she had decided to avoid this. The subjects had already been spooked, and Beck Easton was proving highly adept at playing cat-and-mouse. Marisol was certain that he had left tell-tales—a thread that would fall from a door-jamb or a tiny smudge of flour where a door would disturb it as it opened. It was best not to risk further alarming such a capable individual.

The break-in at the library had been clumsy, unprofessional. Were she the type of person who allowed herself to get angry, she would be livid over how it had transpired. It had alerted her subjects: made them more careful, more elusive. Tracking them here had involved the use of far more assets then she'd cared to employ. If the subjects went any farther underground, nothing short of a manhunt would smoke them out. And she didn't have the authority to call up a manhunt.

Not in this country.

Marisol drove on, Jeep rolling along at exactly the speed limit. She turned her head, checking all three mirrors in one sweep every thirty seconds, making sure that she was not being followed.

Only two possibilities presented themselves. One was that the subjects had traveled someplace completely unforeseen, in which case all she could do was bank on the probability that they would return.

The other possibility was that they had gone someplace familiar, someplace they visited often. Nothing within a single morning's driving distance seemed to match those criteria for Beck Easton, and for Jennifer Cassidy, only two came to mind—her apartment and the university library. And her last visit to the library had been aborted by the investigation of the break-in; it stood to reason that whatever business she had there was business that remained undone.

In Marisol's mind, a two-branched decision tree remained. One branch said that they had vanished and might return to the cabin. The other branch said that they had gone to the apartment or the library.

At the moment, though, the cabin at the lake was unoccupied. Going there would not advance her mission.

As for the apartment and the library, both of those were in Ann Arbor.

Now only a single branch was left on the decision-tree.

Signal on, Marisol turned the Jeep onto M-50 and started north, toward Interstate 94. Even at the speed limit, Ann Arbor was less than forty-five minutes away.

CHAPTER TWENTY-EIGHT

THE UNIVERSITY OF MICHIGAN

"Jen, this is a terrible idea. No—I will not do this."

"All right; then I'll do it myself."

Beck Easton drummed the dash of the Bronco with his finger-tips. He checked the clock on the bell tower across the green—they'd been sitting here for nearly ten minutes. He turned to face the petite blonde conundrum in the passenger's seat. "How familiar are you with the Bible?"

"I don't know." She turned as a couple of students rolled by on in-line skates, books in their hands. "I saw *The Ten Commandments* on TV when I was a kid."

He shook his head. "You won't know where to find it."

"Then I'll just scour every square inch of Booth's Bible until I stumble across what I'm looking for. It'll take days. Whoever's looking will surely spot me, but I will find it. Or you can give me a hand here, and we can be in and out in half an hour. Maybe less."

"Half an hour ..." He squeezed his forehead. "Jen, there is a real good chance that we've lost these people who are trailing you. If they get a glance—so much as a glance—at one of us, they will follow us. They will stick to us like glue, and our safe house won't be safe anymore. These people are playing for keeps. I'm only trying to keep you alive. All right?"

Jennifer crossed her arms. "If you think this idea stinks so badly, then why did we stop and buy that cell phone, and the headset and that phone card? Why did you figure out this plan?"

"I thought about it." He stared through the windshield, not at her. "It's a crummy plan."

"Beck!" She drummed her feet on the rubber matting of the Bronco's foot well. "We ... are talking about billions ... of dollars worth of gold, here. Not millions. *Billions*."

"Not worth it."

"Sheesh!" Her dark glasses didn't conceal the fact that she was rolling her eyes. "What—you think Cecilia popped out into the lake and picked this up a century ago, don't you?"

"Maybe. But even if I was sure that she hadn't, it still would not be worth it. Not even if it was all the gold in the world. It couldn't justify risking your life. Not for one instant." He rubbed his head again, thinking. "If there was just a way I could go in by myself," he said. "If I could keep you out of it, safe and clear—"

"Well, you can't." Jennifer shook her head. "A week ago, maybe—just maybe—I could have called up or sent you in with a note, saying that I was sick and you were looking something up for me. But after that break-in? The archive library's like Fort Knox. I'm pretty sure Mrs. Hunter wouldn't want me in there, if she could help it, but my department head has a lot of say on her funding."

Easton drummed the dash again.

He stopped.

"When we met the curator at the museum, he said that he'd gotten your email."

"That's right."

Easton tightened his lips, thinking. "When did you send him an email?"

"This morning." She shrugged. "I figured it would save us some time."

He drew in a deep breath. "Okay," he said. "I'll go with you."

Behind the sunglasses, Jennifer blinked.

"Just like that?"

"Just like that."

She crossed her arms again. "Why?"

"Because if we initiated an Internet connection from the cabin this morning, I have this sinking feeling that they already know exactly where we're staying. And there's a middling chance that they even know where we are right now. Laying low has become a moot point."

Jennifer gaped. "Oh, no—you don't think."

Easton nodded once, and Jennifer sagged, head in her hands. "But ... no ... they can't really ... "

"Jen. Back during the one period in my life when I actually had a real, regular job, I was a software architect, developing Internet and network security applications. Trust me. If these people can hack the FAA's transponder records, backtracking the University of Michigan's student Internet service to a single dial-up connection should be a very small piece of cake for them."

Jennifer bit her lip. "I'm sorry, Beck."

"Not your fault. You shouldn't have to worry about this sort of thing. You're a graduate student, not a field operative. I should have warned you not to use the phone lines. That's why I used the pay phone yesterday to call Jim about the cabin. I was trying to avoid generating SigIt—signals intelligence—that could lead them to the lake."

"Well," Jennifer was staring at the floorboard. "For what it's worth, I won't do that again."

Easton put a hand on her shoulder and squeezed gently. "I know you won't." He retrieved the black plastic Radio Shack bag off the rear seat. "Okay," he said. "Let's do it."

Easton stood in the library stacks, inspecting the Bibles. They seemed to have every version he had ever heard of—and quite a few that were new to him.

He wondered which translations would have been most popular in 1868. *The King James*, certainly. *The Revised Standard?* He checked the first few pages. No—the *Revised* dated back to only 1885. *The New Translation?* No again—1890. He picked up the *King James*, found a secluded table next to a window, and checked the status bar on the pre-paid digital cell phone. The antenna icon was flanked by three black bars. Not a perfect signal, but good enough. He plugged the headset into the cell phone and set the little silver phone so it could vibrate, rather than ring. Then he began to leaf through the *King James Bible*, placing slips of paper next to likely passages.

Two minutes later, the cell phone burred and danced on the wooden tabletop. Slipping the headset on, placing the slim boom microphone close to his lips, he touched a button on the phone and asked, "You in?"

"Hey." Jennifer's voice sounded clearer than he'd expected over the headset. "Okay, I'm in—up in the archives. Cujo actually checked my bag before she let me go into my carrel. She gave me the third-degree about the telephone—wouldn't let me plug it into the wall jack until I showed her the phone card."

"Well, the card's good for sixty minutes, so we're in business. Got the Bible?"

"It's in front of me." The excitement in her voice was evident, even over the tiny headset speaker.

"*King James?*"

"Let me check the front matter." Easton could hear pages rustling. "'To the most high and mightie Prince, James ... ' Yup," she said, "it's *King James*. Funny spellings and all. Where to first?"

"The obvious one is the verse Booth referred to in his note." Easton turned to his first bookmark. "That's Second Corinthians 11:25, the latter part of the verse: '... thrice I suffered shipwreck, a night and a day have I been in the deep.'"

There was silence on the phone. "Um," she finally asked, "where do I find Second Corinthians?"

Easton resisted the urge to tell her, *Right after First Corinthians.* "Open the Bible anywhere in the back third."

There was the rustle of pages over the phone. The rustling stopped.

"Okay," he said. "Tell me where you are."

"Um ... third chapter of John."

"Good. Read verse sixteen."

There was a short silence, after which Jennifer said, "It doesn't have anything to do with a shipwreck."

"I know," he said. "I just wanted you to read it. Now go forward three books. Acts will come next, then Romans, then First Corinthians, and then Second Corinthians."

The pages rustled again. "There's a date next to it!" Then the excitement dropped out of Jennifer's voice. "No. It's June twelfth, eighteen fifty-eight. Booth was memorizing verses."

"Before he became a Christian?"

"He was an actor," she reminded him. "I remember reading that Junius Booth insisted his family memorize sections of both Shakespeare and the Bible. Sounds as if the practice stuck with Wilkes."

Easton noticed how she had switched to referring to Booth by his family nickname, but he said nothing about it.

"Okay," she said. "Strike one; what else you got?"

Easton glanced at the concordance in the back of the reference Bible. "Well, there's a reference to 'shipwreck' in First Timothy. That's seven books after Second Corinthians. First chapter, nineteenth verse."

"All right, First Timothy ... Nope. No marginalia at all until chapter five."

"Yeah," Easton mused. "The early chapters of First Timothy aren't the most lyric—if he's memorizing, I can see why he'd skip it."

"All right. Strike Two. What's next?"

"Well ..." He flipped pages. "We're running out of the obvious. Those are the only two references to 'shipwreck' in the King James Bible." He tapped the table, thinking, then he moved the little boom microphone closer to his mouth. "Wait a minute ... Booth and Cecilia first went to Cat together in 1865, right?"

"Yeah. Brother Browne's journal said they were married there in October."

"Here's what I'm thinking," Easton said into his cell phone. "Booth is sinking as he writes his final note to Cecilia. He's pretty sure he's going to die, which means that when his body is discovered, whoever it is that finds him is going to go through his pockets pretty well, looking for identification, right?"

"Okay," Jennifer said. "So I'm thinking he's not going to leave any information that a stranger can find easily. He's going to put it somewhere that will only make sense to Cecilia and to him ..."

"And that is?"

"I'm thinking." Easton drummed the tabletop. "All right. Let's say they went on to Cat from Nassau, which would put them on the island in early November. And the *Florida* went down in November of 1868 ... November seventh ... three years, I wouldn't be surprised if it was three years almost to the day. Bear with me ..."

He flipped back in his Bible to the Old Testament.

"Okay," he said. "Here we are. ' ... once in three years came the navy of Tharshish, bringing gold, and silver ...'"

"Sounds good. Where is it?"

"First Kings. That's in the front third of the Bible. It goes Genesis, Exodus, Leviticus, Numbers, Deuteronomy, Joshua, Judges, Ruth, First and Second Samuel, and then First Kings. Are you there?"

"Hang on." Jennifer hummed as she searched. "Okay, buddy. I'm with you."

Where did she get this 'buddy' from? "All right. I'm in the tenth chapter, middle of the twenty-second verse ..."

"Ten ... " Jennifer murmured. "Twenty ... two. I'm there. There's a date. No ... there are numbers. It looks like ... temperatures? And measurements? And it's not Wilkes' handwriting."

"All ... right," Easton said slowly. "What temperatures and what measurements?"

"It says, 'forty-four degrees,' and after that, 'fourteen feet.' And 'eighty-three degrees,' followed by 'eight feet.'"

Easton started laughing.

"What?" Jennifer didn't sound amused.

"The degrees are degree signs and the feet are apostrophes, right?"

"Yeah." Jennifer still didn't sound amused.

"It's not 'feet.' It's 'minutes.' As in 'minutes of arc'—degrees and minutes. What you just gave me are latitude and longitude—map coordinates. That's it, Jen. Booth probably had the captain record his sightings directly; that's why the handwriting looks different. You've found it."

There was a long silence on the phone. "What," she finally asked, "do we do now?"

"First thing, get down here."

"Okay." Jennifer's voice sounded a little weak. Then it picked up again as she asked, "Where do I meet you?"

"I saw some public-access Internet terminals when we came in. Meet me there."

"Whatcha doin', buddy?" Jennifer teased. "Checking your email?"

"No." Easton scrolled and clicked, and a website with light-houses cascaded in on the screen. "Those coordinates you gave me—they're in Lake Huron off Port Austin."

"Well, that's good, right? I mean, Wilkes' ship went down in Lake Huron."

"Oh, it's the right lake." Easton brought up a map of Lake Huron. "But Booth's letter said that when the ship foundered, they could see Fort Gratiot Light to the south. Fort Gratiot Light is down here, by Port Huron, just above the head of the St. Clair River."

"Uh-huh. So they sank just north of there, right?"

"Wrong. I used to dive Huron all the time, back before I went into the service, and I recognized the general area of the coordinator. It's way up here, just above the Thumb of the Michigan mitten."

"Booth said the captain was surprised to see that light. Is there a light on the tip of the Thumb?"

"There is." Easton tapped on the map. "Right here: Pointe aux Barques Light. But a good captain wouldn't mistake the two. The lights are all set up to look different. Some flash every so many seconds. Some are steady. Some change colors. They mark those things on charts—at least, they do now, and I assume they did back then. But a guy I used to wreck-dive with was a real lighthouse nut, and I vaguely recall ... wait, here it is."

He opened a webpage on the Pointe aux Barques Light. Jennifer looked over his shoulder at a picture of a white lighthouse standing next to a prim, white keeper's quarters.

"Okay," Easton said, "in 1867, a number of ships' captains were complaining that the steady, non-flashing light at Fort Gratiot was too easily confused with the locomotive lights in a nearby rail yard. So the third-order, flashing light from up here, on the thumb, was moved down there, and the non-flashing light from Fort Gratiot was mounted in the light up at Pointe aux Barques. I'd bet the house that Easton's captain was using an old chart—and that's what killed them. The *Florida*'s captain couldn't get a star fix at first, so he trusted the light. He thought he was running for the shallow water next to shore, just above Port Huron. But he was actually running parallel to shore above the Thumb, heading straight for the open water of Saginaw Bay. With a rapidly sinking vessel, it was only a matter of time. They were doomed."

"So what's our next move?" The excitement had returned to Jennifer's voice. She had no idea what a "third-order light" was, but so long as Beck knew, she didn't care.

Easton thought for a moment. "It's time we turn this information over to the Coast Guard, I suppose."

"What?"

"Them or the Treasury Department. Maybe the FBI. This definitely crossed state lines."

Jennifer couldn't believe what she was hearing. She stood, hands on her hips. "You—" she tapped her foot—"after all this, you want to just give this all away?"

"No." Easton clicked the mouse and closed the webpage. He looked up. "It's not ours to give away."

"Now wait a minute." Jennifer pulled a chair close to Easton's, sat, and leaned forward, her face not a foot from his. "We know from Grant that some rogue Army officers were skimming this gold from a gazillion different sources out West. It was stolen from people, places, and businesses that no longer exist. Then Wilkes and Baxter stole it from the officers. Then Wilkes—who is already legally dead, by the way, loses it and his life in Lake Huron. Beck, I'd say that gold has been lost, found, stolen, and relost so many times that it pretty much amounts to 'finder's keepers' at this point."

Easton folded his hands. "Jen, I won't say that this question hasn't ever come up on other wrecks. It has; I've read about it. And you're largely right. In fact, there are even special laws in the case of recovered gold or silver. But I still say we hand this off. Two dead people are two too many. We hand it off, and then we steer clear."

"I'll do this myself, Beck. I don't want to, but I will."

Three young women walked by, books in hand, chattering.

"How?" Easton asked after they'd passed. "Even if I was willing to go along on this, there's no telling where that gold is now. Cecilia might have found a salvage company and brought it up. The wreck might have washed on the surface for hours after those coordinates were recorded. It could have drifted as it sunk or rolled on the bottom. You don't just go to that spot on the map and load up the gold, Jen. People have searched for lost ships for years, even decades, with data a heck of a lot more solid than a star sighting grabbed through holes in the cloud cover. I've heard of people spending millions, searching with boats full of high-tech gear, and never finding a thing."

Jennifer sat, thin-lipped and silent.

"And that's in the ocean," Easton added. "In the Great Lakes, visibility can range from a hundred feet to a couple of inches. I've dived wrecks that I couldn't find until I ran into them with my head. In those types of conditions, you can miss a shipwreck by a foot, and it's the same as missing it by a mile."

Jennifer said nothing, and remained silent as they got to their feet and left the library, walking out into the bright sunshine and blinking as they crossed the lawn. Easton turned once, scoping the surroundings, as they neared the street, where the Bronco was parked.

Jennifer swung into the old open-topped truck, sat down, and looked across at him. "You brought a whole planeload of dive gear up here from Florida. I imagine you know tons of people with boats. If not, I've still got the American Express card that Scarvano gave me, and I know that he's not going to object if I rent a boat. Heck, he's not going to object if I *buy* a boat. What does it hurt to go look?"

"It's not the search I'm worried about." He slid the key into the ignition. "It's who'd be following us. And I don't have a planeload of dive gear anymore. We're not going back to the cabin, and were not going back to the plane. That email might have compromised us."

"Then where are we going?"

"I don't know." He slipped the Bronco into gear and then waited as a woman trotted across the street in front of him, digging into a messenger's bag as she glanced toward the library.

Easton checked his outside mirror and was just releasing the clutch when he heard a creak and felt the vehicle shifting. Then Jennifer gasped.

Easton snapped around, but a dark-haired woman, eyes covered with sunglasses, was already settling onto the edge of the backseat, hand up, holding a small, black handgun to the back of Jennifer's head.

"Don't look at me," the woman said. "Drive."

Easton didn't move.

The woman moved her thumb, slipping off the safety on the gun.

"No heroics," she warned. "Drive!"

CHAPTER TWENTY-NINE

Umberto Alcázar stayed well back as he drove. There was no need to crowd them. Even with the top down, the red Bronco rode high off the pavement and could be easily spotted from as much as two blocks away.

Like so many things connected with this project, the satellite photo had been an absolute—what was the word these *americanos* used? Fluke. An absolute fluke. Alcázar had ordered it after his SigIt assets had backtracked the Cassidy woman's Internet connection. Using an identity he'd previously concocted—that of a real-estate developer who wanted a leg up on the competition—Alcázar had sent an email and a PayPal payment of one thousand dollars to a cash-strapped employee in the imaging division of a European defense agency, who in turn had directed an American photo-reconnaissance satellite to image the cabin's coordinates.

Alcázar's intention had simply been to get a high-resolution lay of the land, and he'd gotten that. But in addition, the satellite image had caught the red Bronco driving along the dirt two-track road away from the cabin, a faint dust plume curling up behind it. The resolution had been fine enough for Alcázar to see that the vehicle contained two people, and that the person in the passenger's seat was blonde.

That could have meant anything. It could have meant that the lovebirds were driving out to get breakfast. But Alcázar doubted it. The Cuban prided himself on his predictive abilities, what he called his *nariz*: his nose.

And his nose had told him to come here, to Ann Arbor—the *americana*'s ground, her haunt. It had told him that something would inevitably draw her back, and when it did, he should be there.

A single pass by the library in his rental car had been sufficient for Alcázar to spot the Bronco, parked at the curb. He'd made a second pass and had actually considered stopping to plant a GPS-enabled transmitter on the old SUV, but then he had noticed the dark-haired woman on the sidewalk, walking purposefully with a large bicycle-messenger's bag over her shoulder.

The woman had been on the same sidewalk, walking swiftly in the opposite direction, when he'd driven by the first time.

So Alcázar had parked across the green and, sure enough, this woman had joined the *americana* and this Easton when they'd returned to the Bronco. It had taken a pair of binoculars for Alcázar to spot the gun—the gun that the *mujer sombrio* had held in such a clever way that the ignorant American students strolling by on the sidewalk had not had a clue as to what was transpiring in the open-topped vehicle at the curb.

Alcázar cursed out loud and struck the padded dash of the rental car. The object of this search—which had once been his secret, and his secret alone—was turning into a bag full of holes. And every time he sewed one up, another one appeared.

What was one to do?

Keep sewing, Alcázar told himself. What else was there to do?

He glanced at the duffel bag sitting in the passenger's-side foot well. It bulged with the items he'd purchased clandestinely in a warehouse-district alley in Detroit; at least he still had plenty of needles and thread.

Grumbling under his breath, Alcázar pulled just a little bit closer to the Bronco.

CHAPTER THIRTY

Easton turned the vehicle onto Washtenaw Avenue. His voice was flat when he spoke. "You're not going to shoot us."

"You're willing to bet her life on that?" The woman's tone was as calm as Easton's.

The end of the gun's barrel was tapping solidly, heavily, against the back of Jennifer's head as they drove. If this were TV, she'd turn and karate-chop the woman and wrest the gun away from her. But this wasn't TV. Even in the wind of the open-topped vehicle, Jennifer could smell the musky-sweet smell of the oil on the weapon. It was that close.

She squeezed her eyes, telling herself that she had been more frightened than this in the past. Of course she had. She tried to remember when.

She couldn't think of a single instance.

"The way you got in was professional," Easton said. There was something verging on admiration in his voice. "A final walk-by, and then you moved. That was careful—well-planned. If you were going to pull the trigger, you would have done it right there, where you could have worked out your egress, your options, in advance. Driving along like this? There're too many variables. I'm driving randomly right now. You haven't planned an exit from this situation. You pull the trigger, there's no Step Two. And if you shoot me, I wreck the truck. You aren't going to shoot us. I doubt that you even have a round in the chamber. You wanted us out of there, with you, and you didn't want the delay of a discussion."

It sounded logical, but still, when Easton slowly extended his hand, Jennifer found herself hissing, "Beck ... !" She turned her head slightly, peering out from behind the side of her sunglasses as Easton extended an index finger and gently pressed the muzzle of the gun away from her head.

She turned a little more. The dark-haired woman was putting the gun into a messenger bag. She had the sunglasses off now, and there was something about her face ... Jennifer stared, and then swallowed hard, unbelieving.

Blue tinted glasses. Blonde hair. She blinked, imagined those changes, and considered the woman again. "I saw you," she said. "In the airport in Florida. You were behind those two men."

The woman put her dark sunglasses back on.

"Behind them, but not with them," Easton said. He glanced into the rearview mirror at their unexpected guest. "Let me take a completely wild guess. MI-6?"

The woman didn't reply.

"What's 'MI-6'?" Jennifer asked.

"British intelligence." Easton looked into the mirror again as he spoke.

"*British?*" Jennifer glanced back at the woman, with her dark complexion and jet-black hair. She thought of how the woman's voice had sounded: the liquid "L" sounds, the tiniest hint of a burr when she'd said "willing." It was like the English of the Mexican foreign exchange student that she'd known in high school, and yet it was not.

"You're an American, and you're not suspected of breaking any federal law," Easton told Jennifer. "That means that the NSA can't investigate you directly—neither here nor abroad. The CIA can only concern itself with foreign nationals and matters outside the country. The FBI and the Secret Service have their own portions of federal code that they're concerned with. And DIA and the service intelligence agencies are all similarly constrained. But the intelligence services of other countries are not. And we have several other countries that are only too happy to help keep track of what an American is up to—in return for a quid pro quo. Of those countries, the UK is the one most likely to pop up in Florida, where you first saw …" Easton shot a brief look toward the woman in the back seat. "What did you say your name was again?"

"I didn't. Call me Marisol. To answer the question, yes, I'm British. I was born in London, but grew up here. My mother and father were both Cuban." She pronounced the word *Koo-bahn*, with a hard initial consonant.

"Marisol …" Easton mused as if thinking about the name. Then he turned to Jennifer. "Lots of British protectorates in the Caribbean basin. They like to keep their thumb in the pie." He checked the rearview mirror again. "So, Marisol, I take it you want to talk?"

From the corner of her eye, Jennifer saw the woman incline her head slightly.

"There's a restaurant up here on the left." Easton changed lanes, and then he smiled at Jennifer. "You like Italian?"

More holes in the bag, Umberto Alcázar thought as he saw the woman allow Easton to lower her gun hand. What goes on here? Now these three are going to break the bread together?

He moved into the right lane and drove past as Easton turned the old Ford SUV into the restaurant drive. Signal on, Alcázar drove on down the street and looked for a parking lot or a side street—anyplace where he could pull off and do a U-turn. These two—these three—had become troublesome. It would not do to let them out of his sight.

The server set Jennifer's order, a pasta salad, in front of her, and then returned a few minutes later with huge entrees for both Easton and Marisol; linguine with clam sauce for him and a heaping vegetarian marinara for her.

Having seen the boot-camp-like routine with which Easton seemingly began each morning, Jennifer understood the table-busting lunch for him: he probably needed at least five thousand calories a day just to keep from wasting away.

Marisol, Jennifer decided, was probably equally active and equally fit. She was wearing slacks and a chambray work shirt that pretty much hid her physique, but she had the sleeves rolled up, showing sculpted and muscular forearms.

It was like sitting down to lunch with the Justice League of America.

Jennifer reached for her fork and noticed that Marisol's hands were resting on either side of her plate. She stared at Easton, whose head was bowed.

"Go ahead," Jennifer said to him quietly.

"Father, we thank you and ask you to bless this meal and this company," he prayed. "Grant us, please, your wisdom. In Jesus Christ's holy name we ask this."

"Amen," Jennifer said. And she surprised herself in doing so.

"So, what's the intelligence community's interest in us?" Easton said to Marisol.

"In you?" Marisol shook her head. "No interest. Or rather, no interest beyond the fact that you have attracted the attention of Umberto Alcázar."

"Who?" Jennifer frowned at Easton. If he had so much as a glimmer of what this woman was talking about, he hid it well.

"This guy." Marisol pulled a Sony Clié out of her messenger bag, tapped its screen with the stylus, and then handed the PDA over.

Jennifer studied the playing-card-sized screen with its image of a Hispanic man in his midforties—close-trimmed black beard, hooded brown eyes, thick eyebrows, stern slabs of cheeks. He didn't look like a person who laughed a lot. She passed the silver PDA on to Easton. "And he is ...?"

"The Cuban sub-minister of Information," Marisol said to them both. "What Americans would call a 'deputy director.'"

"Sub-minister of Information," Easton mused. "Are you telling me that this whole thing has an assistant librarian at the center of it?"

"He wasn't always in the information ministry," Marisol said. "Up until five years ago, he was a full colonel in the Cuban army attached to the Ministry of Intelligence. He wasn't shooting up through the ranks, and he never quite got adopted by the Castro family the way so many young Cuban officers do. Alcázar's father was a young lawyer who opposed Batista and wanted change—exactly like Fidel, in that respect. But unlike Fidel, he didn't support the move to communism; most people forget that, until he needed help from Russia, Castro was anti-Communist. So *El Barba*—Fidel—felt he owed Alcázar's family something, but because they didn't support him when he started entertaining overtures from Russia, he didn't feel that he owed them much. Still, Alcázar was doing okay, you know? People in the know thought he was headed for brigadier."

Easton nodded.

"And then," Marisol continued, "five years ago, he resigned his commission and took the job in the Ministry of Information. That raised a red flag with our analysts. This sort of change usually indicates somebody has fallen out of favor, and we watch carefully, looking for people who might want to switch sides." Jennifer noticed that Marisol did not say who "we" was. "But when we asked questions in the right places, we learned that it was Alcázar who had precipitated the change."

"Hard to build a power base in the Ministry of Information," Easton said.

"Our thoughts exactly," Marisol agreed. "True, when he joined, the ministry was running full-tilt, preparing for the fiftieth anniversary of the revolution. The government had really pumped the budget up, setting aside the funds to document the old days—their version at least—while the last living witnesses were still available. We thought that maybe Alcázar moved in so he could siphon some of that budget off. It'd be easy to do, because the chief information minister is an absolute wuss."

Jennifer blinked; it wasn't the kind of word she'd expected this sober, cosmopolitan woman to use.

"The man always defers to Alcázar," Marisol continued. "He lets him speak for the ministry, so it's easy to assume that Alcázar uses him, more or less, as a doormat. But our mole in the ministry said Alcázar wasn't pocketing the ministry's funds; or at least he wasn't pocketing any more than the typical Cuban bureaucrat."

"All right." Jennifer was getting impatient. She wanted to get to the part where she learned why people followed her into airports and showed up in her room in the middle of the night. "We know what he wasn't doing. Do we know what he *was* doing?"

Marisol tried a forkful of her pasta. Then she tried a second taste and a third, chewing slowly as she nodded. The message was unmistakable to Jennifer: *I'll answer your question, but I'll do it on my terms—I don't answer to you.*

Jennifer stifled a sigh and waited. She wasn't about to push the issue with this woman. Frankly, this Marisol person, with her gun and her spooky mannerisms, scared her a little bit.

More than a little bit.

Marisol took a sip of water. "Alcázar did justice to the revolution. He oversaw the production of a documentary film. He produced a picture book, a children's book, billboards, press releases, a series of radio spots. He even hired a Colombian ghostwriter to write a history, and then put his own name on it. Raul Castro personally gave Alcázar the medal for that one."

Marisol lifted her glass again, and the ice clinked as she took another sip. "But Alcázar didn't stop with the revolution," she said, setting her glass down. "He commissioned research all the way back to the nineteenth century and beyond. It looked like he was just being scrupulous about his job, but after about eight months, a pattern emerged. He was looking for abandoned property, clues to people who'd cached money or valuables during various regime changes and then never lived to claim it. That sort of thing. And then he'd find it and seize it. About ten percent of what he found, he turned over to the government. Job security, I suppose. But the lion's share never saw the official light of day."

"Lining his own pocket?" Easton asked.

"Surprisingly, no." Marisol described a tiny loop in the air with her fork as she said this. "At least, nothing that his lifestyle would suggest. But it looks as if that ghostwriter from Colombia always brought an entourage with him when he visited from Cartageña. And we have documentation from Alcázar's intelligence days." She paused, her gaze flicking over both their faces for an instant before continuing. "He was a frequent visitor to Al Qaida and Hamas training camps in Libya."

There was no overt change in Easton, but Jennifer sensed that his whole body stiffened. "So your boy, here . . . ," Easton still held the PDA, ". . . wants to become *el jefé* in Cuba after the Castros bite the dust. Is that it?"

Marisol acknowledged this with a bow—half a nod. "But so do about a hundred others," she said. "The power will go to whoever has the deepest pockets—whoever has the money to buy off Cuba's army, its navy. By our estimate, Alcázar has millions of dollars set aside to fund his coup. But Cuba is a big island, with lots of officers in its armed services. It's not going to take millions. He's going to need billions. And funding a coup is a cash-on-the-barrelhead proposition. People want money to run with, just in case things don't work out."

Uh-oh. Jennifer could sense where this was going and held her breath, hoping Easton would keep quiet about the gold ship.

"So," Easton asked Marisol. "How did Alcázar find out about the *Halcyon*?"

Jennifer fought to keep from falling off her chair. "Beck!" she tried to whisper, but people three tables away turned to look.

"He pieced it together, from what our source tells us," Marisol said, pointedly ignoring Jennifer's discomfort. "There was a harbormaster's report of one of his men being found tied up in a ship's boat in the harbor. That same day, the *Halcyon* was reported hijacked, with two contradictory descriptions of its cargo. The captain referred to it as 'pig iron,' and its supercargo referred to it as 'farm implements.' The next night, a drunk American was arrested for fighting in a cantina in Havana."

Habana was the way she pronounced the word. Jennifer tried again to square it with Easton's "MI-6" comment.

"When the police picked him up," Marisol continued, "they reported that he was bellowing, '*¿Donde es me oro?*'—pidgin Spanish at best, but clearly, 'Where is my gold?' And on the same date, a harbor-front hotel keeper reported that an *americano* named Augustus Baxter owed him a fortnight's rent for two rooms and had vanished in the middle of the night without paying."

Jennifer shook her head. "And on the strength of that," she asked, "this Alka-Seltzer guy has people chasing us?"

Marisol regarded her coolly. "On the strength of such things," she said, "Umberto Alcázar has more than three hundred researchers, pursuing almost an equal number of possible treasures, all over the world. He even has people in the marine archives in Spain, checking stories of sixteenth-century galleons lost en route from Cuba. And why should he not? After all, it's the government's money that he's spending, not his own."

"But—"

"But you drew attention to yourself when you left the nest and went to Florida," Marisol said. "You drew it from those of us tasked to watch Alcázar's *investigadores* for signs of anything unusual, and you drew it from his own people who are tasked to do the same thing. And then, when you jumped your flight and went to the Bahamas?" Marisol shook her head.

"That man in our cottage on Cat Island," Jennifer whispered. "One of yours?"

Marisol shook her head again. "Not ours and not Alcázar's," she said. "There is a considerable Cuban expatriate community in south Florida. Many had lands and property seized by *El Barba*. Many others lost loved ones by his hand. When power shifts, as eventually it must, they have a very short list of who they would like to see in control of Cuba. She paused for emphasis. "Umberto Alcázar is not on that list."

Marisol stabbed another bite of pasta and took a sip of water. "This man is deadly serious," she said, reaching for the PDA. She ticked on the screen with her fingernail and turned it around to show Easton and Jennifer the photos of two men.

"It's the guys from the airport," Jennifer said. She accepted the PDA from Marisol and looked closer. "Their eyes are closed."

Easton adjusted the PDA so he could see the screen. "Mortuary photos."

Jennifer gulped a short breath. The traffic hummed by on Washtenaw Avenue, not a hundred feet outside the restaurant windows, as if it were an ordinary day. "He ..." she took another breath, "... he killed them?"

"They were pulled out of Lake St. Clair this morning," Marisol said. "They are former U.S. Army, with some training in covert action. Working for Alcázar, like your attorney." She gave Jennifer a pointed look. "And at the end of their usefulness—again like your attorney."

"And Alcázar is in Michigan?" Jennifer asked.

Marisol nodded.

"Where?"

Marisol shook her head. "We don't know. But what we do know is that he's killing anyone who knows about this ship. That's why I broke cover."

"That's it," Easton said, setting his napkin at the side of his plate. "We're giving up the location of that gold today."

Marisol looked up, eyes wide. "Then you know where it is?"

"Beck ..." Jennifer stared at him. "No ..."

But Easton's jaw was set in a stubborn line. "It's time to let the air out of this," he said. "Go public with what we know. Scuttle Alcázar's plans—make him give it up."

"Beck ..." Jennifer squeezed his arm. "We can't."

"Actually, she's right," Marisol said. "You can't just announce to the media that there is a fortune in gold and it can be found at ..."

Her voice trailed off, and Easton, to Jennifer's relief, didn't fill in the blank she'd left.

"If you tell that to the press without substantiation, they either won't pay attention, or they'll buzz about it for a week and then drop it," Marisol pointed out. "And I know what you're thinking, but you can't tell the authorities either—not even someone you trust. Our people believe Alcázar has people on the payroll in the American agencies—possibly every American agency. You tell someone you trust, and it eventually leaks back to him. And you can't just sit on the information, because the man is killing everyone who knows about it."

"So we'll tell your people."

Marisol shook her head. "If you guessed who I work for, then you know about Echelon."

Jennifer batted her eyes in confusion and turned to Easton.

"It's an intelligence consortium—the US, the UK, Canada, Australia, and New Zealand," he explained. "The one I was telling you about. They share information."

"That's right," Marisol said. "And that community is far too chummy. Word can leak back. I'm not even going to report to my superiors what we've discussed here today until that gold is secured and out of Alcázar's grasp."

"Then that only leaves one thing left that we can do," Easton said, and Marisol nodded.

"What?" Jennifer looked back and forth at the two of them.

"What you've wanted all along," Easton said, frowning. "Much as I hate to say it, we have to go after this gold."

CHAPTER THIRTY-ONE

GRINDSTONE CITY, MICHIGAN

The Grindstone City marina looked more like a canal than a harbor—a long, straight avenue of water that led out under the pale predawn sky to the broad, flat, steely gray expanse of Lake Huron.

For the tenth time since rising, Jennifer yawned and stretched. She'd felt positively heroic arising when she did, at three in the morning, but the feeling had gone away when they'd gotten to the marina and she'd found the place buzzing with activity. All up and down the concrete seawalls, people—men, mostly—were handing tackle boxes, rods, coolers, and ice chests down to others in boats of all sizes and shapes.

"Weather Service is calling for squalls this afternoon," Easton had told her earlier. "Day like this, you get out and back early, or you stay on the beach."

She had to hand it to Easton and Marisol—once they decided on a plan, they hadn't fooled around. The day before, at the restaurant, Easton had immediately excused himself from the table, saying that he had to make a couple of phone calls.

The women had watched him head to the pay phones near the restrooms. "The first call will be to vet me—to check me out," Marisol said to Jennifer. "To see if I'm ... legit. I'm not sure what the second call is for."

That mystery was cleared up when Easton returned to the table. "Okay. We've got a boat. Ready to roll?"

After they left the restaurant, the rest of the afternoon flew by in a blur.

"All my dive gear's back in the plane," Easton said. "And we still have to assume it's hot. I can pull another set together, but it's going to take a few hours. It's not the type of thing you just run in and pick up; I might have to hit several shops. We'd better split up and then regroup up north."

"Up north" turned out to be the Thomas Edison Inn in Port Huron, Michigan, where Marisol registered for a pair of adjoining rooms after stopping at a Target to buy a change of clothes for Jennifer and Easton, and some toiletries. Once inside the hotel, Marisol had insisted that they stay inside—Jennifer watched movies on HBO, while Marisol sat a few feet back from the window and gazed stonily out at huge Great Lakes freighters plowing up the St. Clair River, under the twin-spanned Bluewater Bridge, and into the wave-swept waters of Lake Huron.

They stayed that way, quiet, for the better part of an hour. Then Marisol, without turning, had asked, "So, how long have you and Easton been together?"

"Together?"

Marisol had turned away from the window, hand on her chin. "You know what I mean."

"Oh." Jennifer's face had grown warm. "We're not."

"Really?" Marisol had kept her hand on her chin. "Then how do you know what size underwear he wears?"

Jennifer's face had turned even hotter.

"Oh. Uh—Beck was wearing jeans the other day when I walked behind him . . . while we were going out to the plane."

"Yes?"

"And his waist size . . ." Jennifer wondered just how red her face was getting. ". . . it was, uh, printed on the belt patch. You know? On the back of his jeans?"

"Uh-huh." Marisol had turned back to the window.

And ever since then, Marisol had acted even more distant than before.

Was it jealousy? Rubbing her arms in the early-morning chill, Jennifer watched the dark-haired spy as she carried a double-set of scuba tanks down to the boat. Jennifer had tried to do that, but discovered she couldn't even lift the tanks, let alone carry them. She watched how Marisol spoke to Easton: direct, brief, all business.

And that, Jennifer decided, was what it was all about; Marisol reeked of professionalism. She probably didn't care for personal relationships among members of her team. And like it or not, that was what they had become: a team.

Jennifer shook a bag of ice into a cooler, dropped in several bottles of Gatorade and a dozen bottles of water, poured another bag of ice in on top of the drinks, and then closed the lid of the cooler. It wasn't much, but it was something that she could do.

Straightening, she looked out at the marina. Boats were moored along the sides of the channel, a few with their engines grumbling, exhaust bubbling up from their sterns. In some of the others, people were lifting radio antennas and clamping them into place, or loosening the lines that ran up to the marina bollards. Even the herring gulls were stirring now, circling overhead in the predawn gloom.

Across the narrow channel and two slips down, Umberto Alcázar busied himself with one of a pair of electric downriggers as he scrutinized the *americana* and her companions.

He was close—so close that, even in this light, he could see that this one's eyes were a particularly vivid shade of blue. Like the sea on a sunny day, next to his native land. And she had an innocent sort of attractiveness to her.

Not like the *latina* who had joined the two lovebirds. That one was beautiful in a way that a man could admire, beautiful in a voluptuous sort of way, with full, red lips and eyes that seemed to smolder. But she was also dangerous; Alcázar could tell that at a glance: the way she carried herself, that confident set to her chin. When the time came—and the time would come soon—he would have to dispose of her quickly. Her and the *americano* as well. But this blonde, this girl; of course, she would have to die as well. But her, he would not kill so quickly. Not right away.

Alcázar worked the switch on the downrigger, lowering a finned lead weight into the dark water of the marina and then lifting it back up again. He found it fascinating that the *norteamericanos* fished for their lake trout and king salmon with equipment that was almost identical to what his uncle and he had used to troll for billfish in the waters of the Gulf Stream. True, his uncle's boat had been wood, while this one that he had rented the evening before was fiberglass, like the bathtub in a cheap American hotel. His uncle's boat had also been powered by a smoky diesel engine, while this one had the Yamaha twin outboards, two hundred fifty horsepower apiece, and that had been his principal reason for renting this boat, as it was sure to be faster than anything Easton would put on the water. And the downriggers on his uncle's boat had been equipped with hand cranks to lower the weights, which in turn kept the fishing line at trolling depth. But this plastic toy had switches. How very American to put motors on them; a real man would crank the downriggers by hand.

Alcázar glanced across the water at the *americana* just as she looked his way, and their eyes met. She raised her hand and waved. Smiling broadly, he waved back and then pretended to adjust the downrigger.

Certainly the *mujer sombria* had shown his pictures to this one. And certainly, if he still looked even remotely as he had in those pictures, she would have recognized him. But the previous afternoon, while the women had done their shopping at that place called the Target—why did Americans call their businesses such very strange names?—he had walked into a *pharmacia* and obtained everything he needed to alter his appearance.

He pushed his hand back through his hair, once jet-black and as long as a military man could have worn it, and now close-cropped and golden blonde. It had disgusted him that these Yankee stores had a whole shelf of products with which a man could bleach his hair blonde. He could possibly understand a man wishing to blacken the gray as he aged, it was only natural—to a point, and then it was not. But to brassen one's hair like a homosexual? It was unthinkable, which was precisely why he had done it.

In addition, he had purchased an electric clipper with which he had shortened his newly blonde hair, and a razor, which he had used to scrape away all residual stubble after he had removed his beard with the clipper.

The eighteen-foot boat had come with flotation vests of the type one might use for water skiing, and Alcázar was wearing one of these under his poplin windbreaker. It made him appear a good thirty pounds heavier: a fat American, ready for a day's fishing on his little overpowered, plastic boat.

To complete the disguise he would have liked to have changed his eye color, as well, but he had not had the time to procure the contacts that would do that. So for now, he just squinted. Later, when the sun came up, he had dark glasses that he could wear.

It was a terrible risk to be so near to his quarry and in plain sight. Every bit of his fieldcraft training told him that. But audacious goals called for outrageous strategies.

Fidel had said that. At least someone had told Alcázar that he had. And he probably had. Four, five, even six hours was not uncommon for one of *El Barba's* speeches. And the man had been giving them ever since the revolution. After more than half a century of such marathon oration, the man had probably said everything at least once.

The *americano* came over to the little blonde one and handed her a duffel bag. Watching furtively, Alcázar bent over a tackle box and pretended to select fishing lures.

"A wetsuit?" Standing on the dock, Jennifer regarded the duffel bag dubiously. "Uh-uh! This girl's staying on the boat." It wasn't that she was afraid of the water. But *cold* water? She didn't even like it when the water heater started running out during a shower.

Easton laughed. "This is for the boat," he said. "If you were diving with me, I'd be giving you a dry suit. In some places, the bottom of Lake Huron never rises above thirty-six degrees Fahrenheit, year-round. This time of year, the surface temperature will be much warmer, probably well above sixty degrees. But it's an open boat. You'll get soaked on the way out. This'll keep you from becoming miserable."

Jennifer took the duffel bag and looked down in the boat, where Marisol was pulling her own wetsuit on over a one-piece bathing suit. The woman had muscle definition that would make Wonder Woman look like the Pillsbury Doughboy. As Jennifer watched, Easton stepped down into the open-decked boat and handed Marisol an orange vinyl dry bag. After a brief exchange between the two, Marisol reached into the boat's helm console, took out her handgun, and dropped it into the bag. She rolled the top shut and snapped the locking buckle closed.

Now Easton, in swim trunks and a T-shirt, was pulling on what looked like a thin, black nylon snowmobile suit. He put on nylon boots after that, and then he donned what he called a "dry suit," a rubberized canvas garment that looked sufficient for a space-walk. It had an attached rubber hood that he'd left down, around his neck, for the time being, but he turned and flexed his arms, à la the Incredible Hulk, and Marisol drew a long zipper shut across his shoulders.

He glanced toward Jennifer who had just finishing donning her own wetsuit. "Um, the legs of the wetsuit should go outside the booties," he said. "Your feet will stay drier that way."

"Oh. Okay." Jennifer rearranged the wetsuit legs and zipped them closed, The suit zipped up the back, but a long nylon-web lanyard made it easy to do that up herself. Her suit and Marisol's were much more form-fitting than Easton's, which looked almost baggy. And wearing the suit made Jennifer feel like she was ready-ing for battle. She grinned at the thought.

"You ready?" Easton asked.

She nodded and stepped over onto the transom of the power-boat. Easton took her hand as she stepped down, and she wondered when she would finally stop feeling that electric surge every time he touched her.

Never, she hoped.

"There's a rubber bulb on the fuel line, there on the right side," he said from the center console. "Squeeze it until you feel resistance, okay?"

Jennifer did as he'd said, and then she watched as Easton moved the throttle lever to neutral and turned the key for the motor. The single Mercury outboard grumbled to life and then burbled smoothly as gray exhaust bubbled up from the water behind the boat.

"Want to cast us off?" Easton asked, and the two women untied the lines, fore and aft. Easton inched the throttle forward, and the boat began to glide down the marina channel toward the break-water and the lake.

Pretending to study a nautical chart of lower Lake Huron, Alcázar watched as the twenty-two-foot Trojan American center-console boat moved slowly down the channel, raising no wake. It looked like a good boat for open water—a high prow, deep V-hull, and a workmanlike helm. There was one seat ahead of the console, and one behind it, and other than that, the deck was open. Neither Easton nor the *americana* nor the *latina* were sitting, which meant that they would be making good time once they cleared the break-water. Still, Alcázar let the other boat get almost to the end of the channel before he started his own engines.

Two other boats made way as he cast off his lines, and that was good. The eastern horizon was red with the coming sunrise, and boats would be departing the marina nonstop for the next twenty minutes. His would be one of several.

Alcázar kept his engines at idling, barely crawling along, acting the part of the good citizen. He did not wish to raise a wake and possibly invite a visit from any lurking law-enforcement vessels. If anyone stopped him, he would be hard-pressed to explain what was sitting in the deck of his boat, behind him.

It was an old-fashioned galvanized washtub, an item that he had had to search for in an age of plastics. He had finally located one at a feed store. Into this, Alcázar had poured half an inch of sand; then he had set a galvanized steel bucket—purchased from the same feed store—into the exact center of the washtub and poured sand around it until it was all the way up to the washtub's rim. Next to this, he had a gallon of gasoline at the ready in a red plastic container.

By itself, the gasoline would be simple to explain: *In case the fishing is good, officer; so I can stay out just a little longer, you see?* But the tub and the bucket and the sand would raise curiosity, and Alcázar did not wish to shoot a law-enforcement official. The Americans were notoriously diligent about tracking down people who did that.

Alcázar rounded the breakwater, and immediately the boat began bobbing and pitching in the rougher water of the lake. He increased the throttle only enough to counter the effects of the breeze, and he scanned the water ahead of him. There was the dive boat, a white wake already rolling behind it. It was headed almost due north, maybe the slightest bit west of north.

Alcázar passed the "No Wake" signs at the marina channel entrance and rolled the throttle all the way forward. Immediately, the bow of the boat pitched up as the two stainless-steel screws bit into the water with the vigor of five hundred horsepower. Ten seconds later, the boat was up on the stepped portion of its hull, drawing a bare ten inches of water and offering little resistance to the might of the two outboards. The wind whistled through Alcázar's newly shortened blonde hair, and he grinned.

At this rate, he would catch the Americans in less than five minutes.

It was like skiing, Jennifer thought. Skiing on hard, moguled snow. It only took her a few seconds to learn to bend her legs slightly and allow them to work as shock absorbers for the rest of her body. The waves on the lake were small—less than a foot from trough to crest—but the boat slammed into them like a stone being skipped across a pond. With the impact of each wave, the loose dive gear on the deck moved back, toward the stern, until it could move no farther.

They hit one particularly high wave, and the handheld marine radio bounced off the console and went clattering down the deck toward the pile. Water sprayed over the side of the boat, splashing the radio, and Jennifer retrieved it quickly, looking around for something to dry it with.

"That's okay," Easton shouted over the rush of the wind. "Radio's waterproof. Waterproof and shock-resistant. We could drop it in the lake, and it'd still work when you took it out. Took me about three radios to figure out that's the way to go."

He grinned, took the radio from her, wedging it into the space between the windshield and the console. Glancing at the GPS readout above the gimbals-mounted compass, he kept his free hand on the throttle, holding it all the way forward.

On the other side of Easton, Marisol was scanning the sky. Looking for aircraft, Jennifer realized. But other than a lone jet contrail, far too high to be following them, the deep blue sky was completely clear.

Suddenly, as if someone had thrown a switch, the red rim of the sun broke the eastern horizon, lighting the boat and the waves with a warm, pink glow. They were moving as fast as the boat could travel, but three fishing boats passed them, and in the third was the blonde-headed man Jennifer had waved to at the marina.

Morning had broken, and it looked as if everyone was racing for the best fishing holes.

Eyes on the rearview mirror mounted on the powerboat's windshield, Alcázar kept the throttles open until the white dive boat was nothing but a tiny dot on the horizon. That was the great thing about following somebody on the water. You didn't have to follow them. There were no alleys, no turns. Once leaving the marina, Easton would have aimed the shallow-draft boat directly at his destination, and kept that heading. So all Alcázar had to do was keep the other boat in sight.

He matched paces with it for twenty minutes, and then the dive boat slowed. That was when Alcázar cut his throttles and went aft to rig his poles. He did everything the way a regular salmon fisherman would do it, because if anybody passed his boat while he was trolling, keeping the Americans just within his sight, he wanted them to see the rods properly bowed at the stern, nothing out of the ordinary. The only unusual thing he did was cut the treble hooks off the spoonlike lures before he cast them into the water.

After all, he only wanted to look like a fisherman. The last thing he needed right now was a stinking fish on the end of a line.

Two hours later, Jennifer was slumped on the seat in front of the center console. Behind her, Easton steered the boat along at a notch or two above idle. A few feet ahead of her, standing in the bow with the tenacity of a Nantucket harpooner, Marisol kept a lookout.

Not that there was that much to look out for. The only aircraft flying overhead were commercial jets bound for Detroit or Toronto. In the last twenty minutes, a high, thin overcast had moved in, hiding even the airliners.

Although three or four fishing boats had dotted the horizon when Easton began running the boat back and forth—"mowing the lawn," he called it—the waves had picked up in the meantime. Now the boat's bow was lifting and dropping three or four feet with each passing wave and only a single fisherman trolled in the distance, his little boat bobbing like a cork on the rising seas.

"What do you mean, we've got to look for it?" Jennifer had asked Easton as he'd programmed the GPS for the first pass. "We've got map coordinates. I read them to you on the phone at the library yesterday. We just go there, right?"

"We are there," Easton said. He pointed to the Lowrance sonar screen, where a gently undulating line indicated the bottom. "But there's nothing down there but clay."

"It's not there?" Jennifer shaded the sonar screen with her hand, and leaned closer, trying to coax the shape of a shipwreck out of it.

"The GPS numbers we use today are expressed in degrees, minutes, and thousandths of a second," Easton said. "With numbers like this, you can lock in any point on earth with an accuracy of ten or fifteen feet. But back in the *Florida*'s day, using star sightings and a chronometer, degree and minute is about as accurate as you're going to get—especially off a pitching deck, sighting between moving clouds."

"So how accurate is that?" Jennifer asked.

"At these latitudes? One-minute accuracy will allow you to locate yourself within a box that's four thousand, four hundred feet by six thousand, six hundred feet."

"Four thousand, four ..." Jennifer silently performed the math while the deck hulaed beneath her feet. "That's more than one square mile of lake bottom."

"That's right. If we had a sidescan sonar, built for wreck-hunting, we could run that in an hour or less. But those are hard to come by, so what we've got is this unit, which is designed for finding fish. It sees a narrower swath of the bottom; it could take us a few days to find this wreck or, if Booth's captain was having a bad day when he shot his star, we may never find it at all. So we'd better get started. Okay?"

"Sure . . ."

So far, the only good thing they'd learned was that no one seemed prone to seasickness. But this tiny victory wasn't enough to ransom the tedium of shuttling slowly back and forth on a rising and pitching sea.

"Half an hour more is about all we're going to be able to do today," Easton said, glancing at the horizon. "Sea's picking up, and we've got more cloud coming in. It's going to get rough."

"He's still out here," Jennifer said, pointing. Out on the lake, now more gray than blue, the distant fishing boat porpoised along.

Easton regarded their distant neighbor through a heavy pair of marine binoculars shielded with thick yellow rubber. "Yeah," he said. "And he's got even less boat than us. More power, but less boat. No sense tempting the laws of physics. And no sense giving the Coast Guard two vessels to rescue, rather than one. We can do one more pass, and then we'd better head back in."

They came about and began the next pass, the freshening breeze meeting them head-on, over the bow.

Jennifer stood when the bumping of the boat striking waves got a little rough on her tailbone. She whipped around at the sound of a shout from Easton.

"Coming about," he said. "We've got something."

"What?" She rushed around the console and peered at the sonar screen. On it, a vaguely rectangular shape was rising from the bottom. Atop the shape were a couple of jagged bumps.

"That's our shipwreck?" Jennifer asked.

Marisol joined them, her eyes on the sonar screen as Easton continued. "It's *a* shipwreck," Easton said. "And it's not charted. Now, as to whether it's the *Florida*, that remains to be seen. Literally thousands of vessels have sunk in Great Lakes waters, but only a few hundred have been located and dived on. This could be the *Florida*, or it could be some grain boat or lumber barge that also ran out of luck. Only one way to find out."

He pushed the throttle forward and leaned the boat around in a big, sweeping oval, running far to the rear of where they'd first made the sonar contact, and lining the dive boat up on the same track.

Throttling back to a crawl, Easton turned to Jennifer. "Take the wheel and keep us on this heading, okay?" Then he said to Marisol, "And you watch the sonar and sing out just as soon as the wreck begins to show up again."

Jennifer concentrated on holding her compass heading. It was harder than it looked with the wind pushing against the boat. She glanced up for just a moment and saw Easton open a small hatch in the nose of the boat. He got out a four-pronged, stainless-steel grappling hook that was about as big around as a basketball. He pulled a big coil of yellow rope after it. After he passed the hook and line under the bow's rail, he stood on the step, hook dangling from his hand.

Jennifer performed a minute correction to their course. Immediately, a big shadow appeared on the sonar screen.

"Now!" Marisol called.

Easton threw the hook in a high arc that trailed the bright yellow polypropylene rope behind it. "Put the engine in neutral," he shouted as the rope paid out of his hands. The rope continued to run for what seemed to be an eternity. Finally it slowed, and Easton tugged gingerly on the rope until it was obvious that he felt resistance. "Back us up, very slowly," he called, and Jennifer inched the boat back for nearly a hundred yards before Easton called out again, "Okay. Cut it."

Jennifer switched the key off, and the engine fell silent, the splashing of water against the hull seeming louder than before. Easton passed the rope through a line-guide on the bow and tied it off to a cleat with a practiced one-handed motion.

"Sheesh." Jennifer shook her head. "How deep is this thing?"

"The wreck's about two hundred feet down," Easton said, and started back to the helm. "But I paid out about four hundred feet on top of that. You want 'scope' on an anchor line—want it running at a good angle. Otherwise, a good wave can come up, put your bow underwater, and next thing you know, you've got two shipwrecks instead of one."

Jennifer fell silent while she thought about that. "So," she said after a moment, "what's next?"

"Next," Easton picked up a weight belt and passed it around his waist. "I go take a look." He looked toward the east, where a wall of cloud was building. "And I'd better be quick. We're going to be racing that front as it is, and weather out of the east is never good up here." He picked up his harness and double-set and balanced the heavy equipment on the edge of the seat. "Here—hold this steady while I put it on, would you?"

From more than one mile away, Umberto Alcázar continued to troll steadily, one hand on his wheel, as he held a small pair of binoculars to his eyes.

The white dive boat had come to a halt; that much was obvious. No wake appeared at its stern, and rather than exhibiting the chopping action of a vessel underway in a rising sea, it was bobbing sinuously: bow up, then bow down; stern up, then stern down.

As Alcázar watched, the *mujer sombria* moved to the bow and raised a staff with two flags: a blue-and-white, V-shaped "Alpha" signal, indicating diving operations in progress; and a red flag with a white diagonal stripe, warning approaching vessels that they had a diver in the water. And there was Easton, standing in the stern with scuba tanks on his back, the little blonde one helping him with his equipment.

Had they found it?

Alcázar thought about that as his boat nodded along on the rolling surface of the lake.

It didn't make a difference, he finally decided. The fact that they were diving indicated that they thought they were close. They were at the limits of their present state of knowledge. They might learn more, but he now knew everything that they knew.

As he watched, Easton sat on the side of the dive boat, setting a regulator in his mouth. He bowed his head and back-rolled off the boat, entering the water in a white, frothy splash.

Alcázar had seen enough. Leaving the wheel for a moment, he slipped a hunting knife from a belt sheath, stepped to the stern, and cut the lines on both trolling rods, causing them to snap upright. He punched the switches on the downriggers, raising the lead weights until they clattered against the stern of the boat. Glancing to make sure that the galvanized washtub and the gasoline container were still within reach, he slid back behind the wheel and pushed the throttle forward, putting the small boat back on the step.

Alcázar had learned all that he needed to know, now, from these people. He had no further need for them.

They could die now.

CHAPTER THIRTY-TWO

The sounds of the surface went away and were replaced by a hollow, muted splash. A thousand shining bubbles danced around Beck Easton. Slowly, they lifted, like a curtain.

He vented a tiny amount of air from the exhaust valve on his left arm and hovered, neutral, in the water. Already, he could feel its coolness on the exposed portions of his face, and on his hands, where water seeped past the cuffs of his neoprene gloves.

Those people who thought that all diving was the same had never dived in the Great Lakes. The difference was not just temperature. It was the color, not blue like the Caribbean, or nearly colorless like the waters in the springs, back in Florida, but green: an opaque, pea green here near the surface, fading to a dim, muddy black deep below. It was the visibility, not the airlike clarity of a Florida spring, or the hundred-plus feet of color that one enjoyed on a Caribbean reef dive, but a shadowed limitation of sight that softened the underside of the dive boat even though he was hovering less than fifteen feet beneath it.

The Lakes weren't always this way. He had made dives in Lake Superior on which he had seen from one end of a hundred-foot shipwreck to another, and he had picked out details on the surface, a hundred and twenty feet above. But the reason he remembered that so vividly was because it had been so very unusual. Take a cup of milk, pour it into an aquarium and view it through green sunglasses. That was what a typical dive in the Great Lakes looked like. And it was what this one looked like.

Arms folded across his chest, Easton finned forward through the green water, passing beneath the bow of the dive boat and swallowing to equalize the pressure on his ears. In a moment, he could make out the yellow anchor line, slanting down through the water and disappearing into the gloom below. He vented a little more air out of his dry suit, oriented himself head-down, and began to glide down, along the rope, slowly falling into the blackness below.

At thirty feet, Easton hit the thermocline, a palpable layer where the temperature dropped a good twenty degrees, the fresh chill shocking to his exposed face. The water around him also became darker as the layering effect of the warmer water, lying atop the cold, acted like a mirror, sending most of the sunlight back to the surface. And the suit was beginning to squeeze now, from the pressure, so he touched the inlet valve on his chest, adding a brief puff of air, and then he unclipped his light from his waist belt and turned it on.

The light was not the high-intensity-discharge variety that Easton customarily used in his cave diving. Those produced a brilliant blue-white light, but they were powered by nickel-metal-hydride batteries that would not yield a full charge until they'd been conditioned by several discharge cycles, and Easton had not had time for that. So he'd purchased an Underwater Kinetics divelight instead, one with a halogen bulb and a lanternlike battery compartment that swallowed eight large Duracell alkaline "D" cells. The yellow-white light it produced was only half as bright as his caving light, but it was perfectly adequate for the more limited visibility of Lakes diving, and the burn time of the alkalines could see him through almost a week's worth of cold-water wreck dives.

The shaft of light poked down through the gloom, the yellow polypropylene anchor line unusually bright in the beam. Passing sixty feet, he added more air to his suit and swallowed again, working his jaw back and forth to get air up his Eustachian tubes and relieve the mounting pressure on his eardrums. There were no fish in this middle water, and the surface had long since faded from sight. When he turned the divelight around and pressed it against his suit to hide its light, everything around him was a deep, dim jade, the angled shadow of the rope the only visual relief in the opaque darkness.

At one hundred fifty feet, he switched off his light and was rewarded with a muted glow from below: the light clay of the lake bottom, reflecting the pittance of daylight that had made it down this far. Ahead of him, a dark form, shadowed and indistinct, loomed out of the twilight.

Seconds later, the dark shape began to resolve into the bowspirit and bow of a sailing ship. Easton turned his light back on and the wood of the vessel, brown and covered with a thin fuzz of moldlike green, reflected a light brighter than anything it had seen in more than a century.

The stainless-steel grapple had caught on a deck rail, the hook nodding and bobbing with the motion of the dive boat, two hundred feet above. Reaching into a pocket on his waist belt, Easton took out a jon-line—a six-foot length of nylon webbing with a loop sewn into each end—and an aluminum carabiner. Clipping the carabiner into the grappling hook's eye, he attached the line to it, passed the line around the deck rail, and then clipped the carabiner to it again. With the anchor line secured, he added enough air to his suit to regain neutral buoyancy and, weightless as an astronaut in space, began finning slowly along the deck rail, examining the vessel.

The foremast had broken off about ten feet above the deck and now lay, like a toppled tree, over the railing, the rigging still holding it to the ship. Skull-like deadheads, used for routing lines, peered back at him from the rail, and the mizzenmast had lifted completely free from the vessel as she sank; Easton could just make it out, lying on the bottom some twenty feet below.

That he was the first diver to visit, or at very least the first to visit in years, was obvious. Silt and algae thickly dusted the deck and rails, punctuated by items from the ship: the shapeless leather of a waterlogged brougham, a signal lantern, its lens clouded and broken.

A two-masted schooner. It was the kind of ship they were look-ing for, and the age was right. Easton swam past the back of the wreck and turned, playing his light on it. But any name painted on the sternboard had disappeared in nearly a century and a half of submersion.

He finned back over the deck, passing above the ship's wheel and a compass in its gimbals, the hemispherical lens clouded over with silt. And just ahead of that, he found what he was looking for: the ship's bell, hanging from a wrought-iron frame rising blackly from the deck.

Easton fanned the bell with his gloved hand, raising a small cloud of silt that hung in the water around him. Slowly, it settled, and the brass bell emerged, blackened with age. Easton held his divelight at an angle to it and was rewarded with letters, simple Roman capitals engraved into the surface of the bell: "F L O R I ..."

Okay. Right ship. He checked his dive computer and his pressure gauge: he'd been down for ten minutes, and still had better than three-quarters of his air left. He'd have to be heading up soon, but there was time to check and see if the cargo had been salvaged.

The *Florida*'s deck cabins and hatch covers had blown off in her sinking, not an unusual occurrence. Swimming forward past an opening where a stair-step ladder ran down to the crew's quar-ters, Easton hovered over a six-foot-by-six-foot opening in the deck and directed his light down into the blackness.

The yellow glow of an eye reflected back at him. It was a bur-bot, one of the deepwater eel-like fish found throughout the Great Lakes, and it was resting atop one of several wooden crates and boxes stacked neatly in the hold.

That got Easton's heart pumping. Wood floats, and wooden boxes, which would trap air for at least several seconds after a sinking, would float even better. For the containers to have stayed where they were as the ship went down? That would mean that they would have to be filled with something heavy. Really heavy, like lead.

Or gold.

Drifting slowly into the cargo hold, Easton lifted the three-foot burbot off the crate-top and set it aside. The lethargic fish, its senses dulled by a lifetime spent at four degrees above freezing, did not struggle at all. It was only after it had been set back down that it began to wriggle, swimming snakelike out of the hold and off into the open water above.

The crate's top was secured tightly with square-headed cut-iron nails. Holding the divelight low and finding a seam, Easton removed a blunt-tipped dive knife from the sheath on his shoulder-strap, and worked the screwdriverlike end of it into the space, lifting and prying.

Slowly, the lid came loose with a low-pitched underwater squeak. He worked the knife all the way around the waterlogged crate top, finally getting it loose enough that he could lift it away and let it drop to the bottom of the hold. Peering through a cloud of silt, he found a layer of burlap that dissolved into dust as he lifted it away.

The visibility went away entirely for the better part of a minute, then it slowly began to clear. The open crate before Easton seemed to fill with the color of a sunrise under the beam of his divelight.

The silt began to settle, and the yellow glow started to resolve into rectangles. He leaned closer and saw row after row of gleaming, shining, unblemished gold bars.

Two hundred feet above and half a mile distant, Alcázar's rented boat was whining across the lake's surface just as quickly as its twin outboards would allow. Steering with one hand, the Cuban kicked the gasoline container nearer and then leaned down and unscrewed the pour-spout to the red plastic container, flipping the yellow nozzle into the white wake behind the boat. Picking up the gas container, he leaned back from the wheel and emptied the gallon and a half of gasoline into the bucket nested in the galvanized washtub. The boat canted and swerved as he worked, but it did not matter: looking out of control was exactly what Alcázar was trying to achieve.

Both women in the other boat were looking his way now. The handsome dark-haired one was pointing at the dive flag and waving her arms, trying to shoo him away.

Bueno. Alcázar jumped up and down, waving both arms over his head, trying his best to look like a man in full panic. He reached into his windbreaker pocket and fished out a full box of farmer's matches.

Relinquishing his hold on the wheel, the Cuban turned, opening the box, and took out a handful of the wooden, strike-anywhere matches. He struck them all at once and hurled the flaming mass at the sloshing, amber bucket of gasoline.

The bars were roughly the same length and width as the one Easton had recovered from Twin Springs, but they were nearly three times as thick, and heavy. Hefting one, Easton had to add three long jets of air to his suit, just to keep from sinking to the bottom of the hold.

He turned it over and examined it in the beam of his divelight. All eight corners were squared; it had not been assayed.

Smart, Easton thought to himself. Booth had melted down the bullion and repoured it. That was the great thing about gold; it melted easily, and, once repoured, no one but a trained metallurgist could tell where it had come from. And a metallurgist wouldn't examine it unless he had a reason.

Easton unzipped his waistbelt pocket and slid the bar inside. He took a deep breath and floated up, out of the hold. Then he came to a hover, kicked forward, and went head-first down the ladder he had passed earlier.

Belowdecks, the crew quarters had not fared nearly as well as the cargo hold. Bunks hung at crazy angles from the bulkheads, and sea chests lay jumbled and overturned. Easton went all the way aft, following a narrow passage until a semi-collapsed cast-iron stove told him that he had found the galley.

Casting the light back and forth, he located a pile of plates and crockery in a far corner, most of them cracked or broken. Hovering above the wooden deck to minimize silt, he sorted through the debris until he found what he was looking for: a saucer.

Hoping that the ship's captain had at least a hint of vanity, Easton turned the saucer over and smiled behind his regulator at what he saw: the name "*Florida*," stenciled into the heavy white china in blue script.

Easton tucked the saucer into his waistbelt pocket as well, not without a twinge of guilt. Removing artifacts from a Great Lakes shipwreck was illegal—a felony, in fact. But Easton was versed on his shipwreck laws. He knew that, in order to claim one—to prevent anyone else from having access to it—he would need an artifact that could be taken into court and symbolically "arrested." An artifact with the ship's name on it was the best possible proof that the wreck had been found. A federal court would require that artifact, and the Underwater Preserve Act was a piece of Michigan state legislation. So, figuring that federal law superseded that of a state, Easton zipped the pocket shut and completed the larceny.

It was as he was emerging from the ladder-well, floating back up to deck level, that he heard it: a distant, high-pitched harmonic whine, growing closer.

Easton knew what it was immediately. It was cavitation noise: the sound of a propeller—no, *propellers*—spinning rapidly through the water far above. A powerboat was in operation on the surface, and it was close, and getting closer.

Placing a hand on the deck to either side of the hatchway, Easton pushed himself up out of the ladder-well and kicked rapidly along the length of the boat, heading for the bow, and the up-line.

◪

"*Muy loco*," Marisol grumbled.

"No joke," Jennifer said. The powerboat coming their way was weaving erratically, its driver in the midst of what appeared to be a major freak-out. But he was definitely coming their way. And that's why they had the flags up; they were supposed to warn approaching vessels to give them a two-hundred-yard berth.

Grumbling incomprehensible Spanish, Marisol stooped, opening an orange dry bag and pulling out a handgun, which she loaded and cocked with a practiced motion of its slide.

"Marisol?" Jennifer's voice sounded shakier than she would have liked. "What's happening?"

"Maybe nothing," Marisol told her without turning. "But stay down, okay?"

Jennifer didn't stay down. She couldn't. The other boat was drawing closer, closer, its driver turning around now.

With a muted "puh-*FUFF* ..." the oncoming boat erupted in flame, a mushroom-cloud of orange that seemed to fill the back of the boat before rolling heavenward. Jennifer heard a shriek, and then realized that it was her.

The roar of the oncoming engines had stopped, and the powerboat was no more than twenty feet away, drifting toward them at a crawl. It was close enough that Jennifer could hear the crackling of flames and feel the heat on her face.

"*Madonna* ...," Marisol muttered, and she set the handgun on the seat in front of the control console. "Stay here," she ordered. And with that, she stepped up onto the transom and leapt, headfirst into the lake.

"Marisol!" Jennifer ran to the far side of the boat. The other woman covered the distance to the approaching vessel in three strokes and reached up high, out of the water, grabbing the powerboat's gunwale. She pulled herself up and pushed down, mantling up onto the boat.

Then there was a loud, sharp crack and Marisol toppled backward into the water. She didn't move.

"Marisol!" Jennifer screamed.

A figure loomed up in the approaching boat. A man, blonde hair ... the guy from the marina. And he had a long-barreled gun in his hand.

It was time to act. And fast. But she couldn't will her limbs to move. She felt like she was in a dream, wanting to scream but unable to make a sound. Terrified but unable to move.

The man leered at her and grinned. He stepped onto the gunwale and sprang, covering the five feet between the boats in one powerful jump, swinging the gun by its barrel as he did so.

The grip hit Jennifer just behind her left ear and the world went gray and tilted. She fell backward and heard, but did not feel, her head striking the base of the console.

When she opened her eyes again, Umberto Alcázar—she knew it had to be him—was punching buttons on the dive boat's touch-sensitive GPS screen, bringing up their position. He reached into his jacket, took out a pen, and wrote for several seconds in a notebook.

Then he turned toward her with that same terrifying grin, and he stooped to pick something up, his back to her. The next sound she heard was a sickening tear of duct tape ... and the man's sing-song humming.

She tried to get up, but he heard her. With a shake of the head and a soft *tsk-tsk*, he lashed out, backhanded, without even looking.

With that, her world went black.

The cavitation noise had grown so loud that it had seemed as if the powerboat were right there, two hundred feet beneath the surface of Lake Huron, bearing down on Beck Easton.

He had known, of course, that it was an illusion. Sound travels twenty-five times more efficiently underwater as it does in air. Things a quarter mile away could sound as if they were happening within arm's reach. Still, Easton had been absolutely certain that the boat was drawing nearer, closer to Jennifer and Marisol.

That had made him hurry. He'd left the jon-line wrapped around the rail and started swimming up the slanted anchor line, wishing that he had gained the surface already.

He'd been passing one hundred feet when the propeller noise had stopped, and that had convinced him to pick up the pace even further. But he slowed when his dive computer began to beep its ascent alarm. Coming out of the water too soon could get him a case of decompression sickness and a trip to a decompression chamber; but coming up from depth too quickly could cause an embolism. That could kill him, and he wouldn't be helping anybody if he was dead.

Then he'd heard a splash–a body hitting the water; he'd heard it often enough, teaching people to dive. And that sickened him.

Father, please, he prayed. *Please. Don't let me be too late.*

Eighty feet.

Sixty.

Forty.

When Easton got to twenty feet, he came to a hover and kicked his way under the dive boat. Rolling over on his back, he looked up.

Sure enough, there were two hulls on the surface above him. And a body on the surface, as well. A woman in a wetsuit. Long hair. Face down.

Marisol.

Every fiber of Easton's being wanted to rush to the surface, to get up there, to come to her assistance.

He knew better than to try. This close to the surface, even with the seas picking up, his exhaust bubbles would be easy to see. Whoever was up there was probably watching them right now, ready, waiting, watching the bubbles.

He hovered for a split second, thinking about that.

Watching the bubbles.

Easton kicked smoothly back to the anchor line, loosening his shoulder straps and unbuckling his waistbelt and chest cinch as he swam. When he got to the line, he wrapped one leg around it, holding himself in place as he took his tanks and harness off, still keeping his primary regulator in his mouth, breathing off that as he worked.

First he wrapped the chest strap of his harness around the anchor line several times, adding air into the harness' buoyancy compensator until it tugged upward and the wrapped webbing gripped the rope like a hand.

Reaching into the waistbelt pocket on his harness, Easton pulled out a zip-strip—a self-cinching nylon wire-tie. He formed it into a loop and passed it around the mouthpiece and diaphragm of his back-up regulator, tightening the strip millimeter by millimeter until the diaphragm was depressed enough to move the demand valve, the thing that caused the regulator to release air.

Air began to trickle from the regulator mouthpiece. Easton tightened the strip further until a steady parade of bubbles was fluttering toward the surface.

Then, leaving his weight belt on, Easton vented air from his dry suit until he felt neutral in the water, took five deep breaths off his primary regulator, and swam away from the decoy he'd just created.

He was well aware of the art of swimming while holding his breath. If he kicked too fast, he'd burn oxygen too rapidly, depleting it before he got to the surface. If he kicked too slowly, the carbon dioxide in his body would cause him to black out. So Easton moved at a normal swimming speed, finning steadily back to where Marisol lay motionless on the surface.

The wound, about a hand's width below her collarbone, was obvious. A thin film of brown blood leached out into the water, spreading slowly. Easton drew closer and saw that, although Marisol's eyes were shut, her mouth moved slightly ... trying to breathe.

She was still alive.

Hovering just two feet beneath the surface, praying that his red dry suit wasn't showing like the proverbial sore thumb, Easton swam to Marisol's feet. Taking one in each hand, he turned her over slowly, trying to avoid any splashing, any noise. As soon as she was face-up, he finned away, trusting the neoprene wetsuit to keep her afloat. It was all he could do for her now. Anything further would endanger both their lives.

Still underwater, he kicked silently back to the dive boat. Whoever was on it was still in the bow, watching the bubbles. That was Easton's hope, at least. But even coming up on the swim step, at the back, was risky. It was like the door of a house, the place where you'd expect visitors to enter. The place to watch.

The more Easton thought about it, the less he liked any approach to the dive boat. Storming a vessel at sea was Marine Corps 101—it was why the Corps had been created in the first place. But sneaking aboard a small boat was always problematic; it was just too easily defended. Marisol had impressed him as a very competent operative, and someone had taken her out.

Someone who was still up there.

But Jennifer was also up there, and Marisol was seriously hurt.

Easton had to move.

And he had to breathe.

So the only thing left was to try climbing in over the side.

And he really had to breathe.

Lungs burning, he swam under the boat, ascended until he was touching the hull, and then finger-crawled his way to the port side, just aft of amidships.

Slowly, gradually, he let his face break the surface, waiting until his chin was above the water before opening his mouth as wide as possible. It was the most silent way to breathe, the way snipers were taught to breathe when the enemy might be just an arm's length away.

Easton exhaled completely, paused, inhaled, and paused again. He did that for thirty seconds, getting the carbon dioxide out of his system, drawing the fresh lake air in as deeply as stealth would allow.

He planned his approach as he breathed. To climb over the side of the boat, he would have to expose part of his body—his hands—before he got so much as a look at his adversary. It went against every bit of training that the Marines had ever given him. It went against every bit of the extensive training that he had received after the Marines, as well. Victory in combat, he'd been taught, was the result of giving yourself every unfair advantage possible. You never gave the enemy a fair fight, and you never, ever went into a situation where the bad guys had the upper hand.

Jennifer changed all that. He had the feeling that her life was measured in seconds now.

If she was still alive.

Easton reached down and slowly undid the quick-release buckles on his fins, and then worked them off his feet left and then right. It would make it harder to get out of the water—he would not be able to kick as he pulled up—but it would be stealthier, and he would be able to move once he got into the boat.

He thought about dropping his weight belt, making him twelve pounds lighter.

He decided against it. The heavy belt might make a noise as he removed it, and he couldn't risk that.

Thunder rumbled hollowly in the distance behind him.

Weather moving in, and there were no decisions left to make. Much as he didn't want to, it was time to move.

He crept one hand up, his left hand, catching just the outside lip of the gunwale at first, working his fingers forward, getting a full grip. He pivoted the left hand until it was solid, and then moved his right, a full grip first time, now that the left hand could help.

He began to pull himself up.

Then his entire left arm shuddered with a sharp, electric jolt of pain. He lost the right handhold immediately, but the left hand stayed put, a seeming impossibility. Easton wanted to let go, wanted to get away from the searing hurt, but he couldn't.

He pulled himself higher, and then he saw why. Sticking up from the back of his gloved left hand was a nine-inch hunting knife, pinning him to the thick, laid fiberglass of the gunwale.

He pulled himself higher still, and a face emerged on the other side of the gunwale. The hair was wrong, the beard gone, but the nose and the set of the forehead was right, as were the dark, somber eyes.

"Alcázar," Easton mumbled in his pain.

"Easton," the Cuban replied. He said it very matter-of-factly, the way a worker might greet a colleague, first thing in the morning. Then he brought up the gun, the .22-caliber Colt Woodsman, and aimed the muzzle right between the American's eyes.

"*Adios*," the Cuban said.

Easton felt no fear. For years, now, he'd wondered how he would feel at a moment like this, at a threshold where philosophy gave way to reality.

How was it the Bible put it? *To be absent in the body is to be present with the Lord.*

That was it. And here, as he watched the tendons move on the back of Umberto Alcázar's hand, his finger tightening on the trigger, Beck Easton knew where he was headed, knew it with full certainty, and that knowledge squelched all fear.

Regret? Of course, he felt regret. Marisol was dying in the water, just a few feet away. And then there was Jennifer—if she was still alive. He hoped she was. But he was powerless to help either one. He was milliseconds away from being powerless to help them for all eternity.

"*Save them, Father*," Easton whispered.

A gunshot rang out.

CHAPTER THIRTY-THREE

It was loud. Way too loud.

That was Easton' first thought. The .22 was a small caliber, the smallest common firearms round in the Western world. It had a report like a firecracker. But what he'd just heard had sounded more like a small stick of dynamite.

And how had he heard it, anyhow? They'd had a saying in the Corps, "You never hear the one that gets you."

Could that be wrong? Could the brain somehow keep running, keep sensing for a moment, even with a quarter-inch hole bored through it?

Almost as if in answer to Easton's question, Umberto Alcázar rolled his eyes heavenward and slumped heavily to the deck.

There, behind him, was Jennifer Cassidy, collapsed in a wet-suited heap against the far side of the boat. Her face was ashen, her eyes wide and petrified. And in her trembling hands was Marisol's Beretta, a thin, gray wisp of smoke curling from its nine-millimeter muzzle.

As Easton watched, the gun roared again, and a bullet snapped past his head, just a fraction of an inch away from his neoprene-hooded left ear.

Put the gun down! That's what he wanted to yell, but one look at Jennifer's face told him that she was still a good two minutes away from being able to do anything like that.

"Okay," he told her gently, instead. "If you don't want it to do that anymore, there's a safety lever just above your thumb. Move it down. Can you do that, please?"

"Huh?" Jennifer whispered groggily. She craned her head, staring at the gun as if it was being gripped by someone else.

"The lever," Easton repeated. "That one. Good. Move it down."

Using her left hand, Jennifer flipped the lever down and safed the weapon.

"Good girl," Easton told her. He pulled himself higher on the gunwale and, holding on with his upper arm, teeth gritted, he pulled the hunting knife free, dropping it into the lake water beneath him.

Thick, red blood welled out of the hole in his neoprene glove, and his hand felt as if invisible anvils were being dropped on it, one right after the other. But when he made a fist, the fingers all curled and then straightened back out again, and he silently thanked his God for that.

Still holding himself up, out of the water, he looked back to Jennifer, crumpled beneath the far transom. "Are you okay?"

She nodded, color returning to her face, the gun still pointed in his general direction. Thunder rumbled again; much, much closer this time.

"Okay," Easton said. "You keep an eye on Junior, here. I've got to go help Marisol. You sure you're okay?"

"I'm ... I'm good," she mumbled.

"All right." Easton slipped back into the cold, gray lake water.

Lying cheek-down on the grit-surfaced deck, water sloshing in his face as the boat rocked and pitched, Umberto Alcázar fluttered his eyelids and fought to roll his eyes back into focus.

Gingerly, he tried to move his left arm. It flared with pain as he did so, and his left shoulder felt like a bag of broken china.

So ... the little *americana* had shot him. Extraordinary. He would not have picked her out as one who could pull the trigger. But it must have been her; who else could it possibly have been?

Absolutely extraordinary.

More cold water splashed against his face as the deck rolled beneath him. It was by no means refreshing, but it was bringing him around.

He remained motionless: listening, sensing. The boat was rocking, but it was not underway. And there was no conversation, meaning that there was no more than a single person aboard with him. The man, Easton, would have turned him over by now, checked him for breathing. Since that had not happened, and the *mujer latina* was in the water, that meant that Easton was in the water again, playing the hero.

The only one who could be left on the boat was the little one, the blonde *americana*. While Alcázar was certain she was the one who shot him, he was equally certain that if either of the others fired the gun, he would be dead. So, if he had to take his chances with any of them, the little *americana* would be the one. She could shoot to save a life, but he doubted she could do it again, in cold blood.

Once Umberto Alcázar made his decision, he did not demur. Taking a deep breath and holding it against the pain, he rolled onto his stomach and pushed himself up on his one good arm.

"Freeze!"

Up on one hand and two knees, Alcázar shook his head. He straightened up, kneeling.

"I said freeze!"

Alcázar got onto one foot, like a man genuflecting, and reached for his pistol.

"FREEZE!"

Alcázar stopped and looked up. "So who do you think you are, now, miss? Clint Eastwood?"

"I'm not kidding." The blonde aimed the gun in a meandering figure eight—his nose, the sky, his right shoulder, the boat, the sky again. "I'll shoot you."

Alcázar got both feet under himself. "You already have." He took a step nearer. Water sloshed at the back of the boat. For a moment, blue-white light washed across the sky; three seconds later, a huge rumble of thunder followed.

"One step more," the *americana* said, "and I swear ..."

He took another step.

The young woman's hand tightened on the gun. She squeezed the trigger.

Silence.

"Señorita," Alcázar smiled. "You are a woman of your word. I wish I had time to appreciate you."

And with that, he took her feet out from under her with a quick sweep of his right foot. She tumbled to the deck, and the gun went clattering to the stern. The thunder rolled again.

Alcázar stooped, retrieved his Colt Woodsman, and put a foot up on the gunwale. His own boat was a good four feet away, the gasoline blaze having burned itself out in its fireproof sand-and-steel nest. Gritting his teeth, he leapt across the gap and tumbled onto the deck of the fishing boat, striking his injured shoulder.

Swaying in pain, he pulled himself behind the wheel, shoved the throttle to neutral, and turned the key. Both engines roared to life.

Still gritting his teeth, he gave the throttle a push. His bow glanced off the dive boat and then jumped to the left, aimed at the open lake. In seconds, the boat was up, on the step, and racing away, leaving the crazy *americana* and her companions where they were, under the approaching storm.

Easton was swimming on his back with Marisol held tightly against his chest. He had his arm around her, his hand pressed against her wound. To keep her head out of the water, he was carrying her high, which pushed his head under as he swam. He was kicking without his fins. That made for slow going, and he pushed down with his wounded hand every five kicks, lifting his head so he could breathe.

The lake water, so efficient a conductor of underwater sound, was equally effective at blocking out noise above the surface. And his thick neoprene hood stopped sound nearly as well as it blocked cold.

So his first clue that something else had gone wrong was when the fishing boat's engine roared, and he got hit by the wash from its props.

He kicked faster. In seconds, his outreached hand was touching metal—the prop of their boat.

"Jen?"

She was there in moments, peering down at him, face red with anger, Marisol's gun in her hand. "It didn't work," she said, waving the Beretta. "I tried to shoot, and it didn't work!"

Easton squinted behind his dive mask. "You have it on 'safe.'"

Jennifer stared at the gun, then back at him. "You told me to put it on 'safe.'"

Easton nodded. "I did. I'm sorry." The wind whipped the waves, rocking the dive boat and threatening to push him away. He tightened his grip around Marisol. "Jen, I need you to come around to the side. Take Marisol while I climb aboard."

The cloud dark sky above her went bright with lightning as Jennifer leaned over the gunwale near the stern, where it was lowest. Easton boosted Marisol, and Jennifer grabbed her under the arms.

"There," Easton said. "Just hold her for a second." He climbed up the swim-step at the back of the boat.

"Is she . . . ?"

"She's alive. But she needs help."

"That guy—he got away," Jennifer said when he reached the top. "He knocked me down, and I dropped the gun. Then he just took his gun and left."

As soon as he was next to Jennifer, Easton leaned over the side. Together, they lifted Marisol from the water. Jennifer held her in a sitting position on the gunwale, and Easton squatted down beside her. Marisol moaned. As if in answer, the heavens thundered.

"Wait," Easton said. He turned and looked at Jennifer, the dive mask still on his face. "Alcázar had his gun? And he didn't shoot?"

Jennifer nodded, her confusion showing on her face. "And when I heard him tearing the duct tape off," she said, "he didn't use it to tie me up."

Easton's pulse quickened. Lightning flashed again, and thunder followed quickly this time.

"Hold Marisol," Easton told Jennifer. He turned to the boat's console. The key was still in the ignition, a plastic-coated orange float dangling from it. Shoving the dive mask down around his neck, he bent low, searching the side of the boat.

He straightened for a moment and glanced toward Jennifer. She shifted her arms to hold Marisol more securely and watched him, her eyes wide with worry.

"What is it?"

"He wasn't going to tie you up," Easton replied, stooping as he searched under the lip of the gunwale on the port side.

"Huh?"

"The tape," Easton said, changing to the starboard side, looking and feeling. "It wasn't to tie you up with. Alcázar wouldn't go off and leave us alive unless he knew that we weren't going to stay that way for long. This is a fiberglass boat—no metal to hold a magnet. That tape was to hold a limpet charge."

"A limpet what?" Her voice was a barely audible shaky croak.

"Explosives . . . a bomb," Easton said. At almost the same instant he said the words, he found it: a black metal box atop a tan, doughy block of Semtex, the whole thing taped under the rail mount on the starboard side, right where the saddle-style fuel tank rose into the gunwale. He bent and took a closer look.

There were three light-emitting diodes on the box—a red, a yellow, and a green. The red was lit, and, as Easton reached for the charge, the red lamp went out and the yellow one began to blink: one flash, two, three . . .

Easton turned and ran across the rocking deck, launching himself halfway across. He hit Jennifer in the back with a flying block that would have made his high-school football coach proud.

All three went over the side. In the millisecond before they hit the water, the shock wave hit, sending them skipping, like stones.

Behind them, the dive boat erupted in a fireball, bits of fiberglass streaking to the heavens, the sound of the explosion answered by the thunder in the clouds.

CHAPTER THIRTY-FOUR

Easton was the first one to come around. He hadn't been unconscious long. Flames still licked the water just a few feet away, the last of the dive boat's gasoline dancing in a shimmering orange sheet that sent black smoke rising into the clouds.

The waves had picked up, big Great Lakes rollers that lifted the three of them five feet with each passing. The wind was howling now, lopping off the tip of each gray wave in a spray of white froth. And lightning played like some celestial galvanic experiment, laces of blue-white flashing and then vanishing. The thunder was nearly continuous.

He held the women as he treaded water, Jennifer in his wounded left arm, Marisol in his right. He knew Jennifer was going to be okay when he heard her sniffling and weeping.

"Hey." Easton squeezed her as tightly as his knife-torn left hand would allow. "It's all right. We're fine."

"No, we're not!" The force of her response was surprising. "The boat's gone, and we're out in this, this storm, and you're hurt, and Marisol's hurt, and—" She stopped, obviously struggling to collect herself, as they dropped to a trough between waves.

"I'm sorry," she shouted over the thunder. "How's Marisol?"

Easton loosened his grip so Jennifer could turn. The three floated in a triangle, facing each other. Marisol's head lolled at an angle, her eyes closed. A small pink froth fluttered on her lips.

"Oh, God," Jennifer breathed.

"Lung's collapsed," Easton said as a wave lifted them and then dropped them again.

"Will she die?"

Easton shook his head. "She'll need surgery," he said. "Close things up, re-inflate that lung—if we get her to a hospital, she'll be walking around by Friday."

Rain began to fall; huge, cold drops that pocked the waves around them.

"I'm so sorry," Jennifer said. "I'm sorry I dragged us out here, got you into this."

"Hey, nobody held a gun to my head. Well, you did, but that wasn't until after we were already out here."

This got a smile, but only for a moment. "The gold's down there?" she asked.

"Yeah. Looks like all of it."

She hung her head. "Guess I got what I wanted," she muttered. The clouds above them opened and rain fell in sheets. Jennifer looked up. "Beck," she said, almost shouting to be heard above the noise of the downpour. "You . . . you need to pray."

"Okay," he gave her another squeeze. "Let's pray."

Rain running down her face, Jennifer floated, tight-lipped and silent. She shook her head.

"Not us," she said. "Just you. God won't listen to me."

Thunder sounded, so loud that it shook them.

"He'll listen," Easton shouted over the noise. "He loves you."

Jennifer turned away. "No," she yelled. "I'm too . . . messed up. Like you said . . . God's never been . . . my Number One. Why would he listen now?"

Easton held her until she turned his way.

"Grace, Jen," he shouted. "We don't deserve it; he gives it any-how. If God didn't listen? . . . To sinners? Then how would he hear us when . . ." A wave crashed and spun them around. ". . . When we ask him to forgive?"

Jennifer shook her head.

"Just pray," she pleaded. "Would you please just pray?"

"Father God," Easton shouted into the wind. "We need—again—your grace. We love you. We know you love us. You made the winds. You can still them. Father, if it is your will, please, take us from this storm. And in Jesus Christ's name we ask this."

The rains drove and the winds howled.

"Amen," Easton added.

Thunder rocked the heavens.

"That's it?" Jennifer said, yelling to be heard over the storm.

Easton nodded. "I think," he shouted, "that covers it."

Something soft bumped against his leg. It bumped again. He looked down.

Bubbles.

A solid stream of bubbles, coming up from below.

He allowed himself the hint of a smile. "Take Marisol," he yelled into Jennifer's ear. "I'll be back in ten minutes, no more."

"Back? What do you mean, 'back'? Back from where?"

"From below," he said. "We're floating on top of my tanks and my dive harness. I'm going to grab them, make a dive. I'll be right back."

Settling the swim mask back on his face, venting the air from his dry suit, Easton jackknifed in the water and began pulling and kicking for all he was worth, swimming into the darkness below.

Jennifer wept.

Marisol felt slack, a dead weight in her arms. Jennifer shifted her position, and Marisol moaned. Jennifer held her more tightly, willing her to live. *Please. Don't die, don't die, don't die, don't die. Please.*

The rain drove down on them, pecking like a thousand icy beaks.

She wept harder. She had never, ever in her lifetime, felt so terribly alone, so absolutely lost.

Lost.

She thought about that for a moment. She remembered a church, and a Sunday school. Her aunt had taken her there, and

Jennifer had liked it because her aunt and uncle had bought her a dress the day before, frilly and pink. A dress and a little white Bible. It had made her feel like an angel. She must have been all of what? Six?

Lost.

What was the song they had sung that day? She remembered that she had liked it—had sung it all the way home in the car. "Jesus paid it all, / Jesus paid the cost, / Paid for all our sins and ... and ..." She couldn't think of the word here but knew the last line: "He came to save the lost."

Jennifer hummed the melody as it came dimly back to her. "He came to save the lost."

"Well," she told the unconscious Marisol. "I certainly qualify."

Lightning streaked across the sky and the thunder rolled. Jennifer could see nothing now but water; the rain was a gray wall around them.

She thought about what Easton had said. She thought about Booth.

She took a deep breath.

"Jesus!" She shouted it into the wind.

Marisol moaned again, and Jennifer blinked away tears.

"Jesus," Jennifer prayed more softly. "I ... uh ... hey. I don't even know if I'm doing this right. But Jesus, you're God, and I've been following, chasing ... well, everything but you. And this is where it's got me. And I know where it's taking me. And I want to forget about that. I don't want that gold. I don't want that life. I don't even want to get even with the jerk who just tried to kill us. I just want ..."

The rains slanted, driven by the wind, and Jennifer shifted her grip on Marisol, trying to lift her higher, keep her face out of the slapping of the waves.

"Jesus, I just want you," Jennifer whispered as lake water splashed around her lips. "And I feel like I'm asking too late, but, well ... What Beck said. You know?" She took a deep breath.

"About grace? Jesus, I need that. I need . . . You. I need you. Can you find it in your heart to forgive me?"

Lightning flashed and the thunder roared.

"I'll take that as a yes," Jennifer whispered. And holding Marisol tightly, she closed her eyes and felt peace within the storm.

Twenty feet below, Beck Easton hovered in the water as he slid the tanks and harness onto his back. He buckled the chest cinch and waist belt, hooked the low-pressure line up to his dry suit, and settled the regulator in his mouth. Then he took out his dive-knife and cut the zip-strip that held the secondary regulator open. It stopped bubbling.

He switched on the divelight and played it on the face of his pressure gauge. Nine hundred pounds. It was not a lot of air. Not at all. At two hundred feet, it would be gone in mere minutes.

He felt for and found his dive reel. They were still roughly over the area where the boat had blown up. He was pretty sure of that. But to descend straight down, he'd need a plumb line to follow. He needed a weight.

He felt in his waistbelt pocket, found the gold bar, and cinched it onto the end of the guideline. Then he dropped the gold and let the line play out, the handle on the reel spinning as the heavy bar fell.

Thirty seconds later, it stopped, and he turned head-down and began descending, reeling in the guideline as he went.

Three minutes after that, he was hovering barely two feet above the hard clay bottom, picking up the bar and zipping it back into his waist pocket, jetting two seconds worth of precious air into his suit to offset the weight of the gold.

The shipwreck was nowhere to be seen, which was what he'd expected. Given the scope of the anchor line, it had to be a good three hundred feet away.

But the bottom was littered with things: the dive boat's windshield frame, its wheel. The outboard was lying on its side, silt still hovering around it from its impact with the clay.

Easton looked at his gauge: five hundred pounds.

I don't have much time, Father. I need you to show me.

He played the light on the bottom. Thirty seconds later, he found what he was looking for, picked it up, and slid it under his waistbelt. Then he took a deep breath, and swimming awkwardly, because he still had no fins, he began making his way back up.

He had two hundred pounds of pressure when he got to twenty feet, and he came to a hover there and just stayed there for a little while, a token attempt at a decompression stop, because he was pretty sure that he was well past his nitrogen limits and somewhere out in no-man's land. Easton had known people who'd dived within their table limits and had still gotten bent like pretzels. And he knew people who had blown off an hour of decompression—or more—and come out fine. It wasn't an exact science, and he just prayed that his case would be one of the latter.

He began to ascend again. Above him was the wave-swelled surface, rising and falling like a loose tent, the circles of a thousand raindrops blinking on it. He surfaced, jetted the last of his air into his buoyancy compensator, and turned as the waves lifted and lowered him. As he came to the crest of one, he saw Jennifer and Marisol through the rain, about fifty yards away and, checking to make sure that he still had what he'd retrieved off the bottom, he began swimming, his injured hand so cold now that it no longer even ached.

"Beck!" Jennifer grabbed him as he joined her, momentarily dipping his face underwater. He came up to a kiss.

"Well," he shouted over the storm. "I'm glad to see you too."

"Where've you been?"

Grinning broadly, he reached under his chest cinch and brought out what he'd found.

"The radio?" Jennifer's eyes widened. Then her face sobered.

"The boat blew up," she yelled over the wind. "That can't still work ... can it?"

"The box said, 'Waterproof and shock resistant,'" Easton yelled back. "If it doesn't work, I'm asking for a refund."

That got the laugh he was looking for.

Easton turned the knob to channel thirteen and turned the power switch on. A burst of static came from the speaker and then stopped. He pressed the push-to-talk button.

"Mayday, mayday, mayday," he yelled into the built-in microphone. "We are in distress ... seven miles north of Pointe aux Barques, medical assistance and evacuation required. Mayday, mayday, mayday."

He released the button and they listened.

Nothing. Nothing but the wind.

"Mayday, mayday, mayday," Easton repeated. "Any station. This is an emergency. Mayday, mayday, mayday. Over."

"Station calling, this is United States Coast Guard," the speaker crackled. "What is the nature of your emergency?"

Parajumper Ensign Collier Westinghouse leaned out from the door of the Sea Stallion helicopter and looked down at the rotor-washed surface of the lake.

"Three people," he yelled to his crew chief, "just like they said. Send me the basket as soon as I'm wet."

The chief nodded, and Westinghouse swung his feet over the edge of the doorway, pulled his dive mask into place, checked the closures on his PFD. Lightning lit the sky like a giant flashbulb. Westinghouse could hear the thunder even over the sound of the helicopter's screaming jet turbines.

Wonderful, the twenty-six-year-old thought. *Oh well. This is why they pay me the big bucks.* Pushing off with his hands, he dropped the fifteen feet from the hovering chopper and entered the cold lake with a splash, popping to the surface seconds later. Moving across the waves with a practiced Australian crawl, he got to the victims and pulled the snorkel from his mouth.

"Ma'am, sir!" he yelled over the noise of the waiting helicopter. One woman looked out cold, and he put his hand on her shoulder as he spoke to the other two. "My name is Col, and I'm going to be your PJ today. Is this the lady with the gunshot wound?"

The man nodded. Neither he nor the short-haired woman looked all that freaked out, which impressed Westinghouse to no end. Storm like this, he'd expected that they'd be crawling on top of him. Instead, they were calm, and the man even seemed to know what he was doing as he helped Westinghouse get the GSW victim into the basket. Westinghouse touched the top of his head and whirled his gloved index finger in the air.

"They're gonna fly that lady straight into the ER," he yelled as the basket lifted and the helicopter moved away, turning and canting in the air like a gigantic, droning insect. "We've got another bird inbound for us as we speak, and in the meantime—" he pulled a thermal flask from a cargo pocket on his survival suit—"I've got hot chocolate."

The young woman took a drink as the Sea Stallion vanished into the rain. The man just smiled and shook his head. They were very calm; this looked as if it was going to be a lot easier than Westinghouse had thought.

"I'm going to be okay," the woman said, her voice strong, even happy, in the wind.

"Yes, ma'am," Westinghouse told her. "Guaranteed. We'll have you feet-dry in twenty."

"No." The woman was gazing at the other man, smiling as the lightning washed pale light over her rain-streaked face. "I mean really okay."

"You mean . . . ?" The man left the question unfinished, but she nodded anyway, and the next thing Westinghouse knew, they were hugging one another like a war had just ended or something.

Wonder what that's all about? Westinghouse thought as he watched them. It didn't matter, he decided. Let 'em hug. Day like this, he could use a hug himself.

EPILOGUE

"Mr. Powell?" The judge peered over a pair of half glasses at the silver-haired, gray-suited attorney. "Would you, Ms. Cassidy, and Mr. Easton approach the bench, please?"

"Certainly, your honor."

Samuel Clayton Powell was the type of attorney that you usually had to be a Fortune 100 corporation to afford. Jennifer hadn't lived in Michigan long, but she'd been there long enough to know that.

Their trip from Lake Huron seemed like a dream now. The Coast Guard helicopter had taken them all to Troy Beaumont Hospital for treatment. There, Marisol had recovered consciousness, and a private physician had arrived to treat her, speaking to the two of them long enough to say that Marisol would recover completely and then clamming up after that.

"Company doctor," Easton had told Jennifer, and that had impressed her. Then she had been astounded when Easton had gone to the phone, made a call, and said, "Samuel Powell, please."

She'd been even more astounded when the attorney took the call, Easton chatting with him as if the two of them had known one another forever.

"Let me guess," Jennifer said after Easton had hung up. "Another wreck-diving buddy from the good old days?"

"Wrong." Easton shook his head and then stopped. "Although you just reminded me—I've got to buy Dave a new boat. But Sam is somebody I know from Florida; I taught him and his son to cave dive a few summers back. They were planning a trip to Mexico, and they wanted to get certified before they left the States."

That phone call had been two weeks earlier. Now Jennifer was wearing her one and only wool skirt with a silk blouse, and Easton was actually wearing a dark blue suit with subtle red pinstripes, a burgundy necktie that looked as if some thought had gone into its selection and—wonder of wonders—a pair of antique scrimshaw cufflinks.

"They were my grandfather's," Easton had said simply when he'd caught Jennifer staring at them. But they weren't all she was staring at; the man cleaned up very nicely—standing tall with his perfect posture, he looked as if he were wearing a dress uniform, but without the brass, braid, and ribbons. As they walked forward, Jennifer wondered how many people in the courtroom realized that the white gauze on Easton's left hand was covering a good sixty-five stitches.

"All right, Mr. Powell," the judge told the attorney. "I know that we went over every bit of this in chambers, but I'm going to review it one more time. I don't want this coming back to bite me because any of the parties later say that they were not fully informed."

"Perfectly understandable, your honor," the attorney nodded.

"All right." The judge pushed his reading glasses higher on his nose and looked at the set of briefs in front of him. "The court arrested the schooner *Florida* two weeks ago Wednesday on behalf of Ms. Cassidy and Mr. Easton here. Which was fun, by the way. First time I've done that in seventeen years on the bench, and it drove my law clerks crazy, trying to verify the statutes cited. Anyhow, Ms. Cassidy and Mr. Easton, by that act, you are recognized as finders of the vessel with the rights of salvage thereunto."

The judge adjusted his glasses again and looked up at Sam Powell. "Now, Mr. Powell, even though you represent these two fine young citizens, I understand that you are also presenting claims on the *Florida* and all properties associated therewith, on behalf of . . ."

The judge looked down at the brief.

" ... The United States Treasury, the Commandant of the United States Coast Guard, the Attorney General for the State of Michigan, the Michigan Department of Natural Resources, the Michigan Underwater Preservation Council, the Thumb Area Underwater Preserve, the University of Michigan, the Henry Ford Museum, Lloyd's of London, the estate of Captain Henry Bircher, the estates of Edwin and Asia Booth, and the Great Lakes Shipwreck Museum. Said claims being a conflict of interest that should have me firing you from a cannon to the Bar Association for review and correction were it not for the fact that I have a sworn affidavit before me affirming that you contacted each of these entities *pro bono* at the expressed written request of your clients, with the wish that you urge these parties to pursue claims against the contents of the *Florida*."

The judge lifted his eyebrows, his gaze fixed on Jennifer and Easton. "Is that correct?"

"Yes, your honor," they answered in unison.

"And I have a further affidavit that you, Ms. Cassidy, and you, Mr. Easton, are voluntarily surrendering all rights to this vessel and her contents to the consortium of claimants for the princely sum of one shiny Sacajawea dollar apiece. Is that also correct?"

"Yes, your honor," they answered again.

The judge took off his glasses.

"Young lady," he said, "and sir, it really is none of my business, but we have discussed the contents of this vessel. I have in my possession a videotape of a portion of those contents, shot by a Coast Guard remote-operated vehicle, and I understand that the Coast Guard cutter *Hollyhock* has been stationed over the shipwreck site ever since the captain saw what was on that video. Folks, this wreck might not place you on quite the same level as Bill Gates, but it will get you in for lunch at the same places. So, let me ask you one more time: Why would you want to walk away from it? Ladies first."

"Because it's not my gold, your honor," Jennifer said. "No more than your money would be mine if I found your wallet lying on the street corner."

"The law would suggest otherwise when there is bullion involved, and when the property in question is a vessel lost at sea," the judge said.

"That's true, but I try not to let legal technicalities get in the way of common sense."

This raised a smile from the judge.

"And besides ..." Jennifer flashed Easton a gentle look, for once, without the color rising in her face. " ... Besides, there are things more valuable than gold. I've found one and ..."

She met Easton's eyes. "And I think I just might be beginning to find another. Plus, there is one terrible man on the run out there, somewhere, and my main priority is just to make sure that he, and people like him, never get their hands on a penny of this, ever again. If I can do that, then I'll feel that I've been very well rewarded, indeed."

"Okay," the judge said. "Mr. Easton, your turn."

"I suppose I could spend the next three decades of my life spinning my wheels in a courtroom, your honor," Easton said with a straight face. "But if it's all the same with you, I think I would rather just high-dive into a dumpster full of broken glass."

"Well put," the judge said. "And Sam, the next time I see you outside a courtroom, I want you to tell me how you convinced the Attorney General and the Treasury Department to accept you as custodian of this shipwreck."

Sam Powell beamed at Jennifer and Easton as the three stood in the hall outside the courtroom. "So, how does it feel to be a couple of billion poorer?"

"Better than you might imagine," Jennifer said. "I'm starting to gain a whole new set of priorities."

"Well, I'm glad to hear that," the attorney said. "I'm also glad you're broke. Because that might put you in a more receptive mood for a job offer."

"Job offer?" Jennifer glanced at Easton, who just shrugged.

"Last night, I had a conference call with representatives for all the parties on our list," he said. "They agreed that, if the judge ruled as we expected him to—as he just did—I should find a competent researcher to assemble as much documentation as possible on the *Florida* and on the *Halcyon* gold. And seeing as we wouldn't have known any of this were it not for your contributions, the group agreed that you would be our first choice for the position."

"Me? But I—"

"I've spoken with Dean Tausch at U of M, and he said that he would be happy to release you from your fellowship obligations. The consortium would fund the rest of your graduate studies and pay you a salary of fifty thousand dollars a year—"

"Fifty thousand!"

"It's not much," the attorney said quickly, his face perfectly straight. "But we have to keep the arrangements here above reproach, and I was hoping that, as the typical graduate stipend is considerably lower than that, you would—"

"Yes!" Jennifer raised her hand as she said it. "Okay! Done! Deal! Where do I sign?"

"There's one more thing," the attorney said, turning to Easton. "We're going to need someone who can liaise with the underwater archaeologists to document the wreck and then captain a crew of salvage divers to bring up the gold. Naturally, I had a one-person list for that, as well. Are you interested, Beck? It would mean being up here in Michigan several more times this dive season and most of next summer. But we'll gladly pay for you to hire someone to run your business down in Florida while you're up here, and we'll make it well worth your while—say twice your usual rate, plus all expenses?

"Plus," the attorney added, "all of the expenses the two of you may have accrued to this point in the pursuit of this gold."

"Me hang around up here?" Easton looked at Jennifer—his mouth was under control, but his eyes were clearly smiling. "How would you feel about that?"

"I ... " She made a show of thinking about it. "... I can be persuaded that it's a good thing," she said.

"Then I'll tell you what ... " Easton grinned. "I'll think about it."

"Well, think quick, buddy!" Jennifer laughed.

And he squinted as she poked him in the ribs.

AFTERWORD

For the record, there is much that is real in this book.

This starts with the premise expressed in the prologue – that a nineteenth-century slave was diving the springs of Florida long before the invention of scuba. Jonah Winslow is based very loosely upon Abe Davis, an African-American slave who once performed feats of spring-diving daring-do to entertain North Florida farmers in the late 1850s. Davis is generally recognized as the first American cave diver, and the Abe Davis Award, granted by the National Speleological Society, Cave Diving Section, to divers who have performed one hundred safe cave dives in succession, is named after him.

Ulysses S. Grant really did resign his commission with the Army and leave California in disgrace in the mid-1850s, and yes, the *S* in his name doesn't stand for a thing. John Wilkes Booth actually did go by his middle name off-stage, did smuggle medications through the Union lines, and really did lead an armed insurrection against the headmaster of his school in Maryland. There actually was a Father Jerome who built stone churches for the people of Cat Island, and he really did create the Hermitage atop Mt. Alvernia, which is still there, and exactly as I describe it, today. Ditto Fernandez Bay Village; it is a real place and much as I describe it.

The rocker in which Abraham Lincoln was assassinated really is kept at the Henry Ford Museum in Dearborn, Michigan, and not in Washington's Ford's Theater. The location of the lighthouses described in the third part of this novel are accurate, and that bit of navigational legerdemain, in which the lights from atop the Fort Gratiot and Pointe aux Barques lighthouses were removed and switched in the second half of the nineteenth century, is a matter of historical record. There actually is a United States Coast Guard cutter called the *Hollyhock*; it was commissioned and replaced the venerable USCG *Bramble* as I made the revisions on this book.

The list goes on.

California gold was once shipped to the East Coast using a cross-Panama portage in the nineteenth century. The legal procedure of "arresting" a shipwreck is a legitimate provision of admiralty law. And the steamship *Central America* is an actual gold ship that sank in the Atlantic in 1857. The wreck of the *Central America* has, by the way, been documented in several television programs, magazine articles, and books, the best of which is Gary Kinder's *Ship of Gold in the Deep Blue Sea* (Random House, 1999).

And it is possible, as of this writing, to buy a legitimate Chilean diplomatic passport through a law firm in Seattle. All it takes is money. Go figure.

That said, while this novel is filled with real history, real geography, and real facts in general, it is nonetheless a novel, and those who attempt to use it as a history book or a geography book or an almanac are going to be sadly mislead. The plot's the thing, and when those niggling things, the facts, got in the way of my story, I simply exercised the novelist's prerogative and changed them.

So, if Grant ever had a conversation in the What Cheer House such as the one described in this novel, the history books are absolutely mute on the subject. That the customs-and-immigrations official on Cat Island might also be the pastor of the local Baptist church is just my having fun with the fact that, on small islands with tourist traffic, individuals often do hold a variety of seemingly unrelated jobs. When the relative position of Mt. Alvernia to Fernandez Bay Village did not meet the requirements for my story, I changed it (I had faith to move mountains, and I did). Ditto the fine points of geography on Michigan's Thumb. And the back rooms and hallways of Dearborn, Michigan's, Henry Ford Museum are, I assure you, not nearly as cluttered as I have made them in this book; the fire marshal need not be called.

As for John Wilkes Booth, I am 90 percent certain that it is he who died of gunshot wounds received in that Virginia tobacco barn in late April of 1865...

... Okay—I'm 60 percent certain ...

This list, likewise, goes on. But the bottom line is, *Deep Blue* is a novel. Read it accordingly.

The one fact I have not messed with one bit, a fact for which I will gladly take bullets, is that Jesus Christ died for the sins of all mankind, no matter how heinous, and that redemption is offered to all who will repent and receive it. You can take that to the bank—and beyond.

On to the thank-yous. Dave Lambert was the original supporter and encourager on this project at Zondervan, and for that I thank him and trust that the confidence he expressed will turn out to be vision.

Karen Ball and Diane Noble did yeoman's service as my editors and remarkably managed to stay conscious when the first draft arrived a hundred pages over length. And if there is a better copy editor on the planet than Bob Hudson, I have yet to meet him. You've got to admire a guy who can get excited over the fact that there is no period in "Dr Pepper," and it's refreshing to get notes from a colleague who takes the time to send an e-mail, just to let you know how much he's enjoying the book.

Curt Diepenhorst and Beth Shagene were art directors and designers on this novel's cover and interior pages, respectively, and their work speaks for itself. My hat is off especially to Beth, who did a remarkable job of maintaining composure when she was informed (rather late in the game) that not only did the author want maps in his novel, he wanted to draw them himself.

Sue Brower, Sherry Guzy, and their marketing crew rendered a hundred services during the development of *Deep Blue* and will no doubt render hundreds more as it rolls out. Jackie Aldridge and Joyce Ondersma attended to a myriad of details, including setting me up in an office that I wish I had at home when I visited Zondervan in midcourse on my revisions.

Captain Luther Alexander, then senior chaplain at the United States Naval Academy, invited me to speak and unwittingly contributed to Beck Easton's backstory during one beautiful autumn week in Annapolis, and Captain Alexander's wife, Jay, was the most gracious hostess possible during my stay there. I'd also like to thank Dr. Anne Marie Drew, chair of the Academy's English Department, for the invitation to guest-lecture to her plebe English class and to gain a bit more insight into the academic life of a midshipman.

Tony and Pam Armbrister were perfect hosts during a research trip to Cat Island, and I can only hope that I have described their resort, Fernandez Bay Village, with sufficient fidelity to capture its charm. I would especially like to thank the owners and staff of Fernandez Bay Village for allowing me to drop the veil of fiction and place them as actual characters in this story. Alas, one of the most colorful of those characters—Francis Armbrister, the regal and delightful "Mrs. A."—passed on as this book was being written. But I am thankful that this grand lady went quite peacefully, in the comfort of her own bed on Cat Island.

And of course, I would like to thank my family for their patience during the extended periods of withdrawal that always accompany the birth of a new work of fiction, and to my extended family, the authors and editors of ChiLibris, who cheered and prayed me on as I worked.

Finally, I would like to thank you. In this time-intensive world, it is a compliment touching and rare when a person decides to devote hours or days to the reading of another person's—a stranger's—work. This is the sort of thing that I do not take for granted, and never will. A life of art and ministry is possible only through the generosity of patrons, and I thank you for the gift of that life.

Beck will be back. I promise you that. And in the meantime, may the windows of heaven rain blessings upon you.

Tom Morrisey
Jackson County, Michigan

What Lies at the Bottom of Cenote X?

Yucatan Deep

Tom Morrisey

Cenote X. The Mayans called it K'uxulch'en, the "Well of Sorrows."

Since the days of the Conquistadors, its exact location was known only to local forest tribes—until its discovery by Mike Bryant and Pete Wiley, cofounders of the Yucatan Deep Project. When their joint attempt to set a deep-diving record four years ago met with disaster, the Well of Sorrows lived up to its name. Now, Mike is returning to the world's deepest sinkhole to finish what he and his late partner began.

Not everyone wants Mike to make the attempt. Bridget Marceau—Mike's team physician, fellow diver, and soul mate—fears losing the man she loves to the same cave that claimed Pete Wiley. She is determined to keep Mike out of Cenote X. And she's not the only one. Someone else is keenly interested in what lies more than 1,300 feet beneath the surface. That person already knows exactly what to look for—and why he must at all costs prevent Mike from discovering the secret hidden in those lightless depths.

Punctuating high-risk adventure with inside glimpses into the world of technical diving, author Tom Morrisey plumbs the depths of the human soul. *Yucatan Deep* is a taut tale of loyalty, greed, and the wellsprings of faith and life.

Softcover: 0-310-23959-1

Pick up a copy today at your favorite bookstore!

GRAND RAPIDS, MICHIGAN 49530 USA

WWW.ZONDERVAN.COM

The Unthinkable Has Finally Happened. Can Chance Reynolds Face a Life without Racing?

Turn Four

A Novel of the Superspeedways

Tom Morrisey

Before he even had his driver's license, Chance Reynolds was racing—and winning. He worked his way up the racing ranks from go-carts to sprint cars to stock cars, exercising a natural talent that made him one of the best drivers in the Midwest. Now he has captured the points lead in stock-car racing's premiere series, and is a favorite to win the championship . . . until an off-track accident shatters his career and his life.

Riddled with doubts and questions, Chance delves into the Bible, looking for answers, a clear path for the next turn in his life. The thought of leaving the racing world is mind-numbing—it's all he has ever known.

Turn Four is an unforgettable ride through the realities of professional racing. Cloaked in the fanfare, it's a life of seeming comfort and glory. But underneath it all, people are searching for meaning in life, for love, for God.

Buckle up and hold on tight!

> *"Not only grabs a reader's attention; the book teaches all you need to know about the inner world of stock-car racing. This book will surprise you with a treasury of life lessons."*
> —Dale Beaver, Nextel Cup Chaplain, Motor Racing Outreach

Softcover: 0-310-23969-9

ZONDERVAN™

GRAND RAPIDS, MICHIGAN 49530 USA

WWW.ZONDERVAN.COM

We want to hear from you. Please send your comments about this book to us in care of zreview@zondervan.com. Thank you.

GRAND RAPIDS, MICHIGAN 49530 USA

WWW.ZONDERVAN.COM